Rafi, Bri, a t
college. Marissa r
but was no less committed to our bond as besties. There was nothing fake about our relationship. It was solid. Genuine.

"Okay, Bri," I said. "You made your point. You feel Rafi had too much to live for, that suicide is implausible."

"Impossible. And I can prove it, Thad." Bri sounded certain like she possessed facts in evidence, that we didn't have.

Marissa picked up on Bri's assuredness, following up with questions of her own. "So, Rafi was murdered? You can prove that?"

"Not directly." Bri leaned forward and got as close as she could to Marissa and me. "What I said was that I can prove Rafi did not *kill* himself."

"We're listening." Marissa pointed to herself and then at me.

I made the left-hand turn from the Pacific Coast Highway onto the California Incline, a slanted road that connects PCH with Ocean Avenue in Santa Monica.

Bri started fidgeting with her engagement ring again. "Remember the Dodge Whitney staffer who conference-called us Thursday night with the news?"

I nodded. Marissa nodded. In my mind, I replayed Jenny Yu's livestream of the crime scene. Her failed CPR attempt. And then my crazy request for her to rummage through Rafi's pockets to look for a suicide note or some kind of clue.

"That night Jenny said something that didn't quite make sense," Bri said.

Praise for Topper Jones

The League of Utah Writers has recognized Topper Jones for his short stories and creative nonfiction. His award-winning work has been published in several anthologies including the *Function of Freedom* and the *Art of Isolation—2020*.

Book Pre-review: *All That Glisters*

Topper Jones takes us on a dangerous ride from the beaches of LA to the streets of DC through the unlikely partnership of Thad Hanlon and Bri de la Guerra. The conspiracies these sleuths uncover remind us that our lives on earth are delicately balanced. Prepare to read into the wee small hours.

—Dorothy Allred Solomon (Author of *In My Father's House*; *Predators, Prey, and Other Kinfolk*; and *Finding Karen*)

All that Glisters

by

Topper Jones

A Thad Hanlon/Bri de la Guerra Mystery

All that Glisters

COPYRIGHT © 2023 by Topper Jones

Cover Art by *Lea Schizas*

The Wild Rose Press, Inc.
PO Box 708
Adams Basin, NY 14410-0708
Visit us at www.thewildrosepress.com

Publishing History
First Edition, 2023
Trade Paperback ISBN 978-1-5092-5168-1
Digital ISBN 978-1-5092-5169-8

A Thad Hanlon/Bri de la Guerra Mystery
Published in the United States of America

Dedication

In loving memory of Luella Odesa Jones, a storyteller's storyteller. Thank you for your boundless faith in me and patience as the narrative unfolded.

Acknowledgments

Lea Schizas, multi-talented managing editor, thank you for your eye-catching cover design and professional editing of the final manuscript. Developmental editor, Chantelle Osman (22 Literary), I owe you a debt of gratitude for helping me reduce the sprawl of an overly long first draft to within a publishable range.

Thanks also to my beta readers (Art Davis, Paul Timm, Kathy Leslie) and to the members of my League of Utah Writers chapter weekly critique group for workshopping the many, many revisions. And finally, I'd like to recognize the late Blake Snyder for his influence on story craft and the folks at Save The Cat Workshops for "beat-by-beat" guidance in plotting my story.

Chapter 1

"Thaddeus Hanlon? It's urgent. 9-1-1 urgent! Please." The caller was female, soft-spoken and young sounding, with a slight Asian accent. She was sniffling.

"Could you speak louder? There's a hum." I stuck the bottom edge of my smartphone flat against my ear. The hum got louder.

"It's about Rafi, I mean my boss, Mr. Rafael Silva. He needs your help or Miss Abril's. I'm patching her in now."

Seated to my left at the outdoor table was Abril, only nobody called her that. She preferred Bri. On the right was my wife, Marissa.

Bri plucked the ringing cell from her evening clutch, straightened in her seat, and said, "This is Bri."

"Abril de la Guerra, Rafi's fiancée?" the caller asked.

"Yes. Who's this?"

The three of us—Bri, my wife, and I—had been sipping celebratory mocktails on the balcony of the Luxe Waterfront Hotel in Marina del Rey, watching the sun drop into the Pacific Ocean. A cool breeze wafted up from the small craft harbor. I pulled Marissa closer, cradling my free arm around her baby bump.

"It's Jenny Yu, Dodge Whitney DC Office, Rafi's audit associate. I'm calling from his hotel suite. I just dialed 9-1-1. Paramedics are on their way. Miss Abril and Mr. Thaddeus, tell me what to do. I want to help. There's got to be something. A work plan. Steps to take. Rafi's–"

That's when Jenny just lost it. First, a single sob, long and painful. Then a sob-stream intensifying into convulsive weeping, followed by intermittent gasps, always muted, always delicate.

Bri tapped her foot. I could tell she wanted to get back to whatever the emergency was and speak with her fiancé firsthand, but every time Jenny paused to catch her breath, every time it sounded like Bri might have an opening to say something, the sobbing resumed.

When Jenny's hyperventilating slowed, I seized a slight gap in her breath, no longer than a hiccup, and said, "Jenny, is Rafi able to come to the phone?"

No answer.

Then Bri cut in. "For me to help, Jenny, I need to know what's wrong. Rafi was supposed to be here tonight. In Los Angeles with me. At the Dodge Whitney LA Office Annual Gala. You need to skip ahead to what's happened. Or just hand him the phone. I want to speak to him. Now!"

"I can't, Miss Abril." Jenny's blubbering resumed, louder this time. "You don't understand."

I signaled Bri to let me take a shot at getting Jenny to open up. Bri wagged her head. I took that as confirmation.

"Jenny," I said, "I'm going to ask you some questions. All you have to do is answer 'yes' or 'no.' Can you do that for me?"

Short gasps followed by a long sniffle. "I'll try." Jenny didn't sound convinced.

Marissa leaned over and whispered in my free ear, "She's anxious. Reassure her." My wife gave me a quick kiss on the cheek.

"Jenny," I said, "I know you're scared. It's natural. I promise the questions will be simple. Just 'yes' or 'no.' Ready?"

There was a pause and then a soft, "Yes."

"Is Rafi able to talk?" I asked.

"No."

"Is he conscious?"

"No."

"Is that why you called 9-1-1?"

"Yes."

My Boy Scout first aid training kicked in. I asked, "Is he breathing?"

"Maybe. I can't tell."

"Bleeding?"

"A dribble."

"So, he's unconscious, might be breathing, has minimal bleeding?"

"Yes."

"Do you know CPR?"

"Yes."

"Do you think you can start compressions?"

"No."

Odd response.

"Can you explain?" I asked.

"It's not safe."

Unsafe?

This twenty-question approach to get anything out of Jenny was taking way too long. I had to come up with a better tactic. A better way to assess the situation. "Jenny, do you have FaceTime on your phone?"

"No."

"Rafi's cell? You still have it close by, right? We can use his phone."

"Yes, but it's locked. It needs a passcode."

"Seven, seven, two, three," Bri said.

We could hear Jenny repeat the numbers as she fetched the phone. She said, "Seventy-seven twenty-three doesn't work."

"So not our wedding date." Bri rubbed her temples. "Okay, try my initials, A-D-L-G. Two, three, five, four on the keypad. That's his default code."

Four taps later, Jenny said, "I'm in."

I pressed the green FaceTime icon on my phone and selected Rafi's thumbnail photo from the contacts listing. Within seconds, the two devices were connected. I could see Jenny's face. The whites of her eyes were red and blotchy.

"Jenny," I said, "press the camera swap button on the lower right and point the phone at Rafi." I could hear a low hum in the audio feed again.

As the image of Rafi came into view, Bri shrieked, then doubled over. Marissa paled, grabbed the sides of her chair, and turned totally white. I wasn't feeling too good myself.

My best friend, Rafael Silva, sat completely still in his Euro-cut suit, head slumped to the left, blood trickling from the corner of his mouth toward the pocket of his pale-blue dress shirt with French cuffs. His face was mottled, eyes bloodshot, lids at half-mast, pupils etched with an irregular star pattern. His lips were a deep blue. The half-Windsor knot of his silver-and-crimson-striped designer necktie was loose, slightly askew, as if he had been interrupted just before he had a chance to straighten it.

Wrapped around Rafi's left forearm was bared copper wire from a section of an electric cord. Enough insulation had been removed to circle the arm three or four times. Where the unsheathed cord had contacted the skin, the flesh was blistered and charred in places. A shaving cream-like lather, white and thinly applied, covered the surface of his arm from elbow to wrist where his suit coat sleeve had been pushed up.

On the floor next to Rafi's chair lay a busted hotel clock radio, the power cord yanked free. A lone cufflink sat atop the radio remains. Stretching from Rafi's chair to the nearby wall socket was the rest of the power cord, with the insulation still intact, the two prongs of the plug connected firmly to the outlet.

Marissa started to retch. And then Bri's gag reflex kicked in. I cupped my hand over my nose to reduce the smell. Stomach acid gurgled up my esophagus. I kept my mouth shut and swallowed hard.

"Jenny," I said, my throat burning, "cut the circuit. You have to pull the plug."

"But 9-1-1 told me not to touch him." In the silence, the low hum seemed louder than it probably was. At the base of Rafi's chair, a yellow pool had formed on the tile.

"You don't need to use your hands, Jenny, if that's what you're worried about. Just kick the plug with your shoe and stay away from the pee puddle."

Jenny cocked her left leg and snapped at the wall socket with the ball of her pump. A couple of sparks flew, and then the humming stopped. She grabbed Rafi's left arm, braced herself, and tugged. He slid sideways, fell from the chair, and landed facedown.

As Jenny struggled to reposition him, the video got jerky. Her breathing was labored. She wasn't able to flip him.

"Use your legs," I said.

Jenny scooched her rear perpendicular to Rafi. She brought her knees to her chest and explosively extended her quads. Once. Twice.

Rafi rolled. Landed face up this time. Jenny flopped on her back and worked on catching her breath. Took a good minute, maybe longer.

Bri jabbed her finger at the FaceTime image of the Dodge Whitney staffer stretched out on the floor tile and said, "Jenny, if you want to save Rafi, you have to get up. Start compressions. Please. Now!"

Jenny stirred, then set the cell phone down next to Rafi's ribs. The video stream blurred. We could hear her counting the compressions. When she reached thirty, I asked, "Is there any chest movement?"

"No. Should I keep going?"

"Jenny," Bri said, "can you feel Rafi's breath on your cheek? Lean down. Get close."

"Nothing." Jenny whimpered.

"Switch to rescue breaths," Bri suggested. We heard Jenny blow two big breaths into Rafi's lungs, and then she started up with another round of compressions, followed by more rescue breaths.

Jenny was on her third set of compressions when she was interrupted by loud knocking. We could hear the faint sound of a doorknob jiggle.

Chapter 2

"DC Fire and Emergency Medical Service." The voice was husky and deep-throated.

Jenny yelled, "In here," and resumed chest compressions. We could hear her counting.

"Ma'am, can you open the door?"

"Five one-thousand…Miss Abril, I can't leave Rafi…six one-thousand…What should I do?…seven one-thousand—"

Before Bri could respond to Jenny, we heard a double thump and the door splinter as the emergency responders breached the entrance to the hotel suite.

"Step aside, ma'am. We got this."

From the number of new voices in the room, it sounded like at least two EMTs, maybe three, had arrived to work on Rafi.

"Jenny, pick up the phone," Bri said. "Jenny, the phone. I want to see what the EMTs are doing."

One EMT was working on Rafi's airway. Another was grabbing a defibrillator. A third, wearing a paramedic uniform, was removing Rafi's shirt, exposing the matted hair on his chest. He shaved the skin just enough to apply the defibrillator pads and shocked Rafi three separate times.

Nothing.

"Calling it in," the paramedic said. He tapped his shoulder mic. "Male patient, approximate age twenty-four to twenty-five, found not breathing…"

Bri yowled—throaty and primal, from a place deep in her diaphragm. I shuddered when I heard it.

The paramedic continued, "No audible heartbeat. No detectable blood pressure. Did not respond to CPR, repeated defib, and epi injection. Never achieved sustainable pulse. Notify CME. Contact Metro PD for possible suicide. Do you copy?"

The paramedic turned away to repack the portable defibrillator and his other gear.

"Copy that," the dispatcher said. "Patrol officers on their way to seal area and secure scene."

Bri crossed her arms tight over her chest. She shook, her chair rocking from side to side, the chair legs clinking on the balcony decking with each movement she made. A mist from the marine layer rolled in off the shoreline. When I tried to hug Bri, consoling her the only way I knew how, she pushed me away. "I'm a de la Guerra," she said. "Warrior strong."

I wanted to believe her, believe she could compartmentalize so easily and go full warrioress, folding and tucking tonight's chaos, origami-fashion, until it formed a paper box that she could pocket deep inside her heart. That way, she could cloister her feelings for exploration another day, far into the future. But I knew better. She was as crushed as I was by Rafi's suicide, probably even more so.

Rafi and suicide? Really?

Self-murder was against Rafi's religion. For the hardcore faithful, end of story. Killing himself? Made no sense.

Rafi had a great ride going, at least it seemed that way. Life better than good. No obvious reason to edit himself out of the gene pool. He had won the California *Set for Life Lotto* when Bri persuaded him that marriage to her was in his best interest. And his career? He loved it.

Yet here we were. Staring at the proof on a tiny screen, Rafi splayed on the floor, dead.

It was so incongruous.

Beyond meaning.

Except for *that* conversation I'd cut short with Rafi earlier in the afternoon. He'd been spooked by something on his new assignment, a hush-hush job in DC. And like an idiot, I'd blown him off. Mocked his conspiracy theories. Disconnected the call before he could finish.

"Miss Abril, Mr. Thaddeus, are you still there?" Jenny inhaled sharply. She had been crying again. "I am so sorry... sorry I couldn't save him...save Rafi."

Bri didn't respond.

"You did everything we asked," I said, "step-by-step, like a pro."

Marissa took the phone from me. "This is Thad's wife. You were amazing. Courage under pressure. Jenny, none of this was your fault. There's nothing to be sorry about." Marissa handed the phone back.

I was hoping Bri felt the same way, that Jenny had done all she could, but Bri wasn't talking. She continued to rock from side to side.

"Mr. Thaddeus, what should I do now? Tell me what to do."

I don't know why I said what I said next, but maybe it was thoughts of compartments, boxes, and pockets. "Check his clothes, Jenny. Can you do that for me?"

"I can't."

"I know it's creepy, but it's important. I have this niggling, a sense. What if Rafi left a note?"

"It's not that I'm afraid," Jenny said. "That's not it at all. What worries me is the emergency medical tech. I can't afford to lose my OPT visa. That's my real fear. What if he gets suspicious and accuses me of stealing? I'm not ready to go back to Guangzhou. Not without my CPA."

Optional Practical Training visas provided a gateway to the H1-B visa lottery and permanent residence. If Jenny was charged with felony theft, her chances of remaining in the United States and becoming a Certified Public Accountant were nil.

"Understood," I said. "That's why it's important to be discreet. Trust me. You're more capable than you realize."

We heard a low moan from Jenny.

Bri cut in. "Jenny, reposition the video."

The livestream refocused. Jenny was on her knees next to Rafi, trembling. The image juddered as she fumbled with his pants pockets.

"Anything?" I asked.

Jenny shook her head. "Breath mints. Room key card. But nothing he could write on. No other electronics."

"No wallet?" I asked.

"Not in his back pocket."

"Rafi no longer carries a wallet," Bri said. "He considers them déclassé. Check his suit coat's breast pockets. That's where he keeps his ID, business and credit cards."

The left breast pocket was empty. Jenny switched

to Rafi's right and withdrew a tan leather billfold. She held it up in front of her, careful to shield it from the paramedic behind her, who was re-packing his equipment. She opened the billfold. Rifling through the inside compartments, she pulled each card and held them one by one a short distance from the phone, showing us first the front, then the back.

American Express. California driver's license. Auto and health insurance IDs. And a mini stack of Dodge Whitney business cards, all of them blank on the back. No writing whatsoever.

"You didn't see an engagement portrait?" Bri asked. "Wallet size? Maybe he wrote something on that."

"Just this beach selfie of you and Rafi on the sand." Jenny cupped a snapshot in her hand, held it a short distance from the phone, and flipped it over. Blank. No note. "Let me double-check his billfold."

We watched as she re-examined each compartment slot, using her fingernails to check if a snapshot might have slipped down inside the leather. There wasn't one. She then opened the currency pocket and pulled out a chunk of cash.

Rafi was carrying a lot of dinero. A jumble, in no particular order. Fifties, hundreds, and even a solitary two-dollar bill.

Marissa whistled. I whistled. The most I ever carried was a C-note for emergencies.

Bri arched her flawless eyebrows. "Focus the camera on the cash. Flip each bill. Look for cursive. He always writes in cursive."

Jenny held twenty one-hundred dollar bills up and turned them slowly so we could inspect them for ourselves. The bills looked like they had just come off the press. No wrinkles. No marks. No cursive. No block printing. No final words.

No clue why Rafi had decided to self-destruct.

Jenny moved on to the fifty-dollar bills. Same result. Perfect bills without blemish. Ten in all.

Just as Jenny started to hold the two-dollar bill up to the phone's camera, we heard the paramedic zip his gear bag shut. He turned to the audit associate and said, "Ma'am, I know this must be hard, but Metro PD will be here soon to take your statement."

Jenny didn't miss a beat. She stuffed the cash back, leaned down to kiss Rafi on the cheek, and spoke his name with tenderness. Then she gave him a farewell hug and re-pocketed the billfold. For someone who didn't know what to do in an emergency, Jenny was surprisingly adept at being discreet.

"Hang in there, ma'am," the paramedic said as he exited. If he saw Jenny return the billfold, he never let on.

Bri mewled. She had flinched not once, but twice when Jenny gave Rafi the final delicate hug. It didn't take much imagination to guess what Bri might be thinking:

What was a Dodge Whitney staffer doing in Rafi's room at 11:47 p.m. Eastern Daylight Time?

How did she get in, given Rafi was in no condition to come to the door?

And if Jenny was improvising a grieving girlfriend to dupe the paramedic into believing she was paying her last respects—all the while surreptitiously rummaging through Rafi's pockets—why, for the love of Saint Michael, was her performance so convincing?

Bri's mewling evolved into full tears. Her once-perfect makeup was now smudged, cheeks wet. She muttered something about "possible suicide," pivoted and took off running.

In heels.

Toward the Luxe Waterfront Hotel Grand Ballroom.

Straight for the annual Dodge Whitney LA Office end-of-busy-season celebration and gala spectacular.

Etched in her eyes was the kind of determination that usually meant she had an agenda.

This could get ugly.

Chapter 3

At the entrance to the ballroom, Bri ducked inside, her champagne-colored evening gown rippling behind her like a superheroine's cape. She stormed over to the open bar, sidestepping the Dodge Whitney professionals with their guests. I wasn't too far behind her. Marissa trailed, waddling along as best she could.

"Two shots tequila," Bri requested.

The barkeep, dressed in waitstaff black, pulled the closest bottle of ultra-premium Añejo. He filled two single shots and slid them over.

Bri lifted the first glass. "*Salud.*" She quaffed one tequila, then the other, and handed the empties to the bartender. "Hit me again?"

While she waited for the barkeep to pour, Bri brought the fingertips of her right hand to her throat, gracefully drew the pads of her thumb and index finger downward, and traced the alcohol burn.

Bri downed the next two shots faster than the first two and ordered refills. These she nursed for a good half hour before flipping the glasses over and pushing herself away from the bar. She swiveled to face us.

"I have a score." Bri wasn't slurring her words quite yet, but close to it. "And after…after I settle it, Thad…" She stepped closer and put her face right up against mine. I could practically taste the tequila on her breath. "I need you, Thaddeus Hanlon, to drive me home. As my designated." She steadied herself against a ballroom column.

I stepped back and cleared the air with my hand. "Bri, whatever you're planning, whatever you have in mind for the rest of tonight, bad idea! We should go now. The three of us."

Marissa extended her hand to Bri and said, "Come on. We'll take you home."

Bri spun on her heels and entered the throng of Dodge Whitney officemates and their partners. Fluidly, she moved through the couples, trying to distance herself from us. Whenever waitstaff with a tray of champagne flutes passed, she snagged a couple of bubblies and gulped.

We trailed her but couldn't keep up. Marissa was too pregnant to speedwalk.

"Thad, I'm worried," my wife said. "What should we do?"

"I think we need to give Bri some space. Let her work through her pain. If she wants to growl, what's the worst that can happen?"

"I hope your approach is right."

So, we held back. Stayed just within earshot.

Turned out my strategy was flawed. Bri was elusive, kept on the move, negotiating her way through cliques and clumps of the 500-plus professionals from the Dodge Whitney Los Angeles office and their guests, jostling through at times, zigzagging in a hunting pattern. She was in pursuit.

It didn't take Bri long to spot what or who the target was. She pulled a compact mirror from her clutch, ran a hand through her hair, and reapplied lip gloss. Then uncapped an aerosol breath freshener, sprayed twice, and swallowed. There was a heightened ferocity in Bri's eyes. It reminded me of the de la Guerra family's motorcar fleet and the purr of her mother's pet 16-cylinder Bugatti, one-thousand horsepower of raw muscle under throttle.

Abril "Bri" de la Guerra was fully revved. She stepped onto the parquet dance floor with just a slight wobble and approached a couple who were slow dancing. Marissa and I edged in behind her, doing our best to be inconspicuous, and ended up on the other side of a foursome showing off their ballroom skills.

"May I?" Bri said as she tapped the shoulder of the woman slow dancing with the managing partner of the Dodge Whitney LA office.

I recognized the woman, a new audit manager in her late twenties who was a climber, a shoo-in for making early partner in the firm. She looked annoyed by the request. "We were just getting started," I heard her say, "but if you insist."

"I'll give him right back," Bri countered. "Promise. I just need a word."

The audit manager withdrew her arms, letting Rafi's fiancée cut in. Before Donnell Warnick could object, Bri put her arms around the Dodge Whitney partner, settling in close while never losing a beat. When the song ended, the band kicked up the tempo.

Warnick said something to Bri—we couldn't tell what—then he tried to disengage, but it didn't look like she had any intention of letting him leave the dance floor. "Come on," she insisted. "This tune happens to be my favorite."

Bri took Warnick by the wrist. She led him to the stage, next to stacked guitar amps and a thumping double-bass drum set, and engaged him in a frenetic response to a popular female empowerment anthem. Pure frenzy.

Near the end of the second verse, the part about floating like a butterfly, stinging like a bee, Bri threw a sucker punch.

Warnick never saw it coming.

Bri's perfectly placed right cross caught the managing partner square in the left eye, sending him tripping over his feet backward onto the dance floor, where he whacked his head. He landed, sprawled on his back, face flushed, his dignity no longer on display. The music stopped abruptly, mid-bridge, the lead vocalist's final roar echoing throughout the ballroom.

Bri sauntered over to the felled partner, stood directly over him, and started growling, "You killed him! You killed my Rafi."

She bent down, got right in his face. "You killed us. Killed my future with him." She then raised her trembling fist. Warnick covered his head with his hands, elbows protecting his good looks, and tried to make himself small by curling into a ball. Awkward for a lanky six feet one inch tall guy.

Bri ripped Warnick's elbows apart with her nails, uncovering his face. She made him look at her. "You can't hide."

Warnick's eye was beginning to swell, the cheek puffy where he had been punched.

"Rafi's death? That's on you, Donnell Warnick." Bri placed her hands on her hips, pelvis out. "Your ninety-hour workweek culture? A total soul suck. Completely unsustainable. And then you compound things for my fiancé. You send him out of town on a prolonged assignment, after he confided in you that he was suffering from incredible burnout. What did he say you called it? *A little vacation? A chance to get away?*"

Warnick started to wiggle, untucking his body to full size. He looked like he might be trying to position himself so he could get up. Before he had a chance to push off from the floor, Bri nudged his ribcage with the tip of her stiletto.

"I'm not finished." She added a second nudge, a little harder this time.

Warnick's elbows slackened. He made no further attempt to rise. Instead, he folded his arms across his chest to protect his ribs. "Bri, what are you talking about? What do you mean Rafi's dead? We talked this morning. He sounded—"

"Did I say I was done, Donnell?" Bri raised the toe of her shoe, not so gently, placing it on his crotch.

"Bri, please. Whatever happened, whatever you think this is, the firm has resources." His voice wavered, making him less than convincing. This was uncharacteristic. Donnell Warnick, though gangly slim, usually had a commanding presence and a deep, controlled voice that instilled trust and spread calm when clients would rage into the office. Tonight, he sounded dazed. Blood was matting on the side of his head where he had hit the floor. "Let me help. We'll sort this out. Bri, tell me what I can—"

Bri tapped her shoe. Warnick flinched, but remained silent.

"Donnell, what I don't get, what I don't understand is, why?"

Warnick looked confused. I was confused.

Was Bri:

a—asking why Rafi had been sent on assignment to DC?

b—posing an existential question about why Rafi had to die? or,

c—plunging headlong into deep philosophical territory about the "why of being" for overworked masses?

Turned out to be d—None of the above.

"Why…" Bri continued, "*why,* when you knew Rafi wasn't partner material, why would you string him along on this fake career path in your wannabe-Big-Four-CPA firm, wringing twenty-five hundred billable hours a year out of him, getting a healthy return on your investment in his training, when all along you never intended to promote him? If you had been honest with him, honest enough to outplace him with one of your clients a year ago, honest enough to let him succeed in-house, as a chief financial officer somewhere, then my fiancé would be alive this very minute! If only—"

That's when Bri cocked her right leg and swung, kicking the downed managing partner, the toe of her color-matched satin high heel, digging deep into the soft flesh of Warnick's floating ribs, so deep I could hear a crunch in between the groans.

"Thad, do something!" Marissa pushed me forward.

"Shouldn't we wait for hotel security?" I stepped back.

"Bri'll kill him before that."

"My wrist." I rolled up my coat sleeve, exposing the seam-like scar where the surgeon had implanted a metal plate a couple of years ago. "It's too risky. I'm sure someone will separate them."

But no one came.

The crowd retreated to the edge of the dance floor, a kind of weird tribal justice that gave Bri all the space she needed to go berserk and inflict maximal damage. Warnick may have had the respect of the LA Office, but apparently no friends. At least none willing to tackle the Champagne Flash as she continued kicking.

Marissa squeezed my face between her hands. "Bri is not going to quit, and if you don't stop her, this is going to splash back on you. There are no innocent bystanders. She's as much our guest as Rafi's. She came with us."

Good point. I couldn't afford a career-ending wipeout for doing absolutely nothing while a woman I brought to the company party crippled the Big Boss.

My wife took my hands in hers and placed them on her baby bulge. "Thad, we need your income. We need your health insurance. You got to stop her. This risk's worth taking."

Deep exhale. And then I rushed Bri, wrangling her to the dance floor with a rear bear hug, trapping her arms and legs. Warnick, now free, writhed.

"Let me go, Thad!" Bri twisted, trying to wriggle out of my hold. She screamed, "I have more! More to tell him!"

"No. You're done, Bri. Enough." I locked my hands around her ribs and tightened my grip. "You need to throttle back."

Perhaps realizing that any further move on her part would produce no net benefit, or perhaps, because, at some level, she realized she had done enough damage to Donnell Warnick for one evening, Bri did the only thing she probably thought she could do—she fainted—

or at least it appeared that way.

As I wrestled unsuccessfully to get Bri to her feet, one of the Dodge Whitney senior managers, Tigran Vardanyan, knelt beside me. "Thad, let me help."

"I got this," I said, but didn't. Although well-sculpted, Bri still weighed 130-plus pounds, more than my surfboard collection combined. Add to that the dead weight factor and—

"I'll take this side." Tigran positioned himself under Bri's left arm. I draped her right arm over my shoulder. Together, we got her to my car and managed to settle her into the back seat. She flopped down face first. The car filled with the dank smell of tequila and sweat.

Before I could thank Tigran for his efforts, he retreated. "Gotta check on Warnick," he said and slipped back into the Luxe lobby.

I ran around to the front passenger seat, helped Marissa get settled, and then hopped in the driver's seat.

"Thad, you've got to crack a window," she said.

I did. All four. The salty night air, thick with moisture, displaced the tang from the backseat. Bri's breathing was now a rhythmic snore, a counter tempo to the rumble of the tires over the cobblestone paving of the Luxe Waterfront driveway.

Not more than a hundred yards from the hotel entrance, before I had even reached the street bordering the Luxe complex, Bri bolted upright in the back seat. The dance of the streetlights on Bri's eyes—now swollen, puffy, and glistening—reflected in my rearview mirror.

"Do either of you blame me?" Bri asked. Her voice

was atypically weak, drained of her usual self-confidence. I could barely hear her.

Much as I hoped we could go gently into what was no longer a good night, the evening wasn't over.

Chapter 4

"Blame you for what?" Marissa twisted the best she could toward Bri, faced the back seat, and said, "For taking your pain out on Warnick? You have a right to grieve."

"I totally agree," I said. "The drubbing might have been a tad intense, but mourning takes many forms. When I lost—"

Bri interrupted me. "Blame me for Rafi?" she asked. Her chin quivered. "Do I share the blame for his suicide?"

That brought the conversation to a halt.

Marissa broke the awkward silence. "This wasn't your fault. This was all Warnick. He never stopped pushing Rafi. He kept holding the carrot of promotion just out of reach, taking advantage of Rafi's ambition. That's not on you, Bri. That's on the firm."

Bri sniffled, placing her finger under her nose to keep it from dripping. "But Warnick wasn't the only one pushing."

Marissa handed her a tissue.

"Maybe I expected too much from him," Bri said as she wiped her nose. "Maybe I made him feel he couldn't live up to my plans for us. Maybe it was the wedding—the pressure." In my rearview mirror, I could see her shudder.

"Don't, Bri. Don't go there," Marissa said. "Every

23

princess dreams of a fairytale wedding to a prince with the potential to become the man she deserves. Rafi didn't have to say yes. He didn't have to commit. You can't blame yourself for wanting a perfectible husband and an HEA. A happily-ever-after is your birthright."

Bri did have a noble history. She was of European Spanish heritage. A purebred descendent of prominent Californios—property-holding elites that controlled Alta California during Spain's rule in the 1800s. The New World's virtual royalty. A magisterial class.

For his service as military *Comandante* of the Royal Presidio of Santa Barbara, Bri's great-great-great-great-great granddad was awarded a mega-rancho along the California Central Coast.

Today, the de la Guerra family's real estate holdings included organic farms, avocado and citrus orchards, and beachfront acreage with development potential.

"It's partly my fault," I blurted. "Some of the blame for this is mine."

Except for slight road noise from the radials on the Prius, the car went dead silent. Nobody said anything, the air heavy with quiet.

I looked over at Marissa. Then, checked my rearview for Bri's reaction. Both looked stunned.

Bri leaned forward. "What does 'partly your fault' mean?"

Marissa said, "Thad, what did you do?"

"I wasn't there for him." My voice was weak. I felt shame. "When he reached out, I wasn't there. He needed a friend and…"

"And what?" Bri and Marissa both said.

"I shouldn't have dismissed him as I did, but I was

24

in a time bind when he called today. If I had just listened…took the time to hear what he wanted to say, maybe he wouldn't have done it." As we neared a construction trench in the zigzag from Admiralty Way to Washington Boulevard, the traffic slowed.

"Rafi reached out?" Bri said. "I didn't get so much as a text today. Not even a sad-face emoji to say he wouldn't be here tonight. Reached out about what?"

"Let me—" I said, but I never got to finish my sentence.

"Thad," Marissa interrupted, "why are we hearing this just now? When did Rafi call?"

"On my way home from the office. It's why I was late to get you. Why we were late picking up Bri."

"When were you going to tell me?" Marissa gave me a look. I could sense her disappointment. I had violated The Rule. Our vow to each other to be honest, to be open, and to never withhold.

Rafi's mysterious phone call had spooked me. Tonight was supposed to be a hang loose affair, a kick-back moment. I wanted Marissa to have a good time, relax, and enjoy the sunset. Telling her about Rafi, or telling Bri, would have ruined any peace possible, disrupting the calm of the harbor and the sound of water lapping the sides of the moored sailboats, halyards clanging on mainmasts.

"I was going to say something earlier. Planned to, at least. But things got away from me." Without thinking, I tightened my grip on the steering wheel.

"You're telling me the timing wasn't right?" Marissa said.

"I am."

"We're doing surf metaphors? Good timing as a

core life principle?" Bri asked.

Good timing does apply to more than surfing. Take off too early, you miss the push of the peak and never catch the wave. Too late and you risk wiping out. There's always that split-second, that perfect moment when the surf gods are in your corner, and the energy of the swell tickles your legs and tells you, "It's time."

My timing today?

Worst ever.

Perhaps if I had said something, told Marissa about the curious call from Rafi, and let Bri know her fiancé was acting strange, they could have intervened and pulled the plug on his self-destruction. As it turned out, my misjudgment, my inaction, my failure to communicate? That made me complicit in Rafi's death, crushing any mellow I had going in my life and making me feel culpable, unworthy.

And perhaps if I had said something earlier, Bri wouldn't have engaged Warnick and we could have taken her home after the emergency conference call. She could have mourned in private if she wanted. Tonight's ballroom dance floor spectacle? That was partly my fault, too.

"Thad, you should have shared something before now." Marissa squeezed my leg. It was a compassionate squeeze, not overly firm.

"I can make this right," I said.

Marissa squeezed one more time. "You always do."

Chapter 5

Early the next morning, Bri texted: —*NO WAY Rafi killed himself. I have proof!!! Help me.*—

Last night on the ride from the Luxe Waterfront to Santa Monica, I said I'd make things right. I was being sincere. But not necessarily bold.

What I had meant was I'd renew efforts to keep my wedding vows to my wife—to be open and honest, sans secrets. I promised to be more forthcoming. With her primarily. And I'd work on conquering my fear of making unnecessary waves, even if it involved bearing bad news.

My knee-jerk commitment to making things right was limited in scope and mostly for Marissa.

It was never intended to be a universal call to action.

Or an offer to undertake a quest.

So Bri's plaintive text had me concerned.

NO WAY Rafi killed himself.

Was Bri simply grieving Rafi's unexpected death? Trying to recover some sense of meaning she'd lost? Or embarking on one of her crusades for justice, in all its many forms? Grief relief, I thought I could handle. But a full tilt at windmills?

Help me.

Truth is, I'm more a loner than a joiner. Crusades aren't my thing. I've never lived up to my namesake,

Saint Thaddeus, the Patron Saint of the Impossible. I was never much help with a lost cause. No friend of desperate times.

With baby Hanlon on the way, a crusade was out. Painting and wallpapering the nursery, going to natural childbirth classes, and monitoring Marissa's IVF pregnancy didn't leave much in the way of spare moments. Bri would have to enlist someone else for her quest.

And if a complicated home front wasn't enough reason not to engage, now Warnick wanted to see me first thing. It could be repercussions from last night at the gala. Or it could be questions about my performance on the last job. I wasn't sure which.

I was waiting in the corner office for a meeting—a meeting for which I had no way to prepare. Lilit, Warnick's administrative assistant, didn't have a clue why the Big Boss wanted to talk to me.

"Does my tête-à-tête with Donnell have something to do with a previous or upcoming performance review?" I asked.

For my midterm review, one of my managers raved about my "positive mindset" and my willingness to "put in the hours" to get the job done. Another complained that I yawned once in an audit team meeting. I'm all about continuous improvement so my solution was simple—doubling up on Diet Coke.

Warnick's admin said, "You want to know if your meeting with Mr. Warnick concerns your personnel feedback cycle?"

"Yeah."

"Can't say. You'll have to ask him."

Cautious response. Lilit was being particularly

tight-lipped today.

Warnick's spacious corner office overlooked the Pacific Ocean from the 53rd floor of the fifth tallest building in the City of Angels. A 450-power telescope stood where the two floor-to-ceiling plate glass windows met. I walked over to the corner and angled the device, peering through the eyepiece at the waterfront. A solitary surfer in a spring wetsuit with neon coral trim was paddling out through the mild chop of the Pacific Ocean.

"Ah, Thad," Donnell M. Warnick said, as he stood silhouetted in the doorway of his office. He was carrying a mug stenciled with the firm logo. The shadows on Donnell's face couldn't hide the purple and brown discoloration around his left eye or the swelling. Bri had placed the sucker punch remarkably well. Warnick's shiner was epic.

The managing partner ambled gingerly into the office. He was well-scrubbed, back to his usual debonair workaday self, but stiff as he moved. I suspected he was wearing fresh athletic tape around his rib cage.

I snuck one last look through the telescope. The sole surfer took off, slipped into the hollow of the wave, and crouched into the curl. Totally tubed. I wanted to trade places with her and get in a little "water therapy" of my own after last night, but here I was instead. I turned back to Warnick.

"Please, have a seat," the Dodge Whitney top dog said. He motioned for me to sit on the couch.

Even though office sofas are an interior designer's attempt to create a "casual" space, I suspected this discussion wasn't going to be all that relaxed. We sat.

Warnick nestled his slender frame into the cushions, leaving a good two-thirds of the sofa for me. Even with ample personal space between us, I was uneasy. The power dynamics were all in his favor. I didn't know what to expect.

"Thad," Warnick said. There was a meekness in his voice that was new to me. "I'm sorry about Rafi. I seriously thought he was the right person for the job when I sent him. I didn't have any idea he was suicidal."

"At the end of 'busy season'," I said, "we're all a little unhinged. The firm's January to mid-April seven-days-a-week audit slog had him working monster-long hours and not coming up for air very often."

Warnick pressed his lips together in a sympathetic smile and nodded. "I have my staff reaching out to his family and his fiancée."

"Are you going to press charges against Bri?"

"For what? Being human?"

Given the circumstances, I'm not sure I would be so forgiving. Warnick was full of surprises.

"The funeral's tomorrow," I said. "Up the coast a couple of hours at the Old Mission Santa Inés. Rafi's parents are Spanish natives and very tied to their culture."

Donnell took a sip of his coffee. "Meaning?"

"In their tradition, burials usually occur within twenty-four hours. They asked for a rush autopsy in DC and were able to have it scheduled this morning. The casket will be on a flight out of Reagan National this afternoon."

"Plans for a wake?"

"Silva family and close friends only."

"Understood." Warnick eased back into the sofa, slowly, chest-cage erect. He was anything but limber. "Please convey my condolences. And if you would, share that the firm has already established a Cal State scholarship in Rafi's name. Dodge Whitney takes care of its own."

With concerted effort, Warnick interlaced his fingers and placed his clasped hands behind his head. He seemed determined to strike a partner power-pose, broken ribs or not. "Thad, what do you know about the audit Rafael Silva was running?"

"Not much. Rafi said it was a new client with a lot of first-time-through work."

Taking on a new audit always required gathering background data, previous financial statements, and former audit work papers.

Warnick looked up at the ceiling. "Anything else?"

"To tell you the truth, since Rafi started the job, I haven't seen him much. He hasn't even been in town long enough for us to get to the beach. Shame, too. Surf's been clean. South Bay's been breaking best all spring."

Warnick pushed himself up from the sofa and crossed over to the desk. He picked up the sole paperweight atop his inbox. Encapsulated in the 5 by 7 inch rectangular Lucite block was the miniaturized cover of the *Sunstake Extractive Industries IPO*—a report announcing the company's initial public offering of seven million shares of common stock. Such deal toys were lovingly referred to as "tombstones" because the embedded financial industry print notice resembled a graveyard headstone.

The Dodge Whitney managing partner tossed the

paperweight from hand to hand, pleasure in his eyes as if remembering some enjoyable moment of the recently completed Sunstake pre-IPO audit, a job I had run as a Senior Associate.

"Ever hear of the Gold Commission?" Warnick asked.

"Which one?" I knew from my Money and Banking class at Cal State that there had been at least two. The first Gold Commission was established in 1981, shortly after Ronald Reagan's landslide election. The new president had inherited a hot mess of an economy. The U.S. markets had cratered. Mortgage interest rates hit an all-time high of eighteen percent. Gas prices had doubled in three years. Voters demanded action.

To attack the problem, President Reagan empaneled a seventeen-member bipartisan task force.

The mission: Tame inflation.

The strategy: Bring the nation closer to a metal-backed currency.

"The second commission," Warnick said. "I'm referring to the reboot." The managing partner returned the Lucite paperweight to the top of his inbox.

All I knew about the sequel to the First Gold Commission was the business press had given it a Hollywood-style moniker. Gold II was shorthand for the Second Gold Commission. "The reboot is our client?"

Warnick didn't answer. He held up a finger, signaling me to wait, and then rummaged through his inbox. He pulled out a manila folder and leafed through the documents. While he searched, I launched into a follow-on question.

"Not to be disrespectful," I said, "but isn't our niche, public accounting for a slice of the Fortune 500? We audit big companies in the financial services sector—All Things Money. Banks, investment houses, precious metals, and hedge funds with offshore ties." I paused to take a breath.

"All true." Warnick returned the first manila folder to the inbox and selected another. While he rifled through it, I kept probing.

"Donnell, tell me this. Hasn't the firm always shied away from government consulting work—federal, state, or local? I thought we didn't do government jobs. The word in the hallways is such clients are too volatile. The public enterprise too subject to politics, agency shutdowns, and delayed payments."

"Also, true."

"How does the Second Gold Commission fit into our scope of practice?"

Warnick focused on a single document in the second folder. "Thad, before I respond, I need you to sign an NDA."

"A non-disclosure agreement?"

"It's a formality, but yes. We've been asked to maintain strict secrecy because of the sensitive nature of the engagement."

From the manila folder he had been searching, Warnick withdrew a form on Dodge Whitney company letterhead. He slid it across his desk and offered me a pen.

I got up from the couch, took a seat in the chair facing Warnick's executive desk, and said, "Can I take a minute to read it?"

"Of course."

It was a standard employee NDA. I had to promise to protect the confidentiality of our client and the firm's engagement. In return, Dodge Whitney CPAs entrusted me with insider information.

I signed and slid the completed form back.

"Gold II is an exception," Warnick said. "Outside our traditional scope of practice. A one-off. Special circumstances."

"And Rafi was working Gold II?"

"Undercover, yes."

"Dude, you're telling me my best friend was a spy? As in Top Secret? For Your Eyes Only?" A snigger slipped from my lips.

Warnick's jaw tightened. He took several deep breaths before saying, "Thad, let me give you some friendly advice. If you want to make a career here at Dodge Whitney, you need to work on being a professional...and not just in front of the client." He took another sip of coffee. "For one thing, I'm your managing partner. Not one of your surf buddies. *Dude* is out of place. And here's the second thing, sarcasm is never appreciated."

My face flushed to match my fire-red sideburns. I fought the urge to be defensive, keeping my mouth shut until the humiliation passed. Warnick's tough love meant I still had a lot to learn.

"Thad, your best friend accepted a challenging assignment," Warnick said, "the details of which he couldn't divulge to you or his fiancée. He was not a spy, but at the request of the client, he was working undercover."

"Special circumstances?"

"Yes." Warnick shifted in his oversized leather

executive chair and rubbed his chin. "Thad, I'm a pretty good judge of talent. I have been building Dodge Whitney's presence in LA for a long time, hand-picking our new hires for almost twenty years. I remember when Rafi hand-delivered your resume to me. He was so insistent I give you a chance."

Right after graduating college, I had taken a gap year opting for a world surf safari. When I returned from Uluwatu, Indonesia, I had absolutely nothing lined up, not one job offer. Rafi had used his connections at Dodge Whitney to get me an interview.

"Rafi saved me," I said.

"He claimed you had financial superpowers. X-ray eyes capable of spotting cooked books, balance sheets that don't balance, and numbers that don't add up. I had to hire you to see if it was true."

"Superpowers are a stretch. A skeptical eye, yes."

"Thad, I need someone to pick up Rafi's baton. With your background in mining and metals, particularly the Sunstake job you did for me, I figure you could slot right in. Take over the Gold II audit. Keep the client happy. What do you say? This would be a good career move for you."

A surprise career move.

For a snap meeting with Warnick, I might have expected a reprimand for hesitating to help while Bri tap-danced all over him in last night's ballroom fiasco. Or a head honcho action list for improving my job performance given my tendency to yawn in client meetings. What I didn't expect was to be reassigned to a clandestine project nearly three thousand miles away in the nation's capital.

"Donnell, do you think I can handle the transition?

The job's a month in and the person most qualified to onboard me is no longer with us."

Warnick gave me a reassuring smile. "Rafi was hyper-meticulous. You'll have access to his notes to bring you up to speed. The work programs, client spreadsheets, and audit tests are on the client's secure server."

"What about Marissa? She's six months along. I can't leave her."

"And we wouldn't want you to. Travel can make the usual arrangements for you, double occupancy standard. For your wife's airfare, I'd suggest cashing in some of the frequent flyer miles that you've racked up with us on out-of-town assignments. Talk to her, Thad."

The managing partner wrapped his right hand around the Lucite tombstone he had toyed with earlier, made like he was a pitcher for the LA Dodgers, and lobbed it in my direction. "That is, Thad, if you're all in? I need you focused."

I juggled the Sunstake IPO deal toy, hot-potato-style. "Give me twenty-four hours to think it through." I laid the Lucite paperweight on Warnick's desk.

"You have until tomorrow night. Oh, and, Thad, take the rest of the day off."

That gave me thirty-six hours. Even better. More time to muse. If taking Rafi's place on Gold II was the best way to honor my best friend, Marissa would tell me. Her yogi soul would bring clarity.

Chapter 6

As I left Warnick's office, I texted Marissa: —
Wanna come with?—
—*With where? Thought u were working?*— my
wife responded.
—*Warnick gave me rest of day off.*—
—*Can't go to beach. I'm prepping.*—
I dropped by the Dodge Whitney bullpen of first-
come, first-served desks and picked up my red combo
briefcase/backpack and my collapsible e-bike. I texted:
—*Switching to phone.*— Then dialed my wife.
"Marissa, I really need this right now. I need to be
on the water. I need clarity."
"And I need to wrap up the curriculum for my
third-trimester yoga class. The poses. The music. The
yogi moments at the end of each session."
"About your class? We need to talk." I ducked into
the elevator on the 45th floor of the Dodge Whitney
office building, lugged in my e-bike, and pressed the
button for the first floor. "Something's come up."
"Hmm."
"Hmm, yes I'll come with? Or hmm, no?"
"Just hmm."
I unfolded my e-bike and put on my helmet. The
call cut over to the built-in Bluetooth headset.
"On my way, Mar baby. Ten minutes." I adjusted
the straps on my red combo backpack, eased into

traffic, and headed south on Grand Ave to our downtown apartment on Pico and Olive. The commute home turned out to be more like twenty minutes. And the trip in the car to the beach took three times that.

Traffic for Friday afternoon was gnarlier than usual. The I-10 freeway to Santa Monica bumper-to-bumper. Marissa shifted in her seat the entire hour it took to go the 15.7 miles, finding little relief for her pregnant form. On the plus side, my recap of the morning meetup with Warnick distracted her from the discomfort somewhat, as did my infinite questions about what she thought we should do, given the unexpected context.

I was hoping for answers.

She preferred to debate, raising issues I hadn't considered.

We parked in Lot 4 where Bay Street in Santa Monica dead-ends into the Pacific Ocean. By then the afternoon breeze had kicked up. Most beachgoers had cleared out. The blue-gray water was dappled but not anywhere near washing-machine conditions. There were some rideable swells, offering some beefy shoulders for carving. The waves breaking to the right looked pretty good.

Marissa helped unload the Prius while I set up her beach shade—a three-sided tent perched facing the shoreline, secured with guy-lines and stakes screwed into the sand. I spread a blanket, a quilt actually, that my mother had made for me before she passed. The repeating pattern featured waves (of course) from fat quarters she had picked up at a fabric shop in some artsy enclave outside Cambria, just south of Hearst's Castle off the Pacific Coast Highway.

"Please," Marissa said. She handed me a tube of sunscreen. I applied lotion to her lightly tanned back and neck, careful not to get any on her white bikini.

When I was done, I spun her toward me and kissed her forever.

"Sweetly spontaneous," Marissa said, as she gently nudged me away to take in a breath. "But as much as I'd like to continue these beach exercises with you, do you think you can do my legs first?"

Given Marissa's sizeable baby bump, self-application of lotion much below her thighs was now a biomechanical impossibility. She sat on the beach quilt, legs extended.

I lathered her up. "Thank you for coming with me."

"Does this mean you're ready to talk?"

California gulls dive-bombed our beach setup. I pulled a bird-healthy organic snack from the outside flap of the cooler bag and tossed the giant seed cake a good fifty yards. At some point, when the seabirds finished the unsalted and unshelled black sunflower seeds, I knew they'd return for more. By then, I planned to be back from the water.

"There're a few things I need to 'surf on' first." I unzipped my board bag, pulled out my red six feet two, and waxed up.

"Clarity ritual?" Marissa said.

"Yes." We'd only been married a couple of years, but Marissa had cataloged my behavior. She knew the pattern. "Surf on it" was my way of sorting through life's options, of making tough decisions, of mixing adrenaline with mindfulness.

The Bay Street afternoon surf report predicted a combination of knee-to-waist high swells coming in every eleven and fifteen seconds from the south, and a secondary swell every thirteen seconds from the northwest. The online surf cam showed modest breaks, mostly cascading to the right, with enough peaks along the shore to avoid bunching the lineup.

I picked a take-off spot, strapped the cuff of my board leash to my right ankle, tossed the leash cord behind me, and waded out. As I paddled I got slapped in the face with one wave after another, saltwater dripping into my eyes. I squinted, wiped my eye sockets, and dug my hands deep into the ocean, thumb and fingers squeezed to form paddles.

I could feel a swell tickle my fingers as I stroked. I lifted my chin and arched my back to get a better look. A four-footer, maybe even a five, was building, the wall taking shape. I spotted a good take-off zone, near enough to the shoulder of the swell but not so close I'd get sucked up the face and tossed off the lip in a classic over-the-falls wipeout. I paddled hard, pivoted 180 degrees, angled my board slightly right and facing toward shore, and paddled some more, arms slicing the surface of the ocean simultaneously while I flutter-kicked my legs to add momentum.

Big surge. The nose of the board popped out of the water, my clue to jump to my feet. I scrambled up into a regular stance, left leg forward, right leg back on the deck pad, and slid down the face of the wave until the tail fins grabbed. That gave me the traction I needed to snap the bottom turn up to the lip, cut back into a reverse with fins facing the beach, and throw rooster-tail spray until I went for my final move—a carving 360—sticking the trick without over-spinning as the swell rumbled through in a flash of whitewash.

Marissa waved. She had waded into the crumbled breakers up to her knees, her camera pointed at me.

I gave her my best pro surfer smile and paddled out to catch another. By now, there were a couple more locals in the lineup out in the water.

"Nice moves," one surfer said as I paddled by.

They *were* nice. Some of my best. Only I wasn't getting stoked and feeling the usual rush.

All I could think about was Rafi. How my surf buddy, being goofy-footed and all, would always take off left every time I took off right. We'd mirror-carve every wave, so it looked like choreography—me right, him left—the tail fins of our boards sketching white water trails in perfect symmetry.

We were inseparable. And insufferable. Whether it was ankle-biters of one foot or less, or double overhead waves twice as tall as we were. The self-proclaimed Dynamic Duo of the Santa Monica surf scene.

When Rafi called yesterday while I was e-biking home from the office, he had asked for help.

"Things just aren't adding up," he said. I could hear him gulp air like he was about to duck dive under a rogue wave at the pier. Then, his voice got small, and he started to whisper. "Thad, it's like one of those smell-test fails from Lutz's Intermediate Accounting. But mondo-sized. Spreadsheets so large they don't talk to each other."

I wasn't sure how to respond. The call was unsettling. I said, "Lutz? Did I hear that right?"

Prof. Lutz was a legend at Cal State. "If the numbers don't smell right," he would say, "chances are you'll need to sniff around."

Rafi had memorized Lutz's lectures on creative

accounting and had picked up some serious skills over the years as a CPA. But my buddy had one major flaw—he tended to overanalyze things.

"Bigger than Enron, Thad. Farther reaching. Maybe even bankageddon!" Rafi was whispering again. "If I'm right, Thad, this touches everyone."

Enron was the mother of all stock frauds—$74 billion in losses spread over 1.5 million people. Pensions gutted. Life savings wiped out. Investors leaping from tall buildings, flailing as they spiraled to their death.

But for CPAs, there was a silver lining. The mega fraud led to the passage of Sarbanes-Oxley, Capitol Hill legislation, fondly referred to as the "CPA Full Employment Act." Ever since then, investigative accounting had been a great gig. It paid my bills. And then some.

"Listen, Rafi," I had said. "No fraud can be that big. You've fallen for the professional skeptic's trap: *Question everything. Before long, everything is questionable.* My point is, dude, whatever you're involved with, it's probably *not* the a-stock-alypse. Not something that's going to tank the personal finances of everyone on the planet."

"Point made," Rafi whispered.

My phone fell silent. We had been friends since college. I knew when Rafi was frustrated.

"Rafi, you still there?"

When he didn't respond right away, I tried again. "You there?" I pressed the phone closer and could hear controlled breathing—Rafi's routine when his civility was working overtime to blunt his frustration. "Sorry, bro," I finally said. "Sometimes I can be a dismissive jerk. But you *do* realize, on occasion, you exaggerate."

"Thad, this is you making nice?"

"Can we do this later, Rafi? I hate to bail, but I'm desperately behind schedule in picking up Marissa. And we still need to dash to your condo to collect your fiancée."

"Bri?"

"Tell me you remembered?" I said.

We had preplanned a week ago that Marissa and I would pick up Bri on the way to the Dodge Whitney Annual Gala that night. Once Rafi landed at LAX, he was to take an Uber to catch up with us at the Luxe Waterfront in Marina del Rey.

"About that—"

"Rafi, gotta go. Catch you later at Dodge Whitney's schmoozefest."

"Thad, Thad, don't sign off. Not yet. There's more." Rafi dropped into a whisper again. It sounded like he said *VersaChem*, *plan*, and something about *advice*. The last word I could make out for sure was *amigo*. That was less than twenty-four hours ago. Surreal.

"Hey, man. You gonna take this one?" A teenage girl in a pink Roxy wetsuit asked. She was sitting next to me on the water facing the horizon. "You all right? You seem zoned."

Startled, I splashed saltwater on my face, brought my hands together in prayer position, and gave a slight bow. "It's all yours."

Roxy edged into position and took off.

The next wave I grabbed, I rode it all the way in.

Marissa was experimenting with third-trimester yoga poses on her mat, her bikini taut against her skin, her belly glistening with sunscreen.

I set down my board, made sure the wax side wasn't facing the sun, and unzipped my wetsuit. I pulled the neoprene fabric off my shoulders and lowered the upper half of the suit down to my waist, long sleeves dangling. After toweling off, I picked up Marissa's camera and snapped a few pics of my wife.

"Did the sea gods grant you any wisdom?" she said. "On your decision?"

"King Neptune was polishing his trident. Couldn't work me into his schedule. So…instead of me thinking through the pros and cons of taking the Gold II assignment, I kept looping through my last phone call with Rafi."

"Only natural. You two were close. And now you have an opportunity to finish what he started. But you have questions?"

"I'm hoping I can count on you to help me sort it all out. Woman's intuition. Feminine mystique. Marissa, I need your insight." I donned my surf poncho, shed my wetsuit, and stripped off my wet compression boxers. Next, I wiggled into some blue jeans, commando-style. "I wasn't expecting Warnick's proposition this morning. I don't know what to do. I don't want to uproot us—"

"When you put it that way, Thad, the answer is obvious. You don't want to go. But…but what if I'm capable of being replanted?"

The gardening metaphor was tempting, at least for someone like me who tends to get into the weeds, especially since Marissa never talked much about how she came to be living with her aunt in the swanky private member community of Malibou Lake, nestled in the Santa Monica Mountains. All I knew was that she was originally from upstate New York. I took another tack instead. "But what about your Bun-in-the-Oven yoga classes? You told me your second-trimester students are expecting you to transition them to third-trimester poses."

"I can arrange for a substitute to cover."

"Is flying even safe for you?" I felt stupid for never having even considered that risk before.

"Under twenty-eight weeks, no doctor's note needed. I'm at twenty-six." Marissa stretched both arms overhead, palms together, striking a tree pose. "Thad," she said, "I can't make the decision for you. What I can say is this: Don't tell Warnick no because of me. I'm your biggest fan. Whatever you decide—"

Before she could finish, I placed my finger on Marissa's lips. "Babe, let me ask one question. And I'm being serious. Big-League serious. Are you really going to be happy living out of a suitcase in some vapid ten by fifteen feet hotel room, day-in-day-out for weeks on end, *ad nauseam*? Not to mention, once Thadpole shows up, things *will* compound."

Marissa began twirling the few red hairs on my chest. "Are you kidding? I'd go crazy, even if the place had a masseuse on-premise and a solid gold crib for our son."

"Good to know. Can we talk about something else then? Something related?"

"Bri's mysterious text?"

"You can read minds, can't you." I wrapped my arms around Marissa and nibbled her ear.

The tide had come in. With the waves crashing closer to shore, the roar was louder. The dive-bombing gulls had returned to our site looking for another handout. And a fire-orange sun sat atop the western horizon.

The late afternoon onshore sea breeze kicked up the sand around us. Bri snuggled in close. "Some minds are easy to read," she said, then kissed me. Her lips were hot on mine, her breath a perfect kind of sultry.

I grabbed another blanket.

Covered us both.

Clarity.

Chapter 7

The sun failed to pierce the gray marine layer that hung over the Los Padres National Forest early Saturday morning. With the thick overcast condition, the normally green hills surrounding Old Mission Santa Inés took on a pasty, languid color. Even those souls gathered near the Silva family mausoleum in the Campo Santo burial ground looked pale. All except Bri.

Her face was blotchy pink and red, tear-streaked, with mascara in the wrong places. Thankfully, her earlier hysteria en route to the funeral had passed. Marissa had calmed her.

Bri de la Guerra, dressed in a dark classic pants suit, head covered with a black lace mantilla, now stood emotionless in front of Rafi's crypt. Her mother, a slightly taller woman, was next to her. Except for the height difference, the two de la Guerra women could pass for twins. Regal features. Perfect skin. Gene pool gold.

The processional music concluded with a boy's choir singing "The Prayer of Saint Francis."

Lord, make me an instrument of your peace.
Where there is hatred, let me bring love.
Where there is offense, let me bring pardon.
Where there is discord, let me bring union.
Where there is error, let me bring truth…

As the flower-covered coffin was lowered onto the

lift table by the pallbearers, I squeezed Marissa's hand. Flanking the handcrafted hardwood casket were Rafael's parents and a few friends of the family. We waited silently for the priest to join us at the foot of the draped opening to the crypt.

Friar Mateo was dressed in an earthy brown Franciscan robe, adorned with a black sleeveless outer vestment and embellished with a modest embroidered gold cross. He began the Rite of Commitment.

"Our brother Rafael Silva has gone to his rest having been taken far before his time. We are saddened by his death for he was cherished as a son, fiancé, and dear friend. May the Heavens now welcome him."

My inability to focus—what Marissa called my "monkey mind"—was working overtime. I found it hard to be fully present during the deliberate pacing of the solemn liturgy. My thoughts raced. Was Rafi really "taken"? Or did he "take" his own life? Was it a suicide as the paramedic suggested?

Friar Mateo was circumspect in his word choice. He was giving Rafi the benefit of the doubt. Self-murder was a mortal sin under church teachings.

"For all of us here present," Friar Mateo continued, "I pray that our hope in eternal life sustains us in this moment of sorrow and prepares us for death when our sojourn on this earth is done. Let us pray as Jesus taught."

As Friar Mateo recited the Lord's Prayer, most of the audience joined in, while a few simply bowed their heads. The three Mission bells atop the tower entrance to the Campo Santo began to peal.

...and lead us not into temptation, but deliver us

from evil.
   Amen.

Friar Mateo bid the small gathering farewell. As he bowed to exit, his black chasuble draped to the ground, calling attention to the handiwork of the embroidered cross with its delicate gold thread stitching. It reminded me of finer things. Made me think of Rafi.

Before long, Mr. and Mrs. Silva excused themselves to make the drive back to the Silva Trails & Equine Center to prepare for the wake with the extended family. I apologized to the Silvas for not being able to stay longer. Bri did the same.

Marissa was my excuse. At six months pregnant, she had been uncomfortable on the drive up, uncomfortable sitting on wooden pews in the mission chapel, and uncomfortable standing for the crypt side ceremony.

Bri, on the other hand, excused herself as being in no condition to be around others and just wanted to empty her tear ducts in private. She took one last look at her fiancé's casket, turned, and started toward the northwest corner of the cemetery.

I was considering going after her so we could get on the road when Marissa squeezed my hand. "She needs this, Thad."

Marissa found a weathered bench to take the pressure off her feet. Mrs. de la Guerra and I kept vigil by the family mausoleum while we waited for Bri's return from her alone time.

Rafi's fiancée was hunched over an old headstone, her back to us. Her shoulders rose spasmodically as she sobbed. Her breathing was uneven. Periodically Bri would raise her fists, clench them until her knuckles turned white, and then double hammer punch the gray sky.

About an hour later, the marine layer burned off. As the clouds parted, a light breeze licked our faces.

"I'm ready," Bri said, loud enough for us to hear her across the Mission Cemetery. From a distance, I could see red rings around her eyes. She joined us and said, "Let's go."

The four of us walked toward the Mission parking lot. As we drew closer to her mom's top-of-the-line Mercedes, Mrs. de la Guerra said, "Abril, dear. Promise you won't wallow."

"Too busy, Mother. It's earnings season. Got to keep Wall Street happy. Next week's booked solid with management meetings for my April thirty fiscal-year clients."

Bri's mother slid into the driver's seat of her platinum-colored V-12 coupe, fired up the engine, and lowered her window. "Always chin up. That's my princess."

With that, Bri's mother raised the driver's window and backed out of the weathered asphalt parking stall. Her tires spun, screeched for a moment, and then she sped away in her overpowered sedan toward the family rancho atop the Santa Susana Mountains, two hours south of the Mission.

We had even farther to go than that. At least a three-to-four-hour trek. Time to hit the road, drive Bri back to her place in Santa Monica, then slog another thirty minutes to our apartment in LA.

I shuffled over to the passenger side of our car and opened the doors. Marissa took her place in the front seat, while Bri angled herself into the back. I helped Marissa buckle in and shut the doors.

Bri pulled out a set of prayer beads, clasped the crucifix, and started working her rosary, chanting softly.

The hybrid was whisper quiet as we took Mariposa Drive to Mission Drive. The internal combustion engine finally kicked in as we jogged onto U.S. Highway 101 and followed the El Camino Real down the coast.

For a hundred and twenty miles, the only sound was the whir of mpg-tuned radial tires on pavement and the muted whoosh of passing vehicles. During the entire stretch, Bri looked straight ahead, transfixed, in deep recitation, fingering her prayer beads one by one as she chanted in Spanish her *Our Father*s, *Hail Mary*s, and *Glory Be*s.

Two and a half hours later, Bri returned the rosary to her purse, opened a bottle of mineral water, and took a sip. We were just south of Malibu on the Pacific Coast Highway—PCH to the surf crowd and those who can afford to live on the beach. The waves pounded the shore.

"I know he didn't kill himself," Bri said. Her voice was uncharacteristically solemn, yet removed like she might be beside herself, literally with her spirit astride her physical presence as she spoke. Her gaze was fixed, a thousand-yard stare down the Pacific Ocean shoreline.

I didn't engage. Wasn't sure what to say.

"Rafi would never do that to me," Bri said. She was louder this time, startling Marissa from her nap.

My wife looked irritated, skipping her usual mewing as she awakened. She was groggy as she spoke. "Never do? What's 'never do?'"

Bri didn't explain. I shot a glance at her through the rearview mirror. She stopped fidgeting with her engagement ring, looked at me and then at Marissa, and said slowly, pausing after each word, "He. Loved. Me."

"He adored you," Marissa said.

True love and adoration? Not the usual formulary for suicide. It was a no-brainer why Bri might think Rafi hadn't killed himself. Or how she might feel she was a secondary victim, collateral damage in a murder that confiscated her future. It made me wonder about the fluidity of narrative. Of perspectives that never overlap. Of stories that never coalesce into truth.

I wanted to believe her alternative storyline, her romantic tragedy. But thanks to Jenny's livestream video, I had seen the inside of Rafi's hotel room that night. There was no sign of a struggle, no overturned furniture, and no obvious defensive wounds on Rafi's face or arms. Granted, the paramedic may have jumped to a conclusion in his assessment, but it sure looked like Rafi had killed himself. And so far, Bri hadn't provided any evidence of foul play.

What if Bri's denial was nothing more than a mental defense against the stigma of Rafi's suicide? Something she had constructed subconsciously to deflect blame for holding higher expectations for their relationship than he could ever meet? Abril de la Guerra was a Type A+ personality. An archetypical striver.

In a vocal rage somewhere between a howl and a scream, Bri shrieked, "You...don't...believe me." Her face twisted with loathing, her eyes moist. "I can see it. I can smell your skepticism." She choked, tried to clear her throat, and choked some more.

Marissa unbuckled her safety belt, used the headrest to pivot herself as best she could so that she faced the backseat, and extended her hand to Bri. "I want to believe it…believe you."

"But you don't." Bri had gone hoarse. She now spoke in a raspy whisper.

Thank heavens, the shrill is gone.

But that didn't mean Bri was done with her rebuke. "I can do this on my own," she said next. "I can prove Rafi did not do it! I don't need incredulous pseudo-friends."

Before either Marissa or I could respond to the verbal gut punch, the seatbelt alarm kicked in. I didn't know which was worse, listening to the car nag about passenger safety or hearing Bri ding our friendship.

"For crying out loud!" Marissa repositioned herself in her bucket seat, fussed with the seat belt, and re-buckled.

When the incessant beep finally stopped and the dash warning light disappeared, I kissed my index and middle fingers and laid them on Marissa's lips. "Thank you."

She made a little heart shape with her thumbs and index fingers, placing it over her left breast. Good to know. At least at that moment, one person was in my corner.

Truth is, Bri's slap down shook me. No one had ever called me a "pseudo-friend" before. I didn't care for the sound of it and suspected Bri didn't really mean it.

Rafi, Bri, and I had been good friends throughout college. Marissa entered the picture a few years later but was no less committed to our bond as besties. There was nothing fake about our relationship. It was solid. Genuine.

"Okay, Bri," I said. "You made your point. You feel Rafi had too much to live for, that suicide is implausible."

"Impossible. And I can prove it, Thad." Bri sounded certain like she possessed facts in evidence, that we didn't have.

Marissa picked up on Bri's assuredness, following up with questions of her own. "So, Rafi was murdered? You can prove that?"

"Not directly." Bri leaned forward and got as close as she could to Marissa and me. "What I said was that I can prove Rafi did not *kill* himself."

"We're listening." Marissa pointed to herself and then at me.

I made the left-hand turn from the Pacific Coast Highway onto the California Incline, a slanted road that connects PCH with Ocean Avenue in Santa Monica.

Bri started fidgeting with her engagement ring again. "Remember the Dodge Whitney staffer who conference-called us Thursday night with the news?"

I nodded. Marissa nodded. In my mind, I replayed Jenny Yu's livestream of the crime scene. Her failed CPR attempt. And then my crazy request for her to rummage through Rafi's pockets to look for a suicide note or some kind of clue.

"That night Jenny said something that didn't quite make sense," Bri said.

At the top of the incline where it bisects Palisades Park, I turned left onto Ocean Ave and headed toward Bri's condo. I was about to ask, "What something?" when Marissa beat me to it.

Bri hunched even closer, positioning herself directly between the two bucket seats. "It has to do with the money," she said. "Remember when you asked Jenny to examine Rafi's billfold, and she held up a wad of mixed bills?"

"Yes," we said.

"My Rafi never carries that much money, even when he travels. He's one of those cashless euro-types. Cards only."

Perhaps Bri had a point. Rafi never seemed to have any greenbacks. He charged everything. He loved his American Express cashback card. It was the only card he carried when he traveled. And he claimed he was saving money every time he used it. "That's your evidence?" I said. "Your proof?"

"I'm not done!" Bri gave me the look. Marissa gave me the look.

I shut up.

"You two remember the old joke about how to tell if someone is an accountant?" Bri said. "Thad, you should know this one."

Actually, there are several such jokes, none of which are gut-busters. The punch line eluded me.

"Check their wallet," Marissa volunteered.

"Yes." Bri explained, "Real accountants order all of their cash facing forward, with bills grouped by denomination, larger bills toward the back. It makes it easier to count your money."

"Bri's on to something." Marissa wiggled in her seat and repositioned her seatbelt, trying to find a more comfortable way to sit. "Rafi's money was mixed up. I remember. A two-dollar bill in the middle somewhere, bills facing this way and that."

"That's our evidence? We're going to expose bogus suicide with his money being out of order?" I gripped the steering wheel as we slowed for the stoplight. "It might be a clue but it's not dispositive. Everyone who's ever worked as a cashier sorts their cash."

"Bri, have you contacted the DC Metro Police?" Marissa asked.

"I called their tip line. They listened. I could hear keys clacking as they took down notes while I talked."

"And? What did they say?" I asked.

"They thanked me. They took my contact info. They tried to comfort me by explaining that in the United States, people take their lives every twelve minutes. Men four times more than women."

Not very comforting.

"But did they say they'd look into it?" I asked. "The information you gave them?"

"Time permitting," Bri said.

Not very encouraging.

I pulled the car up to the covered entrance to Bri's Ocean Avenue complex. By now the sun hung low in the sky, the onshore winds from the Pacific close to thirteen knots an hour. I jumped out and ran around to the passenger side to open the back door.

Bri swung her legs to the ground, knees together. As she stood, she adjusted the jacket of her pants suit so that it once again snugged her waist. "Thad, a moment ago you questioned if my wallet-in-disarray theory was sufficient evidence and I didn't answer. You can be sarcastic at times. I wasn't sure if this was one of those times."

"I can be a dismissive dolt."

"And I can look past your minor character flaws, but what I need you and Marissa to understand is that my evidence—the money thing—is proof enough for me. Until I can find more." Bri folded her arms. "Thad, this was a homicide, not a suicide."

It had been another overly long, emotionally draining day. I was spent. I could only imagine what Bri was feeling, the existential questions running through her head.

Marissa lowered her window and said, "Bri." She held out her pinkie. They locked fingers and stayed that way for a spell. Strength through sisterhood.

Bri turned toward me. She gave me a long hug and as she did, I kissed her lightly on the cheek and whispered, "Listen, I think I may have a way to get closer to the evidence, whatever that might be."

"Walk with me," she said.

I did. As I escorted Bri to the tri-tower entrance, I shared with her the details of my meeting yesterday with Warnick.

"So, you know what Rafi was working on?" she said.

"I do."

"And if Marissa agrees to your plan?"

"Then…if there is something that clears Rafi, I'll be in place to help you find it."

Bri managed a smile. "I just love serendipity."

Chapter 8

"Do you want to hear my proposal or not?" Marissa asked.

We were finally back in LA. It had taken me two trips to the underground parking garage of our downtown apartment to clear the trunk. For a car with a 207-volt battery pack strapped to the frame, the Prius hatchback was still roomy enough for us to take too much with us, even for a day trip. Hospital go-bag, a change of clothing for the unexpected, a donut pillow, and vitamin water.

"I haven't made up my mind yet," I said. As I re-stocked the vitamin water in the fridge to cool, I noticed our inventory of fresh kale was low. "Alexa, add baby kale to my shopping list. Roots on. Hydroponic." The smart speaker confirmed my addition of living goodness.

"If we have enough for a green superfood monster smoothie," Marissa said, "I'd sure be obliged." She batted her eyes. She was seated on her yoga mat doing a butterfly stretch, what she would call Baddha Konasana or bound angle pose. She was clutching the heels of her feet to her pelvis, knees flat. Her torso was stretched to relieve her back pain from the long drive home. She inhaled through her nose and made funny open-mouth breathing sounds as she exhaled, kinda like beach waves crashing.

I pulled out the Blendtec, added frozen pineapple, a banana, half an avocado, two tablespoons of chia seeds, mixed in some greens, and crushed ice. Pushed the smoothie button and marveled as the kitchen tech whirred until what were once naturally occurring solids transformed into a green froth bubbling up to the latching lid of the BPA-free blender jar.

I poured two glasses and handed one to Marissa. "Proposal or proposition?" I asked.

Marissa ignored the double entendre and sipped her smoothie. She held out her free hand. I helped her up.

"A proposal assuming you decided…" Marissa said.

"To take Rafi's place on Gold II?"

"And assuming you couldn't live without me and invited me to take a leave of absence from classes at the gym so I could join you…"

"In DC?"

"In or about DC proper," Marissa said. "And, naturally, we would need acceptable lodging."

"Accommodations that you would find *acceptable*?"

"Given my condition, of course." Marissa gestured from head to toe. She drew closer to me and pressed her bulging stomach and full breasts against my body.

"Of course," I acknowledged.

"Double occupancy in a Dodge Whitney-provided extended-stay hotel isn't my idea of acceptable."

"You made that clear yesterday. When we were at the beach."

"So, hear me out, Thaddeus Jude Hanlon."

"All ears."

"Remember my uncle Leonid Petrovski, the

LUKOIL executive?"

"Yes."

Marissa was Uncle Leonid's favorite. He always called her by her Russian name—Matryoshka. Her parents had named her after the Russian nesting dolls. One mystery inside another.

As head of the Russian oil giant's North American retail operations, Leonid was on the road a lot. And every time he was in LA, he made sure to visit us to sample Marissa's borscht and savory blinis.

"So, my little *zaichik*," Marissa said, "LUKOIL is sending Uncle Leonid to Moscow for three months. Aunt Nika's staying put. Yesterday, while you were with Warnick, my uncle called to tell me he wouldn't be stopping by anytime soon. And…"

"And what?"

"I was thinking their Georgetown brownstone is spacious, has a yoga room, and Nika might like some company."

Marissa and I hadn't been married that long, but in some ways, she knew me better than my mother did, may she rest in peace. Marissa, for instance, knew what a difficult time I had saying no to logic, to reason, and to clever. It was obvious she thought she had such a proposal. But I wasn't ready to concede just yet.

I drew Marissa closer. Without warning, I inched my hand down Marissa's side and started tickling her. One final retaliatory gesture before surrender.

"Thad, don't! Please, stop. You'll throw the baby into a hiccup pattern and I'll be up all night."

"Saint Thaddeus will come to your rescue." I gave her my best-crooked smile, the mainstay of all Hollywood action-adventure heroes. "And if I can't save you and Lil' Thadpole, who can?"

Marissa pushed away my hand. "You can be such a dork." She tried to pinch me but wasn't fast enough.

"Loving dork," I countered, "and on the fast track to becoming a successful dork." I held her for a good long time before I reached for my phone and texted Warnick: —*I can be in DC on Monday.*—

He sent back a thumbs-up emoji.

By Monday morning, I was in the nation's capital. Marissa was safely ensconced in Uncle Leonid Petrovski's brownstone in Georgetown. Aunt Nika was doting on her. And I was three miles away, standing in front of the reception station of the Dodge Whitney Washington DC office, about to check in with the administrative assistant sitting behind the dark walnut and quartz slab countertop, when someone grabbed me from behind.

"Come on, Hanlon. You're with me." The man squeezed my arm.

I recognized the voice and did an about-face. After I caught my breath, I said, "Going where?"

Tigran Vardanyan grabbed for my red combo backpack/briefcase. "Nowhere just yet, Hanlon, as long as you have that ratty thing in your hand. Give it to me."

I tightened my grip and wouldn't let go. "It has sentimental value. You can understand that, right?"

"Hanlon, get a clue. This is Washington, DC, the seat of the Alpha Democracy. The Center of the Universe. Not a Silicon Valley startup where the dress code is 'California casual.'" The senior manager made another attempt to separate me from my bag. "Hanlon, I don't have time to babysit you."

I clutched my trademark bro satchel that had seen me through four years of college. "Red on Red," Rafi called my fashion choice. A red school combo backpack/briefcase to match my red hair. Pragmatic and distinguished. Made it easy for my study buddies to spot me across campus.

"Give it," Tigran reiterated. He yanked harder.

I'm taller than average at six feet two inches, with over-developed shoulders from paddling out into every imaginable size wave, but definitely no match in tug-a-war with a five feet six inches two hundred-ten-pound heavyweight contender in a Brooks Brothers suit. I let go of my hunter red backpack/briefcase duo. Tigran stumbled, narrowly missed a pratfall, then regained his footing. He flung my bag behind the reception station.

I could hear a thud and a tinkle of glass that wasn't encouraging. "Hey, my wife's photo was in there."

"So sorry." Tigran yanked me through the double glass doors of the Dodge Whitney DC lobby. "I'll get you another frame at the Dollar Store. And Hanlon…"

"Yes."

"For Heaven's sake, stick your Pentel pencil in your inside coat pocket. You look like a computer geek."

"But it's my tool," I said.

"We do this my way, Hanlon. Put your tool away where no one can see it."

"Tigran, why are you being so nice today?" I kidded. I had worked with him in the LA office before. He was being more Napoleonic than usual.

"Hanlon, today's a training day. Yours is not to reason why—"

"Yours is but to do and die? Tennyson's *The*

Charge of the Light Brigade? You want I should be more duteous?"

"Something like that."

The Tigran Vardanyan I knew in the LA office had a sense of humor. He told stupid accounting jokes like "How many auditors does it take to change a light bulb?" and recited bawdy financial limericks at the Angels Flight bar—the local watering hole that catered to the Dodge Whitney after-work crowd.

This Washington DC–Tigran was different. He was one hundred percent game-face earnest, sullenly serious like he was saddled with some Atlas-sized weight on his shoulders.

Rafi's death had been a shock to all of us. For Tigran, the loss of Rafi on the Gold II team appeared to change things. And I sensed he wasn't happy to pull me from the bench to substitute for his star player.

For whatever reason, I got the impression I would never live up to my senior manager's expectations. Something about this job was turning out to be a total fun suck for him. Dollars to donuts, I'd bet Tigran hadn't laughed since he took on Gold II.

We skipped the elevator and headed straight for the stairwell. Tigran's hulking footsteps echoed as we passed the large black numbers painted on the concrete walls of each landing.

As I followed the conservatively dressed Dodge Whitney senior manager in a quick trot down the stairs, I tried again to find out where we were headed. "Destination, Tigran?"

"Not now," he said. "When we get outside where no one—especially other DW staffers—can hear us. Then, I'll explain."

Once we reached the first-floor landing, Tigran shoved open the metal fire door leading into the Willard Office Building lobby. We hustled along the crimson, yellow, and gold geometric-design carpet that led to the F Street back entrance of the facility, passing a satellite office of the brokerage house, Goldman Sachs. An LED stock ticker display flashed the latest market prices. The Standard & Poor's 500 index was down a fraction. Gold prices were up.

Tigran stepped through the double glass doors onto F Street. I was right behind him. He scanned the sidewalks for a cab stand.

Across the street at the entrance to yet another DC luxury hotel was the closest taxi queue. The line was short. Businessmen and women milled, dressed to impress.

For a hundred yards in either direction, the sidewalk on our side of F Street NW was empty, probably because of the scaffolding blocking pedestrian traffic where the northwestern exterior of the Willard was being renovated. No one was within earshot. Tigran took the opportunity to school me.

"Listen carefully, Hanlon," he said. "Two years, right? You've been at Dodge Whitney a little over two years?"

I nodded.

"Then, you know it's Dodge Whitney policy not to discuss our clients in public. Our work is confidential. Clients expect us to be discreet. With Gold II it's even more critical."

"Understood. I signed an NDA last week."

"Hanlon, I don't think you *do* understand. At least not the ramifications."

This is getting serious.

"Can you imagine, Hanlon, how the mainstream media, cable news, or even the Twitterverse would react if they knew about the nature of our engagement? It's—"

I held up my hands to call for a time-out. "Tigran," I said, "other than our client requires Department of Justice clearance for me to come on board, I don't have a clue about this job. I've never been fully briefed on *the nature of our engagement.* And much as my wife thinks my imagination is usually overwrought, I am having trouble *imagining* a Gold II media firestorm when I haven't even been read in on the details of my assignment."

"You done venting, Hanlon?"

I swallowed, clearing my throat. "Okay, I may have been a little whiny. I can work on that."

Tigran shook his head. He motioned for me to follow him. "Time to meet the client, Hanlon," he said. "This morning's destination is the Treasury Building for a short status presentation to TSec. It's a short walk from here. We'll be avoiding crowds, so it may take a little longer than usual. Keep close. Don't discuss the job unless we're in the open, no one near enough to listen to us. Hear me, Hanlon?"

"I hear you. What's TSec?"

This was new jargon for me. The accounting profession, like any specialization, is full of acronyms and initialisms. I raised my brows, sporting curious eyes.

"Hanlon, this is about to get real. Think you can handle it?"

"Yeah."

"Just out of curiosity, why'd you say yes to Warnick? To this assignment? Your wife is what, six months along? Oh, by the way, she did look fetching at the annual bookkeeper bash last week, but very pregnant and not entirely comfortable. You could have telecommuted and Zoomed in."

"Warnick invited me. I'm *ever* the team player."

"Really?" Tigran gave me a don't-pull-my-chain look.

We took the crosswalk from 15ᵗʰ Street to the east side of the Treasury Building, threaded through the metal bollards designed to look like antique outdoor landscape décor, and continued south.

I slowed my pace not to outstride the senior manager and his stumpy legs. "Tigran, you want the reason I took the assignment? Warnick said Gold II would be a career turbocharger. And Marissa thought it would help me work through Rafi's death by finishing up what he had started."

We took a right at the southeast corner of the block-long Greek Revival temple dedicated to the coin of the realm. Sightseers holding tiny American flags circled the larger-than-life-size statue of the first Secretary of the U.S. Treasury, Alexander Hamilton. We skirted the tourists taking selfies with the man in bronze and hiked over to the grass, away from everyone.

"I think we're alone now," I said.

Tigran surveyed the southwest corner of the Treasury Building grounds, doing a full 360. "You're right. There doesn't seem to be anyone around."

"Are you going to reveal what 'TSec' means? Before we meet whoever we're meeting inside?"

"Promise you'll behave? I realize some of this 'hiding what we're doing' is going to seem over-the-top. You have a tendency—"

"To be playful. To be a child at heart."

"That."

"Tigran, Gold II is a big opportunity for me. I'm not going to risk doing something stupid."

"Promise?"

I crossed my heart.

Tigran groaned, then proceeded. "The Treasury Secretary is TSec. That's her staff nickname, like POTUS for the President of the United States. And because of the delicate nature of our assignment, we've assigned a stronger nickname—really more of a code name—to Gold II. You'll hear Acting Treasury Secretary Kennedy Beck and anyone else on the job refer to it as National Brick and Foundry."

"These code names," I asked, "are special precautions to keep Gold II out of the press?"

"They're one active measure." Tigran's eyes narrowed.

"What other measures should I be aware of?"

"Safeguards, really," Tigran said. "So, in addition to code names, we have a cover for you. Your background story for whom you're supposedly working. There's even the audit sandwich."

I worked hard to avoid a smirk. Tigran had gone deep James Bond. The next thing I knew, he was going to have us do SDRs—surveillance detection routes—to dodge suspicious operatives in oversized black SUVs. Come to think of it, we had taken a long way around to the Treasury Building. "I know I promised not to be snarky, but you're serious, aren't you?"

"Completely serious, Hanlon." He clenched his teeth, making it hard for me to understand his words. "Thirteen years. That's what I have in at Dodge Whitney. The average time to partner is twelve years at our CPA firm. This is my up-or-out year. Gold II is either my ticket to partner or my pink slip out the door."

"Oh," was all I could say. I looked away for a moment to regain my composure. "Sorry." I hoped I sounded genuine. I was trying to be.

If office rumors about Tigran were true, he still hadn't passed the CPA exam, at least not all four parts. Advancement in the firm to senior manager usually required having been awarded a state-issued certified public accounting license—what in Dodge Whitney office jargon was known as the "License in Hand Rule."

Tigran didn't have his CPA license.

Candidates for licensure need to meet all three E's: Education, Experience, and Exam.

The first two E's my senior manager had more than satisfied.

And he was within a whisker on the third.

He successfully passed three of the four sections of the Uniform CPA Exam.

But AUD, the fourth section, he had just missed the minimum score of seventy-five out of ninety-nine. Audit and Attestation was his nemesis, the part he was short of a passing score.

But apparently not too short to make an exception.

With availability in the job market for experienced senior managers stretched tight, Dodge Whitney gave Tigran a pass on its promotion policy. This one-time.

There would be no exception to License in Hand

for advancement to partner. The up-or-out threat to Tigran's career was real. I wouldn't want to be in his shoes.

Dodge Whitney, like the Big Four accounting firms it emulated, had a pyramidal organizational structure. The vast base of the pyramid was comprised of Associates, competitively recruited from select accounting programs across the globe.

The second layer of the pyramid was proportionately smaller and made up of Senior Associates like me. The proportion dropped even further for the third layer—the Managers.

Tigran Vardanyan was in the fourth layer—the small cadre of Senior Managers biding their time before making the big bucks.

At the top was the final five percent of the pyramid—the Equity Partners—the owners of the firm who got a cut of the profits.

Keeping the top of the pyramid pointy was legend. Up or out was the norm. You either were promoted or were coached out. There were no career managers, no career seniors, and no career associates. Only partners on the audit side and principles on the non-CPA consulting side. Tigran's remaining career at Dodge Whitney had a nearing expiry. I could definitely sympathize.

"Hanlon, you give me pause," my senior manager said. "You genuinely do. But Warnick vouches for you. Says you have skills. Says I can trust you to be a professional in front of the client."

"I won't embarrass you or the firm." I sucked in a deep breath. "Tigran...what's my cover?" I was being as sincere as I could be. "And, just wondering. What's an audit sandwich?"

"I'll get to that, but first, let me explain your cover identity. You're GAO."

Images of two classmates from Cal State flickered through my mind. Both Melia Melkon and Koji Hayabusa had taken positions with the Government Accountability Office. They said the money at the GAO wasn't nearly as good as public accounting. And that there was no real upside, like becoming a CPA firm partner. But at least they had work-life balance, never putting in more than forty hours a week.

"Hanlon, you're working for Uncle Sam now. The Gold II audit team is on loan from the GAO."

My phone vibrated. Marissa texted a blowing kiss emoji. She wanted to know if I was coming back for lunch.

I told her I couldn't make it, that I was deep into the onboarding process. —*Maybe dinner*.— I texted.

"Let's go, Hanlon. We don't want to keep Kennedy Beck waiting any longer." Tigran grabbed my arm and escorted me to the granite steps of the west façade, to the famed Bell Entrance.

Tourists clad in everything from brightly colored shorts and shirts to lightweight cotton suits lined the public ingress to the Main Treasury Building. At the foot of the steps, a docent stood next to a replica of the Liberty Bell, corralling visitors into the next tour group about to trek inside. The smell of magnolia blossoms from the trees dotting the building grounds sweetened the air.

Tigran and I sprinted up the steps. He shoved open the main door and tried to step through. He didn't get far.

Blocking our way was a scrum of visitors huddled around the foyer exhibits. Tigran juked right, whipped out his GAO pass and photo I.D., and flashed them. He charged through the metal detector.

"What about your associate?" One of the security guards, an African-American female protecting the halls of Treasury Headquarters from unauthorized access, pointed directly at me.

"Hanlon, show 'em your creds."

I held up my temporary I.D. badge, my California driver's license, and smiled.

Tigran pointed to his watch. "We got to run."

I rushed through the metal detector and caught up with Tigran. He wound through the lobby toward the curved, cantilevered staircase, then raced up the marble stairs to the third floor and the Treasury Secretary's office. I was as close as his shadow.

Chapter 9

Just as we were about to enter Suite 3330, we heard a voice from inside TSec's office.

"Halt, gentlemen!" It was a man's voice. No-nonsense. Resolute.

I didn't decelerate fast enough from our sprint down the hall and smashed into Tigran's back, knocking him off balance. He teetered on one foot, stumbled forward, but somehow righted himself and then promptly froze.

Blocking the entrance to Kennedy Beck's reception area was a member of the U.S. Secret Service. The Treasury Secretary's security detail was in his early forties, triathlete trim, with skin the color of driftwood. He wore a tailored navy-blue suit draped over a wiry frame, with bulk in just the right places. His prematurely white hair was closely-cropped, Marine style. The agent motioned for us to back up.

Tigran said, "I am so sorry—"

"Drop the briefcase," the agent said, cutting off Tigran mid-apology. "Do exactly as I say. Hands behind your head. Interlaced." The agent's face was expressionless.

With his left hand, the agent systematically frisked us. He made Tigran bend over and open his briefcase. He ran a paddle-shaped wand over the contents. No beeps, no flashing LEDs.

"Not two seconds ago, I got a call that one of you was flagged as you went through the arch metal detector," he said. "So…we're going to do this one at a time." He held up the wand, motioning for Tigran to step forward. He ran the hand-held scanner over Tigran's body, not once but twice. The wand never made a peep.

"You next." The agent pointed at me with the paddle.

I moved forward, hands still interlaced behind the back of my head. "I can save you some time," I said.

The agent ignored me and wanded me anyway. The device chirped.

"Big wave wipeout," I said. "Banzai Pipeline, North Shore, Oahu. I have a plate."

"Show me."

I took off my suit jacket. Rolled up the sleeve of my dress shirt. Exposed a nasty scar from a surfing accident where the orthopedic had rebuilt my right wrist and forearm with titanium implants.

"You can put your jacket on," the agent said. "And next time, gentlemen, follow protocol. Our security screening serves a purpose. Wait for the STEP-THROUGH confirmation before you take off running. Bypass and you force a weapons search."

"My apologies." Tigran stretched his hand out, realized the agent wouldn't shake, and dropped his arm to his side. "I assure you, it will not happen again, sir." Tigran pivoted, made eye contact with me, and said, "Right, Hanlon?"

In awkward client situations, accounting firm protocol is predictably hierarchical: *Keep your mouth shut. Let the ranking professional on the job do all the talking.*

I was glad Tigran was in charge and not me. I said nothing. Gave my best subservient smile.

From behind the reception station, a fashionably dressed man in his mid-thirties popped out. "Agent Jaxon," he said, "I'll take over from here."

The Secret Service security detail nodded. He kept his eyes on us as he retreated to his watch station at the back of the outer office to Suite 3330. There he resumed his vigil.

"Messrs. Vardanyan and Hanlon, Agent Jaxon Casama cleared you. You don't need to stand in the doorway. Please..." The man who intervened on our behalf, motioned for us to enter.

We did.

"Cole Lecompte, Chief of Staff." The man brought his right hand to his chest to signal he was referring to himself. "You may call me Cole." He then mimed air handshakes, first to Tigran, then to me.

Unusual greeting.

Tigran gave a slight nod to acknowledge the introduction. I followed his lead.

Cole had a real flair for color pairings. He sported a slim-fit mocha suit and a white-on-white dress shirt with a teal skinny tie. He delicately grabbed Tigran's arm just above the elbow. "This way."

We took a right turn from the outer vestibule into the Treasury Secretary's formal office. Beck was wearing a fire-engine red high-collar jacket and matching trousers. Coupled with her trademark bowl-cut hairstyle and squatty football frontline frame, she reminded me of a bulldog in a pants suit.

Rather than a presidential cabinet-level player, I

would have pegged the Treasury Secretary as a no-nonsense top-ranked litigator in the Department of Justice or a crack attorney for the enforcement division of the Security and Exchange Commission. She definitely had a prosecutorial look.

TSec turned her attention to the two of us and motioned for us to advance. "Gentlemen, I've been expecting you."

Tigran stepped forward and gave TSec a mom-like hug. They exchanged pleasantries and talked at length about someone named Fitz. While they did, I caught myself staring at the Acting Secretary of the U.S. Treasury, Kennedy Beck.

I was starstruck. Though I had seen TSec's face hundreds of times in the business press, I couldn't believe I was about to meet her—meet a financial demigod, one of a handful who manages the wealth of nations and decides world fate. There was only one thing keeping me from intimidation paralysis. Today Secretary Beck appeared a smidge more approachable than her cable financial news persona, less gladiator in a suit, less pugnacious. It gave me a good vibe.

"Thaddeus," Beck said. She extended her hand, nails perfectly manicured. Her skin was soft. Her grip measured. "Welcome to the Gold II team."

"Madam Secretary, call me Thad if that's easier. Fewer syllables."

Tigran squinted and pursed his lips, looking like he was sucking on a California lemon, Eureka variety, super tart.

I could take a hint. "But…my given name is just fine. I didn't mean to be impolitely informal." I took in a breath. "And, may I say, Secretary Beck, this is such an honor. Meeting you." My cheeks flushed.

Beck withdrew her hand and said, "Thaddeus, I understand you were good friends with your predecessor. My sincere condolences."

Her concern moved me. I stumbled through run-on thank yous, references to Rafi, how he was like a brother, and big shoes to fill. When I finally finished effusing, she motioned for Tigran and me to join her in the conference room adjacent to her main office.

In the center of the space was a walnut boardroom table, positioned over an ornamental area rug of patriotic reds, blues, and white. Eight fabric-covered chairs flanked the table.

"Sit anywhere?" Tigran asked. He stood just inside the doorframe of the conference room. He rubbed his hands and wiped them on his slacks.

I was right behind him. In the overmantle mirror above the fireplace, I could see our reflection.

Tigran's left eye was twitching.

Nerves?

Tigran was normally self-possessed around clients. Today was different. His deodorant was failing. I wondered if I was the only one who could tell.

"Up here," Secretary Beck said, placing herself at the head of the conference table.

Tigran sat to her right. He pointed to the empty chair next to him. I took my place.

Secretary Beck fingered the briefing folder Cole had given her earlier when we transitioned to the conference room. The cover was stamped TOP SECRET NATIONAL BRICK. She steepled her hands, brought them to her lips, and then rotated her wrists until her fingertips pointed at Tigran. "Don't you think it's time we brief Thaddeus?"

Finally!

TSec sat up straight in her boardroom chair. She angled toward me and said, "You like origin stories?"

Given that I was jumping into the middle of an ongoing project, I didn't think it could hurt to start at the beginning. I said, "Yes."

"Good answer." Beck opened the National Brick folder. She flipped to the first tab. "We'll start with the Nixon Shock."

I'm sure I looked puzzled. I wasn't making the connection between the 1972 break-in to the Democratic National Committee headquarters and the first gold commission of 1981-82. "Nixon Shock being Watergate?" I sought to clarify.

Tigran shook his head. "Before Watergate. Before the president's surprise resignation. Pre-scandal."

"A shock of a different kind," Beck said. "Let me explain. Mid-summer 1971, the international financial markets were in turmoil. The Federal Reserve had pumped up the money supply to pay for the Vietnam war. Wages and prices soared. Prompting…how can I put this in layman's terms?"

TSec's backstory about the second gold commission was getting technical. I was hoping we would get to my part in the narrative soon.

"Prompting…," Tigran said, "a run on the U.S. gold window."

"More like a stampede," Beck said. "No one wanted inflated U.S. currency. First, Switzerland redeemed fifty million dollars in U.S. Federal Reserve Notes for gold. Then, France exchanged a hundred ninety-one million dollars. Next thing we know, Great

Britain wants to cash in three billion at the U.S. Treasury gold window. And that was just the beginning of the foreign bank panic. At the time, the U.S. had only three point two billion that could be used to cover such requests."

It didn't take a math whiz to see the numbers weren't going to work. Demand exceeded supply. I said, "So, Nixon intervened?"

"He did. It was a Sunday," TSec said. "Middle of the dog days of summer, right after a secret meeting at Camp David with high-ranking White House and Treasury advisors. Nixon goes on TV, issues a presidential directive, and officially closes the gold window."

Tigran chimed in. "Nixon's so-called 'intervention' broke the link between the dollar and gold for good. The result: the U.S. debased its currency, moving to pure fiat."

I had heard the term "fiat" before. In my money and banking class. And not in a kind way. As a pejorative. My professor, using colorful language, explained that with fiat you take an intrinsically worthless object such as paper, and presto-change-o, like magic, you declare it to be money. No backing necessary. No silver. No gold. Poof! Instant legal tender because the government says so.

"Can we go back to the gold window?" I asked. "Secretary Beck, when you say 'closed,' are you referring to a real-life window? Like a teller's window at a bank?"

"Thaddeus, now we're getting into my dissertation 'In Gold We Trust: Stabilizing U.S. Financial Markets by Returning to a Gold Standard.' I'd be happy to share a copy with you."

I wasn't sure I wanted to do a deep dive into the nuances of monetary policy. I said, "I'm fine with an executive summary. If that's okay. No disrespect."

There was a flicker of disappointment in Secretary Beck's eyes at losing a ready audience, given the depth of her research passion. But she was gracious enough to give me the abridged version, starting with gold confiscation under Franklin D. Roosevelt's Executive Order 6102 and ending with the Republican Party's atonement for the economic fallout from Nixon's Shock when President Reagan convened the First Gold Commission.

I took a deep breath, thanked the Treasury Secretary for the double-digit inflation history lesson, and wondered out loud, "So what happened to the first commission?"

"They punted, at least the majority did," TSec said. "After Federal Reserve Chairman Paul Volcker took a fire hose to inflation, the country's mood shifted. By the end of 1982, the cry for a return to the gold standard had subsided."

Beck pulled a copy of the 1982 commission report from the briefing folder on National Brick. She flipped to the section on domestic monetary policy arrangements and pointed to the first commission recommendation:

Under present circumstances, restoring a gold standard does not appear to be a fruitful method for dealing with the continuing problem of inflation.

"Committee-speak for 'no change in policy,'"

Tigran elaborated.

No wonder any memory of Gold I had faded into the collective unconscious of the U.S. The First Gold Commission had essentially been a non-starter. Whatever the dangers from Nixon's Shock and the resulting embrace of pure fiat currency, Gold I had produced no answers, fruitful or otherwise.

I said, "Madam Secretary, you mentioned the majority punted. Am I to understand there was a minority?"

Beck's eyes lit up. "Perceptive, Thaddeus," she said. "Yes, there were two members of the first gold commission who dissented. One is our link from Gold I to Gold II."

Tigran pursed his lips. He looked like he was about to say something that started with the capital letter *O* or *R* or *W*, but decided against it, and smiled obsequiously at TSec instead.

Beck eyed Tigran, nodded, and continued, "Former Texas Congressman Ron Paul *was* and *is* an outspoken gold bug. Fast forward thirty years to the Great Recession of 2008-2009. Congressman Paul introduces the Federal Reserve Transparency Act into the House of Representatives."

"H.R. 1207," Tigran added.

Hard to fault transparency. It's right up there with other government tropes like "accountability breeds response-ability." I was hoping Gold II wasn't going to be a make-work exercise in window dressing.

"Thaddeus," Secretary Beck said, "care to know what was in Congressman Paul's bill? There's a direct link between the Transparency Act and Gold II. It's another piece of the genesis puzzle. It's why you're sitting here with me today."

Chapter 10

Of course, I was curious. A half-hour into my briefing and I still had no idea what my new responsibilities were. Only that my hush-hush assignment had something to do with an obscure piece of legislation.

"The gist of H.R. 1207," Beck said, "was full Fed transparency—something the Federal Reserve has avoided since its inception in 1913."

There was *that* word again. I wanted to know Beck's definition of the term. "*Transparency* meaning what in this context?" I asked.

"Meaning the bill directed the Government Accountability Office to conduct a full-scale congressional audit. All the numbers. All the policies and procedures. All the gold the Fed claimed to have on its balance sheet."

"That never happened, did it?" I said. "Unless transparency doesn't include letting the public know."

Tigran gave me a play-nice look.

I backpedaled, dropping into my best conciliatory tone. "Being that if there *had* been a GAO audit in the last ten years, the Fed wouldn't be once again under fire. Investors would be less worried about a national debt that has ballooned from five point six trillion to thirty trillion. The price of gold wouldn't be at an all-time high."

Secretary Beck pulled a single page from her briefing folder. "Good guess. The original legislation authorizing the audit never passed. Not then. And not recently, when it was reintroduced. Death by congressional gridlock. That's why the White House decided to act."

She slid the official-looking document over to me.

"Take your time, Thaddeus. Buried in the executive order is a 'sunshine guarantee' clause. See if you can spot the nugget."

PRESIDENTIAL EXECUTIVE ORDER ON THE ESTABLISHMENT OF THE SECOND GOLD COMMISSION

By the authority vested in me as President by the Constitution and the laws of the United States of America, and in order to promote a return to sound money, it is hereby ordered as follows:

Sec. 1. Establishment. The Second Presidential Advisory Commission on Gold is hereby established.

Sec. 2. Membership. The Secretary of the Treasury shall chair the Commission, which shall be composed of not more than 14 additional members.

Sec. 3. Mission. The Commission shall, consistent with applicable law, conduct a study to assess and make recommendations regarding the policy of the U.S. Government concerning the role of gold in domestic and international monetary systems.

Sec. 4. Administration. Until such time as the Federal Reserve Transparency Act (H.R. 24) or a similar bill is passed by Congress, audit oversight responsibilities for the Federal Reserve will be let out for bid to an independent third party.

Sec. 5. Termination. The Commission shall terminate 30 days after it submits its report to the President.

Sec. 6. General Provisions. To the extent permitted by law, and subject to the availability of appropriations, the Government Accountability Office (GAO), on a reimbursable basis, shall provide the Commission with such administrative services, funds, facilities, staff, equipment, and other support services as may be necessary to carry out its mission.

THE WHITE HOUSE

I skimmed. Sunshine guarantee sounded significant, but I was drifting to sleep. The import of what TSec was saying wasn't fully registering. My eyes drooped. I took my Pentel pencil from my inside coat pocket and covertly jabbed my thigh, hoping the poke would offset the onset of more than mild jet lag from my west coast flight. In a reflex jerk, I banged my knee on the conference table. For the moment, I was awake.

As Secretary Beck watched my head-bob-knee-smack blooper, she said, "Oh, how clumsy of me. Would either of you like something to drink? Coffee? Soda? Cole can arrange it."

Salvation.

"Yes. Yes," I said. "Diet cola. Large. Ice. Lime, if you have it."

"Sparkling water, Madam Secretary," Tigran said.

"Thank you."

TSec's chief of staff arranged for the beverages, some fresh scones, and a latte for the Treasury Secretary. While we took a break, Beck stood, pushed her chair back, and crossed over to the fireplace. On the wall to the right of the over-the-mantel mirror was a sheet of U.S. currency in an oversized frame.

"You see these," she said. Beck pointed to the collection of gold and silver certificates that hung on the wall. "Until May 1, 1933, you could take one of these gold certificates to the Treasury Cash Room downstairs and exchange it for gold coins or bullion. That was before FDR's E.O. 6102. It was proof of the financial stability of the United States. Sound money. Hard currency."

I joined TSec to take a closer look at the artifacts hanging on the wall. My eyes roved the framed currency, coming to a hard stop on a one hundred thousand dollar gold certificate, a thing of beauty I had never known existed.

Woodrow Wilson's face was on the front. The back, printed in bright orange, looked like Monopoly money. On each certificate was engraved the phrase "gold coin payable to the bearer on demand."

Pure poetry.

Gold certificates sure would have been nice to have in my Christmas stocking. Growing up, I'd have been happy with a ten-spot convertible to shiny coin, but the Santa who climbed down the Hanlon household chimney had only left a few arcade tokens.

Cole reappeared from the main office. He ushered in a middle-aged man wheeling a serving cart. When the attendant removed the stainless-steel plate cover, steam rose from the scones. My stomach rumbled. Cole noticed. So did TSec.

I massaged my midsection to stifle the growl. "Sorry. It must be the scent of fresh-baked goodies." I snatched the soda from the cart and started to sip. My heart rate began to edge up to normal.

"Fresh each morning," Beck said. "Best to eat warm."

She picked up the plate and offered me a scone, took one for herself, and handed the rest to Tigran. Cole slid a serving tray toward me with locally sourced honey.

"Delicious," Tigran said, wiping crumbs from his lip.

"Even more so with this *honey*," I added as I munched the baked goods. I took another giant gulp of soda and returned to reading the executive order.

After a few minutes, I thought I spotted a possibility for a sunshine guarantee in the phrase "other support services" but before I could confirm, TSec took her napkin and drew an organization chart. She sketched the hierarchy of the U.S. Department of the Treasury.

Reporting directly to TSec was the deputy secretary, the position Beck had held before she was appointed acting secretary of the treasury. And reporting to the deputy secretary were all the operations people and their cascade of boxes.

Beck moved her pen back to the top of the chart. Off to the side of the highest box, she drew two new boxes. These positions reported laterally to the Treasury Secretary. One was her chief of staff. She scribbled in Cole's name. The other org chart rectangle she labeled

OIG. She circled that one.

"Office of the Inspector General," Tigran said.

Clarifying the initialism helped, but still left me confused. What connection could there possibly be between the OIG and sunshine?

"The Treasury Inspector General is responsible for auditing the deep storage reserves," Beck said

Tigran saw my brow furrow. "Mint holdings," he explained. "Deep storage reserves are the portion of Treasury-owned gold bullion, which the U.S. Mint secures in sealed vaults. Over 261.5 million troy ounces. At today's spot market prices, close to a half-trillion dollars."

Big stakes. At a burn rate of one million dollars a day, every day, it would take me over a thousand years to spend through every last troy ounce. Marissa and I could have a lot of fun. Such luck, I only wish.

"Here's my concern," Beck said. "Much as I trust my people, having the Inspector General—a U.S. Treasury Department employee—audit the Treasury's gold stockpile, sounds a lot like the fox guarding the henhouse."

I could see the problem. The OIG was doing an *internal audit*. The Transparency Act specifically called for an *external audit* of the Fed by the Government Accountability Office. "Have there been issues with previous internal audits?" I asked.

"Some gold market watchers say *yes*." Beck told of rumors that had surfaced. Issues regarding audit procedure. Insufficient assays of gold bar purity. Unaccounted-for differences between depositories.

"I think I know what you mean by 'sunshine guarantee'," I said. "It refers to Section 4 in the

Executive Order. The part about having an outside third party shining a light. Guaranteed independence. Riddle solved."

Head nods all around.

Beck said, "Your job, Thaddeus, as 'independent third-party,' is to finish what Mr. Silva started. To conduct the first true audit of depository gold owned by the United States in almost seventy years. Tigran tells me you can fill Mr. Silva's shoes."

All eyes were on me. I gave them my best game face, the one I save for inspiring confidence in a twenty-seven-year-old, ruddy-faced redhead with a surf hairdo. Professionalism personified.

I must have passed the test because Beck didn't push some hidden button under the conference table to have me escorted from the Treasury Building. Instead, TSec sipped her latte, turned her focus to Tigran, and said, "Gold II status?"

Tigran hoisted his briefcase onto his lap, snapped the clasps open, and withdrew a thin sheaf of paper.

"To date, we've finished thirty percent of the work," he said. "We're ready to move into Phase II. The addition of Hanlon couldn't have come at a better time, especially with his expertise in mining and metals."

Kennedy Beck pulled up her phone and checked her calendar. "Can we go back to the thirty percent? Doesn't sound like you're on target."

"We lost a week with the suicide, but…" Tigran shuffled through his papers until he found the pages he was looking for. He displayed a combination of fancy PERT project management and Gantt project timeline charts. Task dependencies over time. "…but we can get it back," Tigran said. "We add bodies. We pump overtime."

"The remaining seventy percent? All of it?" Beck looked to Tigran, waiting for his answer.

A bead of sweat formed above Tigran's upper lip, glistening under the conference room lights. "Yes," he said.

"A bet-your-career yes? Or, Tigran, a yes-maybe-if-the-stars-align? I'm not sensing a lot of confidence. You know you can be honest with me. We have a history." Beck set her phone down on the table, the calendar app still glowing.

"Yes, Madame Secretary. On time. Under budget. As promised."

"No more hiccups?" Secretary Beck slipped her copy of the president's executive order back into her confidential briefing folder. She pushed the folder to the side.

"Agreed."

"And, Tigran...oh, this is for you too, Thaddeus...let me be clear why. The President loves the gold standard. He sees it as a way to fire up his base and build interest for his presidential re-election campaign."

The Treasury Secretary retrieved her phone and thumbed through several screens until she found what she was looking for. She pushed play on an interview clip and increased the volume. It was the president in a video interview before he ever took office.

"Believe me, bringing back gold as a standard for our money, would be fantastic. Hard to do, for sure. But as a defense against inflation, the best. Absolutely the best!"

Before the video segment could loop, Beck shut it off. "Let me see if I can put this in perspective. Your task of auditing the Fed is not about pandering to the 'Audit the Fed' crowd. Nor is it about making the Federal Reserve Board Chairman the scapegoat if inflation spikes further. This is bigger. This is preemptive. The Second Gold Commission is about finding a way to dismantle the printing presses. *Before* we head into hyperinflation."

"Time-critical," Tigran said. "I understand."

I didn't. At least not all of it. Madame Secretary wanted us back on schedule, meeting our milestones. That I understood. Gold II couldn't move forward without hard numbers on the deep storage bullion inventory. Also understood.

Until Dodge Whitney wrapped up its audit, any recommendation concerning the role of gold in domestic and international monetary systems would have to wait. That, too, I could grasp. Two critical steps, sequentially dependent.

But there was more to the TSec's sense of urgency than audit results driving gold's future. This was personal. Her end game seemed to stretch far beyond Dodge Whitney's involvement.

"One more thing, Tigran…" Beck paused.

Tigran was multitasking, carefully arranging his status report papers in the folder while he listened. He stopped. Gave TSec his full attention.

She continued. "In addition to getting National Brick back on track, promise me no more amateur faux pas. We hired Dodge Whitney for a reason. Your man, Rafael Silva, had audit papers in his briefcase. Papers linking my department to National Brick. My people had to work DC magic to sanitize his hotel room and keep his death out of the press. Need I remind you Gold II is *classified*."

Tigran's shoulders sagged for a bit before he straightened up, inhaled sharply, and flexed his chest. It gave him an air of confidence but not necessarily the look. "Madam Secretary, no instant replays. I promise."

"I keep my commitments," Beck said. "I expect the same from you, Tigran. Too much is at stake."

Secretary Beck rose. She motioned for my senior manager to come close. She gave him a quick hug. I got up and shook her hand. She yoked us together between her arms and walked us from the conference room to her office. Through the corner windows, I could see the National Mall and the Washington Monument in the distance.

"Know this, gentlemen," she said. "The only way to make America even greater is to make her money great again. We can't do that if the Fed starts the printing presses. Goosing the money supply has toppled more than one nation. I'm not letting that happen. Not on my watch."

I had my marching orders and a short fuse. Marissa wasn't going to be too happy about the overtime. That was something we hadn't planned on.

Chapter 11

Once outside the Treasury Secretary's office suite, Tigran raced for the nearest drinking fountain. He dropped his briefcase. As he pushed the button on the faucet, his wrist trembled. The water stream dribbled at first, arcing unevenly.

He removed a monogrammed handkerchief from his breast pocket, ran it under the spigot until it was soaked, and used it to wipe his brow.

I caught up with Tigran at the bubbler. "Can we debrief? I have questions."

"I bet you do." Tigran wrung his handkerchief, carefully refolded it, and tucked it into his pocket. He slicked back his cola-brown hair. It had filled with perspiration during our meeting with the Treasury Secretary. Had that funny smell that people who sweat from their heads get. Smoky without being a smoker. My nose wrinkled.

"Would I be breaking cover if I asked what's the plan for the rest of the afternoon?"

"Plant tour," Tigran said. "After the lecture in TSec's office, I could use a change of scenery. Let's get out of here."

Ninety-nine percent of all audits begin with an operational overview. Not only did a tour of the client's facilities help auditors understand the context of their investigation, but sometimes it was more interesting than the audit work itself. Kind of like an on-premises *How It's Made*—the behind-the-scenes science documentary on the manufacture of everyday products. In my short two-plus years with Dodge Whitney, I had toured a gold mining operation in the Rockies, a high-tech handgun manufacturer, and a video game development company.

We traced our path back to the grand staircase. Just north of the circular stairway was the third-floor elevator bank.

"Tour of what?" I asked. "The U.S. Bureau of Engraving and Printing? Or the Philadelphia Mint?"

This could be fun.

"The Treasury Bureau of Fiscal Service, Hanlon. I'll introduce you to Rafi's old team. Get you settled in."

We approached the marble columns that guarded the stainless-steel elevators. "So which floor is Fiscal Service on?" I asked.

"Not here. This building is strictly for policy people. Operations such as the Bureau of Engraving, the Internal Revenue Service, and the Bureau of the Fiscal Service are off-site. Fiscal Service is in an annex building on 14th Street down by the Jefferson Memorial." Tigran pressed the down arrow on the elevator call panel.

We took the elevator to the first floor and headed out the west entrance. As we weaved through the tourists lining up outside the Treasury Building, Tigran took out a slip of paper to write something but changed his mind. He crumpled the paper and tossed it into the rubbish.

"Four zero one," Tigran said. "That's the address

on 14th Street. Do you think you can remember that?"

"Like the retirement plan. Got it."

"I have some errands to run, so I'll meet you there at two p.m. That should give you plenty of time to grab lunch and retrieve that thing you call a briefcase from the office. Do you copy?"

Tigran had dropped into black ops mode, lingo and all. I decided to humor him.

"Copy that, sir," I said. "Permission to speak freely?"

Tigran rolled his eyes.

"Sir, the debrief? The post-mortem following our meeting at ten-hundred hours with TSec, sir?"

"Hanlon, cut the crap. There's a fine line between following orders and being a smartass. This is a serious assignment."

I bowed my head. Got very deferential. "But my questions, Tigran? I really want to know."

"I have time for two."

We returned to the grass area at the southwest corner of the Treasury building where, earlier in the morning, Tigran had revealed to me who our client was. There were no crowds. No listening ears.

"Okay," I said. "Two questions. They're in priority order."

"Hit me."

I pointed to the third floor of the southeast corner of the Treasury building, to the windows facing out from Kennedy Beck's office. "Tigran, you seemed pretty buddy-buddy with TSec. What's up with that?" I mimed giving him a virtual hug.

Tigran slapped away my hands. "Familiar, yes, Hanlon. But I wouldn't characterize our relationship as 'buddy-buddy,' even though Kennedy Beck and I go back maybe ten years. She's more like a bonus mom."

"Okay, same question, part two. Who's Fitz?"

"Her adopted son, Fitzgerald. Fitz and I met in the Chicago Booth MBA program. We were on the same case study analysis team and did all our write-ups together. Really hit it off. Hung out at his mom's house on the weekends for the home-cooked meals. I stayed with them for the holidays while my parents were always on a world cruise somewhere. Kept in touch ever since."

Good to have friends in high places.

Tigran's mention of home-cooked meals had my stomach grumbling again. TSec's fresh scones had been yummy but apparently not enough to curb my appetite. And seeing the parade of food trucks bordering Constitution Avenue only made me hungrier. As soon as we were done with the debrief, I figured I might head over to the National Mall and grab a Philly cheesesteak or some pulled pork BBQ.

"Tigran, what's an audit sandwich?"

My senior manager checked his watch. "The answer's kind of involved," he said.

"It's my last question. Promise."

Actually, I had a million more questions, but Tigran looked like he was pressed for time. I didn't push my luck. Didn't ask why Warnick had never mentioned *beaucoup* overtime was going to be needed to get Gold II back on schedule, or just exactly what was meant when Secretary Beck said Rafi's hotel room had been sanitized, or why Agent Jaxon Casama had been so intense when he frisked us, especially since this wasn't the first time Tigran had been to TSec's office.

"It's a strategy," Tigran said. "The audit sandwich is my creation. You won't find it in the textbooks." There was a gleam of satisfaction in Tigran's eyes, a look I sensed was a grown-up version of what he must have felt as a child when his mother would mount yet another one of his stellar report cards on the fridge and smile. Parental pride building self-esteem.

Tigran continued, "An audit sandwich is a way to perform a clandestine investigation without anyone knowing."

"And this strategy works how?" I gestured for Tigran to keep the explanation rolling.

"Ingeniously simple. An audit sandwich is two to three layers of related but wholly superfluous audit activities surrounding the true meat of the audit." Tigran paused, waiting until I acknowledged the genius of what he had said.

When I nodded, he continued. "In this case, the meat of the audit is the verification of the Mint-held deep storage gold. The collateral. What backs up the eleven point one billion dollars in gold certificates the Fed says it owns."

"The shiny stuff. The gold bricks."

"In layman's terms, yes. Twenty-four-karat glitter."

"So that's the meat. Checking to see if the gold's there. What's the bread?" I asked.

"Right, the bread. How should I say this?" Tigran hooked his pointing finger and rubbed his nose. "The bread," he said, "the bread is how we hide what we are genuinely doing."

"You mean misdirection? Like what magicians do?"

Tigran smiled. "You're a regular Harry Houdini."

I knew something of the dark arts of accounting, had spotted my share of shell games as a forensic auditor, but didn't claim to have any real tricks up my sleeve. "So, are you going to tell me what the bread is or keep me in infinite suspense?" I tapped my watch.

"The bread," Tigran said, "the distraction component of the sandwich, as it were...is a review of a much bigger number on the Federal Reserve's balance sheet. I'm talking about the one point twenty-five trillion dollars in toxic home loans that the Fed bought during the Great Recession as part of the financial industry bailout."

I whistled. "That'll take an army of accountants. Spreadsheets stacked to the moon."

"Exactly. Misdirection perfection." Tigran paused. "You'll be running a huge team of interns with those ten-key calculator-style keyboards and an Excel program. In truth, no one will suspect what you and your team are doing."

"So that's an audit sandwich?" I said. "Two mega-slices of bread hiding the beef?"

"My great and unmatched brilliance blinds me at times."

I wasn't sure if Tigran was being funny-sarcastic or sincere. The grin on his face looked natural without an upturned smirk on the lips. Nope, it wasn't sarcasm. He was into self-flattery. In this case, deserved self-flattery. His diversionary tactic was clever, not something you'd ever expect from a major international accounting firm known for integrity and transparency.

"This audit sandwich..." I said while scratching my chin. "Am I going to be working on the 'meat' or the 'bread'?"

"You'll get a taste of both."

I groaned.

"Rendezvous at fourteen-hundred hours, 401 14th Street. Be prompt, Hanlon." Tigran left.

I made a beeline for the food trucks.

Two hours into my new assignment and I had met the client, had a better picture of what Rafi was investigating, and had some idea of the risks posed by Tigran's audit sandwich strategy. Now all I needed was to somehow access Rafi's files, pick up his digital trail, and get a sense of where he left off.

Time to rifle through Rafi's things at the Bureau of Fiscal Service.

Chapter 12

"Get in, Thad." Bri was driving an exotic rental—a sunshine yellow Jaguar F-type sport convertible with the top down.

I had been hoofing it back to the Dodge Whitney DC office to get my combo briefcase while downing DC's finest pulled pork sandwich, careful to keep BBQ sauce from spotting my tie. As I crossed 15th Street going east on Pennsylvania Ave. NW, Bri had pulled up beside me.

"What are you doing here? And I mean that in a good way." I jumped in the car and banged my knee on the wrap-around console. It felt like I was sitting in a cockpit. The leather seat was comfortable, though. Supple. "I only have an hour."

"Buckle up." Bri punched the gas pedal.

"I have to be down near the Jefferson Memorial at two p.m. near 14th Street, briefcase in hand. Bri, I cannot be late."

"That could be tight. We have to make one stop before I drop you off."

"Can we get something to drink first? I could use another soda to wash down lunch."

"You can get something from the vending machines when we get there."

"Get where?"

"DC Metro Police."

That left me no choice. I reached for the jumbo cup in the rental car console, not caring what was inside the Styrofoam, and took a big swig. I almost spit it out and wished I had. My throat was burning.

"Chocolate habanero chai," Bri said. "Had to go to the Logan Circle District to find it."

"Nasty." I coughed. My tongue was on fire.

Bri fished around in her oversized handbag, pulled out some sugar-free gum, and handed me a piece.

I popped in the gum. Worked it in my mouth until the heat from the habanero chilis dulled. "Aren't you supposed to be in Century City wrapping up the April thirty fiscal year-end for one of your hedge fund clients? You told Marissa you couldn't get away for several weeks until the numbers were in."

"Plans change."

"Hillenbrand and Rose gave you grieve leave?"

"The partner in charge could see I was unfocused. Said I needed to work things out. They gave me the option of mandatory grief counseling or a week off."

"When do you start counseling?" I gave her half a wink. It was as a partial jest meant to be hearteningly witty yet sensitive.

Bri wasn't amused. "A week's leave should be enough, don't you think?"

"To work things out? Or to get your mind back on your clients?"

"To investigate. To find Rafi's killer."

Bri was serious.

We headed east on Pennsylvania Avenue toward the U.S. Capitol. Noonday traffic wasn't bad.

"I can count on your help, right, Thad?" She looked my way for confirmation.

True, the day of the funeral, I had offered her words of comfort, something to the effect that once I was on-premise and had picked up where Rafi had left off, I might be able to help. Rafi was my best friend, and I owed him that much.

I just hadn't expected Bri to parachute into my schedule before I had even been fully onboarded.

"A week?" I said. "You'll be here for a week?"

"Only if it takes that long." Bri was straight-faced.

Abril de la Guerra comes from the declarative world of the elite. Every statement is an illocutionary speech act, a truth to be realized. Confidence born of royal breeding makes it so.

"Just curious. How did you find me?" I said. "No one's supposed to know where I am. Marissa doesn't even know. I'm undercover."

"Location services." Bri handed me her cellphone.

The screen was opened to a friend-finding app. I could see my picture floating on a map of Washington, DC.

"Thad, I've been tailing you most of the morning. Who's the thickneck you've been following around like a puppy dog?"

I gave Bri back her phone. Made a mental note to review my privacy settings. So much for being covert.

"The body builder's Tigran Vardanyan."

"From the Dodge Whitney LA office? The one who helped you manhandle me into the car after I decked Warnick?"

"The same. He's the senior manager on the job. He's helping me pick up where Rafi left off."

Bri gunned the engine. "So, you know who Rafi's client was? What he was working on?"

"It's classified. I could lose my job."

We hung a hard left on 6th street. Bri's long chestnut brown tresses bounced behind her in the wind. "I lost my entire future," she said. "I lost Rafi." She shook her head.

I had seen that head shake before. Recognized it for what it was—patrician disbelief. This was Bri's way of affirming that I was utterly clueless, that I didn't understand the resolve of the rich. No matter how many excuses I could invent, she was going to get her way. I should just tell her everything. Socio-economic determinism was in her favor.

"What if we did hypotheticals?" Bri said.

"Like hypothetically, let's say Rafi was working on a secret audit of the U.S. gold reserves?"

"Like that. Like what might have got him killed."

I briefed Bri on Gold II using theoreticals, conjectures, and suppositions. Made her promise not to say anything or I'd deny everything.

"Does Marissa know any of this?" she asked.

"She will. We don't keep secrets."

We pulled into the parking lot at DC Metropolitan Police Headquarters, a couple of blocks shy of the U.S. Capitol. Lunch hour was apparently a popular time to visit the local police department. Parking was non-existent. I fired up a car park app on my phone. Found a place at the corner of 6th and C street on the backside of MPD, complete with valet service. Bri was charmed by my tech skills.

The Henry J. Daly building has one thing going for it: a classy 1940s art déco façade. Too bad social media reviews for Metro PD were sans enthusiasm. What didn't help, for sure, were the concrete Jersey barriers out front and the stone bollards ringing the entrance. It made the eight-story building look like a distressed fortress rather than a welcome center for a law enforcement/community policing partnership. And although Bri might have been gung-ho about her chances of seeing Rafi's case file today, I had my reservations. She wasn't an immediate member of the Silva family. Being engaged to be married doesn't grant next-of-kin status.

We climbed the steps to the entrance and pushed through the revolving doors into the north lobby marked Public Entry. Bri scooted past me to check the building directory hanging from the greige marble walls. Meager light from a row of pre-WWII sconces lit a memorial plaque for the building's namesake.

"Room 5059," she said.

We took the elevator up.

The main desk for the MPD Command Information Center was swamped. We took a number and took a seat.

The waiting area reminded me of a California DMV office—people filling out forms, clutching documents, and checking their smartphones. This was not Central Booking like I imagined. It seemed to be more non-emergency services, without the calm. I could smell failed deodorant as workaday men and women came and went. For some of those in the queue, personal hygiene had never been a priority.

"Can we talk about that night?" she said. "I want to have my facts straight."

So, we went through the gory details. We talked quietly about the images from the hotel room where Jenny Yu had discovered Rafi's body. I cringed when we remembered aloud the stripped lamp cord wrapped about Rafi's arm, the burn marks, and Jenny's reaction to the smell. Bri shuddered when she shared her panic at seeing Rafi's blueish-purple face, his glazed eyes, unfocused, staring motionless. We played over and over the fruitless attempt by Jenny and the paramedic to revive Rafi. And then balked together at the paramedic's mention of possible suicide. Finality made worse by insinuation.

Gold II had spooked Rafi. He had reached out to me and wanted to talk. In that last phone call, he asked for my advice. Said something about a *plan*. He didn't sound depressed.

Forward-thinking people do not commit suicide. Rafi had everything to live for. None of this made sense.

Fifteen minutes passed before they called our number. The uniformed desk sergeant shuffled some papers, looked up, and peered at us through the bottom of her bifocal glasses. "Yes," she said, "how can I serve you?" Her full lips never moved. Ventriloquism in the most unexpected places.

"My name is Abril de la Guerra," Bri said. She waited just long enough for me to introduce myself, then continued. "I'd like to speak with the detective assigned to the Rafael Silva suicide," she said.

"What's your relationship to the deceased?" the desk sergeant asked.

"Fiancée," Bri said.

"This is a new case, right?" the sergeant said. "Not a cold case?"

"Rafael died last Thursday, April twenty-seven, a little before midnight," I said.

The desk sergeant held up a finger. "Give me a second." She pulled her computer keyboard over and rattled the keys with her French nails. The screen blinked as she paged through the search results. Multicolored lights from the display reflected on her face.

"You'll want to talk with the supervisor of the Family Liaison Specialists Unit," the sergeant said. She looked directly at Bri and then at me. "I'm sorry for your loss." Her voice was deep and reassuring, lips parting to reveal a tangle of orthodontic wires, metal brackets, and pink and white bands. Dental wax had been applied to where the hardware irritated her gums. Painful. A good reason to be tight-lipped.

"This supervisor? Which room?" Bri asked.

"Oh, not here, dear," the sergeant said. "Across town at the MPD First District Station. 101 M Street SW. The old Anthony Bowen brick schoolhouse."

"What about the detective I talked to on the Tip Line?" Bri said.

The desk sergeant gave us an encouraging look and said, "Start with FLSU."

Then she called the next number in the queue.

Chapter 13

"Across town" in DC is nothing like "across town" in LA. Instead of an hour or two, it only took us seventeen minutes via I-395 and that was even with a detour to the Dodge Whitney DC office to get my combo backpack/briefcase.

We parked across from the First District Headquarters and scrambled through the bright blue double doors into the low-slung red brick building. The supervisor of the Family Liaison Specialists Unit had just taken her lunch break, so we met with one of the specialists instead. The name tag on her right breast pocket said A. FERGUSON.

"This can be such a terrible time," the specialist said. "Life-shattering loss punctuated by bouts of grief." She looked directly at Bri, made eye contact, and then did the same with me. I felt like she was trying to give me a hug with her mind and make a soulful connection. "Being a family survivor is tough," she said. "Whatever resources we have, we're here to support you."

Bri wasn't as touched by the comfort-talk. She was looking for answers. "Ms. Ferguson, thank you for taking a next-of-kin meeting with us on such short notice," she said. "This won't take long."

"Can I offer you some bottled water? Coffee? Tea?" Specialist A. Ferguson wasn't going to be rushed.

I was about to decline anything to drink and even got so far as to say "Nothing for—" when Bri cut in.

"The case file?" she said. "We'd like to see it."

I gave Bri my best dirty look. Short-circuiting the FLSU specialist's hospitality right now seemed counterproductive. Formalities have their place.

Bri ignored me. "Ms. Ferguson," she said, "your office provides updates about investigations to family members, correct? We'd like to see Rafi's file or meet the detective assigned to the case."

A. Ferguson got up, went to her mini-fridge, and pulled out three bottles of mineral water, fresh from a national big-box wholesale store. "Ms. de la Guerra, how is it that you are related to Mr. Silva?" She set two of the water bottles in front of us.

"Almost related," Bri said. "We were engaged. The wedding was planned for July seventh."

Ms. Ferguson looked at me and asked, "Mr. Hanlon, are you next of kin?"

"Rafi Silva was my best friend."

"This is awkward," A. Ferguson said. "You caught me off-guard. MPD policy is that a next-of-kin meeting is open only to the decedent's immediate family members or their designee." She emphasized *only*. "We need to back up a step."

Bri pulled a form from her purse and handed it to the specialist. "Would a notarized Limited Power of Attorney form resolve this?" Bri asked.

"It depends."

"This was signed by Rafi's parents. It authorizes me to inquire into police matters regarding their son and to retrieve his personal property seized at the crime scene."

"Can I see some photo identification? We need to ensure family privacy."

Bri flipped open her phone case where she kept her California driver's license.

A. Ferguson compared the photo on the license with Bri's face, which was none too easy given the California state seal covered the top quarter of it. The specialist then matched the signatures on the license with the POA. "You can put away your ID." A. Ferguson leaned back in her desk chair, took a sip of her mineral water, and said, "What would you like me to tell you?"

"What's in the file would be a start."

"Not much. The C.M.E.'s report. The field officer's report. An interview with the woman at the scene. Photos. And some notes."

"C.M.E is Chief Medical Examiner?" I asked.

Specialist A. Ferguson nodded. She lifted the cradle on her desk phone and punched in a four-digit intercom code. "Would you bring me the Rafael Silva case file, please?"

"The C.M.E.? What did she say? What was the cause of death?" Bri asked.

"C.O.D. was low voltage electrocution. We don't get many of those. She also ran a tox screen."

"Rafi was poisoned?"

"For suicides, we always check for prescription—"

"*Suspected* suicide," Bri corrected the family liaison specialist.

"Let Ms. Ferguson finish," I said.

"Ms. de la Guerra, we can do this another time, if you prefer?" the FLSU specialist said. "The circumstances of the death, the photos you'll see in the file, are all so very troubling. This has got to be hard."

Bri is usually not a weepy soul, but her tear ducts didn't know that lately. Her eyes glistened. I reached over and hugged her. She buried her face in my shoulder.

A courier with a file in hand slipped into the office and approached Ms. Ferguson's desk. "Here's the jacket you asked for," he said. A. Ferguson signed for Rafi's case file. The brick-red multi-folder was thinner than I would have expected.

Before the courier had even left the office, Bri snatched the case file from the desktop. She offered no apology to the specialist. Just started flipping through fastened pages of the "jacket," leafing back and forth between the dividers. When Bri turned to the photos, she stopped. The 8x10s were so much larger than the images we had seen on my mobile phone screen that night. I caught my breath. Jenny Yu had said the hotel room had an acrid smell. My nose itched.

Bri removed one picture, the one with the lamp cord wrapped around Rafi's arm. She examined it, pulled out her phone, and then used the camera lens as a magnifying glass to enlarge a section.

"You see anything?" I asked.

"Not sure." Bri slid the photo to me. "You look."

I did. Wasn't sure what I was checking for but held the picture at various angles, moved in close, then held the glossy print at arm's length. If something was amiss, I couldn't see it. I handed the photo back to Bri.

She tucked it into the folder, then flipped to the Medical Report. She checked the summary of the toxicology screen. Then, she ran her finger over the

C.M.E. autopsy narrative, reading it line by line. She stopped when she got to the manner of death and shook her head. Only one had a check mark.

—Natural

—Suicide…Check mark

—Homicide

—Accident

—Could Not Be Determined

"Ms. Ferguson, it wasn't a suicide," Bri said. "I explained that to the detective from the Tip Line." She clenched her jaw. Her knuckles turned white as she made fists.

"Your call-in notes are there," A. Ferguson said. "I can show you." She tapped the back flap of the file folder. "You did see them, right?"

"Yes. I saw the telephone transcript."

"All I can tell you then, Ms. de la Guerra, is that based on the autopsy and lab results—the lack of bruising or defensive wounds, no foreign DNA under the fingernails, a clean tox screen—the C.M.E. checked the box she felt best interpreted the medical evidence. Does that make sense?"

Just as Bri's chin broke into a full quiver, she cupped her hands over her mouth and stifled a faint moan. Whether the C.M.E.'s professional opinion made sense or not, Bri was clearly not ready to hear it.

"Let me help you, Ms. de la Guerra. We have grief counselors. I can book you an appointment this afternoon."

Bri took a tissue from her purse and wiped her nose. She closed the case file and was about to slide it back to A. Ferguson when I stopped her.

"Did you read the inside flap?" I asked.

Bri fumbled with the heavy cardstock of the multi-panel case jacket until she found the Metropolitan Police Department Public Incident Report pegged to the inside flap.

"Take a look about a third of the way down on the face of the report," I said.

Bri ran her finger down the form until she reached the line labeled *Case Status*. "Administratively Closed," she read aloud. She grabbed the folder, cradled it to her chest for a full minute, and then slammed it down on A. Ferguson's desk. It sounded like small-caliber gunfire. MPD staff walking the hallway stopped mid-stride. Conversation ceased. There was an apprehensive quiet in the office.

"Closed? As in no investigation?" Bri was shouting, shaking her fist at FLSU Specialist A. Ferguson. "Homicide Branch isn't going to do anything? No probe? No follow-up on the leads I gave you? The tips?" Bri jumped up from her chair and leaned in to make her point. "This can't be right!"

"Ms. de la Guerra, please sit down. I need you to calm down. Can you do that?"

Bri was shaking. I got up, helped her back to her seat, and coached her to take deep breaths. Her nostrils flared while she oxygenated. Eventually, she relaxed her hands and unclenched her fists.

"Thank you," A. Ferguson said. She leaned back in her office chair, putting distance between herself and Bri. "Believe me, I know how upsetting this must be."

"How could you possibly know?" Spit flicked from Bri's lips. Droplets landed on A. Ferguson's desk. Bri folded her arms tight across her chest.

The FLSU specialist's eyelids dropped, staying that

way for a beat before she spoke. "Honey," she said, "this is Washington, DC, not some palm-tree paradise in sunny SoCal. And my job—my entire career—is to meet with families in distress five days a week. The news I have to share is often gut-wrenching, just like yours and…" A. Ferguson brought her water bottle to her lips, took a sip, and swallowed.

Bri sat rigidly and waited for the woman to continue.

"And every single day, Ms. de la Guerra, I tell those left behind, just like you, the unimaginable. I tell them about some random act that hurts like being shivved, cut when you least expect it," A. Ferguson said. "So yes, sister, I do know *upset*. And aftermath. And especially scars."

Bri relaxed her arms, dropped her hands in her lap, and closed her eyes. She stayed that way for maybe five minutes before returning to the conversation.

"I am so sorry," she said. "This…my behavior…this is not me. It's not who I am. Rafi's death has me all rewired." Bri looked at me. "Ask Thad."

"Not her usual self," I found myself saying. A. Ferguson didn't look like she believed me. I took a swig of my water.

"Control. I am usually in control," Bri said. Her rage-red face had returned to a healthy color. She pushed the case file over to the specialist. "You know, Ms. Ferguson, what would provide some comfort and help me move on?"

"What might that be?" The FLSU specialist was guarded in her response.

"Meeting with the responding officer," Bri said. "If

I could have a few minutes with him to discuss the incident report, that would provide solace."

Ferguson opened the case file and scanned the inside flap. "Officer Ziobro is stationed in Second District. That's where the report was filed. I could check with the District Commander, but it will have to go through channels."

"Where's the Second District Station?" I said.

"Over near the National Cathedral. A good half hour from here."

"What about the detective assigned to Rafi's case?" Bri asked.

"That's a much simpler request. Homicide Branch is located right here in the First District Offices. Let me see if Detective Mapu is riding his desk today or out in the field."

Chapter 14

Homicide Detective Mapu was in his office just down the hall from FLSU. As he plunked away at his keyboard, he chowed on a pressed-rice sandwich wrapped in paper-thin seaweed—Spam *musubi*. Now and then, he licked grains of sticky rice from his fingers.

"*Eh, sistah and braddah*, have a seat," the detective said. "*Wen pau da* paperwork, we talk."

This was going to be interesting. Hawaiian pidgin in Washington DC.

"Long way from home, *brah*," I said. "You Big Island?"

"Nah, Oahu. North Shore. Your face sound familiar. You player?"

"Small *kine*, *brah*. World Surf League poser. Mainland, most time. South Bay, off Santa Monica Pier," I said. "Once I go surf Sunset, Rocky Point, the Pipe."

Bri leaned forward in her chair. "Thad, you keep yakking and Detective Mapu won't be able to finish his report."

Detective Mapu gave me a gap-toothed grin. "*Brah*, we talk story later, otherwise, look like she goin' *pound* you." The detective pushed away his keyboard.

"Detective Mapu, pleased to make your acquaintance," Bri said. She stood, extended her hand,

and squeezed.

"And yours, Ms. de la Guerra. So sorry for your loss. Aliyah Ferguson messaged me about you two. Said you were on your way over." Detective Mapu rubbed his hand as he sat down.

"You speak perfect English," Bri said. "That's not quite what I expected."

Mainlanders! Bri was going to have to work on her cultural sensitivity.

I stood, then rounded Detective Mapu's desk. I shook his hand. "Much call for island pidgin in DC?"

"There's a small population but *ohana* just the same. Island pidgin is useful. Good for Samoans, Tongans, Maori, and Tahitians with Hawaiian ties."

"Incident Report CCN# 17956372," Bri said. "The Rafael Silva investigation. Can we focus on that?" She pointed to her watch.

Timely move. We only had a half-hour before I had to be at the Fiscal Service Bureau offices, so this was going to have to be fast.

"The electrocution at the Foggy Bottom Suites last week? That case?" the detective said. "The C.M.E. ruled it a suicide."

"We know," I said. "But what we don't understand is why the case status is listed as *Administratively Closed.* Are you saying a suicide classification means no further investigation?"

"This may sound harsh, *brah*, but yes. With a confirmed suicide or death by natural causes, there is no crime to investigate."

"But didn't you read the Tip Line transcript? The suicide was staged," Bri said.

"Ms. de la Guerra, here's what we know. Based on

the evidence the forensics team collected at the scene, there was no indication of foul play. There was no break-in. No struggle. And nothing to indicate that anyone else was in the hotel room when Mr. Silva plugged himself into the electrical outlet. But you already know that. Aliyah Ferguson let you read the case file."

"What about my tip about the money? My fiancé never carries any cash."

"The money? The twenty-five hundred dollars? Yeah, we checked into that. Forensics ran prints on the bills. They found lots of partials, fo' sure, but they also found full fingertip images. Mr. Silva's thumb and index fingerprints were on every single greenback."

That was damning. If the cash in Rafi's billfold wasn't his, then why did the forensic evidence indicate otherwise?

"The bills were out of order," Bri said.

"As are the bills in most people's wallets, Ms. de la Guerra. That's not proof."

"Our engagement picture was missing," Bri said.

"This is your probable cause for a fake suicide?" Detective Mapu asked. "Are you sure he ever put the picture in his wallet? Would you swear to that under oath?"

"But I did give it to him." Bri got out her tissues again. She was sniffling. "The photographer must have taken fifty, sixty shots. That pose? The one for the wallet photo? Rafi picked that himself."

The talk of pictures and snapshots had me thinking about the case file, about the crime scene photos we had looked at with A. Ferguson. I closed my eyes, retrieved the mental images, studying the details. I couldn't shake an anomaly that came into focus.

"How is it, Detective Mapu," I said, "a left-hander, such as Rafi, has the dexterity to wrap his left forearm with stripped wire using his non-dominant right, and then plug the cord into a socket? Wouldn't he naturally use his left?" I demonstrated a wire-wrapping motion with a degree of awkwardness that left no room for doubt.

Bri looked pleased by my theory. "The photo in the case jacket," she said. "I knew there was something odd. There's no way Rafi could have possibly killed himself. His suicide was staged by someone who didn't know he was left-handed."

"Mr. Silva was a lefty?" Detective Mapu said.

"Yes," Bri said.

"One hundred percent," I said. "Goofy-handed, goofy-footed. Smudged all his handwriting when he took notes, used left-handed scissors to cut, paste, and assemble—essential skills for a CPA—and surfed right-foot forward."

Detective Mapu didn't look sold on the staged suicide hypothesis. "When you two surfed, he ever take any rights?"

Goofy-footed surfers favor left-peeling waves. It allows them to take off facing the swell. Makes it easier to read the surf, to adapt to changing conditions, to carve like a master.

When lefties take off on a right-peeling wave, their back is to the swell. It's awkward and requires constantly looking over your shoulder, but goofy-footers riding rights is not impossible.

"Rafi was ambipedal," I said. "Left-curling waves, right-curling. He'd take whatever."

"If Mr. Silva was equally skilled with his feet, is there a possibility he may have been so with his hands?"

"Ambidextrous?" Bri said.

"I'm not trying to be unsympathetic, Ms. de la Guerra, but yes. It just doesn't seem like there's enough to go on here. Homicide Branch has a backlog of open unsolved cases. Resources are limited and sometimes we have to move on."

Not what either of us wanted to hear, but for the moment, it did sound like a good suggestion. It was getting late. I couldn't afford to arrive at the Fiscal Service Bureau behind schedule. "Come on, Bri," I said, as I tugged on her arm. "This isn't panning out."

Bri pushed my arm away. "What about his telephone logs, Detective Mapu? You must have pulled his telephone records. Who was the last person he spoke to? Did you interview him or her? And what did they say?"

"Ms. de la Guerra, I truly am sorry. I wish there was more we could do," the detective said. "We are way understaffed."

Bri raised her eyebrows. She looked like she was about to counter but apparently decided against it. Detective Mapu wasn't the problem. At some level, she had to know that. Though by the look on her face, I could tell she wasn't happy about it.

"You got a business card, *brah*?" I asked. "We'll be in town for a while. Thought I'd check out the local waves. Maybe we could catch a few together."

Detective Mapu fished a card out of the plastic holder on his desk, flipped the card over, and wrote his cell number on the back.

"Tough times for both," the detective said. "All the more reason to hang loose, *brah*." He gave me his card. It read DUKE "DOOGIE" MAPU.

"Your parents?" I said. "They named you after The Duke, didn't they?"

"*Fo' sure!* The Big Kahuna himself—Duke Paoa Kahinu Mokoe Hulikohola Kahanamoku—Hawaii's ambassador of surf," the detective said. "It's impossible to compete with a legend, so *da' braddahs* call me Doogie instead."

I slid Detective Mapu's card into my nylon wallet and gave him a quick fist bump. "*Mahalo nui loa*," I said.

Detective Mapu stood up. "I should be the one saying much thanks. It's good to put a face to the case. Thanks to both of you for coming in." Doogie Mapu gave us one big *aloha* smile.

I grabbed Bri's arm and tugged. "We've got to bolt."

Once outside the First District Police Headquarters, Bri dropped any pretense of self-censorship and began criticizing MPD's investigation or lack thereof. "Rafi deserves better," she said. Her pupils narrowed into pinpricks, sucking out any sparkle left in her hazel eyes. As we walked back to the car, she said, "I can't let this go. I won't!"

We were clearly dead-ended at Metro PD. Bri was understandably flummoxed, maybe even indignant. In a perfect world, the police brand—the proverbial to Protect and to Serve—wasn't supposed to be hostage to resource constraints. But in the imperfectness of Washington, DC reality, understaffing meant Rafael Silva's case was officially closed.

When we reached the parking lot, Bri mashed the keyless remote a couple of times. The rental convertible beeped in response, taillights flashing. We jumped in and headed west on M Street. The Jag's quad exhaust growled as Bri raced the beast of a sports car. Definitely not eco-friendly, but brutally potent just the same.

"Bri, can I ask you something?" I said. "Why not hire a private detective? Your family has money."

Bri angled right onto Maine Avenue, gunning the engine. The tires squealed as they grabbed. "My parents, yes. The same parents who think I was about to marry beneath myself. Thad, what you don't understand is that Rafi was *my* darling, not theirs. Mother and Father…they had much bigger plans for me."

Usually, my relationship radar can pick up on these things, but apparently not this time. "I didn't know. I mean, Rafi told me your parents had already dropped hints about grandchildren. That your father was jockeying for naming rights for the first boy. He had even picked out 'Julian.'"

Bri snorted. She sounded like a spirited thoroughbred. "All part of Rafi's charm offensive." She reached over the console and activated the convertible roof switch. The top retracted. "What's sad," she continued, "and this is going to sound harsh, Rafi only seduced himself. His own insufficiency blinded him. You need to know the truth."

"Insufficiency for what?"

"It takes more than charm to be one of us. To be a *de la Guerra*."

"He was a purebred Spaniard."

"It takes more than DNA *and* charm."

"But *you* loved him?" I said.

Just then, Bri slammed on the brakes. I almost hit my head on the dash. The taxi behind us had to swerve to miss us. Bri was trembling. The smell of burnt rubber was in the air.

I reached over and steadied the steering wheel. "Can we move to the curb?"

Bri let up on the brakes. The car sputtered to a stop in a bus lane abutting Benjamin Banneker Park. She released the steering wheel. The sobs came in waves. I put my arm around her and pulled her close. Her chest heaved as she tried to catch her breath.

"He's gone," Bri tried to say.

"I miss him, too." My eyes started to leak. I never knew it would be this hard to lose a good friend.

"Somebody wanted him dead," she said.

"I know."

Bri fixed her eyes on mine. Her eyeliner was a mess, her nose red, cheeks puffy. She looked through me and said, "What are you not telling me, Thad?"

I gave Bri my clean handkerchief, tilted the rearview mirror so she could see herself, and make whatever improvements she could. I said, "Remember the night of the annual dinner when you overhead me telling Marissa that I had talked to Rafi earlier, before the gala?"

"Only vaguely. I was pretty wasted."

"Rafi said he was running late that evening. But that was not all. He said more."

"Like what?"

I told her everything. I shared Rafi's suspicions. And I revealed that he had uncovered something during the Gold II probe. Something sizeable.

"Thad, why didn't you say something sooner?"

"It was easier not to."

Bri slugged me in the arm. I deserved it. Maybe even two slugs.

"So, you do believe me?" she said.

"I believe if the police can't do the policing, we should hire a private investigator."

"Rafi and I don't have much money, Thad. At least, not enough to hire a PI."

"What about life insurance? Dodge Whitney carries term life on all its staff."

"His parents are the beneficiaries. We were going to change that after the wedding."

"But you two are DINKs. You live in a three point five million dollar condo overlooking Santa Monica Bay. And you drive matching Teslas."

"The cars are leased. Rafi was prone to impress to excess. For a kid who grew up mucking stables at his parents' boarding ranch in Central California, somehow he developed big-city tastes."

"The condo? You lease that, too?"

"My parents own it. We rent."

"You could ask your mom and dad for the cash."

"Mother was relieved when Rafi was no longer a contender for son-in-law."

At Rafi's funeral, Mrs. de la Guerra didn't seem overly dour with grief, but there was no hint of relief either. Apparently, I am easily fooled by classy mourners wearing black.

"And Father..." Bri said. "Well, you've met him. The man's all business. From day one, he questioned what value Rafi added to the de la Guerra dynasty. He wondered why I was willing to invest in a life partner with so little upside."

"So, we're back to Rafi's insufficiency you talked about earlier? What you're telling me is that his slim sufficiency quotient wasn't just your opinion? It was the de la Guerra consensus." I fell silent.

Before the Washington, DC assignment, Rafi and I usually talked every day. At work. After hours. Going to and from the beach. And in between sets at Santa Monica Pier. Your typical surf banter sprinkled with the drama of the day. If there had been any tension with the potential in-laws, Rafi never shared it with me. That made me wonder what else I didn't know about my best friend.

"Thad, I wasn't trying to trash talk the dead," Bri said. "I would never speak ill of Rafi. I loved him. Still do. Enough to find his killer."

I checked my watch to see what time it was. "If I'm to make it before two p.m., we gotta move."

Bri restarted the engine. She eased back onto Maine Avenue and passed under the Dwight D. Eisenhower Southwest Freeway overcrossing.

"I didn't mean to doubt your devotion, Bri."

"*No hay problema.*"

When Bri drops into Spanish, it usually means there really is a problem. We rode in silence for a while, wind whipping by.

I finally spoke. "I want justice for Rafi, too."

"I know."

"With MPD Homicide a dead-end, it's going to take a new plan. Any idea what we do now?"

"I'll drop you off," Bri said, "and run out to Evidence Control Branch to pick up Rafi's things. Whatever they seized from his hotel room that night might give us a new clue. Then, later tonight, we regroup, and flesh out the next steps."

"You have the address in Georgetown where Marissa and I are staying?"

"Her uncle's townhouse?"

I nodded.

"Marissa texted it to me earlier."

Bri turned left from C Street onto 14th. She pulled up close to some concrete planters protecting the entrance to the Treasury Department annex and let me off.

I grabbed my hybrid briefcase and rounded the car to the driver's side.

"I'll see what I can find out here," I said. "Rafi had to have left some breadcrumbs. If he did, I'll pick up the trail."

Chapter 15

Just off 14th and D Street in Washington, DC, not far from the awe-inspiring architecture of the National Mall, sat an L-shaped, five-story structure that inspired anything but awe.

The Treasury Liberty Center was a non-descript footnote of a building with crabgrass runners snaking over the granite curbs. The landscaping looked intentionally unkempt in contrast to the showcase U.S. Bureau of Engraving and Printing complex next door. Signage was minimal, in all caps.

The letters of the two-word engraving carved just above the double glass door entrance—TREASURY DEPARTMENT—were so worn they blended into the concrete-colored exterior. A passing motorist doing more than twenty-five mph would have no visible clue as to what took place inside. I wasn't even sure what they did at 401 14th Street. All I knew was that Rafi had been doing his audit from here. That he had sniffed out something that didn't pass the smell test. I was hoping to pick up his trail.

The inside of the facility was almost as depressing as the outside. The windows were old-fashioned, composed of four-inch semi-opaque glass squares set in a thick metal grillwork. Grungy asphalt tiles lined the floor of the reception area. A few chairs were shoved up against a green wall, paint chipped and blotched where the sun had managed to filter through the miniature windows. The side table was bare except for a vase of dusty plastic flowers that might have once been red geraniums. A row of mini-lockers lined the hallway across from the seating area.

Perched on a metal stool behind the reception counter was a heavy brunette in an orange sack-style dress with coordinating eyeshadow in metallic copper. Her nametag said "Gladys" but there wasn't anything glad about her. She looked pitbull mean and wore a permanent snarl.

When I approached the receptionist, the Queen of Scowl peered over the top of the latest issue of *Essence* magazine and said, "Do you have an appointment?"

Before I could open my mouth to respond, she pointed to a sign lettered in red on dingy white plastic, perched on the counter. It read: NO VISITORS. AUTHORIZED PERSONNEL ONLY.

I was about to explain to Gladys that I was here on assignment when I noticed Tigran coming out of the men's restroom at the end of the hallway. He was rubbing his hands together to dry them.

"Hanlon, give me your phone," my senior manager said, "and that backpack thing. You really need to get a grown-up briefcase."

I gave him the backpack, but hung back on the mobile. "Marissa's entering her third trimester. How's she supposed to reach me?"

"This building's a sensitive compartmented information facility," Tigran said. "There's no accessible consumer cell service."

I fired up my phone. Zero bars signal strength. *Lovely.*

126

"Hanlon, I've already ordered a government-issued phone for you. It should be here next week. In the meantime, give your wife my secure phone number." Tigran took my iPhone and handed me his government Samsung Galaxy. "Use this."

I texted Marissa, concluding with an ocean wave emoji.

There was a confirmatory whoosh. MESSAGE DELIVERED. I gave Tigran back his secure phone. He pocketed the device, walked over to a rack of beach-style lockers, tossed in my briefcase and phone, and closed the door. He handed me the locker key.

We approached the reception desk. "Good afternoon, Gladys." Tigran flashed his GAO credentials.

The woman looked at Tigran's photo keycard, checked for facial likeness, and waved him to the side. Then stared at me.

"Where's yours?" Gladys said. She rolled up the copy of *Essence* she was reading and used it to point at the AUTHORIZED PERSONNEL sign. Before either Tigran or I could answer, she raised the rolled magazine.

Whap!

Whatever had been crawling across her desk no longer moved.

"Gladys, this is Thad Hanlon." Tigran filled out the visitor log for us. "He's replacing Rafael Silva. He'll be here on a regular basis."

"Still needs a pass," she said.

I humored the woman and flashed my makeshift GAO credentials.

"Give it." Gladys extended her hand. She examined

the badge, verifying the photo on it was me. Then she took the ID and used it to scrape up the goopy bug remains on her desk. She handed the badge back. "You're good to go."

I took the ID from her with the tips of my fingers, careful to avoid bug juice.

"Tissue?" Gladys' lips arched up a fraction as she handed me one. Evidently, no one is a hundred percent evil. My faith in humanity once again restored.

I wiped down the visitor pass and clipped it onto the breast pocket of my coat. "Thanks."

Gladys took the used tissue from me and used it to clean off the magazine. She reached under her half-height reception counter, chucked the tissue in the trash, and fiddled with a button. I heard a soft click. The entire wall at the end of the hallway retracted. A hidden door rumbled open to reveal the inner sanctum of the Bureau of Fiscal Service facility.

Gone were the chipped and peeling walls of the reception area painted institutional green. Gone were the industrial asphalt tiles and seedy décor of the FSB entrance. Instead, I was now staring at a cavernous workspace, complete with multi-colored collaboration zones and the obligatory bike rack. The concealed sector was all gleam and glass, full-spectrum lighting, and a tropical jungle of indoor plants.

"Hanlon, close your mouth," Tigran said. "You look like a red-haired bullfrog, long sticky tongue at the ready."

I palmed my lower jaw back into place. My corneas had dried out from staring wide-eyed. I fluttered my eyelids and blinked until I could see again.

"I had no idea," I said.

"That's the point. FSB takes serious precautions." Tigran led me down a hidden passageway that stretched several football fields in length. To the right was a ginormous rectangular cage with half-height walls topped with laminated glass panels extending to the ceiling. I could see the data center internals and heard a steady hum. To the left was a maze of open-office partitions filled with polo-shirted techs. Tigran weaved through the partitions to a predetermined cube and stopped.

We stood looking at the back of a lanky six feet six inches tall Nordic man in a button-down, short-sleeve tangerine checked shirt, hunched over his workstation screen. The man punched the ENTER key and the laser printer on his desk began to suck paper. The printer shimmied with a muted thwap, thwap, thwap.

To be heard above the printer din, Tigran shouted, "Edvard, we're here!"

The man swiveled in his chair, flashing an underbite that was a prime candidate for teeth whitening strips. Condensation from a monster-gulp soda slid down the sixty-four-ounce plastic cup on his desk and pooled next to the keyboard.

Tigran approached. He dragged me with him. "I'd like you to meet Thad Hanlon. He'll be senioring our little project."

Edvard stood, his mauve polyester-knit tie swishing like a pendulum from side to side. "Call me Eddie," he said, as he shook my hand.

Edvard "Eddie" Zadelhof was in his mid-thirties, had wrinkle-free skin, and the stoop shoulders that some beanstalk types assume when they're uncomfortable with their height.

"You look busy," I said.

"All an illusion." Eddie grinned, flashing his yellowed underbite. He took a sip from his jumbo soda, then used his mousepad to sop up the condensate from the cup.

"Eddie's the new Site Operations Manager," Tigran said. "Besides making sure the Fiscal Service Data Center servers never go down, he's responsible for processing all U.S. Treasury disbursements—four trillion dollars annually. From IRS refunds to Social Security checks to V.A. benefits. It's all handled here at this centralized facility. Most of it electronically without paper checks."

Tigran was working his diplomatic magic, stroking the client. Eddie seemed to enjoy the flattery. His face brightened. If only Tigran had been six inches taller, he would have made a good politician. He couldn't help that his stumpy DNA made people look down on him.

"Eddie," Tigran asked, "any chance we can get a closer look at the farm?"

"I thought you'd never ask."

Chapter 16

"The first layer of our cybersecurity?" Eddie said, an up lilt in his voice signaling a rhetorical question. "An impregnable perimeter defense." The data center manager came to a stop in front of the entrance to the computer facility.

Through the glass panels atop the pony wall enclosing the server room, racks and racks of pizza-box-sized computers twinkled. Green LEDs blinked in synch with network traffic. It looked like a constellation of holiday lights, minus the seasonal décor.

Eddie straightened his back and assumed the posture of a tour guide. "As you probably noticed when you came in, we have taken certain precautions to secure this facility from break-ins or acts of terrorism. The building itself is purposely unassuming. The granite planters out front? Not mere landscape pots. Nay, nay. Barriers deliberately positioned to protect the entrance from a vehicular assault. And these building walls?" Eddie used his overly long fingernails to flick the polished concrete surface. "Steel-reinforced."

I snapped the walls myself. Tried to look impressed. Eddie smiled.

"Remember those retro glass-block windows you saw in the lobby?" he asked. "Bullet-proof, set in a steel bar mesh."

"What about layer two?" I probed. "Your facility

controls?"

"L2? Right. How shall I put this? Even if someone were able to get inside the building," Eddie assured us, "he or she would have to get past the security guard. That is...to penetrate the inner perimeter where we are standing now."

"So, Gladys is your L2?" No wonder she had been more guard dog than receptionist when we checked in. "Curious. Does she carry?" I asked.

"Yep, yep," Eddie said. "Gladys is our second layer countermeasure. Physical security personified."

Tigran nodded. I nodded. Gladys was a perfect match for her job description.

"And yes, she is armed," Eddie said.

At the entrance to the server farm was a security vestibule with access control doors on both sides of a floor-to-ceiling Lexan tube. Eddie stepped inside the see-through polycarbonate structure.

"Assuming someone was lucky enough to get this far, our computer room controls...," Eddie gestured to the walls of the man trap in which we were standing, "...these defenses make it next to impossible to get inside the server room itself. I'll show you."

Eddie ran his ID keycard over the face of the RFID reader affixed to the right of the door jamb. He spoke directly into a silver metal grill about three by four inches in size, located just above the access card reader.

"Crown Nebula," he said.

There was a short buzz and then the door swung open. The hum of the servers and air handling units intensified. We entered the facility and walked up a short ramp that led to a raised platform, maybe about one to one and a half feet above the building foundation.

"So, Crown Nebula's the password," I said. "Suppose an intruder gets past Gladys, and suppose that intruder has discovered your password by trolling the dark web—what's to prevent them from using the phrase to gain unauthorized access?"

"Voice authentication with AI." Eddie Zadelhof grinned like a middle schooler who had just crushed his opponent in a spelling bee. "The system uses machine learning to recognize your voiceprint, compensating for the occasional seasonal cold or flu or even aging vocal cords. And…" —Eddie raised his hand the way some do to make a point— "of course we change the password monthly."

"Hanlon, it's your classic physical controls strategy," Tigran said. "A defense-in-depth approach."

"Exactly," Eddie confirmed. "Secure the perimeter first. If stealing data were as simple as wandering into the server room and walking out with the right hard drive—BOOM! That would be the sound of my career imploding. Can't let that happen."

Eddie motioned for us to follow him. Our footsteps echoed lightly as we walked on the white raised tile floor.

"What about virtual security?" I asked.

"Firewalls? We got firewalls. My father, as did my mother, always told me 'Good digital fences make good neighbors.'"

I eyed my senior manager.

"Eddie's a second-generation network guy," Tigran said. "Descends from pioneers on the information superhighway."

One of the computer techs pedaled a kid's two-wheeled kick scooter past us, pushing a cart with an open laptop on the upper shelf. The fifteen inch screen had an interactive map of the server farm on the left side and diagnostic graphs on the right.

"Scooter Geeks," Eddie said when he saw me watching the tech disappear down one of the rack corridors. "We have close to twenty thousand server units in this data center. The fastest way to troubleshoot is on wheels. My scooter team ensures we keep our Tier IV certification."

Tigran translated. "A tier-four cert, Hanlon, means this facility runs glitch-free, ninety-nine point nine hundred ninety-five percent of the time. Janie Doe, Anytown, USA never has to worry. Her Social Security check will be deposited on time, every time. And Mr. John Q. Public sleeps at night knowing his tax refund check is on its way. He can start spending it now if he wants."

"I get it," I said. "Uncle Sam's river of cash never stops flowing."

"Almost eleven billion dollars a day, like clockwork." Eddie straightened his tie and took a bow.

Edvard Zadelhof's payment engine spent more money in less time, without hiccup than any other machine on the face of the planet. Self-congratulation seemed appropriate. Even so, the dork-pride gesture made me smirk.

"Looking around the server room," Eddie said, "you've probably noticed these thick gray umbilical-like cords coming up through the floor."

They were hard to miss. Looked like elephant trunks.

"These...," Eddie ran his hand over the monster-thick cables, "power the machines. Megawatts and megawatts. And boy, do they throw off a chunk of heat. But you'll never feel it. We have complete ambient air control. Regulated temperature, ten to twenty percent relative humidity, and anti-static flooring."

I could feel the forced air coming up through the false floors as we walked. Whatever noise the air handling units made was masked by the drone of CPU fans that cooled the thousands of processors on the racks.

"The chillers ensure fried motherboards are never a problem," Eddie said. "Now, a building fire or an explosion? That's a worry. If that happens, it's game over. *Kaputksi!*"

I remembered seeing a fire alarm or two as we walked the corridors of the facility, but no wall-mounted fire extinguishers. That got me thinking. I glanced up. From the overhead bus bars, ropes of multicolored network cables descended. What I didn't see above me was the usual array of water sprinklers poking down.

Eddie spied me eyeing the upper reaches of the server room. "Not to worry, Thad. There's a good reason we don't have any ceiling spigots in this complex." The data center manager brought his hands together and made the sign of the cross, the familiar two-finger gesture to ward off vampires. "That would only make things worse. Water doesn't play well with electricity. Machine death. Not a good thing."

Grisly images of Rafi popped into my head. His charred arms from low-voltage electrocution. His lifeless face. The vacant eyes. My mind couldn't stop tracing the lamp cord from his body to the hotel room wall socket. I shuddered. Tigran noticed.

"You okay, Hanlon? You're kinda pale."

"It's a circulation thing. Runs in the family," I lied.

"I can get bottled water," Eddie said.

"Nah. I'm good." I did a few jumping jacks and felt the color return to my face. "Eddie, talk to me about your spigotless ceiling."

He did. "Thad, we have something better than H_2O," Eddie said. "Instead, we use an eight point five percent concentration of FM200 fire suppression gas. The cooling gas works by removing heat rather than oxygen. It's safe for humans, lethal to fire."

Extinguishing fires without water damage. I couldn't argue with that. "What about smoke and heat detectors?"

"Overhead and underfoot." Eddie stamped the raised floor tile he was standing on. "Fire detection and prevention, we got it covered."

A classic rock ringtone played. "Money" by Pink Floyd. It sounded like it came from Tigran's pants pocket. He pulled his cell and jabbed it, silencing the alarm. "Excuse me, Eddie," he said. "Are we just about through?"

Eddie looked disappointed. "We did hit the high spots," he said, the enthusiasm draining from his voice.

"I'm sorry," Tigran said, "but I have to run back to the office. I've got a recruiting dinner in about thirty minutes. And before I go, I need to get Thad set up with Jenny Yu in the GAO work area. She'll finish onboarding him."

Eddie led the way out of the server farm to a workspace near the back of the open office section. The auditors' accommodations were strictly makeshift.

Several long Samsonite banquet tables served as desks. Mismatched chairs completed the bullpen look.

A minifridge sat in the corner. There was even a locking four-drawer file cabinet. A clutch of interns banged away at keyboards attached to desktop computer monitors displaying wall-to-wall spreadsheets. Another team huddled with the in-charge staff auditor. Jenny Yu looked busy.

"Eddie," Tigran said, extending his hand to the data center manager. "Just as impressive the second time. Thanks for the tour."

Eddie lit up as he shook the senior manager's hand. Outside praise was clearly an ego bump. Eddie turned to me. "Your thoughts?"

"I'm thinking *tight*, Eddie. Your controls are world-class. Your shop super, super tight."

"I prefer 'hardened,'" Eddie said. "I like to think of this data center as fully unbreachable."

"Hardened?"

"Not a soft target for thieves, terrorists, or cyberattacks," Eddie said. "This is a SCIF after all."

"Right. A Sensitive Compartmented, etc. Tigran kind of explained that to me when he lockered my phone."

"Yep, yep. No private carrier cell service." Eddie fished his cell phone from his pocket and held it up. "Did Tigran mention our No BYOD Policy?"

"Not yet."

Eddie dropped his phone into his pants pocket, making his keys rattle. "Every piece of hardware in the secure sections of this building is government-issued and ninety-nine percent of the building is secure except for the lobby. We don't allow you to capital B Bring, capital Y Your, capital O Own, capital D Device. Ever!"

"BYOD," I said. "Not even smartwatches?"

"Especially smartwatches. Anything Wi-Fi-enabled or having a cellular SIM card."

"How do you get to the Internet?" I asked.

"You don't," Eddie said. "There is no direct connection. No Internet, no way to breach from the outside. We run our own secure internal network knit together by our fiber-optic lines."

"Hardened," I said.

"Yep. And we Wi-Fi jam, too. The entire spectrum."

When Eddie said there was no way I was going to connect to the Internet, Tigran could see I was puzzled. Dodge Whitney had its own cloud server, super secure, where client files were double and triple-backed up. All work products. All audit documentation. All stored off-site. Accessed through a virtual private network.

"Hanlon," Tigran said, "security measures on this project require all files to be stored right here on-premise. Local only. Nothing leaves the building. No VPNs."

"So, I'll need a different login and password?"

Tigran scanned the audit work area, spotted who he was looking for, and said, "Yu, come join us."

The staff auditor left the scrum she was conducting with her team. She carried a spreadsheet in her hand, a mechanical pencil tucked behind her ear. Jenny was even thinner than she had looked on camera the night she FaceTimed us at the Waterfront Luxe. Her black bangs danced as she walked.

"Jenny Yu knows the ropes," Tigran said. "She'll

get you logged into one of the Fiscal Service Bureau's rack servers *tout suite*. You'll pick up where Rafi left off in no time."

Jenny extended her hand. We shook. "Mr. Thaddeus," she said, "I am so sorry about Rafi, about your friend." Jenny's eyes started to glisten.

"Please, call me Thad." I gave her a warm smile. "Jenny, you were so brave that night. Doing all that you did. Performing CPR." I wanted to hug her but thought it might be misinterpreted and then decided to anyway. Jenny didn't flinch.

Tigran checked his watch. "Time for me to go," he said. "Yu will show you where to find the work plan and give you a how-to on logging in. Hanlon, I'll be in touch later to answer any questions."

The Dodge Whitney senior manager turned and took off down the corridor toward the building lobby. As he walked, he checked his phone. Looked like Tigran was reading messages.

He stopped and then spun. He shouted at me, "When you get a chance, Hanlon, call your wife. Something about an OB/GYN house call."

"Jenny," I said, "get me an outside line. Now!"

Chapter 17

Evening rush-hour traffic in DC ranked right up there with LA's congestion. It was nothing like the cross-town dash at midday I had taken with Bri from the MPD headquarters to the First District Station. More bottlenecked.

The Francis Scott Key Bridge from Arlington to Georgetown was jammed, forcing the taxi driver to detour. It took twenty minutes just to go five miles at a fifteen-mph crawl. I kept cracking my knuckles until they ached.

"Can't you go faster?" I said. "My wife's hemorrhaging. She might bleed out before I get there."

"Bumper to bumper," the Ethiopian cab driver said. "Giving it my best." He looked in the rearview mirror with sympathy in his eyes.

This day was going from overscheduled to crazy busy and now bordered on overwhelming.

"I'm sorry," I said. "For yelling."

The driver cranked the steering wheel to the left, saw an opening, and kicked the gas pedal. The car jerked forward.

I closed my eyes while fighting to regain control over frazzled nerves. I went to my happy place, visualizing my last time out on the ocean, my last wave. It was a perfect barrel ride with my right hand caressing the face of the swell as the crest arced over me. I could feel once again the exhilaration of being spit from the tube as the barrel collapsed into what I can only describe as Mother Nature's water cannon. The longer I stayed in this waking dream, the less my hands shook. At some point, I stopped nervously flexing my fingers.

The cab pulled in front of the Petrovski residence. I dropped a couple of twenties on the front seat, thanked the driver, and clambered up the steps leading to the front door.

If Uncle Leonid's Georgetown brownstone was any indication of the lifestyle of Russian expats working as oil execs, then they were coequal with their American counterparts. Evidently, it was good to be working for a politically savvy Russian oil oligarch on Putin's "nice" list.

The Victorian rowhouse overlooked the Potomac River and was nestled between multicolored, multimillion-dollar townhouses that lined Q Street NW. The popular jogging trail on the Chesapeake and Ohio Canal Towpath was just blocks away. And the house where John F. Kennedy met Jacqueline Lee Bouvier was just up the street.

"Mar-baby, I'm here," I shouted, as I threw open the front door. The blue four-story retro-colonial townhouse opened into a narrow living room.

Marissa's Aunt Nika shushed me. "You're going to rattle the doctor."

My wife was lying on the couch. Her skinny jeans were splotched from the crotch to her knees. Where the blood had blotted, the spots had already started to discolor, turning a brownish-red.

A sturdy woman in tennis shoes and a lavender lab coat was running a wand the size of an electric shaver over Marissa's distended belly. In the other hand, the OB/GYN held a smartphone cabled to the device. *Ultrasound on the go*. The screen showed a grainy black-and-white silhouette of our son. He looked like he was sucking his thumb. A horizontal pulse rate chart at the top of the display showed peaks evenly spaced.

"Fetus healthy," the doctor said. She had a strong Russian accent. "You can see a regular heartbeat." She held up the iPhone screen so Marissa could look.

Marissa was pale, her sun-kissed light brown hair was limp, absent of its normal sheen. Ghost-like circles ringed her eyes, the whites now yellow. Her crystalline blue irises had turned shadowy.

"But you, darling," the doctor said. "Not so healthy. Much blood loss. Half liter maybe. Not enough for transfusion."

The doctor removed the wand from Marissa's belly and wiped off the ultrasound gel. She then detached her phone from the wand and placed the ultrasound attachment into her bag.

The blood loss had me worried. This wasn't Marissa's first problem pregnancy. She had miscarried once before. That's when we had our blood typed. We were both Rh-positive, so Rh-factor incompatibility wasn't the complication. Marissa's elite athlete BMI level of sixteen was.

Convincing Marissa to add fat to her diet was a multi-month struggle. But eventually, her body mass index eked up to eighteen, the minimum required to ovulate. She wasn't happy her period started again, and she cried a lot when she looked at her body in the mirror. *Baby flab*, she would moan, though I thought it looked good on her. Teaching fitness at a gym had its downside. The daily pressure of physiques on parade.

I tiptoed over to Marissa. Squeezed her hand, leaned over, and kissed her. She attempted a smile but was too weak to complete it. She blinked her eyes instead.

"You must be the husband," the OB/GYN said. She set down her medical bag and extended her hand. "Dr. Yelena Godenko."

"I'm Thad." I stood, took her right hand, and gently placed my left on top. "Thank you," I said. "When I walked in just now, I didn't expect to see a doctor. Total surprise. You had me super worried. In LA, only the Beverly Hills elite get house calls, unless you're on hospice ready to die."

"This is for my good friend Nika Petrovski," Dr. Godenko said. "She asks, I come."

Marissa's aunt had rousted her OB/GYN friend from her rounds to triage her pregnant niece.

"We talk," Dr. Godenko said. She waited for me to focus my attention on her before she continued. "Matryoshka has placenta previa. She needs bed rest."

I mouthed the words "placenta previa." I didn't know what to think. Behind me, Nika groaned, so whatever Marissa's condition was, it wasn't good.

"Her placenta is attached too low," the doctor said. She placed her hand on the underside of Marissa's belly. "Baby sack is here." She tapped just a couple of inches below Marissa's navel which had stretched perfectly flat as her womb had expanded. "Covering the cervix but..." the doctor said, "...should be here." She slid her hand up to the top left of Marissa's baby bump and tapped once more.

"But you just told us the baby is healthy," I said.

"The ultrasound was good. The heart rate strong."

Marissa kept fading in and out during the conversation as she strained to listen. She was now paler than when I arrived.

"The baby, yes. Healthy for now, yes." Doctor Godenko glanced at Marissa, waiting for her to open her eyes. "But…" the doctor said, "the fetus is—how do you say it?—iffy."

There was no response from Marissa. Dr. Godenko then shifted her focus to me to see if I had understood.

"Iffy?" I said, "like in risky?"

"Yes, that. Risky preterm labor. And a risk of more hemorrhaging for Matryoshka."

I wasn't liking the way this sounded. I covered my ears and squished my face. I must have looked like I was trying to avoid hearing any more bad news. And maybe I was. Pregnancy complications were a new kind of risk for me.

Calculated risks I understood. I had a lot of experience taking deliberate chances. Every time I took off on a wave, I risked wiping out. But that risk involved me and me alone. This was different. This was straight-up life risk, my wife's and my son's. A risk I couldn't control. I could feel my cheeks turning red.

Dr. Godenko pulled my hands from my face. "Risk we manage," she said, "with bed rest."

I dropped my hands and began cracking my knuckles.

"Matryoshka must stay off her feet," the doctor said.

"Can she use the bathroom or take a shower?" I asked. Images of bedpans, sponge baths, and catheters leaked into my head. Whatever optimism I had that our

DC trip could be an adventure worth having, that we could help Bri find closure for Rafi, was quickly being replaced by worst-case thinking.

"No standing…" Dr. Godenko said, "more than five minutes." She held up her right hand and counted five on her fingertips. "No sex. And no gym."

This time Marissa groaned. If you factored in the miscarriage, pregnancy had messed with her hormones for more than a year now. For Marissa, no workouts meant an emotional death sentence. No time at the gym meant no endorphins to offset the grumpies and a loss of muscle tone. Marissa's lips drooped, the pink color replaced by a pale blue.

I asked the doctor, "What about the baby? Any special treatment? A way to reposition the placenta?"

Doctor Godenko rolled her eyes. Apparently, baby sacks don't just get up and move back into place at request. "Staying off her feet is good for the baby, too. And forget vaginal birth. We do Cesarean."

At the mention of a possible incision, Marissa whimpered. She had no scars. She had never broken any bones. And her only surgery was to have her tonsils removed. Doctor Godenko's straight talk was crippling her spirit.

The doctor's cell phone rang. "Must go," she said.

"*Dasvidaniya*," Marissa whispered.

Yelena Godenko leaned over and kissed Marissa on the forehead. "*Dasvidaniya*, my Matryoshka." The doctor grabbed her medical bag. Nika hugged her and walked her outside.

Marissa took a deep breath. "Sit with me, Thad." Her voice was weak.

I nuzzled closer to her. We stayed in that position

until sometime later when Nika came back into the house. She was accompanied by Bri, who was carrying a duffle over her shoulder. Nika was rehearsing the details of Doctor Godenko's visit.

Bri gasped when she saw Marissa. "Girl," she said, "we got to get you out of those clothes." She dropped the duffle by the front door and crossed to the couch. Together, we lifted my wife into the guest bedroom. "Thad, I'll take it from here." Bri shooed me away.

So, I ended up in the kitchen with Nika, working as her Russian comfort food sous-chef, until Marissa was done freshening up. Bri helped me move her back to the living room, back to her couch.

After a supper of fresh cabbage soup and dark sourdough rye, Marissa wanted to talk. She sat up. The ghost eyes were gone, her lips now rosy as a ballerina's tutu.

Nika was pleased her niece's color had returned. She took that as a cue to excuse herself to go upstairs. That left just the three of us.

"Tell me, Thad," Marissa said. "Tell me everything. Start from when you left this morning."

I leaned forward in Uncle Leonid's recliner. "What has Bri told you? I'll skip those parts."

"I want to hear it from you." Marissa patted the couch next to her. "Sit."

I sat. Then told her everything. About the classified nature of my assignment and the importance of discretion and avoiding "loose lips" so I wouldn't jeopardize my job. I surprised her with tidbits about my meeting the client who turned out to be a top member of the President's cabinet. I let her know I had finally been briefed on Gold II by none other than Treasury

Secretary Kennedy Beck. And I shared with her that I had learned the job had a codename—National Brick and Foundry—and that my cover was GAO auditor.

"But did you learn anything new regarding Rafi?" Marissa asked.

"I'm getting to that." And then I told her about the visit to DC Metro Police Department, about seeing the case file on Rafael Silva, reading the Chief Medical Examiner's autopsy report, looking at crime scene photos, meeting Detective Mapu from Homicide Branch, and realizing the case jacket was stamped closed because the medical examiner had ruled Rafi's death a suicide.

Marissa looked up at Bri. "I'm so sorry," she said. She held out her palm. Bri got up from the wingback chair where she was seated and treaded to the sofa, gently pressing her hand into Marissa's. She gave Bri a consoling squeeze. Bri reciprocated.

"Today feels like such a failure," Bri said. "Failure wrapped in impotence. I've never felt so powerless in my life." Bri clenched her fist and then apparently remembered she was holding Marissa's hand. She let go.

"Sorry," Bri said. "I didn't mean to smush."

The grimace on Marissa's face faded.

"What I was about to say," Bri continued, "was I don't do powerless. That's not who I am. MPD may consider the case closed, but I don't. Not yet. Not while I'm still breathing."

Bri's declaration hung in the air for a beat before I broke in. "I hate to be the bearer of more bad news, but I came up with *nada* at the Fiscal Service Bureau."

Marissa made a face. "You didn't say anything

earlier about this service bureau."

"Nothing helpful?" Bri asked.

"Diddly." I spent the next ten minutes telling them what I did find. I explained that the last place Rafi worked was a digital fortress, locked down so tight not a byte goes missing. I told them that unless either one of them knew a superhero, we had hit a wall.

Bri wasn't buying the impasse. She retrieved the duffle she had brought in earlier. "Rafi's personal effects found at the crime scene. There's got to be something to go on here."

Chapter 18

There wasn't much in Rafi's duffle. Two sealed plastic evidence/property bags with clothing and toiletries. A third bag with his billfold. And a fourth with a high-end over-the-ear headset. Enclosed in anti-static pouches were Rafi's company-issue laptop and his iPhone, also sealed. For a long-term assignment, Rafi had packed light.

Each evidence bag had been annotated with a description of the contents, date and time of recovery, crime scene investigation officer's name, and chain of custody details. I tried ripping one of the bags open to get to the contents. No luck. The bags were tear-resistant.

Bri played it smarter. She simply popped the evidence seals and dumped everything in a pile in front of Uncle Leonid's couch where we were sitting. She reached into the jumble, pulled out Rafi's billfold, and rifled through it.

Inside was the selfie of Bri and Rafi stretched out on the sand at the beach in Santa Monica. An oversized fluorescent orange towel served as a backdrop against tanned perfection. Bri's white tankini was deliciously fitted. Rafi was in the same nylon board shorts he always wore when he wasn't in a wet suit.

Behind the beach photo were insurance cards, Rafi's California driver's license, and an AMEX cash back card. Nothing else. Definitely no engagement photo like the one Bri had insisted Jenny Yu locate that night.

Maybe Bri was mistaken? Maybe she just *thought* she had given Rafi the wallet-size engagement mini-pic. All Marissa and I had ever seen were the 8x10 proof prints.

Bri had made such a big deal about those proofs. She had even conducted full-scale test marketing by polling everyone—friends, co-workers, and family. She would arrange the photo gallery and then ask which shots we felt best met her selection criteria.

"Bri," I said, "Rafi's iPhone has been erased, everything except–"

Bri grabbed the iPhone from me, handing me Rafi's billfold instead. She swiped through each screen. "Default apps, the ones that come with the phone fresh out of the box. That's all that's on here. Thad, what did you do?"

"All I did was fire it up. The phone went straight to the passcode request."

"So how did you unlock it?"

"Used the same password you gave Jenny Yu that night. The one that worked. Your initials."

"Did you go into the settings? Tweak anything?" Bri sounded frustrated.

I, too, was frustrated by her innuendo. If I had accidentally reset the phone, I would have seen all the activation screens. *Hello. Select Your Country or Region. Choose a Wi-Fi Network.* But I hadn't. Rafi must have done a factory reset. Rafi or someone else.

Marissa cleared her throat in an obvious attempt to get our attention. She had been peacefully reclining on the couch next to me. "Children, children," she said, "can we not bicker? You're upsetting the baby." Marissa caressed her belly.

"Sorry, hon," I said. "We'll play nice. Right, Ms. de la Guerra?"

Bri threw the phone aside. Then she tried to grab Rafi's billfold from me.

I pulled it back before she could get it. "Let me look first." I spread open the bill slot and removed the money. Fingerprint dust smudged my hands silver-gray.

Bri snatched the bills from me and started stacking them on the floor, one on top of the other. When she finished, she snapped a photo with her phone.

"Same random order as when Jenny did the inventory," Bri said. "This is *so* not Rafi."

By my count, there were twenty hundred-dollar bills and ten fifties.

"I'm no accountant," my wife said, "but aren't you two dollars short? I remember Jenny holding up a wrinkled $2 bill when the EMTs arrived."

I double-checked the evidence bags. It wasn't listed. Two-dollar bills are rare. Maybe someone along the chain of custody needed a good luck charm.

Bri snapped one of the hundreds with her fingernails. "Twenty-five hundred dollars in new currency." She was re-organizing the bills by denomination, facing forward, and putting them back in Rafi's billfold. "And no used notes. You're right. We're short two dollars. But what's even weirder is that Rafi never carried cash. This is so out of character."

I wasn't so sure. I could think of at least one reason Rafi was flush with bucks. He was living in DC on a per diem meal allowance, courtesy of Dodge Whitney.

Unreimbursed travel expenses for long out-of-town assignments rack up fast. Rather than be out-of-pocket, Rafi probably asked the firm for a cash advance. SOP. Standard Operating Procedure. And who carries traveler's checks anymore? At the seventy-six dollars a day allowed by the IRS for high-cost locations such as DC, Rafi could pay cash for meals for a month before he burned through the remaining money he had on him. If anything, I would have expected Rafi to have more cash than he did.

And I wasn't so sure the systematic arrangement of the bills by denomination, with all the Ulysses S. Grants and Benjamin Franklins facing forward, was proof positive Rafi had been murdered. Just now it had been Bri who had sorted the cash before placing it back into the billfold. She's an accountant, a CPA. Maybe Bri was projecting her obsessive attention to detail onto Rafi. The Rafi I knew was much more slapdash than anal, except when it came to spreadsheets.

"I'm not buying the billfold theory," I said. "It's too easy to come up with alternative explanations."

Bri sucked in a deep breath. "So now you're the devil's advocate?"

"Rafi could have taken a cash advance for the DC assignment. Or maybe he's not as OCD as you think regarding how he maintains his billfold. What if Dodge Whitney's cashier office shuffled the money when they gave him the advance and he didn't have time to reorder it?"

"Thad's right, Bri," Marissa said, her voice weak but firm. "He's just trying to be helpful. The counter explanations are plausible."

"What?" Bri tilted her head and made dagger eyes

toward my wife. "Now you're double-teaming me? Some friends."

That chilled the investigative chat, making for an uneasy quiet. A minute passed. Two minutes. Finally, I stepped between the two of them. "Bri, listen to me. You're going through a grief dump. The cortisol messes with everything. Trust me, we are not the—"

Before I could finish what I was about to say, Bri slumped to the floor. She went all fetal, curling up into a heap, sniffling but never sobbing, bawling but never blubbering. Her breathing was halting, punctuated by involuntary gasps with occasional choking.

I ran to the kitchen and grabbed a bottle of water and a box of tissues. I offered her both. She pushed the tissue away but took the water. The choking stopped.

"Bri, I'm so sorry," Marissa said. "This emotional roller coaster you're on, it must be terrifying. Come here." She beckoned her to draw closer and Bri laid her head next to my wife's swollen belly.

The two stayed that way until Bri's breathing returned to normal. The ache passed and when it did, Bri spoke up. "The laptop," she said. "He uses the same password. We should be able to log in."

I cracked open Rafi's laptop and punched in the telephone keypad equivalent of Bri's initials: 2354. The launch screen snapped into place. Rafi's on-screen work area was cluttered with files, folders, and app icons. Nothing popped out at me. No VersaChem folder. No unorthodox .pdf file. No unusual Word .docx. But then again, I hadn't expected there to be.

"So?" Marissa asked me. "You find anything?"

"Rafi was trusting but not naïve. He would have hidden his notes. There's nothing on his desktop."

153

"Run a search." Bri was sitting up on the floor now, having scooted over closer to Marissa, and positioning herself against the front of the couch. She stroked Marissa's hair, untangling any knots.

A full hard drive search for "Gold II" turned up nothing. Next, I keyed in the codename "National Brick and Foundry." That turned up a single folder but with little in it. Just the briefing documents on the audit. The same stuff I had been given by Warnick, but no actual work docs. And definitely no interlinking spreadsheets with obvious red flags. Whatever Rafi had found, it wasn't on this machine.

"Total strikeout," I said. "Rafi must have kept everything on the Fiscal Service Bureau servers. He probably couldn't take his Dodge Whitney laptop inside the secure sector of the building, anyway. Gladys would have made him locker it as she did with my phone."

Bri jumped up. She started digging through the pile of Rafi's things she had poured from the evidence bags. "It's not here," she said.

"What's not?" Marissa asked.

Bri looked at me. "Thad, wouldn't Rafi have been issued a secure phone for the job?"

Earlier today, Tigran had said he was going to requisition a government-issued phone for me. He carried one. And Jenny had one. Rafi *must* have had one, too.

I retrieved the property poly bags from the evidence heap and scanned the content descriptions. "There's no second phone listed on any of the bags."

"They took it," Bri said. "Whoever killed him."

"Sure makes checking his call history a little more difficult," Marissa said.

"Or checking whatever he had on the phone. Photos, voice recordings, video," Bri added.

"Most government phones don't have cameras," I said. "They're too easy to use as spycams."

"Whatever. The fact is, it's missing." Bri kicked at the evidence pile, knocking Rafi's overnight kit across the room.

"Or," I said, "MPD overlooked the secure phone when processing the crime scene. Or Rafi kept it in the makeshift audit room at the Fiscal Service Bureau. Or he lost it and hadn't requested a new one yet."

"Missing, just the same," Bri said. She wasn't going to let this thread go.

"Thad isn't trying to dash your hopes," Marissa said. "You understand that?"

"Crush is a better verb." Bri gritted her teeth.

I exhaled loudly. Closed my eyes. "Can we stop with the divisiveness? To be honest, I'm feeling tapped out right about now. Gold II is bigger than I expected. Our research is getting us nowhere. We've seen the police report on Rafi's death and looked through his personal effects. I've even walked the halls where he was working. We got nothing. I can tell you what I do have, Bri. Too many balls in the air. My juggling skills are minimal. Something's got to give. Maybe this quest?"

Marissa extended her foot from where she was lying on the couch, rubbed it along my thigh, and looked up at me.

I patted her foot and smiled back.

"Thad, you're right," Bri said. "I get testy at times. Maybe overbearing, liable to be overwhelmed by my own grit."

I raised my eyebrows. Bri's "make-nice" sounded more like a "sorry, but."

"What if we try something else?" Marissa said. "What if we reflect on what we *do* know, speculation aside? Let's see if we're overlooking something."

Marissa's voice of reason won out. I pulled out my phone and fired up the Notes app. "I'll start." I entered a couple of key points and read them aloud. Bri added her thoughts and then Marissa.

—April 25: Rafi calls Thad approx. 6:15 p.m. PDT. He reports he discovered major fraud. Spreadsheets not adding up. The cell connection goes faulty. Rafi's last words: VersaChem, plan, advice, amigo.

—April 25: Jenny Yu conference calls approx. 8:30 p.m. PDT. Rafi's dead. CPR attempts fail. The paramedic reports possible suicide to police. Rafi's billfold has $2,502 in random notes. Rafi and Bri's engagement photo missing.

—April 26: Warnick invites Thad to take Rafi's place on the Gold II audit.

—April 27: Rafi's funeral. Bri shares her suspicions of foul play. Thad accepts Warnick's offer to join Gold II team.

—April 29: Thad meets client—Treasury Secretary Beck. He's brought up to speed on project, the covert nature of the assignment, his GAO cover, and the audit sandwich strategy. Learns Gold II is behind schedule.

—April 29: Bri and Thad review police file. Chief Medical Examiner rules Rafi's death a suicide. Crime scene photos show bare wire wrapped around Rafi's left arm with plug end inserted into the wall outlet. No defensive wounds. Clean tox screen. Rafi's and Jenny's fingerprints are on cash.

—April 29: Thad tours Fiscal Service Bureau's secure data center. Rafi's work files are stored on the center's servers rather than in the Dodge Whitney cloud.

—April 29: Rafi's personal effects from Evidence Control yield little. iPhone has been wiped. Laptop has generic info about audit. No government-issued smartphone found.

"Did we miss anything?" I asked.

Headshakes all around. Marissa rearranged herself on the couch. Bri stood up and paced.

"We have means," I said. "Electrocution."

"And a possible motive," Bri said. "Rafi specialized in fraud audits."

"Fraud stemming from greed?" Marissa said. "Greed's our motive?"

"Greed. Fraud. And the need to cover tracks," Bri said.

"Which leaves us with opportunity." I looked at Bri.

"What about it?" she said. "If you mean the *opportunity* to make it look like suicide, whoever did this to Rafi had all the opportunity they needed. An entire evening. A private space without surveillance of any kind. A cheap clock radio. And an old-fashioned wall socket without GFI for shutting down the circuit."

Marissa shifted on the couch and reached for her water bottle. She gulped twice and wiped her lips. "Don't we need suspects?"

I nodded. "Someone to link the Means-Motive-Opportunity to the crime."

"So, we've moved to suspects?" Bri asked.

"Yeah," I said

"Everybody loved Rafi. At least, everyone I know. He had no enemies. No one had ever threatened him."

"Somebody wanted him dead," Marissa said.

"What about Tigran Vardanyan?" I started a list of potential suspects and made a note.

"The senior manager?" Bri asked. "Rafi's boss and now yours?"

"I'm just throwing out names."

"Tigran's got an alibi," Marissa said. "He was at the Dodge Whitney Annual Dinner that night. Remember when Bri fainted on the dance floor and he helped you lift her into the backseat of our car?"

Scratch Tigran.

"What about Jenny Yu?" I said. "She had opportunity. She was in Rafi's room." I added her to the list.

"I don't think she did it," Bri said as she swiped the phone from me. She erased Jenny's name and handed it back. "Jenny is a slight, young thing. There is no way she could have overpowered Rafi. What I don't understand, though, and not that I'm jealous, is why was she in his room in the first place?"

I looked at Marissa and she looked back. We both knew where this was going. While Bri rarely felt threatened by other women, she could be territorial. Rafi was hers. One day, Jenny would have to explain herself.

"Eddie Zadelhof," I suggested. "The data center guy. It has to be someone Rafi was working with." As I input the name on my phone, I made sure Eddie's last name had only one *f*.

"That's a stretch," Marissa said. "You honestly

think a Dilbert is capable? You said yourself, Eddie's social skills were marginal. He'd never get past the front desk at the Foggy Bottom Suites where Rafi was staying."

"Without an escort?" Bri said. "But maybe Jenny and Eddie are a thing."

"We've gone from person of interest to collusion in less than five minutes," I said. "Five more minutes and we'll be talking conspiracy, rogue operatives, and deep state cabals of powerbrokers and hired assassins." This whole discussion was edging into thriller territory. Robert Ludlum, may he rest in peace, would be proud.

"What do you suggest?" Bri asked.

"We focus on the motive. Retrace Rafi's steps." I put my phone away.

"How?" Marissa said.

Bri had two ideas. The first, a no-brainer: digging deeper at the Fiscal Service Bureau. Tricky, no doubt. I couldn't afford to be caught on a fishing expedition and get myself canned. Bri said not to worry. That she'd coach me through it. That she'd use her street smarts to make sure I didn't do anything stupid.

The other piece was tangential at best. It involved breakfast with Jenny, assuming she was willing. Bri suggested we meet tomorrow morning early at a local coffee bar.

There was only one problem with Bri's plan. Marissa was now confined to bed rest. Until I could arrange for home healthcare, I wasn't comfortable leaving her longer than I had to.

Bri glanced at me, then at Marissa. "I can meet with Jenny solo. Thad should stay here with you."

"I'll be fine," my wife reassured me. "Nika will

help."

"You certain?" I asked.

"Find out what Jenny knows," Marissa said. "She was the last person to see Rafi."

I bent over and kissed my wife, then kissed her belly, careful not to wake Thadpole.

Chapter 19

"Why were you with my fiancé that night?" Bri locked eyes with Jenny Yu.

It was early morning. We were sitting on the terrace of one of the fashionable coffeehouses in Georgetown, overlooking the Chesapeake and Ohio Canal trail adjacent to the Potomac River. The barista had just filled our order for a morning pick-me-up.

"Mostly, I was with him in the afternoon."

"Doing what?" Bri wasn't even borderline accusatory—she was full frontal.

"Not what you think, Ms. de la Guerra."

"You may call me Bri."

"Miss Bri, Rafi needed to talk."

"About what?"

"Gold II. So, we talked. A lot. He did most of the talking. I listened. I've been practicing my people skills. When he said he had to make a few phone calls, I left his hotel room."

"How did he seem then?" I said.

"When I left him? Or during the time we were talking?"

"When you left."

"He said he felt like he'd been caught in a rogue wave. His words."

Bri looked at me. I could tell she had never heard the term before.

"Every surfer's fantasy," I said. "A rogue wave is two to three times taller than the average breaker hitting the shore. It's an opportunity for a once-in-a-lifetime ride, cloaked in danger, mixed with a healthy respect for the surf sirens." I didn't think it was necessary to tell either of them that another synonym for rogue wave was "killer curl."

Bri seemed to mull over the surf reference but didn't pursue it. She said, "But you called us from his room later that evening. Why'd you come back? Were you taking him to the airport to catch his flight?"

"I was worried for him, Miss Bri. When I left his room earlier, his hands were shaking. My boss never shakes. I texted but he never responded. I called his cell and it went straight to voicemail. So, I came back to check on him."

"He didn't let you in, did he?" Bri said. "When you FaceTimed us, he was still plugged into the wall."

Jenny started crying. I put my arm around her and squeezed. She buried her head. Between sniffles, she mumbled something about the smell in Rafi's room and that look on his face. Finally, she raised her head enough to say, "He gave me a key."

Bri looked at me. She twisted the gold band of her massive diamond engagement ring and made an ugly face.

"Thursday afternoon wasn't the first time you and he talked at length, was it?" I said.

Jenny nodded.

"He gave you a key?" Bri muttered. She shook her head. "You had your own key?"

Jenny didn't say anything. She looked down at her lap and scrunched her shoulders.

I saw a chance to take the conversation in a different direction. "Other than the 'shakes,' Jenny, was there any further change in Rafi's behavior you noticed?"

"He'd become obsessed with a spreadsheet model he was working on." Jenny kept finger-twisting the black hair of her pixie cut. "He kept adding variables, tweaking the input, would say 'hmm' from time to time. If I got within five feet of his laptop at our makeshift office at the Treasury data center, he'd slam his machine closed. I swear, Rafi never told me what it was about."

"Days, weeks?" I said. "How long was he crunching on this thing?"

"Three days solid. On the fourth day, he asked me to be his sounding board. And…"

"And what?" Bri sat up.

"Ms. Bri, I want to be honest and I hope you don't take this the wrong way. So, let me preface. You are stunning, but you already know this. You have the face of a model and curves to spare. Me? I am a slight little thing from Guangzhou in this conservative gray business suit. I look like half a billion other girls in China. Men don't even know I exist unless I clear my throat. When my Dodge Whitney firm sifu…my mentor…asks me to stare at his gorgeous face while all I have to do is listen, I thank Confucius for ears."

Bri ran a hand through her hair. "I sense your relationship was something more than mentor-mentee."

Jenny gave a polite smile, blushed, and folded her arms. Her eyes closed. Tears washed her cheeks.

I too sensed something more, but I was willing to give Jenny the benefit of the doubt. Maybe her admiration for Rafi was a sign of reverence for her Accounting Master, her sifu, or a fantasy crush without reciprocity.

At any rate, we weren't going to get anything more out of Jenny this morning. At least not the two of us by double-teaming her. Perhaps at a later date, when emotions weren't so raw. I downed the rest of my chai latte and said to Bri, "Jenny and I need to get over to the job site. The client thinks we're on the clock."

Jenny looked at her watch. "Is Bri dropping you off or do you need a ride?"

"If you don't mind."

Jenny handed me her rental car keys. "Would you care to drive? DC roadways are confusing. The layout a tortured mashup between a Feng Shui map and a Go board."

"You're sure?"

"You'd be doing me a favor." Jenny rose, crossed over to Bri, and gave her a tender hug. "I'm so, so sorry, Miss Bri. For your loss."

For the first time since I've known Bri, she was tongue-tied. She didn't move. She didn't reciprocate. She just didn't do anything.

We left her there, hands clasping her cooling expresso, gaze somewhere beyond.

Chapter 20

"Thad, I need your help," Jenny said.

We had just cleared security at the Fiscal Service Bureau lobby. Gladys didn't give me nearly as much grief as she had the day before, and didn't use my ID badge as a bug scraper this time. The self-retracting panel to the server farm slid open.

"I'm just getting my feet on the ground. I may not be all that helpful."

"Eddie Zadelhof's people are slow-walking my requests," Jenny said.

No one likes auditors, investigative accountants even less so. We're perceived as the Screw Up Police and the longer we were on the job, the better chance of finding something askew to justify our existence. Small wonder clients were reticent to chat with us.

"The PBCs are dribbling in," Jenny said.

Prepared By Client worksheets are a staple in the audit world. They provide the starting point for verification to ensure what clients say they own and owe is real.

"My interns are just about done tying out the loan listings on one point twenty-five trillion in mortgage-backed securities. What they need now is a schedule of toxic assets for each MBS tranche."

Jenny was deep into her high finance techno-jargon. Sadly, none of what she had described mattered.

Jenny's interns were crunching on the "bread" as a smokescreen for the real audit objective. But she didn't know that, and I wasn't about to let on. "When did you request the data dumps?"

"A week ago. Do you think Eddie's stonewalling? Is it because I'm a woman? A rather young-looking woman? Thad, I can't help it if people think I'm fourteen. What can I do? I want to be taken seriously."

I sensed Jenny was just getting started with her tales of client indifference and wanted a sympathetic ear. She deserved that. Even so, it was keeping me from my plans for that afternoon. "Jenny, let's do this. You keep talking, but while you do, show me how to access Rafi's files? I need to know where he left off. The client isn't paying Dodge Whitney's billing rates for me to duplicate work already completed."

"Deal," Jenny said. For the next four hours, she regaled me with anecdotes about being given the run-around, stories of spreadsheets that never balanced, and chronicles of her crushing work schedule. She wondered if staffers in the LA office put in 70-80 hours a week during "busy season" or if she was being punished as a newbie because she couldn't complete her work within the allotted time. She confessed to *eating* hours to make it look like she had met the objective, but was easily fifty percent over plan.

I had fudged time sheets my first year on the job, though I wasn't proud of it. Like Jenny, I'd worked way more hours than I'd logged. It was the only way I could compensate for not knowing what I was doing. Newbies eating time was common practice in Big Four public accounting, though no managing partner would ever admit it.

"There," I said, "that's it! Must've missed it the first time." I pointed to a listing of Rafi's files on the computer.

I uncapped the top of a USB pen drive picked up as conference swag at the last fraud and forensic accounting meeting I attended. The top half was a handy flash drive, the bottom a gel pen. I jammed the top half into the USB port of the desktop computer and started to download the Gold II audit files from the secure network drive located in the Fiscal Service Bureau server room.

Jenny peeked at the Windows File Manager app on the monitor. "Didn't we look at that folder first thing this morning?"

We had. Jenny'd walked me through Rafi's audit docs one by one. We'd checked everything.

"Here. Let me show you." I right-clicked on several new files appearing in the audit folder to inspect the system properties.

"Rafi hid these files?" Jenny said.

"Yes. And he rebuilt the indexes, so we'd never see the files in a global search."

"Modifying the HIDDEN file attribute? They don't teach that in training," Jenny said.

"Not much of a hide, really," I said. "Any teen who games for hours knows how to cloak stuff from his parents."

The download was sixty-three percent complete, slower than I had expected based on the small size of the files.

"What did he hide?" Jenny asked.

"Not sure. I don't want to leave a content trail, so I haven't opened the files yet. I'll do it offsite."

"Do *what* offsite?" Eddie Zadelhof said. He reached over my shoulder and pulled the flash drive from the port. "Mine, now." Eddie clenched the drive and stuffed it in his right pants pocket. There was an audible clink as the top half of the pen drive landed on his keys.

"Eddie, I didn't hear you behind me," I said. My face flushed.

"Thad, I thought I was clear in your orientation. All personal electronic devices *including flash drives* must be lockered. This is a Sensitive Compartmented—"

"...Information Facility," I said. "I'm sorry. Being a pen and all, it just never registered. I mean I wasn't sneaking it in, trying to break protocol. You understand?"

"I understand one hundred percent secure," he said. "No downloads. We can't afford a data leak from the SCIF."

So much for my pen drive. Without the top, the bottom half was too small to write with. I tossed the gel pen half into the metal waste bin.

Eddie was smiling one of those geek-gotcha grins. "Hard to miss a flashing red network node," he said. "Your machine was flagged by the Network Ops control panel the second you inserted the flash drive into the USB port." Eddie stuck his hand in the waste bin and pulled out the bottom half of the pen I had tossed. He snapped the top and bottom parts together. "Cute," he said, as he inserted the USB pen drive into his shirt pocket.

Jenny Yu was shaking. "Thad, I didn't know USB sticks were being flagged. Really." Her voice cracked.

Eddie said, "Why would we advertise port

monitoring?" The data center manager then recited Sun Tzu from *The Art of War,* "Let your plans be dark and impenetrable as night, and when you move, fall like a thunderbolt." When he got to "thunderbolt," Eddie put his hand on the top of my shoulder and squeezed.

"Man, I am so sorry," I said. "Flash drives are second nature for me. I didn't even think about it. I wasn't trying to hide anything."

"Is this your first job with data lockdown?"

"Yes."

"Mine, too," Jenny chimed in.

"And you've never used a pen drive before?"

"Never," Jenny and I said in unison.

Eddie seemed satisfied with the *mea culpas*. At least, he didn't say he would write me up. Or call my manager.

When Eddie left, I exhaled deeply and blinked a couple of times. Jenny was still shaking.

"That was surveillance-state freaky," I said. "Sorry to put you through that."

Jenny excused herself to go to the ladies' room. When she returned, she was composed. Face fresh. She looked like she was ready to get back to business.

"Where were we before I made a complete fool of myself?"

"Hidden files," Jenny said. "If Eddie didn't already know that Rafi was hiding files, he does now. You might as well look at what's in the files *here*. No need to go back to the Dodge Whitney office."

"Good point." For a first-year audit associate, I'd rank Jenny in the top five percent. Maybe even top three. She wouldn't have to worry about her future.

I re-opened the file browser, double-clicked the

first document in the hidden folder, and entered the Dodge Whitney password for the Gold II audit that would unlock the file.

An error dialog box appeared. That was strange. According to the popup message, the file was corrupted and unreadable.

"Let's try this." I loaded the file into the Microsoft Windows Notepad text editor instead. The screen filled with random letters, numbers, Wingding characters, and international symbols. Nothing readable. Looked like digital junk.

Whatever was in the file before must have been overwritten by somebody else. Eddie wasn't to blame. There was no way he could have gotten back to his workstation by now, tracked down this one specific hidden file, and run a corruption algorithm on it.

"Can you recover the file?" Jenny asked.

"Not likely."

"Rafi's notes are gone, aren't they?" Jenny's thin lips bent into a frown.

I checked the remaining files. Each was filled with a different set of nonsense characters. "Yeah. Looks that way."

"We still have his hardcopy audit work papers," Jenny said. She was trying to ease my disappointment. "I'll help you recreate Rafi's findings."

"You don't understand, Jenny. Rafi had superpowers. He could sniff out bad numbers that mere mortals never catch."

"Rafi was a legend," Jenny said. "But, Thad, how does the saying go? He put his boxers on one leg at a time."

I was hoping she was speaking metaphorically and

not from personal observation. Rafi and Jenny? *Crazy.*

"Between the two of us," Jenny said, "we can rebuild Rafi's files. Mr. Vardanyan told me you passed all four sections of the CPA exam the first time. I did, too. We have the skills. I just need a little direction. We can do this. Together."

I closed File Manager and shut down the computer. I knew Jenny was only trying to be helpful, but I wasn't up for tackling the rebuild right now. "I'm going to take off."

"Oh." Jenny looked disappointed. "What do you want me to do, then?"

"Camp out at Eddie's office until he gets you a copy of every single file Rafi ever requested. Don't let him go home unless he gets you the data. We need to look at everything Rafi ever touched."

"What if Eddie continues to stonewall?"

"Then remind him what's at stake. And if that doesn't work, put him on speakerphone. I'll play the heavy."

Jenny didn't seem completely convinced of my strategy to speed things up. I reiterated to her the client's insistence that we get Gold II back on schedule, no questions asked. I told her, "Worst case if Eddie doesn't come through with the data to recreate Rafi's audit notes, I'll hammer him tomorrow."

The last thing I did was instruct Jenny to ride herd on the audit interns. While she waited for Eddie to produce the toxic assets schedules, she was to have her trainee staff keep plugging away at an analysis of the loans backing the Fed's trillion-dollar-plus investment in toxic home mortgages. Furious activity masquerading as progress. Misdirection away from the "meat" of the audit sandwich.

My afternoon had shaped up like a typical late day at the beach when I'd be on the water, crosswinds creating washing machine conditions, the surf totally blown out. It was the sea gods telling me it was time to paddle in for the day.

I heeded Neptune's message and left the office to ponder. I needed to make sense of the sabotaged files. The night Rafi called, he said he had a plan. Did it include covering his tracks using encryption? Or was his plan something else entirely? I needed time to mull.

Chapter 21

"Hanlon, what are you doing back here?" Tigran said.

I had asked the Uber driver to drop me off at the Dodge Whitney DC office. I wanted to research a way to recover Rafi's munched files.

"I need access to the Internet."

"For what?"

"Jenny and I ran into—" and then I caught myself. If Tigran had been in the loop, if he had known what Rafi had found, he would have said something by now. If Rafi hadn't confided in the senior manager, there must have been a reason. I decided to rephrase. "—some ACL scripts and had trouble with the syntax. So…"

"You want to access the firm's Audit Command Language script library?"

"Exactly. Jenny suggested I copy the files I used on the Sunstake audit and tweak the parameters. She thought it would save us lots of time." It looked like Tigran was buying my tech mumbo jumbo. At least he didn't delve further.

"Hanlon, drop by my office when you're done," he said. "Something's come up."

I could only imagine what that something might be. Just because Eddie Zadelhof was a total geek and was intrigued with my little pen drive, didn't mean he wouldn't report my USB-port system breach to Tigran. I hoped my senior manager would be understanding.

The staff bullpen was nearly empty. Except for a senior associate grilling two first-year associates about client cash accounts that were ten cents off, I was the only one in the shared space. I fired up a desktop computer.

Associate One said, "The bank reconciliations are a dime out of balance. Should I keep looking?"

Associate Two replied, "I wouldn't. It's not material. The client has thirty-eight million in confirmed cash."

The Senior Associate interrupted, "Could be nothing. Could be you've missed an unrecorded deposit for five mill and an offsetting unrecorded check for five million ten cents."

Associates One and Two pledged in unison, "We'll keep looking." Their faces contorted to a solid six on the pain assessment scale.

The senior associate left, and the all-too-familiar post-lecture grumbling started. The audit associates were anything but quiet. I dropped in my wireless earbuds to tune out the unhappy. Then, I started my search for "all things file recovery." I hoped to find a way to turn digital junk into cyber gold.

An hour later, I had zip, unless you count the realization that making sense of Rafi's files was definitely beyond my skill set. Bouncing from weblink to weblink only confirmed it. I exited the Internet browser, powered down the desktop, and headed for Tigran's office.

My senior manager was sitting in his temporarily assigned office, an unlit cigar in his mouth. What was it with short men and cigars? Manliness props compensating for lack of stature? And how manly can you be without the smoke? No fire-breathing, no danger.

"Hanlon," Tigran said, "Travel's already booked your tickets. Don't take off this afternoon without a copy of the audit program."

"Tickets for where?"

"Wall Street. You're going to the New York Federal Reserve Bank. The gold inventory test counts are scheduled for nine a.m. tomorrow. You'll take the Delta shuttle to LaGuardia in the morning."

"Is there some reason you're trying to get me out of the office?" Eddie Zadelhof must have tipped my boss off about the security breach at the Fiscal Service data center.

"What makes you say that?" Tigran said.

"New York? It's the first I'm hearing about this. Why didn't you tell me about the trip yesterday?" I ran my hand through my hair, grabbed the nape of my neck, and massaged.

"I thought Monday's meeting with the client would have cued you in. TSec expects us to make up for lost time. I'm accelerating the work plan."

"But I'm just getting my feet on the ground," I said. "Why not have Jenny go?"

"I have other plans for Jenny. She's also headed to New York tomorrow—West Point. She'll be doing inventory test counts of the deep storage bullion there."

"Oh." I must have looked like Bambi's fraternal twin brother—deer caught in the headlights. "But Marissa? Her condition?"

"I heard her Aunt Nika has that covered."

There were no secrets in Dodge Whitney-land. Word spread at gigabit speed.

An intern popped into the senior manager's office with a sheaf of papers. Tigran handed me my airline tickets, the audit program, and the name of my New York Fed audit counterpart. "Call me midday tomorrow. I want a status report."

On my way out of the Dodge Whitney DC office, I texted Bri:

—We have a problem. Need to talk.—

I didn't have to wait long for Bri's reply. She met me twenty minutes later in the outdoor seating of a popular bistro a couple of blocks from the Dodge Whitney offices. She was sitting under one of the blue umbrellas dotting the al fresco dining that ran along Pennsylvania Avenue. Potted hibiscuses were in bloom, a healthy red. Across the street in Freedom Plaza, a Segway scooter tour group in duck yellow shorts struggled to stay in formation as they dodged protestors waving "End the Fed" signs.

Bri returned the menu to the waitress. "I ordered you a large diet cola," Bri said. "Take a seat."

I sat. "You got here fast."

"At your beck and call."

"What I meant to say was, thanks."

"You mentioned a problem. Talk."

So, I told her about finding Rafi's hidden but very scrambled computer files, about Eddie Zadelhof catching me trying to download them, and my worry that if the data center manager hadn't done so already, by end of day tomorrow whatever Rafi had encrypted would be wiped clean from the server drive.

"Oh, and there's one more piece," I said. "Tigran

booked me a morning flight to New York for a nine a.m. inventory observation in Lower Manhattan. Told me to pack a carry-on. He even dismissed my objection about leaving Marissa."

Bri clucked her tongue, making the tick-tock sound she always did when she was deep in thought. "Midnight audit," she said. "Tonight. You up for it?"

As far as I knew, midnight auditing was accounting folklore, an urban myth. I chalked it up to some dreary accountant's superhero fantasy, more imagined than real.

"You can't be serious?" I said. "You'll get me fired." With Marissa's leave of absence from her health spa job to join me in DC, we were down to one income now. Zero income was not an option.

"You're a virgin, aren't you, Thad? You've never rifled through client files after hours?" Bri sipped her Café con Leche. "Haven't you ever wanted to confirm your suspicions that someone was cooking the books?"

"Investigate suspicions? Yes…" I said, "but by-the-book, no sneaking around, no fourth amendment violations. All my work is admissible as evidence in court."

"Give me a break. You've never colored outside the lines?"

"Not deliberately. Not while I've been at Dodge Whitney. The flash drive thing with Eddie today was an oversight. I hadn't planned it. I forgot I even had the USB. If I had remembered it was embedded in the pen drive, I would have lockered it with my other electronics."

"Fine. I'll get the files," Bri said. "Just get me inside the data farm."

I bit my lip. "Even if I could, Bri—and that's unlikely given security—I'd still be an accomplice."

"My eyes can't take this." Bri put on her sunglasses. "Your halo is blinding me."

Ouch.

"You're upset?" I said. "With *me*?"

"With your naive ethics, Thaddeus Hanlon. All goody-goody." Her voice was getting louder. "Let's talk about ethical duty. You were the last person your best friend calls. He needs your help. You're too busy but promise to get back to him later, except later, he's dead. And now, while trying to clear his name, whether out of guilt or duty, you take the risk-free option, choosing to hide behind a misguided sense of professionalism. You said yourself that if we don't recover Rafi's files before Eddie Zadelhof gets to them, it's all but guaranteed the notes will be erased. Dilemma time—you can do some creative auditing tonight and learn to live with your compromised self or ensure we'll never know what malfeasance Rafi stumbled on that got him killed. You choose."

I hate ethical dilemmas. Hated them when Rafi and I had to do ethics cases in the Accounting Professional Responsibilities course at Cal State. Hated them when the prof made us take a position and then justify our recommendation when there never was a right answer. Only imperfect outcomes.

Bri drummed the sidewalk table with her fingernails. "Does your silence mean you're opting in?"

"I can get you inside the data center," I said. "But that's it."

Bri wagged her head from side to side. "That'll have to do."

"And you can't say anything about this to Marissa," I said. "She's a heavy sleeper. She'll never know I snuck out."

Bri zipped her lips.

"I'm serious. We've never kept secrets before. I'm way off-script here."

"I promise." Bri crossed her heart and held out her little finger for a pinky swear.

I shook my head and took a giant swig of my cola instead.

"So, audit buddy," Bri said, "how do we get inside? You told me the place is hyper-secure."

"I'm working on it." I spent the next fifteen minutes noodling on napkins. On the first one, I made a schematic of the Fiscal Service Bureau data center. I traced through the floor plan with Bri. On the other, I brainstormed a list, scratched a few things off, and circled others while Bri hummed a popular '80s glam-rock tune by Europe.

I handed her the list. "The forensic duplicator I can grab from the office. But these things, I need you to round up."

Bri took the napkin. "What's 10TB SSD?"

"I'm going to teach you how to clone. You'll need a high-capacity solid-state drive."

"Makes sense. But what about the funny hats?"

"My foray into social engineering. Let's hope it works."

I couldn't get the keyboard riff from the Swedish rock band's "Final Countdown" out of my head.

"Three, two, one…" Bri said.

Chapter 22

When I got to the townhouse, Aunt Nika was upstairs, already asleep. Marissa was awake, lying on the couch. There were shadows under her eyes that no amount of concealer would hide. Her lids were droopy, but her eyes focused on me. She extended her arms.

I kissed her cool, but moist lips. "Crazy day," I said.

"How'd your clue search go?"

I gave her the highlights. Well, most of them. I told her about our two steps forward: breakfast with Jenny Yu; uncovering Rafi's digital files. And the one step back: not being able to decipher his notes.

I left out the part about Bri's plan to secure Rafi's files before Eddie Zadelhof had a chance to wipe them off the server, chalking up my sin of omission to Marissa's delicate health. At least that's how I rationalized withholding.

"Nika took me for a ride this afternoon to get some fresh air." Marissa clutched my hand.

"Aunt Nika is a saint."

"You would have loved the cherry blossoms. So restorative. We even saw an in-the-park yoga group doing the Happy Baby Pose."

Marissa tried to bend her knees into her belly, legs extended to the ceiling. She couldn't touch her feet to complete the pose and whimpered. The baby started kicking. She lowered her legs and rubbed her belly. "Not so happy, baby."

I placed my hand on her stomach. Our son was a strong kicker, just like his mom.

"Hon, I need to pack an extra set of clothes," I said.

Marissa sighed, soft but noticeable. "For work?" She covered my hand with hers. "Or is there something you're not telling me?"

"For work. I'm so sorry." I could see Thadpole's foot poke just below Marissa's belly button. "Tigran has me flying into New York in the morning to do a gold bullion count at the Fed. He thinks I can get everything done in a day. I'm not planning on overnight but, just in case, I'm taking a fresh shirt and boxers."

I leaned in closer to Marissa, whispered to her, and described in poetic detail everything I remembered about the first time I met her at the gym. How she glistened in her black workout capris and strappy sports bra, boxing hand wraps tight on her wrists, strictly business, leading the class through punch combos on the heavy bags. Tough, take-charge, no-nonsense. The woman I needed in my life then. And now.

"Come on," I said. "Let's get you to bed. You got to be sick of this couch."

Marissa put her arms around my neck. I gently picked her up, one arm around her back, the other under her knees, and carried her to the master suite. We got under the covers. While I held her, she chanted her nightly mantra— "relax, release, rest" —until she fell asleep. I set a vibrate alarm for 11:30 p.m. Bri would be waiting out front with the things I had asked her to bring.

****

The Bureau of Fiscal Service parking lot behind the Treasury's Liberty Building was a no-go. The lot entrance was gate-controlled, and the exit was guarded by a massive steel road blocker painted to look like an eight by three feet STOP sign. There were two spaces outside the lot running along the curb. The one stenciled ENG was open. We parked there. I affixed the GAO parking hangtag to Bri's rearview mirror. ENG. GAO. Close enough. It was the best I could do to keep the 24-hour parking enforcement at bay.

"You got Jenny's security badge?" I asked.

"It took longer than anticipated." Bri clipped the GAO credential onto the lapel of her one-button notch collar jacket. She was wearing a two-piece black pants suit and a fresh glitter-print blouse with a deep v-neckline. All she needed now was black camo face paint to complete the ninja-chic look. Sneaky elegance.

"The badge modification? Was that the tricky part?" I said.

"Swapping the snapshot was easy." She twisted the photo ID keycard so I could see the finished product. Bri had done a professional job splicing in her photo.

I pulled the card in for a closer look. "You didn't?" I said.

"You like?"

Bri had done something with eyeliner to make her eyes look almond-shaped

"You're no Jenny Yu, but you could pass for Asian," I said. "The makeup? That's what took so long?"

Bri shook her head. "Jenny wasn't keen to let me borrow her badge. You know, the work visa thing. Her fear of deportation back to China. So, we had a long heart-to-heart."

"She agreed?"

"She said she would do it for Rafi." Bri looked away.

"That's devotion." I wished all my first-year associates were that dedicated. For a numbers guy, Rafi's social intelligence was genius. No wonder he had his followers.

"How's this going to work?" Bri asked.

"We use the shift change," I said. "That should get us through the front door. Graveyard comes on at midnight. Security will be preoccupied with personnel clocking in and out, making excess scrutiny less likely."

At the entrance to the Treasury annex building, we fell into line with the other skeleton crew that worked the midnight shift. The guard at the sign-in counter had us log in, took a cursory glance at our photo keycards, and waved us through.

I was totally amped.

We had gotten past the first security ring in Eddie's perimeter defense. The adrenaline rush matched any "feel good" I had ever had from flying off the face of a swell in a superman aerial, grabbing the rails, and reconnecting for a perfect return drop into the wave.

We were halfway to the retracting security door leading to the offices and data center when the guard told us to stop.

"I need to see your bag," he said. The guard pointed to Bri's oversized tote, which had kicked off the metal detector.

She returned to the sign-in counter, spread the handles of her purse, and let the guard take a peek. Wallet, burner phone, keys, make-up kit, mirror, nail file, perfume, pepper spray, sunglasses, a package of snack bars, small water bottle, breath mints, hand sanitizer, tissues, and a modest-sized box of extra-heavy feminine napkins. "That time of the month," Bri said.

"Personal electronic items go in the lockers, miss. You'll need to leave your phone."

Bri obliged, depositing the disposable phone I had her buy earlier as a decoy. She tossed the locker key into her jumbo purse and joined me. My hands were still shaking from the adrenaline dump earlier.

"You can do this, Thad," she whispered.

We passed through the entrance to the data center and headed for the auditor workspace and coffee breakroom.

"Eat this." Bri handed me one of her snack bars. "It will help with the shakes and get your blood sugar back to normal."

I wolfed it down. The trembling eased. My peripheral vision returned. Bri pulled the chunky sanitary napkins box from her purse. She opened it, stuck her hand about halfway down, and pulled out the high-speed cloner, the spare hard drive, and the propeller-head hats. *Clever.* But a whole box of menstrual pads to hide our contraband?

Bri guessed what I was thinking. "The first couple days are a flood," she explained, smiling with half her mouth. "You have to admit, my plan worked, didn't it?" She looked good in a smirk.

I gave her a high-five and then unlocked the audit work desk and pulled a file folder. Inside was a copy of the server farm floor plan. Jenny had found it in the Gold II audit documentation from the data center internal controls review she had done with Rafi. She had circled the area where the computer server assigned to Dodge Whitney was located.

"When we get inside the farm, there will be over six hundred floor-to-ceiling server racks arranged in a horizontal grid. Like a warehouse," I said. "The racks are between seven and eight feet high and each is labeled with a unique identifier. You're looking for storage rack number four-three-eight."

"Got it. Then what?"

"Each metal rack has cabinet space for forty-eight separate 1U computer servers. And each 1U server is about the size of an extra-large pizza box. You want the server unit tagged thirty-seven."

"What else?"

"Remember the schematic I drew on the napkin at the café? The drive ports are in the back of the server unit. You'll need to attach the PCIe cable from the forensic duplicator I preconfigured. To clone, click GO when the control screen comes up."

"Just like we practiced a hundred times."

"Like that."

I put on one of the rainbow-striped propeller hats Bri had bought. "Ready to rock-n-roll?" In my hand, I held a second nerd beanie—the holy grail of geek haberdashery.

"You sure this is going to work? Your social engineering plan to get us inside? It seems silly."

"Has to." I was counting on it. Neither one of our access badges was coded to let us enter the data farm. Nor did we have a voiceprint on file for the current password. Psychological manipulation was our only recourse, and if it took vaudeville silly, I was ready to act the part.

The thing is, people like to help. It's human nature. And for computer geeks, even more so. Playing guru is part of the mystique of being a tech nerd. Couple altruism with expertise, add in a wonky fondness for cool stuff, and you have a prime target for a social engineering con. Trickery 101.

We marched up to the server security antechamber. It was a tight fit with the two of us in the Lexan glass cylinder. Bri brushed up against my back, close. I could smell her perfume, feel her press against me. "Duck," I said as I angled away from her.

As the graveyard shift tech wheeled toward the server room entrance on his scooter, I made my move. I rapped on the glass door. He was wearing wireless earbuds, keeping beat to the tune in his head, eyes focused on the open laptop resting on his utility cart, oblivious to our presence.

I pounded my fists against the glass. The security booth began to shake. He stopped. I waved with both hands. He mouthed "What?"

I showed him my access card and pointed to it. "It's not working," I shouted.

He paused, then slid the door open. He spied Bri. "There's two of you?"

"Yeah, neither badge is working," I said.

He took my card and tried it and then Bri's modified card. He spent a long time looking at Bri, mostly her chest. She arched, accentuating her cleavage. Appealing and revealing.

I edged my way inside the server room. A blast of chilled air made the propeller spin on my cap.

"I can't let you in," he said. "You need to leave."

That was my cue. *Time for a diversion*. I picked up his scooter, put my foot on the metal deck, pulled a Bunny Hop, and then, a quick Tail Whip. The backend of the scooter spun around the front bar while I still had my feet in the air. I landed back on the deck plate and did a dismount.

"You know," I said, "this is not just basic transport for getting you to and fro on the farm. This vehicle...," I pointed to the scooter with reverence, "is a sophisticated trick machine." I did a Fakie, which is like skateboarding backward without the help of a rearview mirror. I was wobbly at first, but managed to keep my balance, landing upright against one of the server racks ten feet behind me. I took a bow. As I did, Bri slipped in from the Lexan antechamber.

"Here, let me show you some basic moves," I said to the tech. "Oh, and you got to have one of these." I offered him the other propeller hat. "I'm surprised these aren't standard issue."

The tech put on the hat. I flicked his propeller.

"Do you have a powder room?" Bri dug through her purse and held up a fresh sanitary napkin.

Propeller Tech looked uncomfortable and pointed to the far end of the server racks. "Just around the corner."

Bri smiled and then disappeared.

I handed back the scooter to the tech. "First thing is the hop. You gotta have the Bunny Hop to do the Tail Whip, Bar Twist, or the three-sixty."

"You can do a three-sixty?"

"Get me on your work counter and I can do a backflip dismount."

"Awesome sauce."

When I heard him use the geek meme for something outrageously phenomenal, I knew I had him hooked. I said, "Let's try the Bunny Hop, first. Are you regular stance or goofy foot?"

"What's the difference?"

I showed him left foot forward and then goofy foot with the right forward. Rafi was a classic goofy footer on the waves and on a scooter. Me, I was more comfortable with regular stance.

"Regular stance," he said. "Right-leg dominant." He stepped onto the scooter deck and attempted a hop.

The scooter went nowhere.

"Jump first," I said, "bending your knees and pushing up with your legs. Then pull up on the handlebars."

Propeller Tech tried again and biffed. He didn't suffer any real damage. But the scooter did. I had to straighten the handlebars so they were once again perpendicular to the deck.

"Like this." I crouched and did a series of Bunny Hops. "Take it a little slower," I encouraged. I had him lean on me while I positioned his feet, adjusting his weight so he was balanced. I flicked his propeller once more. "You'll get it this time," I said.

Propeller Tech hopped up about six inches from the floor. Big smile on his face. I gave him a fist bump. He kept going, Bunny Hopping until he cleared a foot off the ground.

"Practice that. And oh…" I pulled a flash drive from my pocket. "I was hoping you could help me with my ACL scripts. You know, the Audit Command Language, the computer-assisted analysis tool? My boss always says 'work documented is work done' but apparently the audit documentation isn't complete, so he had me tweak the parameters at our DC office this evening and told me to go back tonight and re-run everything onsite but I know USBs brought into the facility from outside must be vetted for malicious code first—"

"Where's your partner?" Propeller Tech asked.

Bri should have been back by now.

Once she found the right rack and server unit, it would have taken Bri less than ten minutes to clone the drive. My diversionary scooter lesson with guided practice had easily given her fifteen minutes.

Just then, the emergency strobe lights above the server racks began flashing. I had to cover my eyes. The siren above the doorway screeched, intermittent at first, and then continuously. Then there was a series of explosions from the ceiling nozzles as pressurized FM200 fire suppression gas hissed, flooding the farm in gas.

It was impossible to see, the fog was so thick, and that constant screeching. I was about to stick my fingers in my ears to mute the sound when Bri ran up to us, arms flailing to get our attention.

"What's going on?" she yelled before covering her mouth with the top of her blouse. The waistband of her pants was askew, toilet paper trailing behind her.

Propeller Tech dropped his scooter. "You two evacuate. Now!" He grabbed our arms, marched us down the ramp to the security entrance of the server farm, shoved us, one at a time, through the Lexan cylinder door, then ran back into the server room.

The hissing slowed. The FM200 gas dissipated but visibility was still poor. Once Propeller Tech was out of sight, Bri and I headed for the retracting metal door that opened into the entrance lobby. The graveyard shift security guard was on his walkie-talkie. He had a procedure manual open on the sign-in counter and was thumbing through it. I was pretty sure this was his first building fire incident. He didn't seem to have a handle on protocol.

"False alarm," Bri said.

The guard stopped reading the manual.

I said, "The data center fire suppression system discharged accidentally."

The guard punched the press-to-talk button on his radio. "Sheldon, you okay?"

The radio crackled and then we heard Propeller Tech say, "Ten-four."

"Shouldn't we be evacuating the building?" the security guard asked the tech.

"There's no fire. I'm working on resetting the alarms."

"What about these two?" The guard examined our badges. "Hanlon and Yu?"

We couldn't afford to be detained. And we definitely couldn't afford a bag search or pat-down. Bri held her chest and wheezed. I coughed.

"Sounds like they're having trouble breathing from the FM200. Let 'em get some air," Propeller Tech said.

Bri smiled, grabbed the sign-in sheet, and signed out. I did the same.

Once outside, we ran.

Bri reached the convertible first and put the top down. I hopped over the side of the car into the front passenger seat. Just as I was about to buckle in, Bri floored it. The tires grabbed, squealed, and smoked. I inhaled deeply, trying to catch my breath. The smell of burning rubber, recklessly laid down for our getaway, tickled my nose.

Bri was laughing, that hysterical in-the-face-of-death shriek she always made when the four of us would shoot through the inversion loop on a rollercoaster in one of SoCal's many thrill parks. Good times, then. Me and Marissa, Rafi and Bri. Tonight had been no less crazy.

My armpits were soaked, my hands clammy. So much for being a mere accessory to the break-in. I was coloring outside the lines now.

Tomorrow I'd be in New York City, away from any fallout from the midnight audit at the Fiscal Service Bureau data center. Technically, we hadn't taken anything that wasn't Dodge Whitney work product. And if Bri was successful, she hadn't left an evidence trail. Still, I had this feeling Tigran was going to be pissed.

I'd have to deal with that *mañana*.

Chapter 23

"I have good news and bad news," Bri shouted over the road noise. She followed the in-dash GPS as she sped over the 14th Street Bridge, merging onto I-395 west. The dank air from the Potomac River below sent a chill through me. Moonlight glinted off the highlights in Bri's long chestnut hair as it whipped behind her in the wind. She looked over and saw that I was shaking.

"Top up?" Bri asked. She didn't wait for an answer, dropped her speed to thirty mph, and pushed the console button to activate the power convertible roof. The cloth top slid back into place. Bri picked up her speed again as we merged onto VA-110 heading north to Georgetown.

"Let's get it over with," I said. "Bad news first."

"There was a second tech. You told me graveyard was going to be barebones staffed."

"According to Jenny Yu, it is. She said one tech's always on the floor doing server maintenance—my scooter tutee with the propeller beanie. And one tech is always in Network Ops, monitoring the wall of display consoles. There shouldn't have been anyone walking the racks."

"Well, I heard someone. Maybe the Network Ops guy got spooked by something on the security cams and decided to check things out. I thought I was being pretty stealthy when I set up the cloner."

"Tell me you got the drive," I said.

"I'm getting there."

"So…"

"When I went back to retrieve everything, I heard footsteps a couple of rack corridors over, so I panicked, and ran to the back of the farm, pried up one of the floor tiles, and was about to shimmy down into the subflooring but…" Bri paused, waiting for me to appreciate the suspense.

I imagined Bri slithering into the netherworld of the data center, encountering sylphs we never expected. "Are you going to tell me this is the part where the bad news gets worse?"

"Red laser beams bouncing everywhere. And it's incredibly cramped down there," she said.

"So, you're telling me the data center subfloor has a laser intrusion detection system?"

Bri nodded.

When Eddie Zadelhof busted me earlier today for using the USB drive port, he said he had other security measures in place. Apparently, rigging the server room subfloor with lasers and beam sensors was what he meant. Smart on his part.

"Bri, tell me you didn't trigger the alarm."

"Not *that* alarm. That would have been stupid. Raise too many questions." Bri's hazel eyes went all fierce on me.

"You pulled the fire alarm, instead?"

"Just like high school. Best way to get out of finals."

I could tell Bri wasn't kidding. "What about the security cams?"

"The one for the zone I was in? I took it out with my hairspray. And any fingerprints? I wiped down the box panel. The FM200 gas cloud provided any other cover needed until I caught up with you and the scooter tech."

Bri exited VA-110 on North Lynn, taking the Francis Scott Key Bridge into Georgetown. We were close to Uncle Leonid's place and although Bri's bad news tales were always entertaining, I was ready for the good news. As we approached M Street, a drizzle moistened the fuchsia-colored petunias in the hanging baskets that ringed the lamp posts.

"What's the good, Bri? You said you had good news and bad."

"Mission accomplished." Bri held up the sealed antistatic bag. A glint of gold from the edge connectors of the standard three-and-a-half-inch disk drive sparkled under the light from the oversized globes of the antique streetlamps.

Now, all we had to do was have Dodge Whitney Tech Support decipher the contents of the drive while keeping Tigran out of the loop. In the meantime, Bri agreed to secure the evidence.

When I finally got back to bed, Marissa was blowing puffs of air through her puckered lips, slow and regular. She was Lamaze-breathing in her sleep. The natural childbirth classes we had started in California wouldn't be of any help now. Dr. Godenko made that clear when she said with placenta previa my wife was in for a C-section. I spooned up close to her. She smelled good. I gently kissed the back of her neck and then turned over.

If I was lucky, I'd get a two-hour nap before I had

to wake to take the Delta Shuttle to New York. And if the midnight audit gods were watching over me, I could avoid having to tell Marissa what I had done last night until I got back later Wednesday evening.

By 8:30 a.m. I was in downtown Manhattan, rounding the corner of Nassau Street onto Liberty. Directly in front of me was a twenty-two-story Florentine-style fortress, headquarters for the Federal Reserve Bank of New York. Eighty feet below ground was the inventory I was to test count—6,350 metric tons of gold, one-quarter of the free world's known monetary reserves.

As the cab driver pulled to the curb, I whisked crumbs of chocolate croissant from my suit jacket and slurped the rest of my protein shake. Marissa would not approve of my breakfast on the run, except for the whey powder. Eating healthy on the road required a maturity I was still cultivating. I over-tipped the driver a couple of fivers for the mess I left.

At the 33 Liberty Street entrance, two Federal Reserve Police officers were chatting across the handrail, one in full dress blue and the other, higher-ranked, in dress blue with a white shirt. Their duty belts were fully configured with a holstered handgun, taser, and collapsible baton. Neither smiled. And neither let me in the building. Instead, they redirected me to the public entrance on 44 Maiden Lane, just around the block.

The visitor entrance was pleasantly quiet this time of the morning. School tours weren't for a couple more hours; public tours started after lunch. There was only one guard out front. She directed me to the security checkpoint inside the building where I had to empty my pockets and have my combo backpack scanned. I stepped through the metal detector. It beeped. The security officer waved me over to her associate.

"Surfing competition accident," I said, as I pointed to my right wrist. "Titanium plate." I unbuttoned my cuff.

"Feet shoulder width. Hands to the side," the second guard said. After putting on a new pair of nitrile gloves, he patted me down, ran a wand over my plate, and then motioned me through with a "keep moving" gesture.

The Executive Vice President-General Auditor was waiting for me at the end of the baggage scanner belt.

"Sigalie Kaddish," she said. She had a firm grip to go along with her sturdy build. She was wearing a black blazer, a career woman's chiffon blouse, and a black and white vertically-striped skirt. A pewter thicket of tight curls framed her square face. Oversized white-gold earrings tastefully accessorized her ensemble.

"Thaddeus Hanlon." I shook her hand.

"I know who you are. I know why you're here."

"Then, you must be my GAO liaison." If she nodded, I missed it.

"If you have to ask…"

Then I already knew the answer.

Translation: I was wasting her valuable time.

This was going to be fun.

I should have expected she wouldn't be happy to see me. Audit clients always resent being examined. But having a fellow auditor—a member of your own profession—scrutinize your shop, run test procedures, and question your work? That's considered an insult, enough so to breed resentment on steroids. And that resentment often turns to enmity. Any cooperation on this visit wasn't going to come easy. I grabbed my briefcase from the gray plastic bin rolling off the scanner conveyor belt.

"Follow me," Sigalie said.

I fell into stride behind her. My street shoes clacked on the black and tan marble tile floors as we walked.

Inside the Federal Reserve Building was like stepping through an architectural time warp into the medieval palaces of the Italian Renaissance. The hallways were spacious, with self-supporting arches of limestone and sandstone girding up massive architectural vaults. The ornamental ironwork that graced the exterior walls of the bank was replicated inside. Wrought-iron chandeliers provided the lighting.

The only signs of modernity were ceiling-mounted cameras that rotated in sweeping arcs to monitor all activity inside the building. If the architects were going for solid, stable, and secure, they had succeeded. The Federal Reserve Bank of New York was one impenetrable castle. A great place to store gold if you were a foreign central bank, international financial organization, or foreign government.

We passed the self-guided displays of the building's financial history museum before reaching the elevator bank. Sigalie summoned the next elevator car.

"Here's what I think, Tad." Sigalie moved in closer to make sure I was listening carefully.

"Thad. With an *h*."

"Okay, Thad with an *h*, here's my point. Every two years we go through this fire drill when the U.S. House of Representatives turns over. Some freshman congressional representative hears from the gold truthers, 'All the gold is fake. We saw it on the Internet. And, by the way, End the Fed!'"

The elevator car opened. We stepped in. Sigalie inserted a security key and punched the button to take us down to Basement E on the fifth sublevel.

"So, then," she continued, "we do this 'audit the gold' dance. In 2011, we had congressional hearings for the Gold Reserve Transparency Act. Then in 2012, the Treasury Office of Inspector General sends his people over to check on us again. And what did they find?"

"Sigalie, I'm not privy to the politics. I'm just the senior associate on the job."

The elevator car stopped. "They found nothing, Thad. Nothing out of order. Think about it. Is this how we should be using the taxpayer's dollar?" Sigalie raised her hands, palms up, in one of those give-me-a-break gestures.

"Thad, we follow the same U.S. generally accepted government auditing standards as everybody else. The Treasury now observes our inventory counts every single year. And then you show up unexpectedly to duplicate the counts. I don't mean to *kvetch,* but at this rate, we'll know each gold bar by name."

That was a stretch. Hyperbole aside, apparently I had been given alternate facts in my briefing. The reality was that an independent observation of the Fed's gold inventory had been done only *five* times since 1985, surely not often enough to develop a personal relationship with the yellow bricks. And those five audits in thirty-plus years were flawed, with a capital "F."

In 2012, in response to congressional pressure, the

Treasury had begun annual reviews of the Fed gold but there was one hitch—there wasn't third-party verification. No external auditors observing the inventory counts. *Highly unusual.*

Yet, when the Treasury Department conducts gold audits of Fort Knox, it always hires outside auditors from a Big Four public accounting firm to be on-site and scrutinize everything. No wonder Secretary Beck had engaged Dodge Whitney under the guise of GAO cover to assure counts were above board.

"You don't believe me, do you?" Sigalie said. "Tell you what. I'll show you the gold. You decide for yourself."

"Fair enough," I said. But I still had my doubts.

I followed Sigalie Kaddish into a ninety-ton cylindrical tube that rotated to provide access to the vaults. Two other professionals joined us.

"The rest of my security control team," Sigalie said. "Thad, this is LaVonna Trennery from Custody and Ron Manchusco from Vault Services."

Both were rather non-descript accounting types, clipboards in hand. We exchanged the customary pleased-to-meet-you greetings. Ron's New York accent was thick but not as heavy as the General Auditor's. He was dressed in the last decade's business fashion. LaVonna had that monied-inflection of prep school and the professional couture to match. Ron and LaVonna made sure to give me their business cards.

"Enough already," Sigalie said. Ron put away his wallet, LaVonna her card case.

"You do everything in threes?" I asked.

"Whenever gold is moved or whenever anyone enters the vault. We divide the responsibilities. No one person has complete access."

When Tigran pulled me into his office yesterday, he handed me the Dodge Whitney audit work program. My job here at the New York Fed was straightforward. Review internal controls and observe the gold inventory test counts.

The controls—the procedures to safeguard the deep storage gold reserves—were shaping up to be by the book. A clear segregation of duties was critical. So far, I had three people from three separate departments sharing responsibility for vault access. Barring collusion, dispersed duties would reduce the risk of fraud, defalcation, or theft.

"Point of fact," Sigalie went on, "this ninety-ton steel cylinder you're standing in is the only way into the vault. There are no doors. At the end of the business day, after all gold movement is processed and the public tours are complete, the three of us are present to watch the rotation of the cylinder, which closes off the vault and seals it airtight and watertight. The cylinder is set in a hundred forty-ton frame, making the vault impregnable."

With only two hours of sleep last night, I could feel myself slipping into a daze.

Sigalie caught me with my eyes closed. "Why do I suspect I'm wasting my breath?" she said. "What happened to notes? Nobody takes notes anymore."

I took out a digital tablet from my briefcase, removed the stylus, and started scratching. That helped. Allowed me to refocus.

The General Auditor looked pleased. A small victory for the effectiveness of berating. We exited the tube and stepped into the vault.

The subterranean space was perhaps a half-football field in length. Much larger than I imagined it would be. And colder. The vault was lined with butter-yellow metal stacked in a series of compartments protected by iron gates painted penitentiary blue. As far as safes go, it looked more like a high-security jail than a home for the wealth of nations. Even so, I couldn't stop ogling at the floor-to-ceiling contents behind the blue gates.

The General Auditor snapped her fingers in front of my eyes. "Such beautiful *gelt* you're looking at. Over sixty-one hundred metric tons of the purest gold in the world. For the most part, nine hundred ninety-nine point nine fine."

"This pure gold, what's it all worth?"

"Between three hundred fifty-five and three hundred eighty-five billion dollars, depending on-the-spot price of gold."

"And the number of bars?"

"Four hundred, ninety-seven thousand."

That could be a problem.

Chapter 24

Nearly a half-million bars. There was no way I was going to test count a number that big in one day or one week. I had promised Marissa I'd be back tonight. I had to narrow the scope of my examination. "What about the U.S. portion?"

"Based on the last count—thirty-four thousand twenty-one bars."

Better. But still a large number. I tapped 34K into my tablet. I rubbed my chin as I ran through options for getting this count done today.

The other two members of the control team were getting restless. Ron flicked specks of dandruff from his navy-blue polyester suit, while LaVonna stifled a petite yawn. Sigalie took careful note.

"See those?" Sigalie pointed to the locks protecting the compartment in front of us. There was a padlock and two combination locks in a metal panel welded to the middle of the security bars making up the compartment door. "Ron is the only one with the combo to the bottom lock. LaVonna has the combination to the top. And a member of the Internal Audit staff always has the key to the padlock." Sigalie held up the key.

"So that's how you control access to the compartments once inside the vault?"

"That and closed-circuit TV. The guards

monitoring the CCTV feed must qualify as marksmen each month in the basement shooting range."

"That would be a deterrent," I said.

Ron chuckled, but cut it short when Sigalie gave him the look.

Sigalie rotated a plastic sheet protector that was double-cabled to the middle panel of the compartment door. There was a document inside. "Are you familiar with the Official Joint Seal?" she asked.

"Somewhat."

"Somewhat? Only somewhat?" Sigalie covered her face with her hands so I couldn't see if she was rolling her eyes. She sighed heavily.

I knew more than *somewhat*. I was choosing to play dumb to get a feel for the security control team's process. "It's a record," I said.

"Not just a record, Thad. It's *the* record*!* The official listing of the contents of the compartment." Sigalie used her finger to highlight key portions of the document. "Here's the number of bars, the gross weight, the total number of fine troy ounces." She let go of the form so that it dangled from the cable. "Each time a numbered compartment is opened, the three of us sign off on the Official Joint Seal."

I made a note. "If the seal isn't tampered with, do you require a recount?"

"What's the point? After you've counted the gold once and checked the seal, the numbers are going to be the same year after year after year."

I could see the logic and scribbled some more on my tablet. Excluding previous untampered counts might help reduce my scope even further. "One last question," I said.

Sigalie checked her watch. "If you must."

"Are your internal controls the same for your foreign depositors? And do they ever request an audit of their compartment?"

Sigalie held up two fingers. "That was two, Thad."

I smiled. Worked on making it as ingratiating as possible.

"The answer to both questions is yes."

I scrawled a few more things on the tablet and closed it. "Sigalie, I think I have enough on control procedures. I'm ready to conduct my test counts."

"How long is that going to take?"

"Depends on the sample size. You're the General Auditor. You know statistical sampling theory. You probably have an idea."

"A guesstimate, yes. But we don't know your scope. Or what differences you'll tolerate."

"Scope I can share with you. Today, we're not doing the whole enchilada. Only U.S. gold held by the Fed in U.S. Treasury compartments A through K."

Sigalie took out her phone and fired up a calculator app. "For a ninety-five percent confidence level with thirty-four thousand twenty-one bullion bars, the sample is three hundred eighty bricks. That would take five days. There's no way you're going to camp out here that long."

I whistled through my teeth.

"Okay," I said. "Tell me this. What did you use for an estimate to move, weigh, assay, and re-shelve the bars?"

"Our norm. Six minutes."

Ron nodded. LaVonna nodded. They both pulled out their smartphones to check their calendars.

Tigran had said this job would be a day at the most. Fly into NYC, do a little ticking, do a little tying, and fly back out. He must have assumed the vault safeguards warranted a smaller sample. All I knew was that Marissa would kill me if I was out of town five days straight.

I flipped open my tablet and re-crunched the numbers. "Sigalie, based on the strength of your internal controls, I'm proposing a ninety percent confidence threshold. What that means is, I only need a random sample of sixty-eight bars."

The General Auditor did the math in her head. "Seven hours," she said. "We can do that."

"There's one condition."

"Listening."

"If there is *one* anomaly, one bullion bar you can't find, one gold brick that flunks the assay, the sample size reverts to the original parameters—ninety-five percent with no more than a five percent error rate."

"Let me get the rest of my team in here," the General Auditor said.

We walked down the vault corridor to a section of smaller compartments, home to the fraction of the gold belonging to the U.S. Treasury. Two older men, gold stackers with protective shoe covers, joined our group. They were wearing gray uniforms, black back-support belts, and white gloves. One of them was pulling an empty hydraulic stacking trolley behind him, wheels squeaking.

"Cool overshoes," I said, pointing to the top of his footwear that looked like Apollo moon landing boots. *One bulky step for man.*

"Magnesium covers," the first stacker said. "They

just strap on."

"Have you ever dropped a brick?"

"Happens sometimes," the second stacker said. "At the end of a long shift, we can get sloppy. The shoe covers saved my piggies more than once." He grinned, flashing two gold-capped front teeth.

Sigalie brought the team to a halt in front of one of the smaller compartments. Gold was stacked floor to ceiling. "We're going to start here with Treasury Compartment A."

I watched carefully as the security control team removed the padlock and unlocked the two combination tumblers. Sigalie took a bolt cutter to the steel cable, breaking the Official Joint Seal. She slipped the seal documentation out of the plastic jacket and handed it to me.

I recorded the basics: vault number, compartment, seal number, the number of bars in the compartment, and the weight in troy ounces—the standard of measure for precious metals, a troy ounce being a bit heavier than the everyday avoirdupois ounce.

Beyond the basics, I was also interested in the seal history. When was the gold last moved? From which compartment? Who signed off?

According to the Official Joint Seal documents, they had transferred the gold in this compartment during the 2014 Treasury audit. No surprise. Inventory migration I expected. The only way to count a wall of bricks, several feet thick, was to relocate it, brick by brick, to an empty compartment. I could see the gold stackers had their work cut out for them today.

As the stackers removed each bar, I verified the serial numbers against the inventory spreadsheet Tigran had given me yesterday with the audit program. The count moved pretty fast once we got into a rhythm. I wasn't planning to stop until we needed to pull a test bar for weighing and collecting an assay sample. I had set my selection criteria at every five hundredth bar.

"If you don't mind," I said, pointing to one of the trapezoidal bricks, "I'd like to start with *that* one." I highlighted the serial number on the spreadsheet. The first stacker handed me some disposable cotton gloves.

I reached over and hefted the thick brick in my hands. Even though it was a little shorter and thinner than a household brick, there was a solid, clean feel, a compact dense twenty-seven-plus pounds. I turned the bar over, running my fingers over the stampings: bar serial number; refiner/assay seal; cast date; melt grouping; and purity.

I used the tablet to jot down the data from the stampings, making sure to get the serial numbers recorded exactly.

"Okay. Let's weigh it out." I handed the gold brick back to the stacker.

"Just one bar?" he asked.

"For now."

I followed the gold stacker as he carried the brick down the compartment corridor to the vault weighing system. He handed it off to the vault custodian, who placed the bar on the Lodestar precision balance scale. The tall industrial-sized instrument was capable of weighing hundreds of pounds of bullion at a time to within one one-hundredth of a troy ounce. It was definitely more machine than needed to weigh twenty-seven pounds. The lone bar sitting on the bullion tray looked silly.

The vault custodian set a group of small counterbalance weights on the other end of the scale until it was perfectly in balance. "Four hundred one point two five ounces," he announced.

I made a notation in my spreadsheet next to the line with the bar serial number.

"You look surprised," Sigalie said.

"Relieved. It's always good when there's a matchup between the inventory listing and actual."

"So, the weight and the stamping *are* the same?" Sigalie had that smug look of an I-told-you-so moment.

"For this *one* bar."

"Right." Sigalie sounded annoyed. She looked at her watch. "Verifying on a one-off basis like this, Thad, we'll never get done. Do you want to finish today? If so, I have an idea."

From the muffled chatter behind me, there seemed to be a consensus from the other two members of the security control team that onesies were not the way to go.

"I'm open. What's your protocol?"

"We do bulk. You select all your test bars. The stackers load them on the hydraulic trolley, and then the vault custodian weighs them, one bar at a time."

"And the assay samples?"

"That can also be streamlined. We shave chips all at once at the assay station, factory-style."

Avoiding the traipse back and forth from the compartment to the scale to the assay table made sense. "You've done this before," I said.

Sigalie Kaddish gave me one of those closed-lipped grins reserved for suffering fools. She fluttered her eyelids in disdain.

"We'll do it your way," I said.

Everything went smoothly with the weigh-in until the sixty-third bar. That's when the older of the two stackers lost control while trying to remove two bars at a time. He fell sideways and rammed into a compartment wall. Fatigue had apparently set in. The gold bricks slipped from his white-gloved hands, crashing to the cement floor. One dull thud after another.

"You okay?" I said as I helped the stacker to his feet. He did a little dance in his magnesium shoe covers, then gave me a white glove thumbs-up.

Sigalie lambasted the clumsy stacker. By the time she was done with her withering screed, gold had become a four-letter word. I thought Tigran had honed his venting skills, but Sigalie Kaddish was in another league altogether.

"Just curious," I said. "Can you give me a sec?" I bent over to pick up the gold bricks. The soft metal had flared out at the corners, permanently disfiguring the trapezoidal bars where they had contacted the ground. I stacked the bricks, one on top of the other, and inspected the stampings.

The gold bars were the same size, inch for inch. They lined up perfectly. And the smelter stamp and melt group were the same. Both bricks had been poured at the same refinery.

I separated the bricks, placing one in each hand. I hefted them back and forth, trying to get a feel for any difference. It was close. The bricks were approximately the same weight. But there had been a difference in pitch when they hit the ground. Two equal bars. Two different pings. I turned them over and compared the purity. Both stamped 999.9 fine.

"Let's weigh these out," I said.

The vault custodian placed the bars on the Lodestar, weighing them one at a time. There was less than one one-hundredth of an ounce difference—a third of the weight of a dollar bill.

I noted the serial numbers: 163466 and 163467.

"Listen," I said as I flicked the bars with my fingernail. "Listen for the high-pitched ping. Lasts about one to two seconds."

"I don't know what you're talking about. They sound the same to me." Sigalie looked to the rest of her team for support. Ron and LaVonna shrugged their shoulders.

"Maybe," LaVonna said.

Ron mimed wearing headphones. "I blew out the top range of my hearing as a teen."

"I wouldn't bet my life on it," I said, "but I'm pretty sure one brick is definitely higher pitched than the other." I grabbed two more nearly identical bricks from the trolley stack. Then, repeated the ping test. This time there was no difference. The sound was the same. Maybe the first set of metal clinks was a fluke? I jotted down the two additional serial numbers just to be thorough.

Off to the side of the scale was another hydraulic trolley. This one was loaded with a shipment of "good delivery bars" that must have come in while Sigalie was giving me the grand tour of the vault earlier. The 400-troy ounce bricks apparently had not been completely processed yet, awaiting a weigh-in, otherwise, they would have been moved into one of the secure storage compartments. Sigalie caught me looking at the stack of gold.

"They're outside your audit scope," she said. FOREIGN was stamped in block lettering, lengthwise across the trolley platform. "Those bars belong to one of our international central bank clients." Sigalie moved in front of the trolley to block me.

I snaked around her. Pulled two look-alike bars from the foreign stack and ran a ping test. Different again. One high, one much lower.

"What? You didn't hear me? Give me those, Thad."

Before Sigalie could get her hands on the bars, I took out a pen and scribbled the two serial numbers on the palm of my hand. Then, I helped her set the bars down on the trolley one at a time.

"Pack it up," she said. "Grab your briefcase, notes, tablet, whatever. We're going back upstairs."

I picked up the two funny-sounding bricks with the mashed corners. "I'm taking these to run further tests." The bars were quickly secured in my backpack.

"Guards," Sigalie said.

Two uniformed Federal Reserve Police with black automatic assault rifles appeared out of nowhere. They were wearing navy-blue uniforms, crisply pressed, gold FR pins adorning each collar, navy-blue ties with gold tie clips, dress caps with gold insignia, and duty belts like their counterparts guarding the 33 Liberty Street entrance.

Chapter 25

I put the bars back on the trolley.

"Smartest thing you've done all day, Thad." Sigalie thanked the guards and sent them back to their stations.

"I was trying to preserve the chain of custody," I said.

"Meaning what?"

"Seizing these bars…as audit evidence of my inventory observation work. My plan was to send the suspect bars to Dodge Whitney's lab."

"These bars? You know how much each one of *these* bars is worth?"

"Close to three-quarter million bucks."

"And in what universe do you think I would let you walk out of here with a million and a half in gold, tucked in your little red backpack?"

Nervous laughter on my part. "I was not going to leave the building *unaccompanied,* if that's what you thought. I would never take that kind of risk, Sigalie. What I should have said is that I was hoping you could help me arrange for armored transport for the suspect bars to Dodge Whitney's assay lab. The bars would be returned, once the tests were done, again by armored car."

"No," Sigalie said.

"I'm just trying to rule out any anomalies. Something's off."

"Hell no!"

"Okay, then let me suggest this," I said. "We call Tigran Vardanyan, the GAO senior manager on this job. Let him decide."

"Get him on the phone." Sigalie handed me her government-issue mobile.

The receptionist for the Washington DC office of Dodge Whitney, CPAs patched me through to Tigran. "Can't talk," he said.

"Tigran, I've got you on speakerphone with Sigalie Kaddish, New York Fed E.V.P. and General Auditor."

Long pause.

When Tigran came back on the line, he said, "Sorry it took so much time, Ms. Kaddish. I had to reschedule the meeting I was in. I'm free now."

"You can call me Sigalie."

"Sigalie, it's been what, six or so hours since Thad checked in? How are the test counts going?"

Before my Fed counterpart had a chance to respond, I said, "I can answer that." I recapped the events of the last twenty minutes, leaving out the part about the guards with the assault rifles.

"Sigalie, is that how you see it?" Tigran knew his way around a fierce conversation. He was trying to hear both sides of the story.

"We have a problem," she said. "The staff member you sent me wants to impound two gold bars. He thought he'd stuff them in his backpack, carry them from the vault to my office and then arrange for armored truck rideshare to take them to your assay lab."

When Sigalie characterized my plan that way, my approach sounded overwrought. Perhaps moronic. I certainly needed more sleep than the two hours I got last night.

"Assay chips," Tigran said. "We only need the tetrahedron samples from the top and bottom of the bars. About four-tenths of an ounce each. Would that be possible?"

Sigalie picked up the two bars, one at a time, and set them aside. "We can do that today."

"But the chain of custody?" I asked.

"Thad, this is an inventory observation," Tigran answered. "Not a fraud investigation. Chain of custody is irrelevant."

"Thank you, Tigran." Sigalie did one of her victory smiles. "I've been here for fifteen years. I'm not about to have the integrity of my office challenged by a twenty-something. Thad is no longer welcome at this facility. He will not be allowed in again."

"Hanlon, take the call off speakerphone." Tigran wasn't asking.

At this point, I was pretty certain the less I talked, the better.

"Hanlon, two things." Tigran was using his outside voice. "First, the fiasco with Sigalie Kaddish. When you get back this afternoon, I want a full report. Every misstep on how you alienated the New York Federal Reserve Bank's General Auditor and Executive Vice President."

"And the second thing?" I tried to sound humble.

"Grab the next shuttle to DC. We need to talk. I have something to discuss with you this afternoon."

That last item didn't sound career-enhancing. I wondered if the second thing on his task list rhymed with "Fiscal Service Bureau Data Center." If so, I was in for a double tongue-lash, perhaps worse.

"Tigran, I'd feel better if we could sequester the bars. At least isolate them on a shelf in the Library Compartment where they house small deposits. What do you think?" I asked.

"Hanlon, you have the bar serial numbers?"

"Yes."

"Then just let it go and get your ass back here."

When I touched down a couple of hours later at Reagan National in DC, an onslaught of new text and voice message notifications popped up on my phone.

Tigran reiterated he wanted to see me as soon as I could get to the Dodge Whitney office. "Absolutely no detours," his voicemail emphasized.

My wife wanted to know why every one of her calls had gone straight to voicemail and why I hadn't returned any of them. Oh, and by the way, where was I last night when she turned over in bed and I wasn't there?

Bri's texts were simple. She wanted to know what to do with the cloned drive and the forensic duplicator.

And Detective Mapu at MPD Homicide wanted to know if I'd be interested in catching a few waves on Saturday. —*Surf's up*— he texted.

Doogie Mapu's beach offer had me stoked. After my audit wipeout this morning, I could use a little water therapy this weekend. Plus, it would give Marissa a change of scenery. I took a deep breath and tried to imagine the smell of the Atlantic Ocean, but was disappointed. Jet fuel odor from the airport runway had penetrated the cabin and filled my nostrils instead.

Over the aircraft-PA came: "Ladies and gentlemen, we have reached the gate. Flight attendants prepare doors for arrival and cross-check."

Before I could get my combo briefcase down from the overhead bin, Marissa called. She was hysterical.

I tried to calm her. "It's okay, baby. I'm on the ground. I'm on my way."

Between sobs, I heard her say something about the police.

"Marissa, please tell me you're all right. Tell me the baby's okay."

Nika was screaming in the background. "Matryoshka. The phone. Give me."

More blubbering, interrupted only when Marissa sniffled.

"Thad, this is Aunt Nika. The police. They are outside. What should I do?"

From the airplane shuttle gate in Terminal B, I started jogging toward the curbside cab stand. "Nika, why are the police there?" I huffed as I picked up my pace.

"We were robbed. Two men broke into the house. I call 9-1-1 when they left."

"Did they hurt Marissa? Hurt you?"

I jumped in the first open taxi, put my thumb over the phone microphone, and gave the cabbie the address for Uncle Leonid's.

"They put tape on us. Mouths. Hands. Heavy tape. Sticky."

"Duct tape? They duct-taped you? Is Marissa okay? The baby?"

"I have to open door. The police. They keep knocking."

"Nika, ask them for ID."

The taxi passed the Arlington National Cemetery. The street traffic on Arlington Boulevard came to a crawl just as the driver was about to turn onto North Lynn. All we needed was to cross from Rosslyn into Georgetown over the Key Bridge and I would be there.

"Thad, the police want to take statement. I have to go."

"Nika don't hang up. Give the phone to—"

There were three beeps and then a call-ended notification. *Thanks, Nika.*

This day was becoming Sisyphean.

First, I'm humiliated by the New York Fed General Auditor. Then I'm escorted out of the bank by Federal Reserve Police.

Now, this. A home robbery!

I was spooked. It was all too coincidental considering last night's creative auditing exercise. There had to be a connection.

I dialed Bri to caution her.

"Thad, where have you been?" Bri sounded flustered. "You haven't been picking up."

"Remember last night? I told you I'd be in New York for the day."

Traffic on the Francis Scott Key Bridge thinned as we got closer to Georgetown. The sky had patchy clouds.

"The clone drive and that machine?" she said. "What do I do with them?"

"Find a bank close by and open a safe deposit box. Ditch the drive and forensic duplicator there. Bri, whatever you do, stay away from your hotel. It's not safe."

"You're scaring me."

The cab crossed over the Alexandria Aqueduct and was now making the turn onto 33rd Street going north.

"Thad, wouldn't it be better if I just met you at the townhouse in Georgetown?"

"Bri, no. Absolutely not. Uncle Leonid's place is crawling with police."

"Now you're really scaring me."

My taxi pulled up in front of Leonid and Nika's townhouse. An MPD patrol car was parked across the street in front of the Volta Park tennis courts. I handed the cabbie the fare and tip.

"Just do it, Bri!" I pocketed my phone and ran to the front door of the brownstone.

The inside of the Petrovski townhouse looked like a Category 1 hurricane had touched down. Cabinet drawers pulled completely out. Bookshelves cleared of any volumes. Holes in the walls where pictures used to hang. The couch where Marissa was confined during the day was cushionless, the poly-stuffing in a heap, shredded fabric in tentacles.

Nika was in the living room doing her best to give the MPD officer a statement. My wife was huddled on the floor in the corner, her feet propped up on what was left of a couple of throw pillows that had been sliced open and gutted.

I got down on my knees and put my arms around Marissa. She was a hot mess, tears cascading.

"I'm right here," I said. "I've got you." I held her until she stopped whimpering.

"They took everything, Thad. Nika's valuables and travel cash. My jewelry." Marissa extended her left hand and wiggled her ring finger.

I kissed the tan line on her knuckle where her custom wedding ring set used to be. "We'll get it back. Promise."

"I can't stay here. I don't feel safe."

If the living room was any clue of what the rest of the townhouse looked like, I didn't blame her. I couldn't protect her here. What if this wasn't a DC garden-variety robbery? What if someone had been looking for the clone drive instead?

"I'll get you out of here, hon."

"Nika, too?"

"Of course." I gave Marissa a squeeze. "Be right back. Just need to check on a few things."

I ran past the cop interrogating Nika and up the stairs to survey the damage on the second floor. The master suite had been ransacked by someone in a hurry. The king-size bed had been dissected, dressers overturned, closets emptied.

Uncle Leonid's den was worse. All the drawers in the desk were upturned, built-in bookshelves cleared of knick-knacks and whatever volumes used to be there. The desktop computer was on its side, the case removed, drive bays ripped out, cables dangling. The laser printer cover had been pried open, exposing a nest of cartridges and drums. If there were any USB drives on either machine, they were missing.

The triptych photography of Leonid and Nika in front of St. Basil's Cathedral in Moscow had been yanked from the wall, shattered glass on the floor, and the backs of the frames removed. There were fist-sized holes in the wall where the three prints once hung. The antique Russian rug in front of Leonid's desk had been flipped over. Someone had taken a hognose saw to the hardwood floor and cut a two-foot square opening, revealing a cavity where a floor safe used to be. The bolts that held the strongbox in place had been sheared.

Whoever had robbed the place had done a no-stone-unturned job. I took the stairs down to the first floor. Nika was finishing up her statement with Metro PD.

"You didn't touch anything, did you?" Officer Isoldi said.

"If you're concerned about my fingerprints, they're everywhere. I'm living here. And no, I didn't disturb any of the evidence."

"You shouldn't have gone up there without the forensic tech's okay."

"She was busy dusting the kitchen for prints. I wanted to see if the stuff I kept in the den was still there."

"And was it?"

"My e-reader is missing. My monogrammed gold cufflinks are gone. And the pain pills for my wrist reconstruction were taken. Minor stuff compared to Uncle Leonid's safe. It's gone."

"We'll add that to the report. What's your name?"

"Didn't Nika tell you?"

"She did when you came in from the street, but I want to hear it from you." The officer was poised to make notes on the incident report.

"Thaddeus Hanlon." I showed the officer my California driver's license.

He wrote the details. "What's the best phone for us to contact you?"

I gave him my cell number. He gave me his card.

"Another five minutes and we'll be done here," the officer said. "Before we leave, see the tech about giving her a set of reference fingerprints."

"What about my wife's wedding ring?" I said. I

showed him a photo of it on my phone. "It has sentimental value."

"Your wife told me. I'm sorry," the officer said. "Send me the photo. We'll check the local shops. It might turn up."

"But not likely?"

"Sometimes we get lucky."

Like you did with the non-investigation of Rafi's murder?

The front doorbell rang. The melody from "Moscow Nights" started playing. Bri appeared in the open doorway. She had the cloned drive in her hands, still in the anti-static bag.

"The bank was closed by the time I got there," she said.

Chapter 26

I jumped over the debris to intercept Bri. I whisked her outside and hustled her to the driveway where she had parked her rental. "You got to hide that. The cops're still here."

She did a quick 360, catching sight of the patrol car across the street. "Completely missed it," Bri said.

"You didn't go back to the hotel last night, did you?"

"I didn't see the point." Bri was wearing the same two-piece black pants suit she had worn yesterday for our little off-book investigation at the FSB data center. She could have used a fresh blouse. Her hair hung in a limp ponytail.

"Couldn't sleep?"

"Needed to decompress. I took the Jag for a cruise." She opened the trunk and slid the drive and forensic duplicator under the panel concealing the compact spare tire.

As we walked into the house, Nika was circling the living room, serving chilled bottled water. Officer Isoldi was still facing the corner, questioning my wife.

"You stated the men were speaking in Russian. Did I hear that right?" the officer said.

"When they weren't threatening us. Yes, Russian."

"And what did they say?"

"If I screamed, they would kill my mother. If she

screamed…"

Nika interrupted, "Ukrainian, Matryoshka. Not Russian. Ukrainian is what they spoke."

Marissa wagged her head. "Okay. Slavic."

Officer Isoldi responded to a call on his two-way. He stood, then yelled toward the back of the house. "Ennis, you finished? Got another call. We need to roll."

Officer Ennis emerged from the kitchen, crime kit in hand. "I'm right here."

Isoldi gave me a copy of the incident report for insurance purposes. The two officers left in a hurry.

Uncle Leonid wasn't going to be happy about the break-in, the scare to his wife, or his trashed house, but I couldn't think about that right now. The Petrovski home was no longer habitable. We had to find another place to stay. Like Marissa, I too didn't feel entirely safe here. I had an idea. Farfetched, but worth a shot.

I pulled Doogie's business card from my wallet and dialed his office. The detective's number rang four times before he picked up.

"Mapu, MPD Homicide Branch."

"Hey, *brah*. Thad Hanlon. The Rafael Silva case." I could hear the thrum of the MPD District One station house in the background.

"Right on, *braddah*. *Howzit*?"

"Shoots, *brah*. You didn't hear?"

"Hear what?"

"We were robbed. Whole house trashed. They tied up my wife. My wife's aunt."

"Never hear about no robbery. *Wen* happen?"

"Just now."

"Man, you know Metro PD is one big Hawaii Five-

223

O, right? Fifty-six patrol areas. Seven districts."

Asking Detective Mapu if he heard about the break-in was kind of dumb on my part. Why would he know about a robbery that just took place in a city with a reputation for eighty-five property crimes per day? Unless, of course, it just so happened the incident took place in District One where Homicide shared offices. Where we were staying in Georgetown was in the next district over.

"Thad, you there, *cuz*?"

"Doogie, I need your help, *brah*. I don't know who else I can trust."

"I try listen."

"I need a safe house, *brah*. Someplace for my wife. Someplace where she won't be threatened. Rafi's at the center of this. I can feel it."

"What you mean? How's robbery tied to suicide?"

I told him. I recounted everything that had happened since Bri and I had met him on Monday. About Rafi's suspicious files. About the midnight audit to clone the data before it could be erased. About the questionable gold bars at the New York Fed. And about the methodical search of Uncle Leonid's home by Ukrainian nationals.

By being open with Doogie, I hoped to gain his confidence. We needed an ally. We needed somewhere safe to crash for the next few days. Detective Mapu was the only one in DC with a badge that I thought could possibly help.

"Whoa," Doogie said. "Some story. You one crazy mainlander."

"Tell me you got something. A place to stay."

"What about the precinct?"

"Marissa's on mandatory bed rest. I was thinking one of your safe houses."

"A clandestine site, *cuz*? That requires official channels. Captain has to approve. He's not going to buy off on theories."

"Conspiracy theories?"

"You have to admit, *brah*, your story is a stretch."

"With no proof to connect the dots."

"Captains do like evidence."

It was getting late. The sun was dropping behind the Littleleaf Linden trees lining Q Street. Across the road, the tennis court lights snapped on, illuminating a dog walker on the brick sidewalk who was cleaning up after his pet.

"Doogie, what about an *unofficial* channel for finding a place? I'll take any *kōkua*." Naked pleading for help sounds the same in Hawaiian as it does in English. Desperate. Pathetic. Toadyish. Pick one.

There was a long pause before Detective Mapu said, "Virginia Beach. I have a friend. Let's me crash at his place as a surf basecamp when not renting it."

"That's four hours from here, *brah*. We just need protection, not relocation."

"Best I can do, *cuz*."

"The place gate-guarded?"

"No, *cuz*. It's just an old cottage two blocks from the beach. Tell you what. I'll arrange to have a Virginia Beach PD cruiser patrol the house."

I didn't know what else to do. We had to have a secure spot to land, something big enough for Marissa, her aunt, and me. And Bri, if she decided to stay. Two hundred miles to the southeast would put distance between us and the immediate threat in DC, giving us some measure of safety. I could telecommute for a couple of days until things settled. If Tigran did call a meeting in the office, the flight from Norfolk to DC was just an hour. My only option was sounding better all the time.

Doogie said, "*Cuz*, do I hear a *mahalo*? You know this could blow back on me."

"Sorry, *brah*. It's been one of those days." I exhaled, filled my lungs, and said, "Thanks, man. You da bomb."

Detective Mapu gave me the address and told me where to find the spare key. Twenty minutes later we were packed and ready to dart. I locked up the disaster zone of a townhouse and the three of us left. Bri followed in her rental.

"Gotta make one stop, hon," I said.

"For dinner?" Marissa asked. "I'm starved. Eating for two is a caloric challenge."

"The office. I need to drop off the assay samples." I also needed to get a backup copy of the clone drive made, but I didn't think she needed to know that. Not until I could explain why I had the drive in the first place.

"How long is that going to take?" Marissa shifted in her seat. She was trying to find a comfortable position in the front of the car but couldn't.

I decided Nika needed to move up to shotgun and then I'd lay down the backseat of the hybrid SUV to create a bed. I didn't see any other way my wife would make the four-hour trip to Virginia Beach in her condition. That meant I would need to get a memory foam mattress for Marissa. So, make that two stops rather than one. First, the Dodge Whitney DC office.

226

The second would be a department store.

"It won't take more than a couple minutes," I answered. "My staffer, Jenny, will be waiting on the curb out front."

"Thad-minutes or sixty-second intervals?"

To play it safe I said, "Maybe more like five minutes." That would give the data tech Jenny had lined up the time to make a forensic copy of the drive Bri had duplicated.

Marissa put her hand on my leg and massaged it. "Chocolate noir gelato, triple scoop," she said. "Can we? I'm hungry."

"We'll make a detour." On the way out of Georgetown, I spotted DC's Finest Italian Ice and drove up to the take-out window. Bri stayed close behind me in her Jag.

While we waited for the drive-thru cashier to take our order, a Dodge Charger Pursuit pulled into the dine-in parking lot. The car nosed into a space ten feet away from us. The driver killed the engine and cut the running lights. No one got out.

The Dodge had the silhouette of an unmarked car—a gaggle of instruments bolted to the dashboard, an external searchlight on the passenger side, and a lightbar embedded into the front grille.

I texted Bri: —*Possible tail. Need to split up.*—

She flashed her brights and messaged: —*Need things at hotel anyway. Be safe.*—

I tapbacked a thumbs-up and texted: —*Watch your six.*—

Chapter 27

"I don't want to rendezvous!" Marissa said. "Why can't we stay together?"

I handed my wife her three-scoop gelato and a mini-spoon. "Too dangerous. We're being followed."

I edged forward out of the drive-thru lane onto Pennsylvania Avenue heading east. Curbside, just ahead of us, was the minivan I had hailed using a new ride-sharing app that guaranteed all female drivers. I pulled in behind the ride-share.

"Can't we just go with Bri?" Marissa sat up and looked behind us for Bri's car. "She's gone. Was that your idea or hers?"

"She went to get her things at the hotel. She knows where to meet us."

I glanced back at the Italian Ice parking lot. The Dodge Charger hadn't moved. Whoever was following us wasn't interested in tailing Bri. Now if I could just get Marissa and Nika safely out of the picture, I had an idea of what to do next.

"I don't like this." Marissa started to sniffle.

I leaned over the seat and took her hand. "I know."

"I'm scared." Marissa fumbled in her purse for a tissue.

"Me, too." I put the car in park, left the engine idling, and went to talk with the ride-share driver. When I returned, Nika helped me move Marissa from our rental into the back seat of the oversized ride-share van.

"Twenty-five minutes," I said. "I'll meet you in twenty-five." I kissed Marissa and then gave Aunt Nika a peck on the cheek.

"All set?" the female driver asked.

"My go-bag?" Marissa said. "Thad, I need my go-bag."

I doubted she was going to need her hospital bag in the next twenty-five minutes but went back for it, anyway.

"Your bag, hon," I said.

Marissa gave me one of her best fake smiles. It didn't take a rocket scientist to know she wasn't happy with me.

"Ready now?" the driver asked.

I confirmed the destination point. The driver nodded and started the van. I watched as Nika and my wife pulled from the curb and continued east on Pennsylvania toward Washington Circle.

My plan to do everything in only twenty-five minutes was tight but doable. All I had to accomplish was drop off the assay chips to Jenny, get the clone drive duplicated for safe-keeping, and scoot out to the Air Force Memorial Diner in Arlington, VA. Easy-peasy.

I squeezed the handle on my rental SUV, opened the front door, and hopped in. When I turned on the ignition, the lights on the Charger flicked on. I did a U-turn back toward Georgetown and sure enough, the Charger followed. I headed west on M Street.

When I got to 30th, I pulled a sharp left. The SUV rocked as I made the turn, right tires lifting slightly, then reseating on the pavement. The Charger was right behind me, gaining fast. If I was going to shake him, I'd have to be more creative.

I floored it down 30th until I hit K street, hung another sharp left, and raced east toward Washington Circle. The Charger was on my bumper now. I sped toward the rotary.

Up ahead, the through lanes of K Street disappeared into a tunnel burrowing under the raised traffic circle. That was a problem. I wasn't trying to continue due east on K street to use the high-speed lanes. I needed to get to Pennsylvania Ave. To do that, I had to stay up top, enter the Washington circle roundabout, and take the third exit.

Just before 24th street, I yanked the steering wheel to the right, hopped the curb, and landed in the service lane running parallel to the tunnel. The K Street alternate fronted St. Paul's Episcopal Church and next to that, a massive hotel.

The Charger stayed right behind me. Less than a block ahead was the traffic circle. I gunned it. As I rounded the rotary, I had to lean to the left to accommodate the pull of the centrifugal force.

In the center of the roundabout, General George Washington looked so calm in bronze. He was sitting on his trusty steed, sword drawn, unflinching in his determination to best the British. I was anything but calm and gripped the steering wheel tighter.

BAM!

And then BAM, again.

The Charger was ramming me from behind. From my rearview mirror, I could see the driver edge closer to my right rear bumper. I guessed he might be trying to get under it, clip the bumper at an angle and force me into a flip. I hugged the center of the traffic circle and increased my speed. I ringed the roundabout three more times before I pulled away and slipped out the Pennsylvania Ave exit going east headed toward the Treasury Building and the Dodge Whitney office.

It wasn't long before the Charger caught up, then tapped my bumper again to let me know he was there. We passed James Monroe Park going seventy mph. At 19th street, I cranked the wheel left onto H Street. The Charger rammed me a fourth time. My head snapped back, then bobbled forward. The seatbelt tightened against my chest, shortening my breath. My hands were clammy. The steering wheel slipped as I tried to hold it tighter. I could feel a massive headache coming on. The Charger pulled back, probably waiting to see if I would regain control, or if another thump was necessary.

We finally entered Lafayette Square. Due south of us was the White House. The pimped-out Charger still hugged my bumper. There was no way I was going to outrun him. I knew I had to try something different.

Across the street to the north was the Hay-Adams Hotel. I made a quick left, and then an even sharper left into the porte cochère of the famous landmark. A uniformed doorman was guarding the wood and glass double doors leading into the lobby. I pulled the key from the ignition and sprinted over to the hotel door attendant.

"Overnight valet parking," I said, as I handed the key to him. "I'm really late." I ran inside, then stopped for a second, and looked behind me. The Dodge Charger Pursuit had pulled to the curb on 16th street across from the hotel driveway.

The Hay-Adams lobby was elegant. No surprise for a legendary five-star hotel overlooking the White House. I slowed my stride to a quick pace hoping not to draw unnecessary attention. I bypassed the registration desk and kept going down the hallway, past the restrooms, and out the back door leading to the alley. Several valets were outback, stacking vehicles for short-term parking.

I headed south, coming out of the alley between the hotel and the U.S. Chamber of Commerce Foundation building, running all crazy, dodging traffic as I sprinted across the street to Lafayette Square. I ditched my suit coat, tossed my tie, and offered a tourist a hundred dollar bill for a Washington Commanders ballcap and logo sweatshirt. Not much of a disguise but something. I slunk along the park grounds until I came to the General Thaddeus Kościuszko Statue.

From behind the monument, I could see the Charger idling in front of the Hay-Adams. My car was still in the driveway, stuck in the valet queue. Not good. Worse yet, somebody had popped the trunk of my rental SUV and was rummaging through it. The doorman was protesting but the man searching the car ignored him.

Just then I heard the engine of the Charger race and the car honk twice.

There were two men.

The man tossing the contents of my rental closed the liftgate, sprinted over to the Dodge Charger, circled to the front passenger seat, and jumped in.

I had to keep moving. At the corner of the park was a Capital BikeShare stand with two-wheel cruisers available. I did the short-term rental thing and took off pedaling toward the Dodge Whitney office.

Bri texted: —*My hotel room searched 2*—

Texting while driving is always a bad idea. Texting while riding a bike is even trickier, but I couldn't be late for the meetup with Marissa. I pulled out my phone and launched the messaging app. Tapped the microphone icon and dictated: —*Where are you?*—

Bri responded: —*Headed to rendezvous point*—

I replied: —*Meet me at Dodge Whitney instead*—

Her one-symbol reply: —*?*—

Asynchronous communication is the worst. Doesn't matter the medium. It's almost impossible to clarify anything. No body language. No vocal cues. Horribly inefficient. I pulled over next to the General Lafayette statue at the south end of the park and phoned Bri.

"Do you still have the drive in your car?" I asked my sleuthing partner.

"Right where we hid it."

"Leave now. Meet outside at Dodge Whitney in five minutes. I'll be on a bike. Jenny Yu will be waiting out on the sidewalk in front of the Willard Building."

"Thad, are you all right?"

"Not really." My voice jiggled while my knees started to buckle under me.

"Thad?"

"Just get there. Make sure you're not followed." I disconnected and dialed Jenny.

The distance from Lafayette Square to the Willard Building is perhaps a half-mile. Less than a minute by car. I made it there on a one-speed bike in a little over a minute, my fastest time ever on two wheels. Gotta love adrenaline!

I pulled the assay chips from my pants pocket and tendered them to Jenny. She logged the custodial transfer on the face of the evidence bag.

"These'll go out tonight," she said. "The courier's on standby."

"Did you arrange to have the tests expedited?"

"You'll have results tomorrow."

"Who approved the special request?"

"That's the thing. Everyone's gone home except for one computer tech, so I signed for you."

Jenny continued to amaze. "Thanks," I said.

"What about the cloned drive from the Bureau of Fiscal Service?" Jenny asked. "Do you have it?"

"It's on the way."

Bri squealed to a halt in front of the Café du Parc. She popped the trunk of the Jag. I pushed her overnight luggage to the side, lifted the spare tire cover, and retrieved the clone and forensic duplicator.

"Be right back." Jenny ducked into the Willard Building, data drive in hand.

"You a Commanders fan?" Bri asked. She pointed to my head.

"LA Rams New Century Gold and Millennium Blue through and through." I took off the ballcap that had been part of my makeshift disguise but kept the sweatshirt on. I offered the logo cap to Bri. "You want?"

She batted it away. "You look like crap, Thad."

I felt like it, too. This was one Wednesday I could have done without. As I repositioned the cap on my head, I recounted for Bri the car chase through DC and the Dodge Charger attack. She filled me in on the hotel room search and toss.

"Whatever Rafi found?" Bri said. "Whatever is on that drive must be worth killing for." She twirled her hair with her index finger.

I let out a nervous laugh even though none of this was comical. Playing detective wasn't fun anymore. Ten minutes earlier, I had narrowly escaped being rear-ended into a rollover.

"Bri," I said, "I'm sorry I ever doubted. But…and it hurts me to say this…I can't do this anymore."

"You can't bail now, Thad."

"We need to turn this over to MPD Homicide. Detective Mapu can take it from here."

"Turn what over? The clone drive? Is that your plan?"

"I have to protect Marissa and the baby. You understand that?"

"I understand that Rafi is *dead*. I understand his killer or killers are still on the loose. And I understand that *they*—whoever they are—have dragged you and Marissa into this now. But I also understand MPD Homicide Branch can't make a case on speculation. Thad, I need your help. Please."

Bri wasn't going to budge. And bailing on my best friend? At some level, I knew I couldn't do that. Rafi and I were like brothers. But then again, I had bigger responsibilities. To Marissa. And to the baby on the way. I couldn't risk my family.

"What is taking Jenny so long?" I said. "I promised Marissa I'd meet her soon." I turned to get a better look at the 7th floor of the Willard Building. The lights were still on in the Dodge Whitney offices. There was movement inside. Shadows through the windows.

Bri tugged the bill of my Commanders cap. "We

were having a discussion," she said, "before you switched subjects." I turned back to her.

She was right. I was stalling, trying to redirect the conversation. Anything to buy some time. I needed to think.

"Bri, we don't have enough evidence to ask MPD Homicide to reopen the case. I'm not even sure the drive's readable."

"What the hell does that mean? You told me the files were encrypted."

I rubbed my eyes with my palms. "At the Fiscal Service data center, all we saw was gibberish on the screen. I guess I wanted to believe it was encryption. I'm sorry."

Bri yanked off my Commanders cap and rapped me with it. "Tell me there's still a possibility that just because *you* can't read the file there *is* someone who can." She handed back the hat.

"There is a chance it could be deciphered. Or a chance it could be *nada*. The thing is, Bri, we take a 'nothing drive' to Detective Mapu and in less than a nanosecond he'll excuse himself to get back to work clearing real cases involving real homicides."

"Rafi's suicide was staged. Bonafide murder. I know that. You know that. We're getting close."

Close to getting ourselves killed. I didn't know what to say. Rafi deserved justice. Marissa and our son-to-be deserved protection. I couldn't see a way to reconcile both.

"Got it," Jenny said. She was panting from having sprinted from the building. She handed me the duplicate. "The original forensic clone is in the office safe," she said. "Secure."

I took the drive. "One last favor." I toed the kickstand of the red bikeshare.

"I'll return the bike," Jenny said, "but please call Tigran. He's being prickly. He wants a word."

No doubt.

"Tell him I'll call once I have Marissa settled."

Chapter 28

"For me, Thad, controlling worry is a struggle."
My wife was seated sideways in the diner booth, feet
stretched out on the faux-wood bench. She didn't look
very comfortable. She was practicing nadi shodhana
pranayama—alternate nostril breathing—right thumb
on right nostril, breathing through left, then right ring
and pinky on left nostril, breathing right.

"You had us scared," Aunt Nika said. She was
sitting across from my wife.

"I'm so sorry. I didn't mean to alarm either of
you." I pulled up a chair at the end of the 50s-style
diner table covered in Air Force blue laminate. Bri
scooted in on the other side of the booth next to Nika.

"Thad, where's the SUV?" Marissa asked. "And
your jacket and tie?"

I leaned in and gave Marissa a quick kiss. "Long
story."

From the restaurant window, I could see the three
stainless steel spires of the Air Force Memorial, arcing
up and back like shiny jet contrails. It was twilight now.
The pink of the sunset had long faded.

"Our luggage?" Marissa asked. "Tell me you have
our luggage."

"I can explain everything," I said. "At least, I think
I can."

"I'm listening." Marissa repositioned herself,

bringing her knees in and resting her feet on the end of the bench.

"Can we order first?" I opened the menu and thumbed through to the dinner entrees. "I'm feeling lightheaded. I need to eat something."

The waitress came over. She was wearing a bouncy red, white, and blue uniform, complete with a 1950s-style apron and a pillbox hat, bobby-pinned to her pink hair, side ponytail swishing.

"My name is Betty Lou," she said. "I'll be your server."

The Air Force Memorial Diner was the real deal. A likely candidate for a review on Diners, Drive-ins, and Dives. Authentic diner-style comfort food to go with the period costumes. Betty Lou was even wearing roller skates. She took our order and left to get us drinks.

"Thad's lucky to be alive," Bri said.

I held up my hand. "Bri, stop. Let me tell it."

"Why don't you start with Tuesday night," my wife said. "When I turned over in bed, you weren't there. And when you came back, you smelled like another woman."

"It's not what you think, Mar."

"Being duct-taped by armed Ukrainians, then watching them systematically ransack Aunt Nika's house, and now leaving town for a safe space, has got me a little edgy. Time you start 'splainin'."

There was so much to tell Marissa and so much I needed her to hear. And so much I didn't understand and hoped that she would help to decipher. Unanswered riddles that led to the precarious. I began the chronicle of events.

When Marissa heard about the break-in at the

Fiscal Service Bureau Data Center, she snapped, trading her yin calm for yang warrior. She picked up the salt and pepper shakers on the dinner table and threw them at me. If I ducked, they would hit the family in the next row of tables. If I didn't duck, my face would never be the same.

I raised both hands and caught the glass shakers, one in my left and the other in my right. I handed the salt and pepper to Bri, who gave the shakers to Nika, who replaced them in the chrome-plated condiment rack. In Little League, I wasn't much good on offense, no home runs, few base hits. But on defense, as the team's shortstop, not one fly ball ever got past 'Golden Hands' Hanlon.

"Who had the lettuce-wrapped double bacon cheeseburger, fruit on the side?" Betty Lou was balancing four dinner plates on her forearms and hands.

I took my plate from her and started chewing. The long story would have to wait. Betty Lou handed off the other entrees.

"May I get you anything else?" she asked.

"Refills," I said, handing her my glass.

"Diet?"

I smiled and nodded.

Betty Lou topped off my soda and brought the check. I gave her my Lockheed Credit Union debit card with the background picture of the F-22 Raptor. "Everybody loves a good fighter," she said, tapping the airplane image.

No quarrel there.

Marissa barely touched her meal. That wasn't good. The triple-scoop chocolate noir gelato she had eaten earlier couldn't have been that filling.

"Go-box?" Betty Lou asked when she returned with the charge slip.

"No, I've lost my appetite." Marissa pushed her plate away.

"Matryoshka, you need to eat *something*," Nika said. She handed the plate to the waitress, who returned with the dinner boxed to go.

I signed the charge slip, added a healthy tip, and gathered up the crew. There was no way we could fit four people into the two-seat Jaguar. I took out my iPhone and requested another ride-share to the nearest twenty-four-hour car rental desk.

By 10 p.m. we were on the road to Virginia Beach in a late model minivan. Marissa was nestled in the back seat, lying down, feet propped up. If she could keep the potty stops to one per hour, we would be in the beach house by a little after two in the morning.

The minivan had satellite radio. I put on some ambient jazz. The background music put everyone in a trance but me. Thank goodness. I didn't think I had any more energy for another round with Marissa. My attempt to explain my every move since Tuesday eve had only made her edgier. I had to get her settled. Help her regain her center. And bring some stability back into our lives.

****

"You can't expect me to stay here," Marissa said. Her shoulders shuddered. "The energy's inauspicious. I need to smudge."

The Virginia Beach house was underwhelming. The gray clapboard two-story Classic Cape was perched below high-tension power lines. Inside the cottage, the floors were gritty with beach sand. The furniture was dated—maybe late 1970s, early 80s—and not particularly clean.

"If you can wait until morning, I'll look for a white sage kit. We'll smudge together." I grabbed a broom and started sweeping. Nika brushed past me to check out the rear of the house.

Marissa frowned, eased over to the brown couch, and sat. "Thad, how is this place safe? I'm not seeing any deadbolts."

"I'll get some locks tomorrow," I said.

Nika returned to the living room. "No bed bugs, Matryoshka. I check."

Marissa tucked herself into a fetal position on the faux leather. "I don't want to be here."

"Nor I," Bri said, dragging her overnighter through the front door. "But I don't have much choice. DC isn't safe for any of us right now."

Marissa groaned.

"Let's get everyone to bed," I suggested. "We all need sleep."

"I'm not tired," Marissa said. She had rested most of the four-hour drive from Arlington.

I closed my eyes and started to sway, and then snapped awake. Marissa was still angry and wasn't about to let me get any sleep until we had finished the conversation we had started at the diner. I had an idea. I put away the broom and dustpan and made my way to the couch.

"Marissa, put your arms around my neck," I said. She did. I lifted her and carried her gently to the rental minivan. I laid her on the bench seat in the back. A light breeze drifted onshore, fluttering the fronds atop the three palms overlooking the beach house.

"Where're you taking me?" Marissa asked.

"Surprise. Keep your eyes closed." I jumped in the driver's seat and when I did, I checked the back to see if Marissa had shut her eyes. She had.

Three minutes later, I pulled the minivan in front of the jumbo Neptune statue on the Virginia Beach boardwalk, right where Doogie said it would be. The Roman God of the Sea was at peace. The only sound was the lapping of waves on the shore. The bike path and walkway were deserted. I scooped up my wife and carried her to the playground equipment in the sand, a few steps away.

"Now," I said. "Now you can look."

Marissa's lips curled into a faint smile. "Swings! We haven't done this in, like, forever."

I lowered Marissa into the rubber seat and gave her a wee push, nothing vigorous, nothing to upset Thadpole. The sand was cold between my toes, but it felt like home. I jumped into the swing next to Marissa and pumped. I caught up with her and reached for her hand. The moon waxed gibbous, lighting the crest of the waves, filling in the dappled surface of the ocean with pockets of gold.

"Thad, I want to go back."

I was just starting to connect to the shore, my zen place. "Hmm," I said, a little disappointed—maybe *a lot* disappointed. I wasn't ready to return to the beach house.

"Back to California, Thad."

"Oh."

"Coming to DC with you was a bad idea. I'm sorry I even suggested it."

"How can I make it work?" I wasn't ready to

concede.

"You can't. Uncle Leonid's house is not an option. The so-called 'safe house' isn't. Nika is well-meaning but over-doting. Bri has brainwashed you into believing Rafi's suicide was fake and that you can out-sleuth the DC Metro Police."

Marissa let go of my hand. "Thad, stop this investigation. Take me back to our home in LA."

"I can't," I blurted.

Marissa dragged her feet in the sand until she came to a stop. She twisted in the seat to look at me. The chains of the two swings clinked together.

"I'm not surprised," she said. "What you don't see is the downside of playing amateur detective. The adrenaline buzz won't last forever, Sherlock Hanlon."

I inhaled sharply. "Ouch."

She pulled on the chain of my swing, brought me close to her, and slugged me in the arm. "Now, you can say ouch."

Marissa has a mean left cross.

"Ouch, for reals." I tried to kiss her, but she pushed me away.

"Thad, when you showed up in my cardio-kickboxing class the first time, you were all negative vibes, suffering from bad chi."

Self-defeat can do that. I had failed in my attempt to break into the pro circuit with the World Surf League. It seemed I had developed a talent for cracking under pressure going into the final heat of every qualifying series competition. The judges took notice. The fans took notice. The press was brutal. Every glossy surf magazine began running cover pictures of 'Choker' Hanlon's colossal wipeouts. Becoming the next World Tour Champion was a dream too far.

"You feared further failure," Marissa said.

"Yes."

"You dropped out of pro surfing, cut your dreams down to size, and enrolled in community college to become a CPA. Your first wife was so bored with Thad two point oh and your lowered expectations, she left you for a competitive eater with his own YouTube channel."

"Defeat: The Sequel."

"But it brought you to me. Made space in your life for my yoga class. We worked on rebuilding your confidence and muscle tone."

"We did."

"Progress has been slow."

"It has."

"That's why I supported this trip to DC at first. I saw it as a way to nurture good chi. To foster bigger dreams. To get you back in the competition by taking over Rafi's place on Gold II."

"Nice to have fans in the stands." I hoped I didn't sound snarky, but I was afraid I did.

"Thad, what you're doing...this investigation...it's become too dangerous. Bri has you making unnecessary waves. I need you. Our *son* needs you. You can't do that from prison or, God forbid, if you're dead."

Making sense of Rafi's suicide had risks. That I understood. But so far, no one had been hurt. Shaken up maybe, but no actual harm. And whatever threat there had been was now safely four hours away in DC.

"Given how this day went...packing up to go back to California sounds pretty good right about now, Marissa." I scrunched my toes in the sand. "Except, dropping everything, leaving Bri in the lurch with nothing more than a cloned drive, possibly encrypted, is the easy way out. It feels like just the opposite of *bigger dreams*. Feels like settling for a low-stakes life."

Marissa flinched when I used her own words to make the case for not backing off the probe. She started into alternate nostril breathing for the second time tonight.

I said, "You'll be safe here. I can protect you. I can protect the baby."

"Thad, I need you alive."

"For sure."

Marissa punched me in the stomach. It was her way of showing me how much she cared. Love taps for St. Thaddeus, Patron Saint of the Impossible.

I pulled her closer to me and held her until the feistiness ebbed. We stayed that way until the morning fog rolled in.

When we returned to the beach house, it was completely quiet except for the hum of the high-tension lines overhead. A Virginia Beach police cruiser was parked across the street, headlights off, inside lights on. The patrol team was sipping coffee while chatting. I gave them two thumbs-up. The driver doused his overhead light, cranked the ignition, and rolled away.

The air was now heavy and wet. Marissa was shivering as I carried her in the back door, past the rack of well-used surfboards. I tiptoed in. Bri had taken the first bedroom and Nika the big game room with bunks, leaving us the master with the big bed.

Using my right foot as an extra hand, I pulled back the covers of the king-sized bed, then positioned Marissa the best I could. She turned on her side, pulled the sheet over her head, and pushed me away. So much for the romantic swing in the moonlight.

I stripped down to my boxers and climbed in beside her. I don't remember anything after that. No pleasant dreams. No recurring nightmares.

The next thing I knew, my slacks were vibrating on the floor. The mobile had gone off in my pants pocket.

Not now, please.

I tumbled out of bed, silenced the ringer, checked the caller ID, and punched the green accept button.

"Hanlon?" The gruff voice was familiar.

"Let me take this outside," I whispered. "Marissa's asleep." I walked out to the backyard. I wasn't looking forward to this conversation.

"Okay to talk, Hanlon?"

"Tigran, I'm sorry. I should have called."

"*Call?* You promised you'd report to me when you returned from New York. That was eleven, twelve hours ago."

I wandered back to the kitchen. The clock on the microwave read 4:05 a.m. Tigran was up before sunrise. Early bird and all that.

"I can explain."

"Hanlon, if you aren't in my office by nine o'clock a.m., you'll need to freshen your resume."

"I'm four hours out by car. I'll never make it."

"NMP, Hanlon. Not my problem."

Chapter 29

There was only one way I could meet Tigran by 9:00 a.m.

I tiptoed into the bedroom where Bri was sleeping and shook her shoulder. "Bri, wake up."

Nothing. She was lost in slumberland.

I shook her again. "You have to help me, Bri. I'm begging."

"Thad, stop." Bri rolled over and clutched the covers to her chest. "What?"

"It's Tigran."

"He found you? How did he know you were here?"

"He's not *here* here at the safe house. He called. He wants me in the office this morning. By nine. Can you hang with Marissa? She's still freaked."

"She has Nika."

"She needs more. Someone who understands her."

"I can't. I'm following a lead. Yesterday, I found something while combing through Rafi's emails. Correspondence with someone he thought could help him unravel Gold II. I've made arrangements to meet the contact in DC at noon."

I hung my head, pressed my thumbs into my temples, and focused for a few seconds. "Okay, okay," I said. "What about this?" I told her Plan B.

"That could work," she said.

"Got to run." I scampered over to the master

bedroom, found my rumpled clothes, tossed them on, and kissed Marissa on the forehead. She purred, opened her eyes, then closed them tight. I kissed the ends of my fingertips and gently placed them on Marissa's belly. Thadpole jumped. Marissa slowly swiveled in bed until her legs were pointed at me. She kicked but only lightly grazed me.

"Love you," I whispered as I backed up.

Marissa kicked again, but by then I was too far away for her to connect. Last night's fierce conversation on the beach had left her unsettled. It would take more than moonbeams at low tide to restore her calm.

The shuttle flight from Norfolk got me to Reagan National in Washington a little before 7:00 a.m. Plenty of time to make some phone calls and pick up the SUV rental I had ditched at the Hay-Adams hotel yesterday.

I phoned Jenny Yu from the cab. She was getting ready for work. I could hear a hair blower in the background before she switched it off. Jenny listened. I talked. I told her everything that had happened since the meetup last night when I gave her the assay chips and got a copy of the cloned drive from her. I asked her to help me out with Marissa so I could make my meeting with Tigran. Then explained that Bri could only take my place at the beach house helping Aunt Nika care for my wife until mid-morning.

"I don't know, Thad," she said. "They're expecting me at the Fiscal Service Bureau this morning. We're trying to wrap up the mortgage-backed loan analysis."

"There's a one-hour non-stop flight at eight thirty-five a.m. out of DCA. Please," I said. "You'll be back by seven thirty tonight."

"Tigran's not going to be happy."

"I got you covered."

"Meaning you'll find me another job when he fires me."

"It won't come to that."

"I'm only doing this for Rafi," she said.

I booked the tickets for Jenny and emailed her the confirmation. Five minutes later, my cab pulled into the Hay-Adams Hotel driveway, dropping me off at the valet stand. The line wasn't too long. The hotel was a popular breakfast spot for the Washington DC power elite but not this early on a Thursday morning. I inched forward until I was at the front of the line.

"I'm here to pick up my car. Overnight valet parking," I said.

"You have a claim check?"

"No. I was in a hurry. Had to run inside."

"What kind of car?"

"Late model Toyota Highlander hybrid. Metallic red."

"MPD towed it. The Secret Service said you were a possible terrorist suspect, not being a registered guest at the hotel and all."

"What Secret Service?"

"You know, the United States Secret Service. The Senior Agent who searched your car."

"He showed you a badge?"

"He did."

"Do I look like a terrorist?"

"We don't take chances. Take it up with hotel security." The valet attendant looked past me to the next patron holding up a stub, a pushy lady ready to reclaim her car. "Now, if you'll excuse me," he said.

"Impound lot phone number? You have it?" I asked.

"Try 4-1-1, sir. I'm sure they can help you." The attendant smiled his world-class service smile and took the claim ticket from the businesswoman who had made it clear she was more important and in more of a hurry than I was.

I had been shunted aside. Maybe it was my clothes. The Commanders burgundy hoodie over yesterday's wrinkled business ensemble sans tie. Or the day-old fuzzy red stubble and musty body odor. With my rental sitting in an MPD impound lot somewhere, all our luggage and my laptop locked inside, access to a change of underwear and a fresh shirt would have to wait.

Besides I was starving. It was a good hour and a half before my nine o'clock with Tigran. My boss expected a full explanation of yesterday's adventure at the New York Federal Reserve Bank and the midnight run to the Fiscal Service Bureau. A quick breakfast would give me time to prepare what I planned to say. And ponder the next moves. I had an exact duplicate of the original cloned drive with me but no idea what was on it.

I wheeled around, walked directly into the hotel, joined the Washington elites, and took my herbal infusion tea and *pain au chocolat* with the privileged few. For slow-burn carbs, I downed a bowl of steel-cut oatmeal and fresh cranberries. That added a little potency to my step. I straightened up and strode outside, jumping into the first available taxi.

"You're early," the Dodge Whitney receptionist told me. "Mr. Vardanyan isn't expected for another forty-five minutes."

I had been counting on that. It would give me the time I needed. "Could you point me in the direction of our tech support?" I held up the hard drive Jenny Yu had given me.

Dodge Whitney's Washington DC Tech Support was a two-person helpdesk. One technician was out on a call. The other had a virtual reality headset on, the kind used in firmwide audit training. He couldn't see or hear me. Now and then he groped the air with a haptic glove in a silly dance. I tapped on the wrap-around glasses covering the top of his face. He lifted one earcup of his headphones so he could hear me.

"You do file recovery?" I asked.

The tech grinned like it was playtime. "Roger, but you got to try this, first," he said. "Eight-K ah-mazing!" The tech removed the VR headset, ran an antiseptic cleansing wipe over the unit, and handed it to me.

Cool nerd toys. It couldn't hurt to spend a few minutes geek-bonding. I nabbed the goggles and took the hyper-resolution VR unit for a test drive.

White-Collar Mega-Sting. I had seen this VR simulation before. It was a training role-play about an FBI multi-raid on a financial crime syndicate. Big Four forensic accountants go undercover wearing wires and Kevlar vests. White-collar crime takedown at hyper speed. Lots of action.

In the original 720p version of the sim, the first-person point-of-view graphics had been as blocky as a Minecraft world. In this high-def reboot, it was like I was actually there, dodging bullets, bobbing and weaving, landing screw punches, and putting the bad guys into submission holds. If this 36x-resolution of the original version had been available when I took the Dodge Whitney Fraud Investigation course, I might have scored higher on the simulation.

The VR screen went blank.

I removed the unit. "What happened?"

"You tell me," the tech said. "You almost decked me with one of your jabs." He snatched the headset away from me.

I didn't know what to say. The 8K wrap-around glasses and surround sound headset had made the otherworld immersion so complete. "If I told you I was a recovering gamer would that explain it?"

"What's your gamer tag?"

"St.Th@d."

"The defender of lost causes?"

I raised my hand over my head and made a pick-me gesture, repeatedly pointing my index finger at my skull.

"Sweet." The tech grinned as if he had just made an 8K convert. "People forget it's virtual. They become one with the storyline. Before they know it, they assume the persona."

"The simulation *did* get away from me," I said. "Sorry."

"Never apologize," the tech said. "It doesn't look good on you."

I slid the solid-state drive I had been carrying across the worktable. "Here's the deal. I need a little of your help with my own reality. Can your technerdistry crack this?"

"Isn't this…?"

"Yeah. The same one. The duplicate drive you gave Jenny last night."

"Have you hung it on a box yet?" He tapped the desktop computer on the worktable.

"No."

"You didn't plug it in?"

"No. I mean 'yes.' Never plugged."

"So, it's a virgin forensic duplicate? No digital activity?"

"Yeah. Unadulterated. A one hundred percent bitwise copy of the original client files. The master copy is in the Dodge Whitney safe."

The tech guru rummaged through his cables, dongles, and charging bricks and pulled out a universal hard drive adapter. He plugged the specialized connector cable into the clone drive and a high-speed Thunderbolt cable into the desktop computer on his workstation. He fired up the desktop. The screen flickered on. He ran a virus scan, which came up clean. I cheered. For a disk drive cadged from a Sensitive Compartmented Information Facility, I wouldn't have expected anything to be infected.

The tech dropped into a command-line interface—the backdoor to the computer disk operating system. The screen went black with white text and a blinking cursor. He typed in several short DOS commands. A list of files popped up on the screen.

"That one," I said, pointing to the National Brick folder. "You'll need to make the files visible. They're there but Rafi hid them."

"You mean these?" the tech said, as he fiddled with the file attributes. "Not very concealed." He typed out the contents of the first file. The screen filled with digital trash—random characters, numbers, symbols. "The files are corrupted," he said.

"I know. This is where I need your tech magic." I drew a circle on the screen with my finger, circumscribing the digital nonsense. "Is there a way to uncorrupt these files?"

"Wouldn't that be sweet," he said. "An 'Uncorruption Utility.'"

"So, there's nothing you can recover? You're sure?"

"On this screen, I'm sure. But I'll keep scrolling." The technician paged down through the remaining screens. The results were the same. Junk bytes.

"Maledictions," the tech said, followed by a short whistle. He threw up his hands.

Apparently, the tech wizard was out of spells. I felt like cursing too. We were back to square one. Whatever Rafi had discovered was munged beyond recognition. I started putting the drive back in its protective sleeve.

"Hobby hacker, huh?" the tech said.

"What do you mean? I thought we were done. The drive was blitzed. You said yourself nothing was recoverable."

"Yes, the default stream attached to that file. It's corrupted."

"As I said, unrecoverable."

"Uh, that stream, yes. But—" The tech paused and then his eyes lit up as he gave me one of those wouldn't-you-like-to-know-what-I-know geek grins.

I had maybe ten minutes before my meeting with Tigran, and Techboy was toying with me. "But...what?" I was losing patience.

"Are you always so sarcastic?" the tech said. "It creates a hostile work environment." His right eye twitched and then his left. It made me uncomfortable to watch.

"You're right," I said. "I can be mouthy under pressure. My apologies." I drew in a deep breath. "You okay with a redo?"

The twitching stopped.

I followed up with, "So if the default stream is mangled, is there something like a non-default stream? Something else that might be readable?"

"Give me the drive back," the tech said, "and I'll show you."

He launched into a quick course on Alternative Data Streams, files behind files, and meta-data. When he took to the whiteboard in his computer workshop and began drawing me pictures, I cut him short, making a wrap-it-up gesture.

"I have five minutes, max."

"I get it. You want me to fast forward." The tech plugged in the drive and brought up the directory with the hidden file. He ran some kind of streams utility app against it. A cascade of text filled the command-line window one line at a time, cataloging the attachments to the original file. Each concealed text stream was marked with a $DATA tag.

"Bingo," the tech said. He accessed the first hidden stream and clicked to open it. A yellow triangle warning icon popped on the screen with the message: Access is denied.

"Try the second hidden stream," I said.

Same message for the second stream, the third, the fourth, and fifth.

"Whoever created these streams encrypted them," the tech said. "You're going to need a password to decrypt."

Figures. If Rafi went through the trouble of hiding the data file and streams, he would have safeguarded them with a security code as well.

"Bring up the password screen. Let's try something," I said. "How about *letmein?*"

"Nah, I don't think so," the tech said. "Too obvious." He keyed it anyway.

The tech was right. A dialog box appeared with the message:

The password you supplied is not correct. Verify that the CAPS LOCK key is off and be sure to use the correct capitalization.

"I'm pretty sure I keyed it correctly," the tech said. He checked the SHOW PASSWORD box so that we could read what he had typed. The mask of bullet characters disappeared. "Yep, not a caps problem."

"Try this instead. Key in *trustn01.* The letters t, r, u, s, t, n and the numbers zero and one."

"How appropriate," the tech said as he entered the character-letter combo. "Could work."

The computer didn't agree. The incorrect password warning reappeared.

"Okay, let's try *VersaChem.* All one word. Initial caps."

The tech punched in the phrase. "No luck. Not even with all caps or all letters lowercase. Tried a couple of other substitutions. Nothing."

That was disappointing. I thought for sure there had to be a connection to Gold II. VersaChem was one of the last things Rafi had said the night he died.

"Okay," I said. "Time for a Hail Mary. Let's go with a dollar sign. The letter m. The numbers three, one, one. The plus sign. The number three again.

Another dollar sign. And another plus sign."

The password textbox read: *$m3ll+3$+*

"That works," the tech said. The contents of the stream flickered on the screen:

1J,40415,1924,1614689.99,8/25/2010,1982
A,41182,10697,4314775.3,9/30/2012,2003
1,40442,27975,9791843.44,9/21/2010,1980
10A,40430,13566,5416236.08,9/9/2010,2005

The file contents looked familiar but without column headings, I wasn't sure. Maybe Bri might be able to decipher. I snapped a picture with my phone and texted her.

"You want to see the other streams?" The tech took a swig of his Jolt Cola.

"Sure."

There were three more streams with the same number of comma separators. Only the number of rows varied. Two streams had eleven rows, one fifteen rows, and one sixteen.

The fifth and final stream had six columns and hundreds of rows:

U.S.ASSAY,4448,1,395.87,0.9967,1932
U.S.ASSAY,1922,19,7742.06,0.9959,1950
U.S.ASSAY,1963,24,9987.95,0.998,1965

"Dump the screens for me, will you?" I asked. "One for each stream. And throw a copy of the file and attachments on a flash drive."

"Aha! *smelltest*," the tech said. "That's the password in plain text. The one that worked, isn't it?"

I nodded. The night Rafi called he mentioned Dr. Lutz. He had referred to a mondo-sized sniff he was conducting that didn't smell right. The audit practice of smell tests—relying on investigative intuitiveness to

258

spot financial fraud—was a perennial question on every Lutz midterm.

"How'd you come up with the right character substitutions...the dollar sign, the plus sign, and numerals for letters?"

"It's how Rafi would have done it. He loved strong passwords. He was clever that way."

"Genius," the tech said.

The workshop printer burped. I fetched the screenshots the tech had sent and pocketed the flash drive.

Bri texted back: —*I have a hunch about your screenshot. Sidewalk café outside your bldg. Noon. I'm bringing a guest.*—

The timing could work. If my morning meeting with Tigran lasted more than two hours, I'd be surprised. And if it went longer, then that would mean the men in gray suits had chomped my career and I would be looking for another job.

No time for self-doubt.

I confirmed the meetup with Bri and a plus one and swaggered upstairs to my senior manager's office and walked in, stopping just shy of Tigran's desk. I raised my right hand for a high-five.

Chapter 30

"Yo, yo, whatup, Tigger, my mentor."

Tigran Vardanyan swatted my hand away and went back to flattening the clasps of an 8x10 manila envelope to seal it. His fingers were shaking. Two empty venti dark roast to-go cups from the corner barista sat next to a pile of audit folders on his desk.

"Sit your homeboy-ass down, Hanlon." Tigran put the envelope aside. "This isn't Junior High. And what's with the Commanders hoodie?"

"Just trying to fit into the DC pro sports scene." I gave him my best mentee smile hoping to melt his heart. "If 'up high' be out," I said, "I can do bro-hugs." I moved in to give Tigran a manly embrace.

He pushed me away. "Sit," he said. "You're not funny." He picked up a pink While-You-Were-Out message with his name at the top, filled out on both sides, and stapled to two pages of handwritten notes. He waved it in my face. "This isn't funny."

"I can explain."

"Start." Tigran pushed away from the desk and folded his hands in front of him. I had seen this pose before. Third grade. Seventh grade. Ninth grade through senior year. It was *The Principal Pose*. A thoughtful mindset for detecting derp, of sifting through stupidity.

"Would the truth be okay?" I asked.

Tigran kept his hands folded. He nodded.

"What seems far-fetched at first, may on closer look, not be so outrageous, implausible, unbelievable, dubious, absurd…" I had settled into a bout of verbal hiccups. Synonym after synonym after synonym. Couldn't help myself.

"Quit stalling."

"Water? Do you have any water?" I pointed to my throat.

Tigran jiggled the cardboard to-go cups on his desk. He handed me one.

I downed it, fingers crossed I wouldn't contract some hoary virus. My whole body shook. The expresso aftertaste was nasty, but the bottom-of-the-cup dregs did the trick. I could talk once again.

"Can I say something, Tigran? All joking aside, I could really use a mentor about now." I was earnest. I needed advice. And an ally inside the firm.

"Hanlon, you are in deep *kimchi*. Tell me how you buggered this job so badly I have a two-page telephone message from the Site Operations Manager of the Fiscal Service Bureau Data Center, Eddie Zadelhof, and a formal complaint from Sigalie Kaddish, the Executive Vice President-General Auditor of the New York Federal Reserve Bank. Everything, Thaddeus Hanlon. I want to hear every misstep leading to the end of your career at Dodge Whitney, Certified Public Accountants, the international leader in discreet audit and assurance work."

And so I told him about Rafi's cryptic phone call the night of his murder, about the video conference call from Jenny Yu, about Bri's suspicions and Rafi's funny money, about DC Metro Police, the closed case file, about the digital bread crumbs at the Fiscal Service Bureau Data Center, and about the forensic clone Bri made of the hidden files on the FSB server assigned to Dodge Whitney. I showed him the screenshots of the data tables Rafi had encrypted, and I recounted what happened at the Federal Reserve Bank of New York during my observation of the gold inventory counts. I made a big deal of the failed ping tests.

Tigran twiddled a roller-ball pen in his hand. He had been taking detailed notes on a yellow legal pad. He looked up at me and said, "That's your evidence of a conspiracy? Tell me there's more."

I did. I shared the break-in at Uncle Leonid's. The search of Rafi's hotel room. The car chase through DC.

"I admit," I said, "some of this is conjecture, some of it hypothetical, but some is solid." I rustled the printouts the tech had given me a few minutes earlier. "When you put it all together, Bri and I are convinced Rafi was murdered. He found something in the Gold II audit that wasn't kosher."

"And this something is what got him killed?" Tigran arched his eyebrows. He wasn't buying any of this. I could tell.

"I'd stake my career on it."

"If you still have a career at Dodge Whitney?" Tigran pushed away from his executive desk. He stood. "Hanlon, sneaking into a secure federal data center and making an unauthorized duplicate of one of the server drives is a criminal offense. We're talking trespassing in a Treasury Bureau facility, unauthorized access to federal financial information, and copying nonpublic data. Felonies. Up to ten years in prison." Tigran shook his head. To date, I was probably his biggest failure as a mentee.

Visions of orange matching Department of Corrections jumpsuits with D.O.C. stenciled on the back popped into my mind. Not quite the look I was going for. Bri, on the other hand, could make anything look good, and easily give Martha Stewart a run for her money. In fashion, skin color is everything.

"You think jail time is amusing, Hanlon?" My senior manager returned to his seat.

"No, sir. I'm sorry, sir. I tend to smirk when I get nervous." I tried next for serious but I'm afraid it looked more like I was constipated.

"You know, Hanlon. You don't fool me. Since the moment you arrived in DC, you've been using this assignment to play detective."

I didn't say anything.

"Warnick warned me you might try to do this."

I wasn't surprised. "What else did Warnick say?"

"About your latest misadventure?" Tigran slapped his hand down on the while-you-were-out note. "I scheduled a call with him but we haven't talked yet. I've been waiting to hear from you first. I am your mentor, after all."

I just stared at Tigran. I couldn't believe it. He was giving me a chance to explain myself *before* consulting the higher-ups.

So, this is what it feels like to have a career advocate.

"I want to go over the facts before Warnick and I connect." Tigran made bullet points by key passages on his notepad. "You said Bri snuck into the FSB Data Center with a forged ID?"

"She did."

"Bri cloned the server drive, not you?"

"I might have lent her the forensic duplicator and high-speed cables, but she made the copy of the Dodge Whitney work files."

"And Bri was the one who pulled the fire alarm?"

"She did."

"Where's the cloned drive now?"

"In the office safe." I held up the anti-static sleeve with the duplicate. "I had a copy made for our tech guy to analyze."

"And?"

"It's all Dodge Whitney work product—audit documentation, ACL scripts and listings…and Rafi's encrypted notes."

"Any FSB files that don't belong to us?"

"The tech didn't see any."

That seemed to please Tigran.

"Bri has some *cojones*, doesn't she?"

"That's one way to put it," I said. "She is privileged, after all. Takes whatever she wants. A purebred Californio with heritage on her side."

Tigran's ringtone blared. Incoming phone call. "Got to take this," he said. "This'll be Warnick." He motioned for me to stay seated. He scurried outside and down the hall to one of the open-plan office standalone soundproof phone booths.

This day had definitely crossed over into the ominous. For the time being, Tigran was the only thing between me and a jail cell in federal prison. Maybe honesty had been the best policy. At least I wasn't wearing handcuffs just yet.

Tigran's desk was spotless. A place for everything and everything in its place. Neat beyond OCD.

Except for the manila envelope. When I had stepped into his office, he tucked it under the audit folders. But it wasn't a tidy tuck. The corner triangle protruded. The clasp was caught on some of the file pages. And the pile was askew. It was driving me crazy. I fingered the envelope to align it with the stack of folders and snagged the clasp, slicing my finger. Blood smudged the envelope seal flap. I stuck the finger in my mouth, sucked it, and tried to wipe off the envelope.

I don't believe in signs, but a bloody envelope is generally not a good omen. And hard to explain, mentor or no mentor. I panicked, folded up the envelope, and stuffed it into my hoodie pocket. Then I inspected the desk to see if there were any other telltale scarlet drops. None. So far, so good. I sat back down and waited for Tigran. The shaking stopped when I was able to visualize the perfect swell on the perfect day at the beach—glassy, serene, totally connected.

When Tigran returned to his office, he announced that Warnick was reassigning me to Buenos Aires. "He wants you on Patagonia Mines—our big gold client. Says you're perfect for the job."

"You got to be kidding." I started cracking my knuckles. "This is about the midnight audit at Fiscal Service Bureau, isn't it?"

"Warnick thinks Dodge Whitney has plausible deniability. From what you told me, Bri did an amazing job covering her trail. But if there is any blowback, she'll have to own it."

I cringed. In being forthcoming, I hadn't meant for my best friend's fiancée to be thrown under the bus. Not my proudest moment. I'd have to sort things out with Bri later. Take my share of the blame at some point. But now seemed less than opportune. "Warnick's not taking any chances, is he?"

"He thinks distancing you from Gold II can minimize your peripheral involvement. Be thankful."

I closed my eyes. Tried to think what to say next and feebly said, "When am I going to BA?"

"Tonight. Travel is booking everything as we speak. You need to pack."

I got up and paced. My pulse pounded in my ears. My face flushed. "Tonight? We can't. Marissa's in no condition to travel."

"Who said anything about your wife?"

"Tigran, please. I can't leave her. It's not safe. *She's* not safe. They might try to kill her. They already tried to kill me. I should have told you this part earlier."

"Thad, what are you talking about? Who is 'they'?"

I told him the rest of the story. What I knew about the armed robbery at Uncle Leonid's. How Marissa and Aunt Nika had been tied up. How the burglars gutted the house in their search for valuables. How MPD showed up and by the time they had finished their investigation, I had worked out a plan to relocate somewhere safer. But before we could get out of town, I noticed we were being followed. So we split up.

And when we did, a car chased me through DC. Rammed me four times before I could shake the driver by ditching our rental in valet parking at a hotel. Then this morning I find out the SUV had been impounded by the DC police after being thoroughly searched by whomever "they" were.

Tigran looked at me like I was beyond buzzed. Like I was some kind of tweaker, rambling at hyper-speed. "Are you done?" he said.

I nodded, maybe six or seven times.

He fell silent. After what seemed like a good five minutes, all he said was, "Someone followed you?"

"A team."

"The 'they' of this grand conspiracy?" Tigran closed his eyes, breathed slowly through his nose, and massaged his neck. When he opened his eyes, he scanned his desk, picked up the audit folders, and shuffled some papers. He went through each drawer.

"You got to admit, Tigran, the chain of coincidences is long. More than happenstance."

"Hanlon, I don't have to admit anything. Did you see an envelope? About this size?" He signaled with his hands to give me approximate dimensions. Tigran started rummaging through the credenza behind him.

I acted like I was checking the floor around my chair, but instead smoothed the muff pocket of my hoodie. I had to make sure the crease in Tigran's envelope that I had borrowed laid flat so there was no tell-tale sign. And I had to distract him from his search. I changed the subject of our conversation.

"Seventy-two hours," I said. "Give me that. I can wrap this up. Produce hard evidence. Incontrovertible. You'll see."

Tigran turned around. He had a manila envelope in his hand. It was the same size and color as the one in my hoodie muff pocket. He undid the clasp and extracted what looked like a report. He rotated it so I could read.

"You mean incontrovertible evidence like this?" he said.

It was the expedited assay report Jenny had

267

requested for me. Two samples from each suspect bar. Four lab samples in total.

All the samples had come back within the London Good Delivery Bar standard of 99.5% fineness or greater. The Inductively Coupled Plasma Optical Emission Spectrometry results meant I had been wrong about the fakes. The two bars from which the New York Fed's General Auditor had shaved the assay samples were, in fact, solid gold.

Tigran could see I was deflated. If I was not mistaken, he actually looked like he might be concerned about my well-being. Humanity was sneaking up on him.

"Speaking as your company-assigned mentor, Hanlon, I'm not seeing a conspiracy here, but if you still want to take a few vacation days to be with your wife, I can talk to Warnick. I'll ask him to delay Buenos Aires until you can focus on your career, assuming you still want partner track at Dodge Whitney."

Vacation days sounded like a good option, but they weren't. I had burned through all my accrued days going to the fertility doctors, accompanying Marissa to her OB-GYN. "What about FMLA?" I said.

"I can talk to HR but, you know, Family and Medical Leave is unpaid."

"Unpaid," I repeated. "Right." I did the mental math, figured out the cash drain, and knew we didn't have a savings buffer. But I couldn't shake the feeling that Rafi was counting on me. By reaching out to me that night, just before he was murdered, Rafi had entrusted me with his secret, his discovery.

"Thad, you there?" Tigran asked.

"I'm thinking." My temples throbbed, my face felt warm, and my stomach was making unruly noises. I started to gag, rounded Tigran's desk, pushed him away, reached under the desk for the trash can, and hurled my entire breakfast.

Tigran handed me his handkerchief. "And I'm thinking…you don't look so good. Go. Take a couple of sick days. I'll tell Warnick you're out for the next forty-eight."

I left.

It was 11:55 a.m.

By the time I reached the outside seating of the Café du Parc, I was able to stand up straight again. I reached into my pants pocket where I usually kept a mint or two but couldn't find one. For the next forty-eight hours, I was fairly certain barf breath would be the least of my concerns.

Chapter 31

"Do you have any idea what this is?" I asked.

I spread out the screenshots of the hidden file streams that the Dodge Whitney tech support had printed for me. The pages took up half the sidewalk café table. Bri's surprise guest turned out to be Jorma Sarudin, Gold Blogger Extraordinaire. The three of us sat under the shade of a red logo-covered umbrella that flapped in the light breeze. The breakfast bunch had thinned. We had empty tables on both sides.

"The Holy Grail," Jorma said. She whistled, picked up the pages, and started pouring over them. She whistled again.

I looked at Bri. She looked at me. We both raised our eyebrows.

"You have this in electronic form?" Jorma asked.

I pulled out a flash drive. As I did, Jorma booted her laptop and then inserted the drive.

"Are you okay if I change the file extension?" Jorma didn't wait for an answer. She changed the file type from straight text to comma-separated-value and opened the file. Instead of a word processing document, an Excel workbook fired up. Rows and columns.

"Clever," I said.

Jorma froze the column headings, paging down from the top to the bottom of the spreadsheet. Every so often she would highlight a cell and say "Hmm" or

"That's curious."

"Curious how?"

"It fills in the gaps," Jorma said.

"The missing records from your Freedom of Information Act requests?" Bri asked. "Your blog site touts you as the FOIA Queen."

"Gaps, yes. Everything that was redacted on the pages the government released to me," Jorma said.

"So, this is a complete data set?" I said. "*That's* your Holy Grail?"

"Yup. This is every single Official Joint Seal action at every U.S. Mint gold depository. The entire record." Jorma punched some keys and took a screenshot. There was the click of a camera shutter and then the captured image disappeared. "My readers will love this."

"If they ever get to read it," I said. "I'm going to have to say no."

"Soft no, right? No attribution for my source?"

"Hard no. This stuff is classified. I need you to purge the file."

Jorma shook her head and started to close the lid on her laptop. "I don't think—"

I jumped up, reached over, and wrangled the laptop from Jorma's hands. I found the spreadsheet screen image she had snapped and erased it. Then I cleared everything from the trash folder. "No one's publishing anything." I yanked the flash drive from the USB port and handed the laptop back. "Least of all, not high-level classified data!" My hands were trembling.

Bri and Jorma both inched away from the table, distancing themselves from me. My outburst must have scared them.

"Thad, truthfully you need to lay off the caffeine,"

Bri said.

"I overreacted, didn't I?"

Bri nodded.

Jorma looked at me with interest. I sensed she was taking mental notes. Maybe building a character profile for her next online post.

"Thad, we don't even know what the data mean. Right now, it's just numbers."

Jorma took a long sip of her iced tea. "What if I attribute the information on your data grid to an anonymous source?"

I stuffed the flash drive into my pocket. "Nope. No grid. I'm not going to jail."

Bri swirled the ice cubes in her drink. I found the clinking irritating. "You're worried about Tigran?" she said. "That he'll know you leaked—"

"Bri, stop," I said. "We had ground rules. Or have you forgotten?"

"Who's Tigran?" Jorma said. She pulled out a pen, making notes on her napkin.

I reached across the table and grabbed the napkin from Jorma's hands. "Bri, we agreed. No names, no references to my firm, and no mention of my client. Ground rules." Then I snatched the file printout the Dodge Whitney tech had made for me.

Bri swiveled in her chair and faced the online journalist. "Jorma, this is my fault. I invited you here. I thought you could help with deep background. I promised Thad I wouldn't break confidences."

Jorma leaned back in her chair, swept her textured black hair from her face, and wrapped a hairband around it. The tight curl ponytail made her look younger. "Whatever you're involved in must be major big. I've never seen a twosome so twitchy." She wagged her pen between her thumb and forefinger. "I smell a story."

We weren't getting anywhere. The clock was ticking and my edginess was raising unnecessary suspicions. I slowed my chew rate on the gum in my mouth and took a cleansing breath.

I held up the flash drive. "This little confidential tête-à-tête we're having, it's all off-the-record. You've got to promise."

"I'm an investigative journalist…"

I palmed the drive.

"Thad's right," Bri said. "No blog posts until we know what we don't know."

"Ooh, ooh. Riddles. Love 'em. Tell me what it *is* you don't know. Maybe I can help." Like an unruly imp, Jorma crowded in to listen.

"Terms and conditions, first," I said. I spelled out the agreement—a gag on her blogging in exchange for an exclusive interview, once we had proof. "Do we have your word?" I asked.

"For the Holy Grail…" Jorma took the drive from my fingers and plugged it back into her laptop. She rebooted. "…my readers can wait another couple of days."

Jorma's screen filled with a fresh copy of Rafi's hidden stream files. She jumped from screenshot to screenshot, one worksheet for each deep storage gold location:

Ft. Knox, KY
West Point, NY
Denver, CO
New York Federal Reserve Bank, NY

She seemed to be looking for patterns, eyeing specific timelines. "This is going to take some serious grinding," she said. "Has anyone crunched this yet?"

"Rafi," Bri and I said in unison.

"Then why do you need me? Why not ask Rafi?"

"He's dead."

Jorma took her fingers off the keyboard, gripped both edges of the screen, and lowered the lid until the laptop powered down. "Is there something I should know before we go on?" Jorma's eyes narrowed as she spoke.

Bri looked at me. I rubbed my temples and shook my head from side to side. "Jorma, you're right," I said. "We haven't explained the connection. Why your expertise matters or what's at stake." I searched her face for a tell, some kind of hint, or even a micro-expression that might confirm that we could confide in her.

Jorma must have caught on to what I was trying to do because she batted her blue eyes and gave me her best camera smile. "You know, trust isn't the issue. My safety is. Do I need to renew my concealed carry permit?"

I had to think about that. Rafi had been electrocuted. Marissa and Nika had been bound and gagged. Someone had tried to ram my car off the road. But no one had shot at us yet. No need to go full N.R.A. Not just yet.

"Pepper spray might be a good idea," I said.

"There could be risks," Bri added.

"Let me be the judge," Jorma reopened her laptop. "Start at the beginning. Don't leave anything out."

I gave her a full accounting. If there was something

to all this, some connection between Rafi's death and the audit of the United States' deep storage gold, some "plot" for want of a less melodramatic term, then it couldn't hurt to have some insurance. Someone with an online megaphone. An expert in fact-checking. A truther. Jorma could be an asset.

"Your surprise assay results?" Jorma said. "That one's easy."

"How so?" I said. "I was there when they took the assay samples from the two suspect bars. I watched everything. There was no sleight of hand. No switcheroo."

"They gave you tetrahedron-shaped chips, shaved from the top and bottom of the bar. Right?"

"Yeah."

"We call that 'corner-shaving.' The Mint abandoned that technique for sample collection back in nineteen seventy-seven. It was deemed insufficient for detecting salting. For the main depositories—Ft. Knox, Denver, and West Point—audit guidelines require bore samples. This involves drilling a hole near a corner of the bar using a 6mm carbide drill bit."

"What's salting?" Bri asked.

"Long version or short?" Jorma pushed her laptop to one side, looking ready to elaborate. Before Bri could answer, Jorma launched into the etymological backstory, "During the California Gold Rush…"

I raised my hand. "Jorma, can we take a rain check? Bri and I have to go."

"We do?" Bri said.

I winked at Bri. Made an it's-late gesture by pointing to my watch. "I can explain salting to you later."

Jorma closed her laptop and handed me the flash drive.

"You made a copy?" I asked.

"I'm an honorable woman." Jorma took my hand and wrote down her cell number on my palm. "I won't post anything until I hear from you. In the meantime, I'll massage the data." She squeezed my biceps and smiled.

Bri gave me the stink-eye. Jorma just laughed, took her hair out of the ponytail, and shook her curls until they once again framed her face. The tiny drops of sweat rolling down from my armpits tickled.

I rose, pulled a twenty-dollar bill from my wallet, and pushed it under the check for the beverages. "We have to talk," I said, as I grabbed Bri's arm and excused the two of us. Jorma blew me a kiss as Bri and I left. *Cheeky.*

We walked west on Pennsylvania Avenue. In the distance, through a slight haze, I could see the southern tip of the Treasury Building, rimmed by the thirty-six feet tall rock-solid Greek Ionic columns, pure gray granite from Dix Island, Maine.

There was a break in traffic. "Run," I said.

I took Bri's hand as we hustled across the street to Pershing Park. We ended up at a parched pond, sitting on the terraced steps overlooking a dry waterfall. The splash of water would have provided a soothing soundscape, but the park had fallen into disrepair. Instead, the din of midday DC traffic echoed off the sunbaked concrete.

I scanned the tree line of the little urban park, doing a complete 360 swivel and making sure there was no one within earshot.

"The park's empty, Thad. We're the only ones here."

I sucked air between my teeth. "Dodge Whitney's taking me off Gold II."

Bri shook her head, her hair bouncing back and forth on her shoulders. "Tigran's such a lifer. He's protecting his *ass*et."

"This goes higher."

"Warnick? The managing partner's reassigning you?"

I told her about Warnick's plan to ship me out of the country, down to the tip of South America to honcho the audit of a new mining client. I relayed how Tigran actually played mentor during the drama, negotiating on my behalf for additional time in DC. And I made sure she understood the short fuse. How I had less than forty-eight hours before I would be on a plane to the Southern Hemisphere.

"Marissa doesn't know about Argentina, does she?" Bri asked.

"Not yet. Can you drop me at the airport? I'm headed back."

Chapter 32

Short-hop flights are never short enough. Marissa wasn't answering my texts. Likely indisposed. Nika's phone went straight into voice mail, meaning she was taking a nap. And Jenny Yu's line was busy, probably on a call with the office. All I was trying to do was let my wife know I was on my way and that she could expect me soon and then I'd share with her the craziness of my day. Hold her, let her hold me. Cuddle and spoon and listen to the baby's heartbeat.

The flight from Reagan National took less than an hour. The ride-share from Norfolk and to Virginia Beach was quick.

When I arrived, the front door of the beach house was standing open. The place was more of a mess than when I had left in the morning. The TV was blasting an episode of the *Hawaii Five-O* reboot. Wet beach towels were twisted in odd shapes all over the cheap laminate flooring.

Jenny was slumped on the overstuffed couch, unconscious, blood crusting her swollen face. Nika was missing. Marissa was gone.

There was a light trail of blood leading from the house to the front yard, winding around the palm trees, and continuing toward 29th street. Small drops at first, getting larger as I rounded the corner of Arctic Ave and 29th, and larger still on the path to the Virginia Beach

Boardwalk. Erratic spatters zigzagging from one side of the street to the other. *Marissa was running away from someone.*

I sprinted to the entrance of the ocean-front bike path. The blood trail continued to the left, running parallel to the shoreline.

Bunched around the King Neptune statue were several police cars, news vans, and tourists snapping photos. An emergency vehicle sped off, its siren dropping pitch as it pulled away from the crowd. Above the roar, I could hear Nika wailing. It looked like one of the responding officers was trying to comfort her, but she was pushing him away, shrieking in Russian.

"Aunt Nika, it's me," I said, as I put my arms around her. I was breathing hard from the run.

Nika untangled herself and slapped me, open-handed, backhanded, with her left, and then her right. "All your fault. *Da!*"

"Ma'am, please," the officer said as he separated us. It didn't take much effort. A body camera hung around his muscular neck.

"It's okay," I said as I rubbed my cheeks. "She's family."

Nika started crying again, more softly this time. I held her close.

"Where did they take Marissa?" I asked.

Nika whimpered something but I couldn't make it out.

"Virginia Beach General," the officer said. "Not far. About four miles, just off Colonial Road."

"Can you take us there?"

The officer agreed, escorted us to the back of his cruiser, and kicked on the siren.

We made it in seven minutes, and that was including radio calls to the ER room and the dispatcher to request medical attention for Jenny Yu at the safe house.

By the time we arrived, Marissa was already in the OR on transfusion, the fetus in severe distress. A Caesarian section was underway.

Nika collapsed in the waiting room, totally sheet-white. One of the on-duty CNAs crushed an ammonia popper and waved it under her nose. She coughed and came to, massaged her throat, and asked for water.

I was sweating, my dress shirt glued to my back, the armpits of my hoodie dripping. The nurses' aide offered me water too and encouraged me to hydrate. I chugged it and asked for another. The aide pointed me to a vending machine by the elevators.

We settled in to wait. An afternoon soap opera played on the flat-screen TV in the family lounge adjacent to the operating room. Some visitors watched, some knitted while watching, and some completed Sudoku puzzles instead. The rest stared at their mobile phones.

Me? I just worried. I concocted one worst-case scenario after another. Getting Marissa into this mess was my fault. I was to blame. No one else.

A long text from Bri interrupted my fret-fest: — *Secured Rafi's iPhone logs from wireless carrier. Some unusual calls. Working on reverse lookup.*—

I texted back about Marissa and the C-section. I let her know Jenny had been attacked but was in recovery. I ended with: —*Be wary!*—

Triple sad face emojis from Bri and then: — *Leaving NOW!*—

I must have fallen asleep during the wait because when the nurse tapped me on the shoulder, I startled, brought my hands to my face to protect myself, and growled.

The nurse backed up.

"Sorry," I said, fumbling to explain myself. "Flinch response. I know, kind of weird."

"Did you want to see your son?" she asked.

I couldn't stop smiling. Beaming really. "I'm a dad!" I said, a little too loudly.

That woke Nika. I explained Marissa had given birth and that we could see the baby.

"*Oy, oy, oy!*" Aunt Nika said, then kissed me full on the lips.

I grabbed her hand. "Let's go see him."

The nurse led us to the neonatal intensive care unit.

Lil' Thad had a breathing tube taped to his tiny wrinkled face. A scruff of wispy red hair covered his crown. Sensor pads were taped to his chest. Wire leads crisscrossed his body. He was dinky, no bigger than the size of my foot. Couldn't have weighed more than two pounds. Fragile but with great color—a healthy crimson.

"Can I hold?" Nika asked.

"Once he stabilizes," the nurse said. "Right now, he's too vulnerable. We'll work with you on skin-to-skin contact when he's up for it."

I couldn't stop staring at the little man. As his chest rose and fell, I watched the monitors and counted his breaths. Pulse 120: Respiration 60. I examined his bitty face for likeness. He had Marissa's mouth and perfect eyebrows. My rounded chin. I pulled out my phone and snapped several pics to show Marissa.

"Can you take me to see my wife?"

"Let me get the OR doctor," the nurse said. She stepped over to the NICU nurses' station and made a call.

A thirty-something woman in jade scrubs and a matching cap showed up five minutes later. Her surgical mask hung around her neck. She said, "Congratulations on your new son," and extended her hand.

We shook. I said thanks and introduced Aunt Nika, who rambled in Russian, eyes smiling, cheeks raised.

The surgeon turned to me and said, "What do you know about your wife's condition?"

"You mean the placenta previa? We were aware of that. The gynecologist had her on complete bed rest." I put my arm around Nika and pulled her in closer.

"Mr. Hanlon, your wife arrived at the ER unconscious, with severe blood loss. She had apparently tripped and hemorrhaged. We did everything…"

Deep in some untapped vocal chamber of my soul, woe crawled up my throat, transmogrifying into a cavernous shout, a sputtering guttural articulation, unrecognizable as human—a primal *NO* that almost drowned out the surgeon's final words.

"… to resuscitate her and keep the baby alive during the emergency C-section. I'm sorry to tell you this…"

I left Nika and ran. Down the corridor to the east elevators. Punched the call button, over and over, and when the doors didn't open instantly, I headed to the stairs instead. There, I jumped down the steps two at a time. When I hit the first-floor landing, I busted onto the street through the exit. I fled on foot, putting distance between myself and the OR surgeon's discomforting words.

I left the hospital parking lot and sprinted east on First Colonial Road toward the beach house. My lungs were on fire. Feet pounding. I dashed through stoplights. Sidestepped traffic. As I got closer to the beach cottage, I gained speed, making it in record time, setting a personal best for a four-mile run.

The front door was closed this time. I scavenged until I found the spare key. I grabbed one of the surfboards, shed all but my boxers, and hoofed it to the north side of the pier. Had to get in the water. Had to find solace.

The ocean was bracing cold. It didn't matter. Soon, I didn't feel a thing. I paddled out to the surf so fast that my nose started bleeding. I stuck my tongue between my gums and my upper lip, growled, and spit blood.

The waves were chest high, coming in every four to eight seconds. A classic beach break, peeling to the right and left. I took off on everything, every wave in every set. Fast lefts. A couple of mushy rights. And a close-out swell that thumped the shoreline when it hit the backwash from the retreating tide. I lost my footing, went airborne, and touched down on a sandbar, butt-first.

I shook the sand from my boxers and paddled back out. By now my arms had turned to rubber, making each stroke a struggle. I considered going back to shore and was about to turn around, when I saw a five-foot swell, twenty feet out on the horizon.

I paddled like a madman to get into place for a take-off, found a slot near the lip of the curl, and dug my hands deep into the water. I stroked hard, hard enough to feel the certainty, the lift, the moment the board and the wave connect to become one.

Scrambling to my feet, I pumped the board, slapping the underside against the water, one, two, three times before dropping into the shoulder. I slid down the face of the swell until I reached the base of the monster and made my bottom turn, climbed the foam and headed to the lip, raked the back end of the board across the top of the curl, throwing off a rooster tail of spray, and then cut back to set up for a 360.

As I climbed the glassy wall that peeled to the left, I realized I had misjudged the distance to the pier. There was no way I could kick out of the wave in time.

I smashed into the concrete pilings.

The board snapped in two.

The ankle leash connecting me to the board's tail wrapped around one of the barnacle and mussel-encrusted pilings. I went under. My mouth filled with saltwater. I coughed, wound up snorting water into my lungs, and coughed again. I thrashed until thrashing didn't make any sense. And then heard voices. Harsh, judgmental, exhortative.

You can't repent for getting someone killed.
Playing detective isn't an excuse.
Only profound penance will save you.

The ear daemons jabbered non-stop, reciting my sins, and enumerating my crimes against Marissa. Indictment after indictment followed by endless prodding for expiation, until I sensed a plan forming—a purifying passage from purgatory.

My path forward?

Simple. Self-flagellation so extreme that I would

bleed from every pore in a watery atonement for Marissa's unnecessary suffering and death, her needless sacrifice because of my clumsy attempt to regain my mojo by continuing the probe, against her wishes, into Rafi's death.

I hit bottom, found purchase on the seafloor with my feet, bent my knees into springs, then pushed off from the hard pack sand, breaching the ocean surface, and arced into the pier pilings, back first so that the barnacles and blue mussels could scrape away my mistakes, leaving lashes as big as tine marks from Neptune's trident.

I braced for the pain. But it never came. No knife-like stabbing as the razor-sharp shells raked my spine. No sting from the saltwater. And none of the expiatory relief I sought. I chalked it up to moral numbness.

Tainted seafoam dribbled from my wounds. The water churned with spadefish. A brown pelican began to hover, scaring away the Atlantic gulls. A fresh wind swell made its way to shore, snagging the chunk of surfboard leashed to my right ankle as the backwash from the tide smacked the oncoming wave, barreled up, and crashed, driving the chunk underwater and wrapping me around the closest pier piling. I went under with the swell, down two, maybe three feet.

I grabbed at the leash and pulled the quick-release ring that held the fastener in place on my ankle. Nothing happened. I pulled again. The plastic release ring shredded this time. That meant I was still tethered to the ankle fastener, the leash was still wrapped around the concrete piling, and the busted surfboard and I were still submerged.

My air was going fast. I needed to surface before it

was too late. I did a big frog kick. Wide breaststroke. The ankle leash stretched and then snapped back like surgical tubing. The mucus-colored elastic was too short for me to breach the waterline.

So far, my penance wasn't going according to plan. I had never intended to completely self-destruct. Even as a lapsed altar boy, I would never have considered something so final as suicide. I just needed a good flogging to recover my senses.

But here I was, self-chastened with stripes aplenty and about to drown. That gave me pause. Sharpened my focus. I thought about my son, his tiny hands wrapped with a swaddling cloth so tight he could grasp nothing and wondered if he would live long enough to hold my finger, feel his father's touch, grow into a toddler that would ask me to swing with him someday at the playground or ride tandem at the beach on a longboard built for two, float through adolescence, and carve his own path across the face of life's surf.

That's when I saw it.

I dreamed I was thrashing, flailing, reciting a twisted catechism, some doctrinal mumbo-jumbo that had a perverse soothing effect while I gnawed on kelp, a superfood salad of stipe, blades, bladders, and fronds with a salty connection to the bottom of the food chain, taking inordinate pleasure in popping the polyp-like kelp bladders between my teeth.

The vision must have taken forever because the sea went dead silent, my sight failed, and I was left with only darkness I didn't know possible, a soul-sucking coal-black murkiness where light was inconceivable. My jaw cramped. And then I entered limbo.

"Is it the red hair?" Bri asked. She was kneeling

beside me. "Your Irish luck and all?"

I had no idea what she was talking about. My back felt like I had wiped out while attempting an off-the-lip scooter trick in an empty Olympic-sized swimming pool and had slid shirtless down the coarse gunite-lining on my backside, giving me an epic road rash that had scraped my spine until it was freckle-free.

I reached over my left shoulder, worked through the sharp pain, and felt slimy gauze.

"Over whole back," Nika said. "We did best we could." She looked like she wanted to say more but chose not to.

"Looking for this?" Bri asked, holding up two halves of a busted surfboard. The ankle leash had been chewed through.

I scanned the room to get my bearings. I was at the beach house, in bed, on Marissa's side of the California King.

My eyes started to water. I wanted to pull the covers over my face but instead asked, "How's Lil' Dude?"

"The NICU nurses are fussing over him," Bri said. "He's so cute. Has your nose and Marissa's chin." She flipped through the photos on her phone and showed me a close-up of my son.

I was about to say "my chin" but thought better of it. Things were starting to come back to me…my come-to-Jesus meeting with Tigran at the Dodge Whitney office earlier in the day…the scene at the hospital…and my flight from the truth.

"Arrangements?" I said. "For Mar?"

"I take care," Nika said as if I no longer had a say in the matter. Marissa was Nika and Leonid Petrovski's only niece. I had taken their Matryoshka, the family's Russian prodigy in a pink tutu.

I tried to sit up but had to ease back onto the mattress. "What day is this?" I asked.

"Same as it was this morning," Bri answered. "Thursday."

"So, I still have time to see my son?"

"Thad, you're in no condition." Bri fussed over me and tucked the sheets in tight so I couldn't move my arms, something I would have expected from Nika. Instead, Marissa's aunt grunted "humph" and turned her back. She must not have liked the way Bri was pampering me.

I threw off the covers. "Come with me," I said to Bri. "I know how to solve this. Know how we can get the evidence we need and find Rafi's killer." I stumbled out of bed and groaned as my feet hit the floorboards.

"You'll need more than boxers if you're going anywhere." Bri pointed to my shorts.

"They're outside," I said. "I left my clothes next to the surf rack."

Bri ducked out for a second, returning with a pile of rumpled street clothes and the burgundy hoodie. As she handed me the items, the manila envelope that I had filched from Tigran's desk fell to the floor. Bri picked up the folded envelope, smoothed it out, and peeked inside. She looked confused by what she saw. Side by side portraits of my senior manager. Before and after makeover shots with timestamps.

"Another piece of the puzzle," I said. "Not sure where it fits. But I have an idea."

Bri put the folded envelope on the nightstand by the bunk. "Do you need help with your clothes?"

Moving slow and creaky, I must have looked like I was incapable of dressing myself. "Nah, I got this." I pulled the pants from the clothes pile, shook them until the legs straightened, and then stuck one foot through. As I inserted my other leg, I said, "There are a couple things you can do to help."

The first was simple. I needed a coat and a tie. The hoodie had served its purpose and for what I had in mind, would only draw unneeded attention. Bri went out to the car, dug through Rafi's things she had picked up from MPD Evidence Control, and brought back a blazer, a fresh dress shirt, and a bow tie. Spiffy.

"And the second thing, Thad?" Bri handed me the change of clothes.

"Fire up your rental car. Put down the top. And give me the keys."

Bri said, "Joyriding in a convertible? That's your plan to bust this case and find who fried my fiancé and chased Marissa until she bled out?"

"I'll explain on the way to see Thad, Jr."

I finished putting on my shoes. But getting the shirt, tie, and jacket on? Not so easy, especially the shirt. Nika jumped in to assist while Bri went out to warm up the Jag.

A manual transmission 575-horsepower V8 Jaguar F-Type can lay down some serious rubber. In all six gears! The tires spun with crafted precision, grabbed, and then screamed as I painted black patches on the pavement leading to Virginia Beach General Hospital.

Silly stunt, yes, but I was feeling loud.

And ready.

Ready to make waves.

Chapter 33

"I don't know, Thad. The midnight audit at the Treasury Data Center was one thing, but this?" Bri settled into the passenger seat of the convertible and buckled her three-point belt.

I was back at the wheel after our quick stop-off to check on my son. Lil' Dude was sleeping, peacefully oblivious in the infant incubator. The NICU nurse said it would be hours before the next feeding. By then, Nika would have returned to keep vigil.

"You have to trust me." Once the words left my lips, I realized how cliché they sounded. *Superhero Saint Thaddeus dawns cape, hatches an invincible plan, gathers a team to expose gold fraud, and forces the killer to reveal himself.*

Bri screwed up her face. She definitely wasn't feeling the trust. The balmy night air rustled through the convertible, hashing her hairdo and drying out her contacts. "What if Sigalie says no?"

Fury pumped through my carotids, making my cheeks flush. I blurted, "I'm done with NO!"

When I realized what I had just said, replaying in my head every word of my response to Bri's oh-so-legitimate question, I could only come to one conclusion—I was being possessed by a bad trope: *If you can express your emotions, you can address your emotions.*

"Wow! Courage under pressure, Thad." Bri smiled with her eyes. "Absolutely bravo-worthy. Marissa would have liked that answer."

I up-shifted the manual trans of the Jag. "Marissa would caution against overconfidence."

"She *would* point out the danger. Me? I'm glad to see the old Thad, the pre-wipeout Thad who had little respect for limits."

Maybe there was an upside to rage. A laser-like clarity displaced the muddle that had become me. "Bri, what I'm trying to say is we don't need to worry about Sigalie. She identifies with her career. She'll say yes…eventually. I have a dozen comebacks if, at first, she says no."

I reviewed for Bri every possible objection the New York Federal Reserve Bank General Auditor might raise. Then rehearsed my counterproposals, the steps I would take to convince Sigalie Kaddish to meet with us this morning.

"Thad, you'd seriously file a disciplinary complaint to have her CPA license revoked?"

"I don't think it'll get to that. But yes."

"That would blacklist her. She'd never be able to work in any fiduciary capacity."

"The only way we're going to get to the bottom of this—find out who's responsible for killing your fiancé and my wife—is to go to the top. Sigalie's an Executive Vice President. We start there. But before motoring on to New York, we need a few things."

"We're driving? Norfolk to LaGuardia is only an hour thirty-five by air. You sure you're up for a six-hour road trip?"

"Surest I've ever been."

I set the cruise control to 90 mph and adjusted the radar detector. The wind whipped my surf-do and played havoc with Bri's curls. Not once during the 365-mile trip up US-13 to I-95 did my back ever give me grief.

Except to stop for gas, we only made three detours, all in DC—a swanky luggage retailer, a photocopy shop, and Dr. Godenko's.

****

"Did you miss me?" I said.

Sigalie Kaddish gave me the fakest of smiles. "Don't push your luck, Tad."

"It's Thad."

"Tad, turd, whatever." The New York Fed General Auditor nodded toward Bri. "Who's she?"

"We'll get to that." I collapsed the handle of the aluminum business case and parked it along the wall in Sigalie's office. "May I?" I asked as I took a seat in one of the two side chairs in front of the executive desk. "Thank you for taking this meeting." I motioned for Bri to take the other side chair.

"I didn't have much choice." Sigalie repositioned the silk scarf accessorizing her three-piece chalk-stripe suit. Her gold hoop earrings swayed.

Earlier this morning on our trip up the Atlantic Seaboard from Virginia Beach to Lower Manhattan, Bri had used my phone to email Sigalie asking if she wanted to comment before we went public. Attached to the email was a sample of Rafi's spreadsheet with the Official Joint Seal activity for the New York Federal Reserve Bank gold bullion depository. Bri had highlighted a questionable pattern of bullion movement.

Bri unlatched the case. She withdrew a hard copy

of the report she had sent to the Federal Reserve Board Executive Vice President/General Auditor. "My name is Abril de la Guerra. We need your help."

"How so?"

"My fiancé, Rafael Silva, was working on these data when he was killed." Bri waved the Official Joint Seal analysis.

Sigalie shrugged. "I don't know what 'these data' are, but I can tell you Mr. Silva and I never crossed paths."

"He was the senior associate on Gold II." Bri rested the spreadsheet on her lap.

"As I said, I never met him. What makes you think I'd be privy to any of his work product? I'm not seeing any connection."

"We're hoping you can help us piece that together." Bri picked up the spreadsheet and laid it on the desk, calling attention to the figures highlighted in yellow. "All we need is access to two specific bars."

I handed Sigalie a sticky note with the serial numbers of the gold bricks that had failed the ping test two days ago.

"Thad, I cannot believe we are having this discussion again. I gave you the assay samples for these."

"Tetrahedron chips, yes."

"And…"

"The results came back ninety-nine point ninety-nine pure."

"As I told you they would." Sigalie stood, placing her hands on the edge of her desk. She looked like she was ready to usher us out.

"Shaving the ends of bullion bars doesn't rule out

salting," Bri said. "That's why taking core samples is standard audit procedure. But then, you already know that."

Sigalie glowered. Her cheeks pinked before turning bright red.

I said, "I can prove at least one of the bars is counterfeit."

"By snapping it with your fingernail?"

"With a simple experiment. Non-intrusive. Non-destructive. No metal loss." I opened the briefcase, extracted a plastic carrying case, and showed her the lab-grade equipment inside. "We'll be using this."

Sigalie removed her glasses, squinted, and rubbed her nose where the silicone eye pads had dented her skin. "The dilemma..." she said, repositioning the heavy frame on the bridge of her nose, "...the dilemma is if I agree to let you conduct your experiment, it could set an ugly precedent."

I waggled my head. "Extended audit procedures are fairly routine."

Bri nodded. "When there is inconsistency in, or doubts about the reliability of, the audit evidence."

"I know generally accepted auditing standards. I don't need to be schooled." Sigalie's textured gray curls bobbed as she spoke. "And if I say no to the experiment," Sigalie continued, "you'll parlay everything into an audit report exception, which will eventually find its way to Treasury Secretary Beck's desk. Am I right?"

When I had pressured the General Auditor into meeting with us this morning, I hadn't thought that far ahead. I chose not to respond to her question. Smiled instead. Held that smile forever.

"Don't make me regret this," Sigalie said. She shifted in her desk chair, sat up straight, and punched a couple of keys on her intercom. She got LaVonna Trennery from Custody and Ron Manchusco from Vault Services on the line. "Protocol calls," she told them. "Vault. Now."

Sigalie signaled for us to follow her. We took the elevator below ground to the vault. Along the way, I rehearsed to Bri the internal controls over vault compartment access. The Rule of Three. Recited the names of the security control team and their roles. Bri rolled the wheeled business case behind her.

LaVonna and Ron were waiting for us in front of the vault's library compartment. They didn't look thrilled.

"This is my lunch hour," LaVonna said. "How long is this going to take? I just sat down to keto zoodles Alfredo."

"Just finished." Ron had a PB&J smear on the corner of his mouth.

"Five minutes, tops," I said.

"Sigalie, you know zucchini noodles get soggy when reheated." LaVonna made a face.

"I'm sure you'll get over it, Trennery." Sigalie held up the opened padlock for the Library compartment. Using cable cutters, she snipped the galvanized steel cable of the Official Joint Seal, pulled the seal certificate, dated, and signed it. The rest of the security control team did likewise.

Sigalie herded us to the rack where she had isolated the two bars that I had flagged during the inventory observation. I verified the serial numbers. Same flared edges where the bar had been accidentally dropped.

Same shaved corners where the assay samples had been sliced off. I ran another ping test and listened for the difference.

"Now I hear why you had doubts." Bri opened the briefcase, withdrew the portable ultrasound, and hooked it to her iPhone. "Let's test the high-pitched bar first and use it as the control bar to establish a baseline."

From the carrying case, I removed the ultrasound gel and squirted it on the underside of the first bar, laying down a blue bead from the top to the bottom. "Ready?"

Bri swiped through the screens on her phone until she came to the dedicated scanning app for the handheld probe. She fired up the ultrasound. The screen danced with cloudy gray images. Bri ran the tip of the wand from one end of gold bar serial number 163466 to the other. The image never changed. No oohs, no ahs from the control team. Ron yawned. LaVonna used her reflection in the gold bar to primp.

I wiped the gel with the cloth provided in the kit and replaced the bar on the rack.

"Serial number 163467." I applied a long bead of gel to the underbelly of the second bar.

Bri did her magic with the portable wand.

"Did you see that?" Ron pointed to a dark rectangle in the image that ran the length of the bar. "That blip?"

LaVonna nodded.

Sigalie said, "I didn't see anything. And supposing I did, how do I know we aren't watching a desktop video you made earlier?"

"You take the wand this time." Bri handed the ultrasound probe to Sigalie.

The General Auditor re-traced the shape of the bar

from one corner to the next, testing the entire surface. The blip was no fluke. The inside of the bar was composed of something other than gold. She returned the wand to Bri and then snatched the cloth from me. She handed the cloth to Ron. "Wipe off the gel. Restock the bar on the rack."

The vault services member of the control team ran the cloth over the suspect bar until it was no longer slimy. The gold cladding shined.

Sigalie jotted down the smelter stampings on the top and sides of both bars. "I'm impounding these."

"As in 'the bars stay here'?" Bri asked. "I'm not liking the sound of that. We're only half-done with the experiment."

Sigalie ignored Bri and closed the compartment door. She was about to throw on the padlock when I stepped in front of her. "We stop now, and we won't know the extent of the impurities. Only a full wet assay will reveal how much of the twenty-seven pounds of serial number 163467 is pure gold."

"What, you think we have a metallurgical lab in the vault? We send our audit samples offsite for assays like everyone else, Thad. Takes weeks."

"I can get it done today," Bri said. "Interested?"

Sigalie glanced at the ZERO Halliburton. "Just curious. What else do you have in the case?"

Bri revealed the customized gray foam inserts at the bottom of the case where the bars would nestle. She detailed how private armored transport would ensure safe transit to the East River Heliport at Pier 6 in Lower Manhattan. And she described in satisfying detail the full-scale lab awaiting them just minutes from Reagan National in DC.

"Only on one condition," Sigalie said. "The gold never leaves my sight."

Chapter 34

The pilot banked right toward the Hudson River, sending the helicopter into the airspace beyond Manhattan. The Statue of Liberty glimmered below.

I got really queasy. And then nausea hit full on. I reached for the inflight motion sickness bag.

"Feel better?" Bri asked.

I wiped my mouth with the back of my sleeve and closed the bag fasteners. "I'm sorry."

"Happens," the pilot said through his headset. I heard him loud and clear through the over-ear noise-canceling headphones.

We were gaining altitude fast and were now at least a mile above sea level, en route to DCA. The chopper, on loan from Jorma Sarudin's father, was an armored Robinson R44. The pilot, first name Cruz, had that ex-military look.

Sigalie was riding shotgun next to Cruz, thumbing away at her cell phone. The case with the two gold bars rested at her feet.

Bri leaned over and waved her hand in front of my face to get my attention. She mimed writing a note.

I pulled out my mechanical pencil and gave it to her.

Bri fumbled through the seatback pocket of the pilot's chair until she found something to write on. She scribbled: —It's a trap. Sigalie caved too quickly. She's setting us up.—

I took the paper from her and wrote back: —I'm counting on it. —

Bri's eyes widened. She grabbed the paper: — What do we do? —

I had to think about that for a while. We had no idea who Sigalie was texting. Could be her boss. Could be my direct superior, Tigran Vardanyan. Could be anybody. Whoever it was would have associates on the ground in Washington, DC. That would complicate things.

I wrote: —Play dumb until we see who surfaces. —

Bri: —Is that safe? —

Me: —It's a risk. Are you still in? —

Bri gave me the wickedest smile.

"Follow me," Cruz said. We exited the helicopter cabin, keeping our heads down until we were a healthy distance from the spinning rotors. Sigalie rolled the aluminum case behind her.

At the edge of the helipad, an armored SUV with company markings for the Aurum Capital Group was parked. Cruz popped the rear hatch and helped Sigalie secure the case in the cargo area. We clambered in and headed for Crystal City, a little over a mile to the west of Reagan National. Cruz was behind the wheel.

Jorma was waiting for us just outside the lobby of the Lofts at Courtyard Green. We took the express elevator to her parents' 26th-floor penthouse. Using a remote fob, she unlocked the suite. "Follow me," she said.

Spacious would be an understatement. The apartment was the size of a mini-mall, easily 10K square feet with a 360-degree view. From the floor-to-ceiling glass panels lining the east wall, I could easily see the DC skyline across the Potomac River. To the southeast, dimly lit, was the Treasury Bureau of Fiscal Service Building, where Bri and I had conducted the midnight audit two days ago.

Jorma crossed to Bri, leaned in, and gave her a faux peck. "I'm glad you reached out. This is going to be so much fun."

"Where's the lab?" Sigalie asked. She parked the metal business carry-on in the tile entry.

"I thought you all might like a cup of tea first." Jorma ushered us to a free-standing island with a silver tea set, pot steaming, and shortbread biscuits on the side.

"This is going to sound impolite," I said, "but I'm in just as much of a hurry as the General Auditor. My employer has me on an incredibly short timeline."

Sigalie smiled and grabbed the handle of the case. Bri filled a hot drink cup, added a pinch of stevia, and secured the lid. I grabbed a few shortbread cookies to go.

"If you'll excuse me," Cruz said. He held a service revolver in his right hand and a tactical flashlight torch high in his left. "I need to check the security cams and run a perimeter check."

"Right, right. You can never be too sure." Jorma gave Cruz a confirmatory wave as he made his way to the entrance of the suite. "Everyone else, we're going this way."

Jorma guided us downstairs to an industrial-size metallurgical lab that took up the entire 25th floor. With the recent tech renaissance, prime Crystal City real estate was now in short supply. Whatever Jorma's parents did for a living, capitalism had been good to them.

"Let me gear up and then we can start." Jorma donned a shop apron over her chambray halter jumpsuit, swapped her leather sandals for color-matched protective shoes, and hung a pair of safety goggles around her neck.

I helped Sigalie hoist the metal briefcase to the top of the built-in workbench that stretched from wall to wall. The General Auditor twiddled the briefcase lock and then snapped open the latches. The sound echoed across the polished concrete floor.

While Bri positioned herself on one of the shop stools, I assisted Sigalie in removing the two gold bricks from the briefcase.

"Jorma, any way to make cross-sectional slices of the bars? The tetrahedron chips shaved for the audit only proved the edges were solid gold." I handed the bars to Jorma.

"'With the right equipment, anything's possible,'" she said. "My pop's words, not mine."

"Is your father an engineer?" Bri asked.

"Metallurgical. Colorado School of Mines, class of 1990, summa cum laude."

Bri nodded. Sigalie looked impressed.

"Okay, then," I said.

Jorma took the first bar, walked over to a radial diamond-wheel saw, and cut the yellow trapezoid in two. Picking up the half without the serial number, she ran the bar through the saw again, this time slicing off a thin wafer no more than one eighth of an inch thick. She did the same with the second bar. She took the two samples, flipped on a high-intensity lamp, and began examining the wafers.

Fondly, as if each slice of gold was a dear friend, Jorma inspected the metal samples under the bright light. Her full eyebrows arched until the creases in her forehead furrowed. She turned the first assay sample over and ran her fingers across the surface. Near the outer edge of the gold wafer, and at a few points toward the center, she dug her thumbnail into the soft metal. She picked up the second wafer and ran the same visual and malleability tests.

"Mm-hmm, ahh." Jorma's lips separated into a hard-to-read grin. "Yummy."

Assuming *ahh* might be an initial conclusion drawn from her visual check, I asked, "*Mmm-hmm* and *yummy,* I know. What's ahh?" I stepped over to Jorma's magnifying lamp to get a better look at the wafer samples.

Jorma swiveled to face me. "*Au*," she said. "Capital *a*, Lower-case *u*."

"The Periodic Table two-letter abbreviation for gold?" Bri said.

"Force of habit," Jorma said. "Had I been examining platinum I would have muttered '*Pt*' or silver '*Ag*.' My pops made sure I knew all my precious metal friends by name."

"So, the bars are solid?" I asked. "Gold through and through? You can tell this already?"

"A 'look and feel' and a hardness test will only get you so far. If you're asking for preliminary purity results, it's too early to tell. You're interested in truth, right?"

What could I say to that?

Jorma began fiddling with a row of vials. "We're going to do a little wet extraction. It's time-consuming. But it always produces the best results." She adjusted her safety goggles and dropped each wafer into separate glass beakers. Then, she pulled on rubber gloves, positioned the goggles over her eyes, and hung an industrial vapor respirator around her neck.

"You're welcome to watch, but I'd stand back. I'll be mixing up a batch of *aqua regia*. Nasty stuff—a mixture of hydrochloric and nitric acids. Then…" Jorma put on the mask and removed the lid to the hydrochloric acid.

I could already smell the HCl, a close cousin to muriatic acid. As a kid growing up, I used it to lower the pH in our above-ground pool. I backed away. Bri followed suit.

Jorma continued talking. It was hard to make out what she was saying behind the protective respirator, but I got snatches— "precipitate out the gold" and "spectrophotometer."

"How long is this going to take?" Sigalie asked.

"This is science, Ms. Kaddish. It takes as long as it takes. Have a seat. Make yourself comfortable."

Bri's stomach grumbled. She massaged her belly and looked at me.

"As long as this wet assay process is going to take some time," I said, "maybe you could steer us in the direction of some grub. Other than those little tea cakes you served, we haven't had a bite since we dropped in on Sigalie this morning."

The General Auditor gave me the cheesiest of smiles. "That's putting a positive spin on your visit." She obviously didn't think our unexpected meetup this morning in her office was a mere social call. Perhaps my threat of extortion if she didn't volunteer to help had colored her perspective.

Bri stood and took me by the arm. "Come on. I think I saw a juice bar and a bank of blenders by the tea set as we came in. You want anything, Sigalie?"

"I'll pass."

"How about you, Jorma?"

The gold blogger lowered her mask. "Bring me back a baby spinach and açaí juice blend, would you?"

Bri and I headed for the stairway.

"Oh…and," Jorma called out, "make it a power smoothie. The muscle powder is in the cupboard above the sink."

Serious metallurgy and power smoothies.

A perfect combination for unearthing strong evidence.

We had a burly evening ahead of us.

Chapter 35

"Bri, do you think we should have left the two of them alone? I'm worried about Sigalie." I searched the Sub-Zero minifridge below the bar. It was well-stocked.

We helped ourselves to deli-sliced corned beef sandwiches, gourmet Kosher dill pickles, and wonder of wonder, Ding Dongs. Foodie peccadillo, but comforting, nevertheless.

"Jorma's in science mode. She's harmless." Bri juiced some fresh spinach, poured in açaí concentrate, then added ice and a measuring cup of organic plant-based proteins. She mashed the smoothie button on the Blendtec. The ice clattered in the machine before the blender settled into a steady whine.

"Worst case, Thad, is that Jorma will be tempted to pepper Sigalie with questions. It's not often an investigative reporter has direct access to an insider charged with monitoring three hundred seventy billion in gold."

"Death by confrontational inquiry," I said.

"That's a little hyperbolic. Sigalie seems tough. She won't crumple under hard questioning."

"Yeah, maybe, but we should get back, anyway. Sigalie is our best lead. Can't afford to have Jorma's muckraking bias muck this up."

I grabbed a 32-ounce tumbler from the glass-faced galley kitchen cabinets. Bri filled it with the purple power drink that plopped like thick gruel. I garnished the smoothie with a kiwi fruit slice, positioned it on a silver serving tray, and added a cocktail napkin from the bar. *Presentation is everything.*

We took the stairway back down to the lab.

I was anxious.

Anxious and uptight.

Uptight and on edge.

Everything hinged on the assay results. If my hunch was correct, Bri and I could flush out Rafi's killer. And possibly put a face to the man who chased Marissa from the beach house, pursuing her until she tripped and hemorrhaged to death. If my hunch was wrong?

Before I could finish my thought, Bri's hands flew to her face. The silver tray she was carrying clattered to the lab floor landing. Purple-green smoothie splattered everywhere.

"What the hell?" The knot in my stomach tightened into a fist.

To avoid being slimed, the General Auditor stepped back. In Sigalie's hand was a lightweight Glock 42, barrel pointed directly at us. "I was going to say, Ms. de la Guerra, place the drink on the workbench next to the briefcase. But now that won't be necessary." Sigalie waved us over to the lab stools where Jorma had been bound to a chair and gagged with a shop rag.

We complied. Didn't say anything. Jorma smoldered, eyes fierce.

Sigalie handed Bri a roll of duct tape. "Wrap Thad's wrists."

"Sigalie," I said, "I know we haven't been the best of friends, but I thought we were on the same side.

Guardians of the financial markets. Enablers of capital formation entrusted to assure investors that whatever's reported is fairly stated, the numbers 'true and fair.'"

Sigalie rolled her eyes while Bri finished taping my hands behind my back. I was wrapped tight. Couldn't wiggle an inch.

"Ankles," Sigalie said. "Do his ankles next. Now!"

As Bri wound the tape, I splayed my feet to the sides, hoping to keep some space between the ankle bones. Sigalie wasn't sympathetic. She pistol-whipped the top of my right thigh, then kicked my feet together. Bri squeezed my ankles as she wrapped.

I wanted to massage my right quad with my head to relieve pressure on the knot that was building. Marissa's yoga classes had made me more flexible, but I wasn't a contortionist. When it became obvious I would never be able to touch my leg, I raised my head and addressed Sigalie. "Help me understand why you're hijacking the evidence. Who're you working for?"

Bri finished with my ankles. She handed the duct tape back to Sigalie. The General Auditor put her handgun in the back of her waistband, used her clear-coat fingernails to peel back the end of the cloth-reinforced tape, then ripped strips from the roll and positioned them on the lip of the workbench.

"Turn around, Ms. de la Guerra." Sigalie made a 360-degree gesture with her right index finger. "Now sit!" She pushed Bri down onto one of the lab stools. "Hands behind your back." Using the precut lengths of duct tape, the General Auditor bound Bri's wrists and then taped her ankles to the legs of the stool.

"Thad, what makes you think I'm working with someone?"

"Are you?" Bri asked.

"What? Now you're Nancy Drew?"

"The helicopter ride down from New York. You were texting nonstop." Bri tried to flex her ankles. She ended up making her stool wobble but remained upright.

"Both of you. Give me a break."

From the other side of the lab, Jorma squirmed, then started squealing, reminding me of an injured kitten, paw caught where it shouldn't have been. The sound was muffled by the rag used to gag her. Sigalie ordered Jorma to stop mewing, her language less than delicate. Jorma returned to quiet smoldering in the chair.

"Thad, one of the pitfalls of our profession is over-attention to detail. Bean counters are notorious for being analytically myopic."

"Myopic?" I repeated. As an accountant, I was accustomed to insults, but *myopia* was new. "So, what am I overlooking?" The Charlie horse in my leg was killing me. I grit my teeth.

"The possibilities, Thad. Thanks to you, and your shamus playmates, I now have information that no one else has. Material nonpublic info."

How could I have been so dumb?

"Material nonpublic information" was code for insider trading. The practice of buying and selling securities before juicy news—in this case, failed assay tests—was available to everybody. Perhaps I really was myopic and hadn't seen the big picture. I hadn't figured Sigalie for an opportunist. A hardass functionary, maybe. But not someone tempted to monetize an information windfall.

"Blackmail?" I said. "Is that what I'm missing? You're going to use the results of our two-bar gold sample to pad your pocketbook?"

"One possibility," Sigalie said. "Blackmail at the highest reaches of government could be lucrative. Let's see? Who benefits from burying the assay results? The CEO and president of the New York Federal Reserve Bank? Hmm. An obvious candidate, but shallow pockets, likely to only have chump change for responding to payment demands."

"My guess would be the Treasury Secretary," Bri said.

"A better candidate. Especially because she's ultimately responsible for safeguarding the nation's deep storage gold. It would be very embarrassing for acting Treasury Secretary Beck if the word leaked. But Beck's personal net worth is barely into the low seven figures. She spent far too much time in academia to accumulate any wealth. Of course, Beck does have substantial influence. I could leverage that."

Sigalie was enjoying toying with us as she flexed her brilliance. It was a power move. A cue as to who was in control of the moment, of the conversation, and its pace and pedantry.

"Thad, you haven't mentioned the Chair of the Federal Reserve Board? He might like to keep a lid on this."

A 1930s-style bank run would be a disaster for the chairman. Tens of millions of ordinary people, spooked by the collapse of global financial markets, rushing to draw down their savings. It'd make the economic fallout from the jumbo recession of the early twenty-first century look like a Labor Day picnic.

"That I could see," I said. "Not pretty."

Sigalie flashed her teeth, lips curled into a smug smile. "I have one more potential blackmail target for you, Thad. My favorite, actually. The one person with the most to lose. He's a cheerleader for a return to the gold standard. He loves the spotlight. And he would have a hard time tweeting his way out of a scandal in which, under his watch, the nation's gold disappeared."

It didn't take a master sleuth to realize Sigalie was referring to the President of the United States. His re-election bid would never recover. Questionable business practices and serial womanizing were one thing, but losing the people's gold? His claim to populism would vanish. The "forgotten middle" living in the flyover zone would never forgive him.

"And lest we forget," Sigalie continued, "the president has a history of being a blackmail victim. He knows the drill. He could easily tap U.S. Federal Government dark funds to pay extortion demands."

"Dark funds like the Treasury ESF?" Bri asked.

Unless you were an economic historian or had direct ties to the world of high finance, the Exchange Stabilization Fund bordered on the obscure. The balance in the ESF slush fund was now close to $100 billion. Sigalie wasn't into financial small ball. She was swinging for the fiscal fence.

"Major league blackmail is too messy," I said. "Leaves an evidence trail any forensic accountant would spot on day one. I think you're bluffing."

"What? You think I don't have the chutzpah?" Sigalie racked the slide on the Glock. She stuck the gun to my head, hand steady.

Sweat beaded on my forehead, dripping from my

brow. "Chutzpah and then some," I said. "Never a question. You're smart. I'm guessing you have a better idea, one that leaves no trace."

"Like what?"

If we were going to get out of the lab alive, we needed a plan. Right now, I couldn't even think straight. The cortisol dump from my adrenal glands was scrambling my brain. I had to buy some time, so I went with a tactic made famous by Scheherazade, Queen of Persia. A classic life-prolonging ploy. *Story at its finest*.

To keep Sigalie from shooting us, all I had to do was keep her preoccupied with 1,001 strategies for making a killing with her hot tip about Fed gold. If I kept her guessing long enough, perhaps I'd lull her into getting sloppy, and then maybe—

I winked at Bri. She arched her brows. Bri probably thought I was having an anxiety attack, complete with nervous tics. So much for cueing her in. I inched my stool closer to Sigalie. "Instead of blackmail, what about cashing in using a market strategy? Eliminates the downside of extortion," I said.

"Markets have risks."

"Hear me out."

Sigalie jammed the gun barrel further into my left temple. "Talk."

"Market Strategy Number One: buy low, sell high. You purchase options in gold futures at the current price. Leak the assay results to the press. Sell the options when gold prices spike on the news."

"A single buyer or multiple?" Sigalie's voice was steady.

"Multiple buyers to avoid suspicion."

"The buy orders would need to be spaced days

apart. What else you got?"

"Market Strategy Number Two," I said. "Short the stock. Borrow shares of Sunstake Extractive Industries, the only refiner big enough to have a government contract to supply working stock for American Eagle gold bullion coins—"

Without warning, the bloodied body of Jorma's security director hurtled through the air, landing face-up on the worktable, arms dangling to the sides, twisted at odd angles. I couldn't tell if Cruz was still breathing. His chest wasn't moving.

The impact of the body slam scattered lab specimens, instruments, and vials. Glass shattered. The surface of the workbench bubbled from the acid spill, the fumes noxious. I dropped to the floor to take cover.

With her ankles taped to the shop stool, Bri didn't have that option. Instead, she rocked the stool side to side until it wobbled to the lab floor. She crashed on her back, stool strapped between her legs. I covered her face with my body.

Sigalie whipped to the right, attempting to duck a bank of busted test tubes that had gone airborne. She wasn't fast enough. The glass fragments struck her head. Where the jagged slivers pierced her skin, blood flowed freely. She dropped to the floor, pointed her Glock in the direction from which Cruz's body had come, and squeezed the trigger twice.

The crack of the first shot only added to the cacophony of confusion in the lab. But the second shot must have penetrated the target. There was a low-pitched scream, followed by a mix of profanity, salted with religious incantation. Sigalie fired, again and again, emptying the remaining four rounds of her magazine. The scream became a wail, crescendoed, and then abruptly stopped.

Except for the bubbling of the acid draining from the workbench to the concrete floor, the lab fell silent. We had to move. To escape the nitric and hydrochloric drip, we scooted like inchworms. Bri kept her duct-taped hands and feet raised above the floor to avoid broken glass. I too kept my feet up but slid my fingertips behind me along the cement until I snagged a test tube shard. It took me several seconds before I was able to conceal the glass inside my duct-taped wrists. Sigalie was too busy peering into the void beyond the lab to notice.

From the darkness came a command, unequivocal, no-nonsense. "On your feet. All four of you. Now!"

The voice was familiar. I had heard it once before.

Chapter 36

The Treasury Secretary's Secret Service detail, Agent Jaxon Casama, was taller and broader than I remembered. In his right hand was a Sig Sauer P229—the same style weapon he pulled on Tigran and me for skirting the Treasury Building's metal detectors. Hard to forget a bullmastiff with a crew cut.

"Cuff them," Jaxon said. He used his pistol to gesture toward Sigalie, Jorma, Bri, and me. A second, much younger, agent emerged from the shadows of the staircase. He unhooked four pairs of ASP hinged handcuffs from his duty belt.

This could go one of two ways.

First, Agent Jaxon Casama was just doing his job as Kennedy Beck's Secret Service detail. His mission was to protect her against threats in her role as Secretary of the U.S. Treasury. He was here to reclaim the two bullion bars and keep Gold II out of the press. TSec had promised the president the secret audit of the nation's gold supply would be discreetly completed on time and on budget. Emphasis on discreetly.

The second possibility related to the U.S. Secret Service's investigative mission. With direct responsibility for safeguarding the U.S. financial system, Jaxon, as a sworn agent, could be probing potential counterfeiting of custodial gold bullion. He would be obliged to seize evidence.

Trouble is, neither scenario was acceptable. I wasn't about to surrender our evidence. We had risked too much. I couldn't let that happen. And Bri would *never* let it happen. I had to buy some time.

I turned my back to Jaxon and his accomplice, then wagged my duct-taped wrists. "No need for handcuffs. Same for them." I tilted my head toward Bri and Jorma.

Bri showed them her taped wrists and ankles. "See. Already in restraints."

The second agent returned two pairs of cuffs to his belt. He moved on to Jorma, examined the tape job Sigalie had done to secure her, and muttered something that I took to mean "sloppy" because the next thing he did was rip the tape off her feet and hands, yank Jorma's wrists behind her, and lock a pair of cuffs in place. He manhandled Jorma over to one of the free shop stools, plopped her down, and told her to sit still or he'd bind her ankles and do it right this time. Even with the gag in her mouth, Jorma wasn't shy about her displeasure.

The agent ignored her muffled pleas, turned, and headed for Sigalie with the next set of cuffs.

"For the love of God, this certainly isn't necessary." Sigalie kept her hands to her side, choosing not to extend her wrists. "*I'm* the one who raised the Code Yellow alert. National Brick mean anything? We're on the same team."

Sigalie no longer looked as fashionably commanding as she did when we arrived less than a few hours ago at her office this morning. Flying glass had lacerated the shaved side of her undercut hairdo. There was a dribble trail across her tawny headscarf where blood dripped onto the shoulder of her blazer.

The second agent unlocked the hinged handcuffs, spun Sigalie a hundred and eighty degrees, and was about to notch the cuffs in place when the General Auditor said, "Before you two arrived, I had everything under control. Can't you just wait?"

The agent didn't. The cuffs clicked, and then he glanced over his shoulder at his partner. Jaxon Casama gave him a thumbs-up.

"Sit." Jaxon shoved Sigalie onto an open stool.

Sigalie gritted her teeth. Her eyes narrowed and then closed for a second. She wiggled her wrists. "Do these things have to be so tight?"

"Brief us. Leave nothing out. Especially loose ends."

Sigalie clocked through the chronology of the morning with an auditor's attention to minutia—the unexpected visit from Bri and me, the demand to test the suspect bars, the ultrasound results, the helicopter shuttle from Lower Manhattan.

"Such extortion," she said. "You've never seen blackmail like this." And then Sigalie launched into a rant about how she had been forced into helping, how she feared for her life, and how she was only thinking of her mission to safeguard the bona fides of the depository gold and the integrity of the inventory counts when she realized her only path to deliverance from ethical bondage was to "cooperate."

Jaxon's gaze wandered during Sigalie's monologue. He was eyeing the workbench, glancing at the oversized electric cable that powered one of Jorma's lab instruments.

"It's Agent Jaxon Casama, right?" I tried to get the agent's attention. "Do you go by your first name, your title and last name, or sir? What's your preference?"

The Secret Service Agent looked annoyed. He shook his head.

Taking that as confirmation for his given name, I said, "Okay, then I'll go with Jaxon. Well, Jaxon, I wouldn't call our conversation with Sigalie extortion. More like a request for a professional 'assist' to answer questions raised from my inventory observation on Wednesday."

Bri was more direct. "Nobody forced Sigalie to do anything," she said.

Jaxon crossed over to the conduit snaking from the utility panel. He looked like he was gauging the length of the line, yanked on it, and when it didn't budge, he focused instead on the boxy apparatus to which it was attached.

"How do you work the furnace?" Jaxon asked. He was staring at a benchtop lab-grade fire assay furnace—a boxy thing about twice the size of an office fridge, connected to a 240-volt electrical conduit. On the workbench next to the furnace was an assortment of graphite crucibles, stir rods, ingot pouring molds, and safety equipment.

"Ask Jorma." Sigalie nodded toward the penthouse suite host. "It's her lab."

Jaxon continued to play with the dials, banged on the instrument console, and shook the furnace.

Jorma sat up straight on the stool and animatedly tried to talk with the gag still in her mouth. We couldn't understand a thing she was saying until the second agent walked over, pulled a knife, cut through the knot holding the rag in place, and let it fall to the cement.

"Thank God," Jorma said, but it came out muted.

She worked her mouth, stretched her lips, and cleared her throat. "Jaxon, can I ask you to please stop with the banging and shaking? My pops will kill me if you wreck his equipment."

Jaxon gave her a threatening look, kind of like "not if I kill you first." No doubt, he was capable.

"Furnace operation is a little tricky. It requires caution," Jorma said. "I might be able to help, but you have to tell me what you're trying to do."

"Gather information," Jaxon said. "Do you like games, Ms…did I hear your name right? Norma?"

Jorma didn't answer the question or confirm her name. She looked down instead. I glanced at Bri. She shrugged her shoulders in one of those I'm-not-sure-where-this-is-going-either gestures.

"Everybody likes games," Jaxon said. He scoured the workbench for a gold brick and spotted one of the halves sticking out from under Cruz's torso. "Fetch the bar," he told his partner. "Do something with the body. I want a clear gamespace."

The second agent retrieved the half brick and handed it to Jaxon. Then, as ordered, he dumped Cruz's bloodied corpse onto the lab floor. He then dragged it over to the far wall near the emergency shower station and left it.

Jaxon picked up the gold sample, opened his mouth wide, and sank his canines into the half bar. He inspected the results. "Malleability test: CHECK. Softer than I imagined." Saliva dripped from the teeth impressions in the gold bullion.

"You know," Jaxon said, "information gathering can be such a tedious process. And a royal time-suck." He fiddled with the control panel on the front of the furnace. He played with the RESET, up/down arrows, and the MENU buttons. As he did, the green LED display listed the menu options:

OFF

MINIMUM SET POINT

MAXIMUM SET POINT

There was a toggle switch next to the display. Jaxon flipped it. A tiny square power indicator began to glow red.

"At the Secret Service," Jaxon said, "we have found if we gamify the gathering process, information flows faster. And bonus, we can have a little fun during interrogation."

Gamify?

Interrogation?

Jaxon must have overheard everything from the shadows while just minutes ago, Sigalie had her gun pointed at my head. From that conversation, he would have gathered at least one of the gold bars was fake. Sigalie wouldn't have tied up Jorma unless she had been sure there was sufficient proof my audit had uncovered something.

What Jaxon likely didn't know was the scale of the fraud. How fake was the fake? Only the final purity numbers from the assay tests would give him that info.

"You're not going to tell me how to work it, Ms. Jorma, are you?" Jaxon cycled through the next menu options.

SET LOW TEMP

SET HIGH TEMP

Jorma shuddered. She wriggled her wrists, but couldn't find any way to reduce the pressure from the metal cuffs. She said, "Hell, no."

Jaxon pressed the up arrow until the temperature couldn't be set any higher—twenty-three hundred degrees Fahrenheit.

"I hate games," Jorma said. "I'm opting out."

"I was afraid of that." Agent Jaxon tapped Jorma's handcuffs with the tip of his gun. "You do realize that you aided and abetted fugitives, received stolen property, in this case, U.S. Mint deep storage gold, and—"

"That's not the way it was explained to me." Jorma was getting feisty. "Contrary to Sigalie's negative spin during her debrief to you, she came to my pop's lab willingly. My understanding is that she volunteered to have the two bars wet assayed."

Jaxon lifted the vertical door of the furnace. The heat from the glowing coils bathed his arms in a soft red-orange light. He wrenched back, dropping the door and sealing off the high-powered oven. "Damn!"

The Secret Service agent blew on his fingertips while scouring the workbench. When he found what looked like a pair of elbow-length safety gloves, he set them next to the diamond-wheel chop saw. He flipped the switch on the saw, letting it whir. Then he strutted to Jorma, yanked at the safety goggles on her head until they wiggled free, and put them on himself.

"You don't have to be so rough," Bri said.

"Humph." Jaxon positioned the goggles on his skull and adjusted the eyepieces till they fit. He eyed Bri and said, "So, does this mean Ms. de la Guerra, you're volunteering to take Jorma's place and go first?"

Jorma licked her lips. They had cracked from being stretched ear to ear when she was gagged. "Bri, back off. I got this," she said. "I can handle rough."

Jaxon pivoted to face Jorma. "So, you've changed your mind and are willing to play." He picked up the half gold brick he had bitten into earlier and positioned it atop the table plate of the chop saw. "Let's see if you're up to the challenge."

Using the radial diamond blade, Jaxon crosscut a good-sized chunk of gold, flecks flying. He inspected the sample and then dropped it into one of the larger graphite crucibles. He set down his gun, donned the safety gloves, and using the tongs, placed the crucible with the blocky sample into the furnace. The temperature on the controller read 2,000 degrees Fahrenheit.

For the benchtop furnace to have heated that quickly, Jorma must have used it earlier while Bri and I were out grabbing grub. No doubt she had gotten further along in the wet extraction process than I had anticipated. She might even have precipitated out enough gold with the *aqua regia* to run the spectrophotometer.

"Interrogation game begins in ten," Jaxon said. He took off the gloves, raised the goggles, and checked his phone for messages. We watched as he sent a text, thumbed through pics on social media, and laughed once. It wasn't a Santa Claus belly chortle. More a gurgle, like how I imagined a self-amused gargoyle might make. Jaxon pocketed his phone.

Smack in the center of the furnace door was a small peephole. Jaxon peeked in at the crucible and smiled. "Jorma," he said, "you are going to love this game. The rules are simple. There are two players. The object of the game is to get your challenger to reveal secrets. If you find out what he, she or they know, you win."

Jaxon put the safety gloves on again, repositioned the goggles, picked up the tongs, and lifted the furnace door. Even from a few feet away, I could feel the air blast. Jorma scooted her stool away from the heat. That left Sigalie closest to the fire assay furnace.

The General Auditor's face pinked with the unexpected warmth, her cheeks rosy red. "Jaxon, this isn't what I had in mind when I raised the Code Yellow."

"You were expecting a Presidential Medal of Honor?" Jaxon was obviously no stranger to sarcasm.

"You're off-book, aren't you?" Sigalie said. "Your conduct? This mission? None of it is sanctioned by Madame Secretary, is it?"

Jaxon ignored her. "Player one has an advantage. He, she, or they start with a small pot, not too big, just enough to get things rolling."

Jorma didn't flinch, eyes steady on Jaxon.

Jaxon then wrapped the tongs around the middle of the crucible and lifted it carefully from the furnace. The graphite cup was now bonfire red. The molten gold inside the crucible was even redder. Jaxon let the furnace door drop. The counterweights that kept the door aloft eased the descent while it lowered back into place.

Jaxon raised the crucible, brought it within inches of Jorma, and held it there. "My pot," he said.

Chapter 37

"I'm pretty good at this game," Jaxon told Jorma. "In fact, no one has ever beat me in *Gold Lust*." He did a little pun-snicker. "I kind of like the name of the game. Rhymes with poetic irony."

Jorma scrunched her eyes and raised her brows.

"You'll see the connection soon enough." Jaxon's hands were a little shaky from holding the red-hot container at arms-length to avoid the heat. He set the crucible onto a kiln brick and turned to face Jorma. "Oh, and did I mention it was *my* game? My brainchild? Enhanced interrogation practice has never been the same since."

For Jorma's sake, I was hoping *Gold Lust* was a mind game and nothing more. Compassionate waterboarding without the possibility of drowning, followed by a spa massage and an exfoliating scrub. More good cop than bad cop. And if not—

Jaxon lifted the crucible once more. He tilted it a tad until a dribble of gold streamed down, splattering the top of one of Jorma's color-coordinated safety boots. The smell of burning leather stunk as the gold sizzled, masking the odor of fresh pee.

Jorma jumped off the stool, shook her boot, and did a little dance. Right foot in. Right foot out. A crazy Hokey Pokey made even crazier with her hands cuffed behind her back. She almost slipped into the puddle at

324

her feet. "Psycho bastard! I can feel the burn."

"That's the point," Jaxon said. "It's supposed to be hot. How else can I get you to tell me what I want to know?"

"Yo, dude. This is sick." I had slipped into surf speak and was starting to lose control of my anxiety.

Jorma stomped her foot until she dislodged the drizzle. The solidified gold clinked as it hit the floor. "Agent Casama, if you're looking for the final assay results, I don't have them. I wasn't finished yet." She winced and stomped her foot again. "My boot. I'm taking it off."

With Jorma's hands still cuffed behind her back, any attempt to remove her footwear was going to be awkward. But she tried anyway. She bent at the knees, threaded her bound hands between her legs, and extended her fingers until she just reached the boot heel. She toyed with the Velcro straps but ended up losing her balance, fell backward, did a reverse summersault, and lurched to her feet.

Then Jorma ran.

The second agent removed a collapsible baton from his duty belt. As Jorma tried to flee up the stairs to the penthouse level, the agent extended his baton and swatted the back of her legs. Jorma sunk to her feet. The agent holstered the baton, jerked her upright, and returned her to the stool to continue the interrogation.

"This is a two-player game," Jaxon said. "Running off just when it's starting to get fun is rude."

I felt a twinge of guilt. This wasn't Jorma's fight. This was mine. Mine and Bri's. We had gotten her into this crusade. At least one of us had to get her out. Bri didn't look like she was about to make a move anytime soon. Me? I was terrified, almost certain of another epic fail, of orphaning my preemie son. I wanted to flee, avoid the unavoidable but knew at some rationale level that a "flight response" was just me running from myself again—something Marissa had labored to help me manage and that's when I sensed her near, felt Marissa's presence, heard her whisper her yogi wisdom:

You are not your anxiety.
Commit to the rogue wave.
Take off.
Drop in.
Ride.
I'll be waiting on shore, watching you.

My hands trembled. My throat was dry, but not too dry to say what I said next, "Agent Jaxon Casama, if you're looking for a gamer ace, I'm the one you want to challenge. Board games—chess, Monopoly—I win every time. Then there's video. I have leaderboard rankings in *Grand Theft Auto*, *Call of Duty*, and even *Guitar Hero*. I'm the year-over-year reigning champ of the first-person shooter game *Doom 2025*. That makes Thaddeus Jude Hanlon an FPS legend."

I stopped jabbering for a moment to let it all sink in.

"What I'm saying, Agent Casama, is I can be pretty competitive." I gave Jaxon an alpha male up-nod to let him know I was a contender, chin tilting higher, then slowly returning to level.

"Counting on it." Jaxon snickered. The Secret Service agent clearly wasn't buying my bravado.

But I really was telling the truth. I used to be pretty good at games. Could always read my opponent. Stay one move ahead.

Jaxon's game, though, this torture tease, was different. Nothing like any tourney I'd been involved in. He held all the cards, odds always in his favor. And he seemed to be the only one having any fun.

Our part in his sadistic match was as sacrificial gladiators. Best case, when my turn came, I could entertain him long enough to come up with a strategy and devise a series of moves that would allow the three of us to escape the lab. Worst case, I'd lose everything, including the chance to see my son become a man. I had no intention of giving him that thrill.

"When I start riffing on you…" Jaxon mimed an air guitar solo, "…I bet your *Guitar Hero* skills are going to come in real handy." He gave me the cheesiest smile.

"Pre-game trash talk. I love it!" I rocked my head from side to side, cracking my neck like they do in bad Kung Fu movies.

"I will be your *doom*," Jaxon countered. Another cheesy smile. He was enjoying this.

I didn't know how many more bad puns I could take. I said, "Yo, Agent Jaxon. How 'bout we make this the final round of *Gold Lust*? Just you and me? We leave Bri, Jorma, and Sigalie out of any further fun and games. Whaddaya say?"

"Depends," Jaxon said.

"On what?"

"If you tell me everything you know and everything they know."

"I'm sure we can come to an understanding. You in?"

Jaxon fixed his eyes on me, carefully lifted the

crucible, and poured a dribble of molten gold onto my tan brogues. My insides churned, my stomach distended.

The leather sizzled. Before I could fully tighten my butt cheeks together to keep my bowels in check, there was a muffled whoosh. A runny brown discharge leaked from my trousers onto the laboratory floor, compounding the noxious odor in the lab.

Bri whimpered. She was still dry-eyed but not far from tears.

Sigalie opened her mouth and looked like she was about to protest when Jorma spoke up. "You don't need to do this. Thad doesn't know anything."

"Enlighten me, then."

"He was upstairs while we performed the wet assay. He and Bri both. They don't know the results." Jorma glanced at Sigalie. "Only we do."

With his free hand, Jaxon made a "come on" gesture, made classic in every low-budget action film. "And…"

"The first bar is nine hundred ninety-nine point nine fine and…" Jorma paused just long enough to kick my wingtip with her safety boot, trying to dislodge the gold splatter smoking my foot, and almost slipped in the muck on the cement. When she found her balance, she repositioned herself on the lab stool as if reality could be rewound and the last sixty seconds hadn't happened. "And…" she said, "the purity matches the stamping on the gold itself."

No overt reaction from Jaxon, either on the bar one assay result or Jorma's clumsy dance following her failed attempt at kindness to me. The Secret Service agent seemed to be expecting something else. Some other intel.

"What about the second bar?" he asked. He moved closer to Jorma with the tongs and glowing crucible.

"Based on a visual inspection of the wafer sample…" Jorma drew a breath between her teeth, "I'd say the second is at best twelve percent gold— fine on the outside, zero-karat on the inside. The bar's a high-quality fake, better than anything I've seen out of China. I'd say it's gold-cladding over base metal."

"All this from a visual?" Jaxon looked over at Sigalie. "You agree?"

The General Auditor flinched. "You know, Agent Casama, I'm not comfortable with any of this…this game of yours."

"But is she right?"

Sigalie's gaze shifted up and to the left. It looked like she was doing mental math. "Could be."

Jaxon switched the crucible from his right to his left hand. "Tell me how you got your numbers, Jorma. How'd you arrive at sub-three karat purity for the second bar?"

"You honestly want to know?" There was a slight upturn in the fledgling crow's feet around Jorma's eyes. She looked eager to launch into her role as the world's premier gold reserve explainer. "Tell you what, Agent Casama. If you loosen these cuffs, I'll answer the question you should have asked."

"Such as?"

"Such as, how would you counterfeit a gold reserve bar in such a way that it would pass inspection?"

Jaxon looked intrigued by the bonus information offer. "Loosen the cuffs," he told his partner. The second agent did as instructed.

Jaxon gestured for Jorma to keep talking as she massaged her wrists.

"First," she said, "I'd start with a slug slightly slimmer all around than a London Good Delivery Bar. It would have to have the same density as gold. Say...tungsten."

"So," I said, "that would explain why it would be impossible for an auditor to tell by weight alone the difference between the counterfeit and the solid gold bar?"

Sigalie was quick to comment. "Impossible for an *ordinary* auditor," she added.

I ignored the dig.

Jaxon glanced at his watch.

Jorma took a deep breath, refilling her lungs. "There's one more critical step in counterfeiting. The tungsten must be clad with pure gold to bring it up to the U.S. Mint bullion standard. Successful deception requires one-sixteenth inch minimum surface thickness but could be as high as one-eighth inch all around. That much gold wrap would be enough to fool any x-ray fluorescence scanner."

Bri closed her eyes and pressed her lips together. She got that far-away look again like she was in accountant mode noodling numbers. "The one-sixteenth inch gold coating," she said. "That's how you arrived at three-karat purity for the fake? How you got twelve percent gold content?"

Jorma looked pleased. "Yeah, three karats gold, twenty-one karats base metal. Three twenty-fourths. Maybe a hundred thousand dollars in gold cladding. Enough to avoid detection under examination. Versus what? Five hundred dollars total for the tungsten. For a single four hundred-troy ounce bogus brick, the net profit would be a half mil to six hundred thousand dollars. Depending on the spot price."

I whistled. One of those exclamatory we-are-talking-big-bucks whistles.

The night Rafi called, he mentioned a mondo-sized discovery. Fraud bigger than Enron. I didn't believe him then. Dismissed his story as a product of hyper-skepticism. But apparently, when Rafi reached out, he was onto something. If only half of the 508,000 bullion bars in the New York Fed were fake, somebody had made off with $115 billion and change. That qualified as mega, for sure.

With the crucible still at arms-length, Jaxon's arm started to shake again, muscles tiring. The crucible no longer glowed. By now, the gold had to have started to solidify. But instead of setting everything on the kiln brick trivet to finish cooling, he re-opened the furnace and stuck the crucible inside to reheat.

The next round of *Gold Lust* was about to begin.

I tried putting on a poker face but was too dispirited to fool even myself. So, I squeezed my eyes shut and muttered one of Marissa's self-affirmations.

Bri kicked my good foot to get my attention. She mouthed, "Ready?"

I mouthed back, "For what?" I strained to hear over the foot shuffling in the lab. There were no furtive creaks on the stairway. No subtle sounds coming from outside the windows. My hearing isn't the greatest, but if a rescue operation was underway, I couldn't tell.

"Answers," she mouthed.

I arched my brows.

"Before. It's. *Game Over*." Bri over-enunciated

each word, slowly, silently.

I screwed up my face and tilted my head toward her in a classic what's-that-supposed-to-mean? gesture.

"Have to try," she responded.

Chapter 38

So, now I was on high alert, but for what?

I had no idea what Bri was planning. Running? Our ankles were bound. Fighting back? Our wrists were restrained. So, I did the only thing I could think to do: I repositioned the glass shard I had palmed when Cruz came flying into the lab and worked it awkwardly behind my back, gnawing at the duct tape. I was discreet, shielding my micro-movements from Jaxon and his sidekick. To avoid cutting myself, I didn't press too hard, careful not to draw blood. Couldn't afford to drip. Spatter would raise suspicion.

The restraint gave slightly. The grip of the duct tape had weakened, but not enough. At this pace, I'd be wearing more gold soon if I couldn't answer the questions Jaxon had in mind for me.

Sigalie broke the silence. "Jaxon, give me a couple of hours," she said. "With Jorma's assistance, I can separate any base metal and give you an exact purity number." The General Auditor's proposition sounded more like a plea than a genuine offer to help. If she was trying to stall my interrogation, she must have had her reasons. Sigalie was hard to figure.

Jaxon put on the safety gloves and lowered the goggles ripped from Jorma earlier until they fully protected his eyes. He opened the furnace.

"I just need to heat a new batch of *aqua regia*,"

Sigalie continued. "Jorma, do we have any more hydrochloric and nitric acids?"

Jorma nodded toward the first locker in a row of metal supply cabinets lining the north wall of the lab.

"Not now," Jaxon said. Using the insulated tongs, he grabbed the glowing crucible and inched closer to me. He tilted the crucible a fraction. The heat made my head sweat.

Sigalie shuddered. "Jaxon, I'd like to believe I have a well-tuned moral compass. Thad may be a nuisance, but as a fellow auditor he doesn't deserve—"

"Shut up!" Jaxon tilted the crucible another fraction.

Beads of perspiration dripped into my eyes, blurring my vision. My cheeks blazed.

The General Auditor's jaw tightened. "Jaxon, you've got to stop this."

Another tilt of the tongs, a fraction of a fraction.

Sigalie's eyes steeled, pupils narrowing. "I can't. Can't be part of this. I can't just be a bystander. For God's sake," she screamed, "STOP!" When Jaxon didn't, she lunged from the stool, her hands cuffed behind her back.

Jaxon sidestepped the clumsy attack, losing control of the crucible. Liquid gold splashed Sigalie's crown. Her skin boiled as the metal slid down her face. Super-heated steam flooded her nostrils. That's when her yelping ceased and her shoulders slumped. She collapsed, hair and clothes afire. As the gold continued to cool, an agonal gurgle parted Sigalie's lips.

"Oops." Jaxon sucked a breath between his teeth. "That wasn't the plan." He used his shirt to put out the flames, checked Sigalie's pulse, and listened for signs of breathing. Her skin sizzled. It gave off a sick metallic smell as if someone had forgotten the oven was on and melted the roasting pan holding the pork-shoulder dinner.

"Oh, well," Jaxon said. "One less loose end."

Bri fainted and fell backward, the lab stool still strapped to her legs. Her head bounced on the concrete. Her silky chestnut locks turned blackish red, matting with the blood on the floor.

My mouth filled with stomach acid. I choked it down. Felt the gastric juice burn as it sluiced through my esophagus.

"This was not my fault," Jaxon said. "You all saw that. We expect the interviewee to complicate the interrogation process. As professionals, we count on it. All Sigalie had to do was follow my lead. Instead, she converts information gathering into a lethal exercise. Such a tragedy. If only—" Jaxon closed his eyes and took a deep breath. "If…if…what I'm trying to say is, it didn't have to end this way. Now I'll have to get the information another way. This makes my job so much tougher."

With that, Jaxon tossed another cube of gold into a second crucible and loaded up the furnace. "We'll begin shortly."

Jaxon ran a hand through his crew cut, grabbed the back of his neck, and massaged it. The hairs on the top of his head were thick and stiff, springing back into place instantly. While his interrogation techniques might not be working to his satisfaction, his mega sculpting styling gel definitely was.

"I have to confess," Jaxon said, "my average this year sucks. Can you believe it? I'm now zero for three if you count the unfortunate accident earlier this week as a quasi-interrogation." Jaxon made the number '0' by pressing his thumb to his fingers. Then he switched to holding up his index, middle, and ring digits. "If my boss and I didn't have such a long history," he said, "I'd be *history*." He pun-chuckled at his play on words.

Hilarious.

"It's a good thing I don't get *any* satisfaction from my failures. That would be callous." Jaxon sent the second agent upstairs for a blanket to cover Sigalie's body.

From the stairwell, the agent called out, "Anything else?" He had a funny accent, maybe Eastern European, possibly Slavic.

"Water. Bring bottles for everyone."

The agent, if he really was Secret Service, conducted a headcount, making a tally in the air with his index finger. "Six I bring."

"Make it an even dozen," Jaxon called out.

"Each two?"

"Our guests may be thirsty." Jaxon turned to face us. "You see, I'm not a monster. I too have a well-tuned moral compass." With that, Jaxon launched into a soliloquy, passionate at times, about his approach to criminal justice, the greater good, and just about any philosophical argument popular on the Internet that justifies taking another's life.

Jaxon's discourse gave me time to continue working with the glass shard. The duct tape wrist restraints were now so weakened, I was able to snip the tape and wrap the glass, fashioning it into a shiv.

I was ready.

I swallowed hard, put on my best game face, and

recalled what Marissa had always said:

Control is possible if
you manage your breathing.
The secret:
A dancing diaphragm—full, fluid, rhythmic.

I took the deepest breath of my life, relaxed, and got ready to pounce when Jaxon said, "Shall we keep going?"

My body tensed. My legs cramped. I lost my nerve. *My timing's off.*

And there was something else, a niggling at the back of my mind.

Jaxon stepped over to the furnace. Instead of using the peephole to check the contents as he did before, this time he made a show of lifting the vertical door to reveal his fresh pot of gold.

His theatrics failed.

Although the second crucible was red as a fireplace poker, the new cube hadn't completely melted. The pyrometer display on the controller read 2,100 degrees. The furnace was more than hot enough to liquefy gold. But this chunk of the bullion bar had been considerably bigger than the previous cube.

"Well," Jaxon said, "it looks like we have more time to get to know each other." He let the door drop to seal off the furnace. I could feel the heat dissipate slowly.

The niggling in my brain returned. There was something Jaxon had said earlier, a phrase, that kept replaying in my ears. His language, his choice of words made me think about my original plan. It was simple.

Direct. Flush out Rafi's killer by going for the gold.

Securing the two suspect bars from the New York Fed had, in fact, given us a solid lead: Agent Jaxon Casama. But…and this was an intractable *but*…I had no way of knowing if Jaxon's surprise visit to the lab was proof he was involved in Rafi's death somehow…or if Jaxon's SWAT-style attack on the lab was a sanctioned Treasury op in cooperation with the Secret Service to seize the bullion bars as evidence of possible counterfeiting.

For what seemed like forever, I couldn't decide which.

I went with my gut.

"Jaxon," I said, "the night Rafi Silva was electrocuted, was that your first botched interrogation?" I was lathering on the confidence, pretending to know for sure. "You said you were zero for three."

"Is Mr. Silva the guy you replaced on the audit?"

Jaxon wasn't expecting me to answer. He was faking ignorance, being purposely evasive. The Treasury Secretary was responsible for the clandestine audit. She had requested it in the first place and was closely monitoring its progress. Jaxon was Beck's security detail. He knew I had taken Rafi's position on Gold II.

Before I had time to respond, Bri had come to and hijacked my Q&A with Jaxon. "Agent Casama," she said, pushing herself up from the lab floor clumsily, "I have a few questions myself I'd like answered."

"Sit down, Ms. de la Guerra."

Bri blew the hair from her eyes. On the lab floor where she hit her head, there was little blood. She wasn't behaving concussed and likely had suffered only a nasty bump. Now she was face-to-face with Jaxon, the stool still strapped to her legs, but not as tightly as before the fall. There was some wiggle room in the ankle taping. Enough for her to stand awkwardly, even with her wrists bound behind her.

"How is it a digital wallet guy like my Rafi, who never carries cash and uses his Amex card to pay for everything, is found with twenty-five hundred dollars in his billfold, all the banknotes having his fingerprints—right hand only—with no attention to the order of the bills, fifties mixed with hundreds, some facing forward, others reversed? CPAs are nothing if not anal-retentive when it comes to detail. If Rafi *ever* did have cash, all the bills would be tidy. Efficient. A wallet organized like a cash drawer at a bank—every bill in its place."

"I told you to sit down."

Bri shook her head. "He never carries cash. And bills in disarray? That's not my Rafi."

Jaxon nudged Bri with his forearm. She geisha-walked backward, straining against the weakened duct tape, working the play between her ankles and the legs of the shop stool. She came to a stop next to me and sat down hard and loud. Hard enough to rip the tape some. And loud enough, with the banging of the stool legs on the concrete, to cover any sound the torn tape made. Clever maneuver. Except for snapping her stiletto pump in the process. Bri spat at Jaxon as she kicked the five-inch heel of her broken shoe his way.

Jaxon snorted. "'Your Rafi,' as you so dearly refer to him, was a greedy little pissant."

Bri scrambled back to her feet. She locked in on Jaxon, her eyes like flint. Her nostrils flared, then she charged him in a wobbly hop, duct tape shredding as she drew closer. She bent at her waist, lowered her head, and then rammed Jaxon in the solar plexus.

There was a loud "oof" as Jaxon's lungs emptied. He fell backward, landing hard on the concrete. Bri landed face down, sprawled across his chest crosswise, her knees and hips at a right angle to Jaxon's torso.

Jaxon tried to push her off to take in a breath, but Bri just stayed right where she was. She used her knee closest to Jaxon's hip to drub his kidney. Nonstop. Each knee strike fiercer than the last. He opened his mouth and tried to speak but couldn't. He gasped, one, two, three times before regaining his breath and then balled his fist, and hook-punched Bri's right breast, like a jackhammer. Over and over.

Bri shrieked, rolling off Jaxon to protect herself. She repositioned until she was face up, her body perpendicular to his, her feet within inches of his head. She lifted her leg and dropped her heel on his throat. He started coughing non-stop.

Now.

I finished wiggling from the wrist wraps, brought both arms in front of me, and rolled my shoulders to get them moving again. In my right hand was the makeshift shiv. I sliced through the ankle restraints. Then, I grabbed Jaxon's Sig Sauer from the workbench, tapped the magazine, and racked the slide. While I pointed the gun at him, I quickly cut Bri's wrists loose.

We had to hurry. The second agent would be back any minute.

Just as Jaxon was about to regain his breath, I gun-butted him to the temple. He slumped to the concrete. Bri found the duct tape and started wrapping his wrists, ankles, and mouth.

She almost finished.

The second agent grabbed Bri from behind and put her in a chokehold. He pulled his firearm with his right and pointed it at me. "Drop weapon."

Bri thrashed, but every time she did, the agent tightened his grip. She started to droop. The agent relaxed pressure on her windpipe and yanked Bri upright, making sure her body shielded his.

I leveled the Sig Sauer at the agent's head. "I have a better idea. Let's talk."

"Put gun down. Then we talk."

Bri's face went pasty white, body slack. She slid from his chokehold to her knees and spewed, covering the agent's black lug-soled dress shoes with purple-gray hoark. The agent's upper body was now fully exposed.

I fired.

Two shots to the chest.

The first went wide, ricocheting off the workbench. The second grazed his arm. I hadn't held a gun in years and was seriously out of practice.

The agent checked his forearm and spit twice. Then he brought his pistol to level and was about to aim when I fired again.

Two more shots.

The next slammed into his gut.

He doubled over with a strangled howl. As he did, the final round took out his left knee. He collapsed sideways, thwacking his head. His firearm jangled as it hit the cement.

I kicked his weapon away, grabbed the worktable, steadied myself, and surveyed the lab. Some blood had pooled where the agent landed, but not a flood. His chest was still moving. But not the rest of his body.

Concussion maybe.

Bri was just inches from where she had thrown up. I thought she was unconscious until I saw her eyelids flutter. She stretched her arms and wiggled her feet in little circles. Her eyes were fully dilated. Her speech was slurred. "Dizzy," she drawled.

I helped her over to the workbench and got her into a sitting position leaning against one of the wall-to-wall tables. She started to catch her breath when Agent Jaxon Casama stirred. Apparently, the pistol-whipping I had given him earlier had worn off.

Jaxon extended his bound wrists so that he could touch his duct-taped ankles, and using his fingers, he fumbled awkwardly with the unrippable cloth-backed tape. He was muttering something to me, but with his mouth taped closed, it was hard to make out what. It didn't sound like words of praise.

Ordinarily, I won't kick a man when he's down, but for Jaxon, I made an exception.

Jaxon doubled over to protect himself, drew into a fetal position, rump extended, and vulnerable. *Perfect target.* I cocked my leg and kicked his ass.

Jaxon's extreme interrogation had killed Rafi. And for what? For a little information about funky audit outcomes on Gold II. I had to make things right, even if it meant conjuring street justice for my best friend.

Before I knew it, I had tapped into dark energy from unexplored reaches within, toxicity that possessed my quads and my calves, and found myself jackbooting Jaxon, inflicting jurisprudence to within a stomp of his life when I had an epiphany.

There weren't just two data points in Jaxon's record of interrogation fails but three. I could see a pattern now—an ugly, grisly shape—in what happened in the lab today, and what had happened at the extended-stay hotel with Rafi, and…

Jaxon had killed Marissa.

I hung my head and sobbed. Couldn't stop. My chest heaved. Bri put her arms around me and held me tight—a comfort move I didn't find comforting, so I broke from her embrace, fell to my knees next to Jaxon, and raised my fists. I hammered his face with the fleshy ridge of my palms, striking the bridge of his nose until it melted, and blood squirted from his nostrils. This I found comforting.

Bri nudged me with her head and tried to push me away from Jaxon. She was crying, running all her words together.

"You'regoingtokill'imThadisthatwhatyouwant?"

Other than the comfort of taking action—any grief-relieving action—I didn't know what I wanted.

Then suddenly Jorma joined Bri, using her shoulder to push me away. "He's not worth life in prison. Because if you don't stop…"

I couldn't stop.

I kept pounding with the bottom of my fists, drumming Jaxon's face. Right, left, right, left, then right again, until Bri jabbed me in the calf with the only spiky heel she had left. When I didn't stop, Bri jabbed my other calf, full warrioress. She drew blood. It hurt like hell.

It took five minutes to stop quivering. And another five to finally sit up. My shoulders sagged.

"The *quasi-interrogation?*" I said. "Jaxon was referring to my wife. The *unfortunate accident*? That was Marissa tripping and hemorrhaging out."

Bri sat next to me. "Thad, I'm so sorry. I wish to God I could take this hurt from you, but I can't...because..." There was a catch in Bri's voice. She choked on a sob.

Because you're still raw from losing Rafi.

That I could understand now. Bri's shuddering gasps made me ashamed of the meager empathy I had shown her after the love of her life was taken. I felt a wave of remorse for not believing her earlier when she maintained Rafi would never commit the unpardonable. Tears washed my cheeks. Stress hormones flushed my nervous system, bringing me to the knees of vulnerability. I was immobilized—physically and emotionally spent.

Bri looked equally wasted. And then there was Jorma, traumatized before our eyes. I could only imagine how she was processing everything.

We needed a place to recuperate. And it wasn't the penthouse. Nor was it a lab littered with the dead and the nearly dead.

And we needed an exit plan.

Agent Jaxon Casama wasn't looking too good. I bent over him and ripped the duct tape from his lips. He coughed, drooling blood. The tip of his nose was sitting on his cheek, like someone had nailed it there, flat. He was still breathing, short and shallow. Every ten seconds, he licked his lips. Parched white sputum collected at the corners of his mouth. He opened his eyes.

"Tell me where you parked." I fumbled around in Jaxon's right front pocket, searching for his keys. "Make, model, and color."

Jaxon tried to spit at me but couldn't. His tongue

was thick, covered with stringy saliva and drying blood that had drained from his nose. He coughed.

"You're dry," I said. "I'll get you some water." I gripped Jaxon's feet and dragged him to the emergency shower, pulled the activation chain, and let the water run. The caked blood on his face cracked and thinned into a watery paste and then drained into his mouth. He sputtered. "You trying to drown me?"

I supposed I could have tied the triangle handle from the pull chain to the shower pipe so the water would never stop and let his nostrils fill until he aspirated and choked to death, but I was looking for answers.

After fifteen minutes of impromptu interrogation using the emergency shower, Jaxon broke.

Black Chevy Tahoe SSV.

Parked out front in a red zone.

Chapter 39

"Grab the cuffs from the other agent," I said.

"Both sets?" Bri unsnapped the leather handcuff pouch on the downed man's duty belt.

"Yeah, let's not take chances."

She retrieved the remaining pair of hinged restraints and together we cuffed Agent Jaxon Casama, hands behind him, to one of the metal legs of the wall-to-wall workbench. We then cuffed his feet. He wasn't going anywhere soon.

"Good time for a photo. Might come in handy." Bri composed a selfie with the three of us and thumbed the iPhone shutter. Jaxon didn't smile.

"Let's get gone." I undid Jorma's handcuffs, used them to secure Jaxon's sidekick, and then tiptoed over the glass and debris to make my way to the furnace.

"You have a plan?" Bri asked.

"I do. You're going to love it. And do me a favor. Send me the pic you just took."

I toggled the furnace power switch off. The status light dimmed. The controller display disappeared. When I raised the furnace door, it confirmed what Jorma had speculated earlier. The fake gold ingot did, indeed, have a tungsten core.

The crucible glowed red-orange. The stick in the center hadn't melted. The tungsten blank was a funny yellow-white color, sprinkled with a tinge of incandescence. It looked like a couple of fused bars of cheap margarine.

"Higher melting point, huh?" Bri said.

"Oh yeah. Almost sixty-two hundred degrees Fahrenheit." I reached for the tongs, wrapped them around the middle of the crucible, and carried the super-heated carbon bowl over to the emergency shower. I pulled the chain.

As the steam rose, the crucible crusted. It turned a volcanic gray. While the shower spray doused the glowing blank, the tungsten sizzled. The bar dimmed gradually from white-hot to a burbling yellow, then more quickly from orange to red. Eventually, the core of the faux bullion achieved a dull gunmetal color.

I set the crucible down on the workbench, used the tongs to remove the tungsten bar, and set it aside to finish cooling. The shiny gold cladding was still stuck to the bottom of the crucible. I flipped the carbon bowl over and tapped it.

The cup-shaped casting slid out, clinking when it hit the table. If Jorma was right, this was 24-karat gold. For the cladding of the counterfeit bars to pass the chip assay test, it had to be.

I gathered up the gold and the tungsten blank and whatever was left of the two bullion bars and put everything in the aluminum case, rearranging the foam inserts. Then, I thumbed the lock. Briefcase in hand, I took a step toward the stairs. The case was considerably lighter this time.

"What about Sigalie?" Bri asked. "And Jaxon and his sidekick? Those two are going to need medical attention."

"We can sort that out later. And we can't stay

347

here."

Loud "ahem" from Jorma, then a fake cough to get our attention. "Nor can I, Thad. This plan that Bri is supposedly going to love, does it include a role for me?"

"And then some," I said. "You do what we ask and I'll give you that exclusive you wanted for your blog."

"Let's hear the 'ask'," Jorma said.

"It involves access to your dark resources."

"You want me to cyber snoop?" Jorma's eyes twinkled. "I wondered when the fun was going to begin."

Jorma agreed to deep dig into Secretary Kennedy Beck, Agent Jaxon Casama, and my immediate supervisor, Tigran Vardanyan. She was tasked to unearth any linkages and if she found anything, she was to ping me pronto with the results. Once I heard back, I promised that within the hour I'd text a meetup address.

"I need to get cleaned up and grab my MacBook before we go," Jorma said.

"*We* go?" I echoed.

"You're taking me with you, aren't you?"

That wasn't the plan. At least not for our first three stops. "You need Wi-Fi, right? For the research?"

"I don't have a high-speed cellular data card, if that's what you're asking."

"We'll find you an Internet café close to where we're going to rendezvous."

"With espresso? And a breakfast sandwich?"

"Whatever you want."

"Egg, corned beef, and Swiss on a sesame potato bun. Extra-lean on the corned beef."

I gave Jorma two thumbs-up. She headed up the

penthouse stairs and stopped halfway. "Bri," she said, "just a thought. If I brought back medium flip-flops, would you wear them? My mom wears a medium."

Bri looked at her feet. She had on one good stiletto, the other had a busted heel. I had never seen her in flip-flops before—she was more into designer slides. "This one time?" Bri said. "I can make that work." She kicked off her shoes and dropped them in the lab rubbish bin, replacing the metal lid. "Thanks."

"Jorma, any chance your dad is close to my size?" I asked. There was no way my plan was going to work with me stinking as I did.

"I'll bring pants, a belt, and a sports coat. Oh yeah—and some tighty-whities." With that, Jorma disappeared up the stairs, taking them two steps at a time.

Bri scanned the lab and said, "Are we done down here?"

Jaxon's color was good, but he wasn't moving. His breathing was labored. Broken ribs will do that. I checked his cuffs. Tight. Secure. "Yeah. Done."

I lugged the briefcase over to the stairwell. Bri joined me at the bottom.

While I followed her up the stairs, she cranked her neck to the left and spoke over her shoulder. "I haven't heard your plan," she said. "Other than that improv you did just now to get Jorma out of the way, redeploying her to do deep background."

We reached the penthouse level landing and settled onto the stools at the juice bar.

"Let's recap the knowns and known unknowns." I opened the briefcase, retrieved my mechanical pencil, and removed the copy of the spreadsheet with the serial numbers of the suspect gold bars. I flipped over the paper and scratched out some column headings on the back. We brainstormed.

WHAT WE NOW KNOW

—The New York Federal Reserve Bank is safeguarding fake bullion. The evidence? Two serial numbers from U.S. Compartment A and two serial numbers from a recent foreign shipment. At least one gold bar is salted with a tungsten slug. We have proof.

—Agent Jaxon Casama failed to find Rafi's secret spreadsheets. Rafael Silva, my wife Marissa, Cruz, and Sigalie were collateral damage in the wake of his failed search.

WHAT WE STILL DON'T KNOW

—Was Jaxon working at the direction of Treasury Secretary Beck or did he go off script? Until we surrender the phony bullion and Rafi's data analysis to the authorities, who else will be hunting us?

—What does my senior manager, Tigran Vardanyan, have to do with all of this? And what about the peculiar photos of him I lifted from his office? What are they all about?

By the time I had finished with the fourth key point, it was no secret where we needed to go next. We just had to get Jorma set up in an all-night coffee house with a fat pipe to do her research, then pick up sweet incentives for our first meetup.

I felt a tap on my shoulder, jumped, and almost stabbed myself with the mechanical pencil. I pivoted.

Jorma had scrubbed her face, tidied her curly bob, and changed her outfit. Tucked under her arm were clothes for me and a blood orange leather tech carryall. "Sorry," she said. "I didn't mean to startle you."

"We're all a little jumpy." Bri pulled out a pocket compact and, using wet wipes, smudged away the caked blood in her hairline where she'd hit her head. "A breakfast sandwich could take the edge off. I think I know an upscale place with a twenty-four-hour menu. When Rafi was stuck in DC for the weekend, he'd hang out there for brunch."

We took Jaxon's ride—the black special services vehicle—to a bakery in Foggy Bottom. For her breakfast sandwich, Jorma had to forgo the corned beef for brisket instead. We got her settled in a corner booth and grabbed a quick bite ourselves while Jorma re-caffeinated with a double espresso.

"You ready?" Bri wiped deli mustard from the corner of her mouth.

"Almost." I motioned for Bri to follow me to the pastry case at the front of the café.

For a bodybuilder, Tigran Vardanyan had only one weakness–muffins. I wasn't sure what his favorite was. So, I picked one of each—honey bran oatmeal, blueberry, double chocolate chip, low-fat cranberry, and almond poppy seed. And just in case, his muffin palate had developed a craving for old-fashioned cake donuts while living in DC so close to so much financial history, I ordered both plain buttermilk *and* chocolate French crullers. Tigran was our passport to our last and final stop before dawn. We needed every possible incentive.

Bri grabbed three bottles of OJ while I grabbed a barista box of joe. It was 2:30 in the morning when we knocked on my senior manager's door, bait in hand.

Chapter 40

Tigran didn't open the hotel room door the first time I knocked.

I ignored the elegant DO NOT DISTURB sign hanging on his doorknob and knocked louder.

This time I could hear him bumble around and then stumble to the door. When he flipped on the hotel room light, the peephole for suite 1109 lit, but within seconds went dark. Tigran had to be standing directly in front of the peephole, obscuring the glow. There was no doubt he was looking out at us.

I gave Tigran my winning smile, the one I save for job interviews and annual performance reviews. Bri batted her eyelashes.

"I'm calling the cops," Tigran said.

I showed him the muffin box. I opened the lid, picked the one in the middle, and tore it in half. As the steam rose, I took a big whiff and ended up smearing blueberries on my face. Then I rubbed my belly, opened my mouth wide, and inhaled the whole half.

Tigran opened the door about three inches, just enough for the U-bar security lock to engage. I stuck my hand through the crack and gave him the other half muffin. "Tigran, may we come in?"

My senior manager stuck his hand out the door and said, "Another. A whole one this time."

I let him reach into the box and forage with his

fingertips until he found a muffin he liked. He picked the double chocolate chip, took a bite, and licked his lips.

While nibbling the top of the chocolate-chip muffin, Tigran stopped long enough to say, "Have you seen the news, Hanlon? There's a BOLO out or APB or whatever they call it. I can't afford to be an 'accessory after the fact.' I've got too much invested in my career. Make sense?"

Bri drew her phone from her hip pocket and did an online search on Thaddeus Hanlon. Sure enough, every mainstream broadcaster had a video clip of us leaving the New York Federal Reserve Bank in an armored limo. That was followed with a quick cut to the East River heliport and me dragging an aluminum business carry-on behind me as we boarded an unmarked bird.

Being the face of a nationwide manhunt somehow brings clarity. I said, "I need your help, Tigran. This is your mentee begging his mentor."

"What kind of help?" Tigran stuck his hand out for another muffin. I turned the carryout box sideways and held it up to the opening to let his fingers forage.

"I need you to set up a meeting with TSec," I said. "Do me a favor. Look out the peephole."

I raised the ZERO Haliburton, unlatched the briefcase, and showed him the contents.

"You're making a mistake, Hanlon. Making unnecessary waves."

Bri pushed me out of the way, looked straight into the peephole, and said, "I need to tinkle. Open the damn door."

Tigran complied, unlatched the U-bolt, and let Bri into his hotel room. Before he could shut the door behind her, I muscled past him. Bri headed for the water closet. I pulled out Jaxon's service pistol and pointed it at Tigran's chest.

"About that meeting with Secretary Beck," I said. "I'm hoping you'll reconsider."

My senior manager couldn't take his eye off the all-black Sig Sauer in my hand.

"Sit," I said, motioning for Tigran to find a place on the studio-sized sofa adjoining the mini-desk. He was dressed for bed in an off-white long-sleeve Henley sleep shirt. It reminded me of Ebenezer Scrooge and the night the ghost of his business partner, Jacob Marley, appears.

As Tigran sat, I unplugged the landline running to the hotel telephone. On the nightstand were his wallet, rental car keys, and mobile phone. I confiscated my senior manager's cell and keys. We settled in for a chat.

"I can make some calls," Tigran said. "If you give me the phone back, I'll arrange a discreet meeting, just the four of us." He had chocolate chips smeared on his cheek. Tigran held out his hand for the phone. "Hanlon, how about we schedule this first thing Monday? I can set up the discreet meeting for then."

"Nah." I stuck his cell in my pocket. "How about first thing today? Better yet," —I held up the keyring to his rental— "how about now? Throw on some shoes."

"She is *not* going to be happy," Tigran said. "I can tell you this. She's a morning person. *Not* pre-dawn. And definitely not weekends? Weekends are sacred. They're off-limits...except for...except for an occasional appearance on a Sunday Morning News show."

The three of us appearing with Secretary Kennedy

Beck on *Face the Nation* while three million viewers watch a spot news story about fake gold at the Fed? That could be interesting. But probably not the kind of discreet meeting Tigran had in mind.

And not my style.

From the briefcase, I pulled the manila folder with the 8x10s that I swiped from Tigran the day before. I undid the clasp and withdrew the photos. One by one, I laid the purloined pictures down on the dinky cocktail table across from the sofa where Tigran was sitting.

"Care to explain?" I asked.

Tigran played with the ribbing of his sleep-shirt collar, rubbing the fabric back and forth between his thumb and forefinger. His tongue kept peeking out from between his lips while he concentrated. I figured he was running through every worst-case scenario, examining his options. He finally spoke. "Who have you shown these to?"

"I was saving them," I said.

"Saving what?" Bri emerged from the bathroom. She sat next to me. "Oh," she said, "saving those. This should be good." She picked up one of the glossies from the table.

Most of the shots were make-over photos with a before and after image. Each picture was split frame, with side-by-side headshots of Tigran. I could have sworn they were studio portraits with an identical twin if he had one. Or of a clone. *Weird.*

The last two pics in the bunch were action shots. The first was Tigran entering the official CPA exam test site. Across the bottom was stenciled a date and timestamp. The second photo was Tigran in a reunion shot in TSec's office with Secretary Beck and her son,

Fitz. This picture was also date and timestamped.

Doubly weird.

The date and timestamps of the two action photos matched. Same exact day, same exact hour, same exact minute.

"Tigran, how were you in two places at once?" I picked up the side-by-side headshots and took a closer look.

Tigran lowered his eyelids. "What if I told you—" He stopped short, looked at me, then at Bri.

"It's not you, is it?" I said. "The guy in the second mug shot barely has any eyelashes."

Bri took the photos from me. She compared Tigran's face to the close-up photo. "I'd kill for lashes like yours," she said. "Who's the doppelgänger?"

Tigran's cheeks turned shame red. "You want the whole story?"

"Everything," I said.

"But talk fast," Bri said. "Maybe double speed. We have a BOLO on us, after all."

So, Tigran ran through the details—how Beck offered to help with his "License in Hand" problem. How she'd ensure he finally passed all four sections of the CPA exam so he could meet state requirements and receive his official license to practice as a Certified Public Accountant and, at last, be eligible for partner at Dodge Whitney.

It was a clever plan, even if completely unethical. Secretary Beck had hired a professional test taker, a surrogate, to sit for the exam in Tigran's place. She called in favors from her friends who do *Mission Impossible* kind of things with latex masks and silicone fingerprints.

Testing center security at the authorized CPA exam site was no match for the scam. Tigran's surrogate waltzed through the facial recognition system and finger biometrics. On the exam itself, the hired gun scored a respectable 87%, well above the 75% required to pass AUD, but not so high as to raise suspicion.

I said, "And you want me to believe that Beck did all this because you and her son were grad-school buds and the three of you were like 'family'? Is that right?"

"It's not like I hadn't passed the audit portion of the CPA exam before," Tigran said. "The rolling eighteen-month window—it's absolutely unjust." Tigran was jumping onto his soapbox.

I wasn't about to get into a philosophical discussion over the morality of the National Association of State Boards of Accountancy limiting test score shelf-life to a year and a half. Although it was true Tigran had passed all four parts of the uniform CPA exam, he just hadn't done it within NASBA's allowed eighteen-months timetable. That meant his scores had expired and he was required to re-take the lapsed sections.

"Tigran, let's continue this in the car." I held up his car keys.

"We're switching vehicles?" Bri asked.

"I think we need to."

"Then, I'm driving." Bri swiped the key fob from me. She headed for the hotel room door.

That left me to ensure Tigran didn't balk, or try to run. He was still our passport to the Treasury Secretary.

I let the Sig Sauer do the persuading. I trained the muzzle on Tigran while he grabbed his moccasin slippers and a pair of denim jeans. He dressed in the elevator. I handed the gun to Bri to guard him. That gave me just enough time to text Jorma the Treasury Secretary's home address before the elevator doors opened to the underground parking. Jorma responded by texting the results of her cyberspying—dark arts shedding light on TSec from an Internet that never forgets a connection.

At three in the morning, Embassy Row had zero traffic. Bri gunned Tigran's rental, straining the engine. At this pace, we'd be at TSec's in less than ten minutes.

"For the assist with nailing the exam," I asked Tigran, "what did Beck expect in return?" My senior manager was sitting in the back seat with me where I could keep an eye and a gun on him. I had to twist sideways to get enough legroom.

"You mean the *quid pro quo*?" he said. "Hanlon, that's where you come in."

"Oh? How?"

"Simple. Gold II was supposed to be a seagull job—swoop in, collect the data, and swoop out. Do enough number-crunching off-site to verify what everyone in the Treasury already knew. Then issue a clean audit opinion confirming everything."

"You guaranteed an unqualified audit?" I said. "That was your *quo* for her *quid*? You promised Beck that Dodge Whitney CPAs would sign off on the U.S. gold inventory as being all rainbows and unicorns?"

"I wouldn't characterize it quite like that," Tigran said.

"And my role? Where did I come in?"

"Hanlon, we needed someone like you with precious metals cred, with your auditing background at Sunstake, and…"

Bri tapped the brakes. "Did I miss it?" she said. "The turn?"

"Make a U-turn at the Islamic Center," Tigran said. "Then double back to Belmont Road and take a left. If you pass the Belize Embassy, you've gone too far."

Bri spun the car and squealed down Belmont.

"Tigran, what else? Mining, metals…and what?" I needled Tigran to finish his explanation for why I had been chosen to staff Gold II.

"You're a Kolbe Fact Finder personality type." Tigran paused to let that sink in. Like the other big international accounting firms, Dodge Whitney was into personality tests for facilitating team communication across types. Managers knew everybody's profile.

"And so, as a fact finder," he continued, "you tend to gather information before taking action. You research everything. So much so, you get bogged down in the details and never quite see the big picture." Tigran took a deep breath and said, "Hanlon, please don't take this the wrong way, but Beck and I wanted someone who would get lost in the weeds, someone who would miss the proverbial forest for the trees. Your personality fit the bill."

Hand-picked by the client! What else had Secretary Beck orchestrated?

"But Rafi was assigned to the Gold II audit first, not me. If I was your first choice, what happened?"

"Managing partner's prerogative. Donnell Warnick intervened, not that I didn't argue against it. He was so sure you wouldn't take the assignment unless Marissa could go with you and…"

"He's cheap," I said.

"Frugal. Mr. Bottom Line would never cover anywhere close to a hundred percent of Marissa's travel costs, and I didn't have any way to squeeze it out of the Gold II audit budget. I had to staff the job with Rafi instead. And he screwed everything."

"Thad, we're here." Bri parked a few houses down from Secretary Beck's address behind Jorma's car. The investigative reporter had beat us there.

Bri shut off the subcompact, popped open the little car door, and said, "You sure this is going to work?"

I said, "One way or another."

With that, I marched Tigran to the foot of the double-curved staircase leading to the front porch of Secretary Beck's mini-mansion. The brushed aluminum briefcase was in my left hand, the pistol in my right.

Chapter 41

The motion detectors worked.

As soon as Tigran put his foot down on the northmost steps of the circular staircase, the vintage pendant light flicked on. The raised porch to Secretary Beck's red-brick Beaux-Arts home illuminated.

I was right behind Tigran, the muzzle of the Sig Sauer P229 pressed to his spine. Bri and Jorma ascended from the southmost steps using the wrought iron rails.

We huddled in the middle of the porch under the gabled-roof pediment framed by the oversized front door. Affixed to the engaged pilaster was a video doorbell. Tigran pushed the button. The doorbell wall plate lit up and after a short lag, Westminster chimes rang.

Tigran stared into the camera and said, "Madam Secretary, we need to talk."

Thirty seconds went by. That should have been time enough for TSec to activate her smartphone and engage the one-way video intercom ID. There was no response from the doorbell speaker.

Tigran rang the chimes again.

"It's three in the morning," Beck said. "This better be good, Tigran." She cleared her throat and dislodged some mucous.

"It's about the audit, ma'am," Tigran said. "We

have a problem. The figures aren't adding up."

"Nonsense. We'll discuss this on Monday."

"I'm afraid it can't wait." Tigran stepped to the side so that TSec could see the entire delegation.

I smiled and waved Jaxon's gun. "We have some news about your security detail. Disturbing news." Then, I showed her the selfie Bri had taken of the three of us in the lab where Jaxon wasn't up to smiling.

The arched fanlight above the door lit up. The front windows began to shimmer. We heard the deadbolt unlock.

Secretary Beck opened the front door and ushered us into the vestibule. "I'll take your weapon, Thaddeus." She was pointing an identical Sig Sauer P229 at my head.

Some women command presence even in a muted floral sleep robe, hair tousled, face sans makeup. For a millisecond, I considered ignoring Beck's request to disarm, but there was no way I could get a shot off before she pulled her trigger. Instead, I complied.

I stepped out from behind Tigran, discharged the clip, and handed over Jaxon's gun and ammo. Beck chamber-checked the service pistol, verifying it was unloaded. She thumbed the rounds from the magazine until it was empty.

"Let's put these toys away." TSec shoved her gun and the one she had taken from me into the middle drawer of the antique secretary desk just inside the entryway to her home. "Now we can talk."

Beck led us down a hardwood floor hallway to a set of doors on the right. With diplomatic grace, the Treasury Secretary swung back the French doors to her study, careful not to rattle the antique glass panes. She gestured for us to take a seat. "Please."

Tigran, Bri, and Jorma did as they were bid. They walked in, settling into side chairs and the settee near the desk.

I just stood there at the entrance, briefcase in hand.

Secretary Beck turned to me and said, "You noticed?"

How could I not? Her study was an exact duplicate of her office in the Treasury Building, Suite 3330, complete with replicas of her 1920s-style walnut double-kneehole desk with identical drawers on the front and back, the brass bankers dual-bulb desk lamp, and her modern ergonomic executive chair.

A reproduction of the portrait of Alexander Hamilton by Caroline Ransom hung over the fireplace in a colonial revival frame. In the corner were three draped flags, identical to the ones in her office—the American Stars and Stripes, the mint-leaf green ensign of the Department of Treasury, and the flag of rank for her cabinet position—a swath of old glory blue, fringed in gold, with thirteen crested stars circling crossed anchors. In the center of the anchors was a white shield, emblazoned with blue measurement scales and the Key to the Treasury.

Heady stuff.

"Helps me focus," Secretary Beck said.

"I bet," I said, *sotto voce*. But not nearly as hushed as I imagined.

TSec ignored my whispered sarcasm. "My high-performance coach suggested 'outcome visualization,'" she said. "She encouraged me to imagine having achieved my goals. But the mental exercise of imagining didn't work for me. I found I needed something palpable. So, when I moved to DC to take a position with the Treasury Department, I decorated this study exactly how I wanted my office to look, every last emblem."

Beck then went all Napoleon Hill on me, reciting the Law of Attraction from *Think and Grow Rich*. She counseled me, "Act as if you have already achieved what you want."

What I want, Madam Secretary, is to know why.

Why my pregnant wife?

Why my best friend?

Why the U.S. deep storage reserves aren't "good as gold"?

And what secret calculus spawned these "whys"?

Beck continued to prattle on about her journey to a cabinet position in the current administration with her appointment as Acting Secretary of Treasury, ensuring that I developed an appreciation for the challenges, reversals, and speed bumps women like her face along the way.

But I wasn't here for a feel-good moment. Truth was, I was more than tired. My hands were swollen from the drubbing I had given Jaxon. I pressed TSec, mentioned V*ersaChem,* and waited for her reaction. I studied her eyes, watching for tells that she recognized the mystery phrase.

Secretary Beck brought her hands together, thumbs-to-thumbs, fingers-to-fingers, and rested her elbows on the glass top protecting her walnut desk. She brought her prayer hands to her lips and tapped twice. "VersaChem? One word or two?"

No micro-twitches. No arched eyebrows. It was the same response I had gotten from Tigran Vardanyan just a half-hour ago and the same response Jorma had given us when Bri and I had met her for deep background on gold markets. It was even the same response Donnell Warnick gave when I asked him point-blank what secret assignment Rafi had been working on before I was ever assigned to Gold II.

I must have heard Rafi wrong on my way home that night. And I was getting no closer to making sense of Rafi's murder and Marissa's accidental death. I went for brazen. "The night Rafi died, the second to the last word he said was *plan*. Something about a way forward."

"That's what he called it?" TSec said. She interlaced her tiny fingers. "Your honored friend was not so honorable. His *plan*, a not-so-clever euphemism really, was to redistribute wealth. When Rafi reached out to me, he alluded to a whiff of jugglery in the U.S. Mint. He claimed to have evidence of financial legerdemain from the Treasury Department's Bureau of Fiscal Service."

Beck apparently had been taking lessons from the Federal Reserve Chairman in obfuscation. I had hoped for insight. Instead, she offered shrouded meanings cloaked in Fedspeak.

Everything pointed to Rafi having stumbled onto monetary magic. Mondo-scale. I was certain of it. But what I was not so certain of was what had transpired when he confronted Beck with his audit findings.

"Thaddeus, you claim you were good friends with Mr. Rafael Silva," Secretary Beck said. "Did you know he was in default?"

I ran the math in my head. Bri's parents owned the condo. She and Rafi paid token rent. Their matching

Model X Teslas were leased. That left, as the only defaultable debt, Rafi's—

Before I could finish, Bri challenged Beck. "I don't believe you," she told the Treasury Secretary. "Rafi would have said something."

The Treasury Secretary swiveled in her chair to face Bri. "So, you were aware your fiancé had borrowed the aggregate maximum—well over a hundred thousand dollars—to finance his undergraduate degree and his Master of Science in Accountancy."

"Well aware," Bri said. "We discussed every federal direct loan. He was up on his payments. Never late."

I did some more mental math. I ballparked the car lease, the monthly payment on the student loans, and his share of the rent. He was budget positive, but barely.

"Did your fiancé discuss his cards?" Beck asked.

When she heard "cards" plural, Bri's forehead scrunched.

"Rafi only had one card," she said. "He used Amex for everything. He paid it off every month."

"A single card?" Beck said. "Hmm. Let me see if I can explain it this way. Your fiancé's annual salary as a Senior Associate at Dodge Whitney was ninety-five thousand. This is a respectable sum, but insufficient for his lifestyle. My staff reviewed his financial records, all of them. What they found was Mr. Silva spent money like a Big Four accounting firm partner. He maxed out his Amex *and* every other credit card he owned."

I knew Rafi stressed over Bri's taste. Whenever we were out surfing, he'd worry out loud about their socio-economic compatibility and whether he'd be able to hang on to her and I'd reassure him of his long-term income potential as the brightest of rising stars. I knew he was smitten with Bri. But I never suspected he was financing his upscale ways to keep her in his life by using undisclosed plastic beyond his cash-back card. Even the best bean-counter has a hard time juggling multiple minimum monthly credit card payments, not to mention fending off school loan debt collectors.

A negative cash-flow spiral could explain why the night Rafi phoned, he so urgently asked for advice. Friend that I wasn't, I was too busy to listen. I cut the call short. If I had stayed on the line, I might have been able to talk Rafi out of his desperate plan. Beck's snarky comments earlier about Rafi wanting to "share the wealth" now made complete sense. His plan for debt-free living was coming into focus.

"Extortion?" I said. "Rafi was going to blackmail you to cover his debt?" I watched TSec's face to see if my suspicion was right.

No one said anything. Tigran shifted in the antique side chair he was sitting in while Bri closed her eyes, chin quivering. Secretary Beck offered Bri a tissue. Jorma played with her pen. She had stopped writing in her notebook. I just sat there ashamed over how clueless I had been about my best friend.

Bri stood, wadded the tissue, and threw it at Beck. "You didn't have to kill him," she said.

"That was never our intention, I assure you."

Bri rushed the Secretary's desk, sidestepping me, but before she could get her hands on TSec, Beck opened the top drawer of her desk and withdrew a Charter Arms .38 caliber Pink Lady revolver. TSec pointed the muzzle at Bri.

"Sit," Beck said. She waggled the gun. As Bri returned to her chair, the Secretary fumbled through the papers in the wooden organizer tray resting on the upper right corner of her desk.

"Your fiancé, Ms. de la Guerra, threatened me with…how shall I say, a 'dirty opinion.' With this."

Secretary Beck slid forward a mangled sheet of paper.

Chapter 42

The paper had obviously been crumpled into a ball and smoothed out later. Bri and I leaned forward to read it.

INDEPENDENT AUDITOR'S REPORT

Basis for Adverse Opinion

We were unable to obtain sufficient appropriate audit evidence supporting the physical counts and valuation of the inventory as recorded. Consequently, we were unable to determine whether any adjustments to these figures were necessary.

Adverse Opinion

In our opinion, because of the significance of the matter described in the Basis for Adverse Opinion paragraph above, the Schedule of Custodial Deep Storage Gold Reserves does not present fairly, in all material respects, the balance of the United States' gold bullion in the custody of the Mint, in accordance with U.S. generally accepted accounting principles.

A *dirty opinion*—auditor slang for an adverse outcome report to the client—is rare. Clients loathe them and would rather shop for another auditor than get one. In the world of public accounting, dirty opinions are the business shame equivalent of the *Scarlet Letter*—A for Adulterated Financials. Caveat emptor.

"May I?" I picked up the wrinkled paper and showed it to Tigran. The face of the document bore the firm's DRAFT—INTERNAL USE ONLY watermark and had been initialed and dated in the upper right corner by Rafi.

From the look on Tigran's face, he apparently had never seen the draft opinion letter. "This comes as a shock," he said. "I didn't know." He handed the paper back to Beck. "Rafi clearly went rogue. No other way to explain it."

"As you can see, most indelicate," Secretary Beck said. "I couldn't let it happen. I asked my staff to follow up."

"Agent Jaxon Casama?" Bri said.

"Yes. Jaxon, my security detail. He's very good at what he does. Trustworthy. He doubles as the office petty cash custodian."

With Jorma present and taking notes, Secretary Beck was being guarded, circumspect in everything she said. And with a stubby pink gun in her hand, she was controlling the pace of the conversation. But I wasn't willing to do this tango all night. Bri was smoldering, I could tell.

I whipped out the briefcase, flipped the latches, and eased the two half-bars from the foam inserts. I covered the tungsten slug and the cup-shaped gold casting so TSec couldn't see them.

"I hope you like science experiments," I said.

Beck trained her revolver on me, a crimson dot from her laser sight wiggling on the left breast pocket of my blazer. "No abrupt moves, Thaddeus."

I laid the two half-bars on Secretary Beck's desk, the cut-away edges facing me. From her perspective, the half-bricks would appear to be standard issue London Good Delivery bars, albeit sliced widthwise across the middle.

"Let's begin with serial number 163466. We'll run a couple of simple assay tests. That way, we can verify the purity stamping is legit."

And so, I performed a malleability test by digging my nails into the brick. I had the Secretary do the same. Then, I asked to borrow a magnet. TSec handed me her paper clip holder, a magnetic mini-statue of A. Hamilton covered with fasteners. I brushed off the clips dangling from the founding father's tri-foil hat and ran the magnetized statue over the bar. There was no attraction. Pure gold is non-ferrous.

I repeated the tests for serial number 163467.

"Hold out your hands," I said. "We're going to do a scale test. I'll place one bar in each palm. All you have to do is tell me if they have equal heft." I picked up the two half-bars to offer them to her.

TSec declined to hold out both hands. Instead, she offered only her left palm. "I'm not a moron, Thaddeus." With her right hand, she kept her gun leveled at my chest.

So much for tricking her into laying down her weapon.

"Okay, then. We'll do one bar at a time." I swapped the first half brick for the second. "Madame Secretary, based on the tests, what do you think?"

"You rousted me out of bed for this? There isn't a difference. None that I can feel. Both bars are equally soft. Neither sticks to a magnet. They weigh approximately the same."

"Listen carefully." I flicked bar number one. Nice ping. I flicked bar number two. No resonance. "Did you hear that false ring?"

I didn't give TSec a chance to respond. I flipped the end of bar number two around so she could see the cross-section.

Beck took it from my hand. She tried digging her nails into the center of the crosscut. When she busted her nail, she made her displeasure clear without any of the usually affected grace of her office. Then she said, "So this one has a non-gold slug." She handed back the fake gold bar.

"Gold-clad tungsten. We did a fire test." I pulled the cup-shaped gold casting and the primer-gray tungsten slug from the briefcase. "We used a furnace to separate the two. The gold liquified. It looked like melted butter. The tungsten, however, heated to a blinding white but never changed shape."

"That's your evidence? A single bullion bar?" Kennedy Beck wasn't impressed.

"Ooh, ooh," Jorma said, "let me say something. There's precedence for this kind of thing. In October 2009, China received a shipment of fake gold bullion. The serial numbers traced back to Ft. Knox. Five thousand, six hundred bars total. And then there's Rafael Silva's mysterious spreadsheet."

"I'm sorry. Who are you?" Secretary Beck now pointed her gun at the gold blogger.

"She's with me." I walked over to Jorma Sarudin and stood between her and Beck's Pink Lady. I was counting on TSec's willingness to hear me out before she pulled the trigger. Hoped I was right. I turned my head to the side and spoke over my shoulder, "Jorma, remember our agreement? I ask the questions. You take notes."

"Fly on the wall. Nothing more," Jorma said. "But

did I mention the one point four million four hundred-ounce tungsten slugs Sunstake Extractive Industries manufactured for a prior White House administration? Rumor has—"

I said, "Be the fly, Jorma."

"Sit down, Thaddeus." Secretary Beck wagged the revolver. "I want to hear more about this so-called mystery spreadsheet that Jorma mentioned. Move so I can see your friend."

I didn't budge except to say, "You mean this so-called spreadsheet?" I held up the USB flash drive with Rafi's hidden files on it. "Or would you prefer a hard copy?"

"I'll take that." Beck gave me a give-me gesture.

I tossed the drive at her. Beck blinked, giving me just enough time to jump across the desk to attempt a disarm.

There was a loud crack. Then my legs buckled. I bounced off Beck's desk and face planted on the wood floor, cracking my nose.

Instead of taking her gun, I had taken a bullet in the thigh. I lay prone for what seemed forever but was probably only seconds. If I tilted my head just right, I could see the bloodstain at the top of my dress pants blossom. The pain in my left thigh burned like a blistering-hot tungsten poker had shafted me. Worse yet, I realized I was still in Beck's line of sight. I had to move, had to take cover.

I worked my right leg until I was able to flop over on my back, then tucked into a front roll, and ended up doing a sloppy dive instead, crashing into the front of TSec's desk. I pulled myself up against the front-facing walnut drawers on the right side of the double-sided antique. Beck could no longer see me. For now.

But I could see her. At least her legs. Through the kneehole I watched her push away from the executive desk. She stood and said, "No sudden moves, Ms. de la Guerra." As Bri's chest heaved, the red laser from Beck's gun danced on her heart. She had crazy in her eyes.

I said, "Bri, don't—"

Bri ignored both of us. She dropped to a crouch and leaped. Full Superwoman pose with hate on her lips.

Beck fired her second round, grazing Bri's right arm, catching her mid-flight, and throwing off her trajectory. She landed in a belly flop on the Nantucket red and slate blue Persian area rug in front of Beck's desk.

Jorma freaked and went all "active shooter defense." She tossed her reporter's notebook, flung her purse, and then grabbed the oversized paperclip holder. She caught Beck just below the ribs.

TSec doubled over. She massaged her solar plexus until regaining her breath, then straightened and lit Jorma up with her laser sight. Beck was about to pull the trigger when Tigran body-tackled the blogger, shoving the investigative reporter beyond Beck's line of sight.

The Treasury Secretary's third shot caught Tigran with his head down, mid-charge. Blood spatter misted Jorma's lap. She cradled what was left of Tigran's face and attempted to stop the bleeding by applying pressure. The odds were not good. There was a funny look in her eyes. From her contorted lips, a throaty wail.

The Charter Arms .38 Pink Lady is a petite woman's handgun. It chambers only five rounds. Beck had two bullets left. Enough to finish off me and Bri.

Chapter 43

Maybe it was the 31-hour sprint to find Rafi's killer that had started Thursday night after leaving the NICU, or maybe the searing hole in my leg, or even maybe my inaugural daddyhood, but there was no way a bullet with my name on it would take me out before I had raised my son.

I made a deal.

If my namesake patron, St. Thaddeus Jude, Defender of Lost Causes, could work out an accord with God to let me parent Lil' Dude, I promised I'd do Marissa proud by teaching our son her truths.

Jorma was still cradling Tigran, applying pressure with fabric strips she tore from her blouse. Bri was sitting up now. She made eye contact with me. Using winks, eyebrow raises, and head feints, she tried to give me an idea where Beck was in relation to her desk. That just confused me. For all I knew, Beck could be standing on top of the antique with her gun pointed down at my crown.

But she wasn't. Beck surfaced to my left. She kicked my bloody leg where the bullet had entered. "Get up, Thaddeus."

I pressed my back against the desk for support, hitting my spine on the drawer handles. Sharp pain shot through my nerves. I powered through it to push off the floor with my hands, then wiggled myself up. When my left leg buckled, I was able to catch myself on the edge of the desk.

Beck tiptoed over Tigran to where Bri was sitting. She waved her pink revolver. "You, too, Ms. de la Guerra. Stand up!"

Bri wobbled to her feet and smoothed out her skirt. There was a half-dollar-sized stain on her blouse, just above her elbow, where Beck had nicked her.

"And you," Beck said, pointing to Jorma. "Up!"

Jorma must not have heard her. The online journalist was rocking back and forth, running her fingers through Tigran's thick brown hair, singing "Somewhere Over the Rainbow." Her raven curls dangled just above his deep black eyes, still open.

"He's dead, sugar." Beck bent over Tigran. She used her fingertips to close his eyelids. "Such lashes," she whispered. With reverence, the Treasury Secretary used her free hand to roll Tigran's head from Jorma's lap. With her right, she kept her revolver steady on Bri.

When Beck was done repositioning the senior manager's body, she retraced her steps to within a few feet of her desk. She searched the floor for something. When she didn't find what she was looking for, she studied the credenza behind her.

In the crevice between the back of the antique and the wall, TSec spotted the reporter's notebook. She dislodged it and flipped through what Jorma had written. She held the words at arm's length to read them and then slapped the cover closed. Beck slid the notebook into her bathrobe pocket. "Finders keepers."

My leg throbbed. On the floor under the desk, blood continued to pool. I was pretty certain the bullet had not hit the femoral artery, but I wasn't willing to risk bleeding out before I could get us out of here. I fumbled with my belt.

"What are you doing?" Beck painted my waist with her gun laser.

"Making a tourniquet." I looped the black leather around the top of my thigh and cinched the belt tight.

"We need medical attention," Bri said. "Please." It wasn't quite a pretty-please or a pretty-please-with-sugar-on-it-and-a-cherry-on-top, but for someone used to imperatives only, I sensed Bri had crossed over into unfamiliar territory. Her pleading was sincere. Whether enough to move the Treasury Secretary, I could only hope. Any future with my son depended on it. Jorma was still singing.

Beck stayed a safe distance from the three of us while she aimed her weapon, first at me and then at the other two. She sidestepped until she was behind her desk, picked up the handset from the multi-line telephone, and dialed. She put the call on speakerphone.

"Hello, 9-1-1, what is your emergency?" a female dispatcher said.

"I have them at gunpoint," Beck said. "One of them tried to kill me. I had to shoot."

"Ma'am, the one you shot? Is that person breathing?"

"No." Beck sniffled. More tears formed. This wasn't playacting. Tigran had meant something. Their relationship had meant something to her.

"Ma'am, is anyone else hurt?"

"One of the fugitives. The one all over the news," Beck said. "I think he needs an ambulance. And the girl he was with, she's bleeding. God, you have to hurry. HURRY!" TSec screamed.

"Ma'am, I need you to stay calm," the dispatcher said. "We have an ambulance on the way. Officers should be there soon."

In the background chatter at the 9-1-1 call center, someone mentioned the caller had said she was armed and someone else advised the dispatcher to keep the caller on the line. "Ma'am," the dispatcher said, "I can help. I'll walk you through what to do. Can you tell me your name?"

I don't know if the Treasury Secretary ever told them who she was because my ears stopped working when I heard these three words:

Officers.

There.

Soon.

Bri and I weren't finished, and I wasn't about to get arrested, not before we had all the answers, and definitely not before I knew who ordered Rafi's hit and Marissa's deadly chase. If Beck wouldn't confess, I had to get her to talk on the record or find some way for us to escape before the cops showed.

From six feet away, I couldn't make anything happen.

I needed to get closer without taking another bullet.

Needed to make myself less of a target.

Needed to become a non-threat.

I moaned, stiffened, then fake fainted, collapsing on the floor in front of Beck's desk. I tucked into a small ball so she couldn't see me and lay inert for what seemed like two centuries but was probably only two hundred seconds—long enough for the Treasury Secretary to lock into deep conversation with the 9-1-1 dispatcher about emergency first aid response.

Time to make my move.

I forearm-crawled inside the kneehole running through the center of Beck's antique desk, then wormed my way out to the back where she was standing. Before she realized I was at her feet, I lunged, wrapping my arms around her muscly calves. In a double-leg takedown, I lifted her off the hardwood floor and slammed her bulldog body onto the desktop.

Beck's handgun discharged into the ceiling. Plaster rained everywhere. The telephone handset clattered to the floor.

That's when the Treasury Secretary kneed me in the groin, causing me to loosen my bear hug grip so she could use her free palm to push off my hips, creating just enough space to shove her stubby .38 revolver in my gut.

The barrel felt warm. Hard. Unforgiving.

Only a few inches separated Secretary Beck's final chambered round from any future in which I would take Lil' Dude to his first day of kindergarten.

I don't regret what happened next.

And I'm not sure I could ever bring myself to do it again.

It started with a growl—a primal sound deep within the folds of my DNA. I bared my teeth and curled my lips under. Saliva dangled from my incisors. I snarled and snapped. Beck's eyes darted. There was fear in her face for the first time.

I slapped a hand on her desk and, using that as leverage, rolled to the right, free of the gun muzzle. Before she could re-aim, I reached into my left inside coat pocket, pulled my mechanical pencil, and jammed it into her right eye.

I'll never forget her yelp before she pulled the trigger, burying her fifth and final bullet in my left shoulder.

The impact felt like getting belly-whomped bodysurfing at Pounders Beach when a big wave closes out, smacking me on the hard-pack sand. I couldn't feel my left arm.

With my right, I fumbled with the wet pencil in Secretary Beck's eye socket until I was able to remove it. Flung the pencil, watching it careen off the other side of the study. I offered Beck a tissue to dab her eye.

She took it. Beck was alert, but clearly in pain, her robe splotchy with bloodstains, a little of hers, but mostly mine. I repositioned her so she wouldn't fall off her desk. It seemed like the right thing to do. By now, she had lapsed into ordinariness. She became pliant. Was even willing to talk.

Bri walked haltingly, zombie-like over to Tigran. She tore the bottom of his combed cotton nightshirt into bandage strips. She made a sling for me. I gave her my cellphone and asked her to call Detective Doogie Mapu. I told her to tell him I'm sorry. Sorry, I pulled a total Quimby move. That I didn't mean for things to get so physical.

I could hear ambulance sirens. Faint, maybe a couple of miles out, somewhere south on Embassy Row. The neighbors were not going to be happy.

"Madam Secretary, a few questions," I said.

She shrugged.

"VersaChem?" I pressed. "How long do you think you could have kept it from the President?"

Beck wet her lips and shook her head. "You still have no idea." She talked through her teeth. Some of her bulldoggedness was back.

"Enlighten me," I said.

And so, she set me straight, *sotto voce*, so softly only I could hear.

I have never been so wrong in my life.

And then I fainted for real.

Chapter 44

The paramedics were the first on the scene. Detective Mapu and the cops, a close second. Secret Service after that. And then the FBI arrived and took jurisdiction. Total love fest. Crime scene investigation by committee.

At least that's what Bri said.

I was sad to have missed it. The last thing I remember before I blacked out was a subdued Treasury Secretary connecting all the dots for me, holding her damaged eye while she shared her version of the truth.

And then the next thing I knew, I was in a hospital bed with an IV in my arm.

When I woke, Bri said, "You owe me, Thaddeus Hanlon."

"And me," Jorma echoed. The blogger was sitting in a waiting chair in the corner of the room.

"Ditto that, *braddah*." I didn't recognize Detective Mapu in his off-duty Hawaiian shirt. He was standing near the window. The midday sun was shining, blue sky, a dusting of high clouds.

"When can I see Marissa and the baby?"

Smiles drooped all around. The hospital room got quiet. Bri grabbed my hand. Held it tight. She searched my eyes.

"I have some good news and not so good," Bri said. She was all serious-faced. I realized this wasn't a setup for a joke to lift my spirits.

"You're crushing my hand, Bri." She eased her grip but continued to hold her breath. She was probably afraid I was in denial about the bad news, about my wife's fatal slip and fall. In the helter-skelter of the last two days, I had not forgotten that Marissa had hemorrhaged out. I was in shock, yes. And emotionally numb, for sure. "I just need some time with her, one last kiss," I said.

There was a collective sigh of relief from Jorma and Detective Mapu. Bri resumed breathing.

"We can make that happen. In fact," Bri said, "that brings us to the good news. You're in Virginia Beach right now rather than the G.W. University Hospital or the DC Jail. Detective Mapu has considerable influence."

Doogie Mapu gave me a *shaka*—a surfer hand signal meaning "It's cool." He twisted his wrist slowly, thumb and pinkie extended. "Ms. de la Guerra arranged medical transport, *brah*. You same hospital as *keiki*."

"Lil' Dude's here? I want to see my son." I grabbed the bedside rails, attempted to monkey myself up, and collapsed. My left shoulder wasn't cooperating. And my left leg wouldn't move at all. Worse yet, my right leg had a police ankle monitor attached.

Bri eyed the ankle bracelet. "The not-so-good news." She looked apologetic.

"Under house arrest, *brah*." Detective Mapu explained I had been released to his custody while I underwent medical care. The judge had agreed I could be reunited with my son while I worked out an immunity deal for my testimony against Kennedy Beck and her cabal. Bri offered to put up bail.

I settled back down in the bed and tried to wiggle the toes on my left foot. Only the baby toe twitched, ever so slightly, but enough it made me think about Lil' Dude's micro-preemie feet, how they were half the size of my little finger, pink against the hospital-white bedding of the incubator, and I teared freely, and soon was sniffling, chin trembling.

Jorma found a hospital tissue and handed it to me.

There was a light knock on the metal door jamb of my hospital room. "Lunch is here." A nursing assistant stood in the doorway with a tray. She stepped into the room and set the meal on my bedside table, and then asked if there was anything else I might need.

I lifted the tan plate cover from the entrée, thought about taking her up on the offer for "anything else" and dreamed about asking for a double-double burger, animal style, light fries, with a mondo-size diet cola but decided she wouldn't find it funny. Nor would anyone else in the room. So I settled for the red Jell-O, hummus, and veggie sticks instead. I gave my PB&J sandwich to Detective Mapu. In-N-Out Burger would have to wait until I was back on the West Coast.

Bri and Jorma decided to head off to the hospital cafeteria while Detective Mapu set up a tripod and digital video camera. It looked like I was going to give my official statement on the events of the past ten days.

"Ready, *brah*? The doc gave her okay to proceed."

The power light on my ankle bracelet flashed green. I wasn't going anywhere until I handed off the investigation to the authorities, at least not without Detective Mapu shadowing me everywhere. The sooner I could make my case for immunity, the better. "Let's get this over with." I fiddled with the remote control for my hospital bed and adjusted the frame so I could sit up, facing the camera.

Detective Mapu read me my Miranda rights, cautioned me that I didn't have to answer all the questions, then asked me if I understood.

I nodded, then eased my head back on the pillow.

"By nodding, you mean yes?"

"Rights, yes. Any questions I answer are admissible, yes."

The MPD detective punched the record button. "For the record, Thad, would you state your full name, date of birth, and street address?"

I did.

"Let's start with the Thursday night that MPD Second District Officer Ziobro found Rafael Silva's body. What was your involvement? Tell me everything."

I did that, too. All the details. Rafi's mysterious call to me earlier that Thursday evening, Jenny Yu's conference call to Bri and me, the failed attempts at CPR, and the cash wad in my best friend's billfold.

We were about to move into the events of Friday when Bri and Jorma returned with an extra-large diet cola for me.

I took a small sip and felt the carbonation tickle the back of my throat. I wasn't up for gulping just yet. "Can we take a break? I'm feeling a little ragged."

"I could use a break myself, *brah*. Need to get some real grinds and call MPD Homicide Branch. Give 'em an update." Detective Mapu swiveled the video cam on the tripod so the lens was on him. He annotated the recording with a timestamp to indicate we had paused the interview and then shut off the camera. He popped out the digital memory card and secured it.

"Try rest, eh?" Doogie Mapu gave me a fist bump and made for the door on his way to the cafeteria. He talked briefly with someone outside my room before his voice trailed off.

I nodded off shortly after that.

When I woke around 2 p.m., I was in a supine position rather than sitting up. My pillows had been rearranged and fluffed.

Lunch had been cleared. There was a note on my bedside table from Bri letting me know she had gone down to the NICU on the second floor to check on Lil' Dude. Jorma was in the corner of my room working on her MacBook Pro. And, Detective Mapu was still on break.

Jorma welcomed me back from dreamland. She asked if I wanted to give her the exclusive interview I had promised.

"Maybe later," I said. "I haven't forgotten. I keep commitments, Jorma."

"How about a pull quote, then? Something I could use in my next blog post to call attention?"

"Sure, but first, can we focus on the loose ends? I'm still trying to make sense of the last twenty-four hours. Of what Beck confessed. Can you get the team together?"

"Fair enough." As Jorma texted, Detective Mapu stepped back into the room and pulled up a chair.

"Just heard from HQ," the detective said. "Other than the loss of her right eye, the Secretary sustained minor scrapes and bruises. She's being held in the medical care facility at DC Jail."

Bri returned from the NICU and jumped right into

the conversation. "You still haven't arrested her? Why not? She was the one that sanctioned Rafi's interrogation. Agent Casama was only following orders."

"All I can tell you is the Silva case has been reopened. I can't disclose details now that it's ongoing. You understand."

"What about Marissa?" I asked. "Did you open a case file on my wife's death? Beck was behind that too."

"Jurisdiction, *brah*. Metro PD Homicide Branch is handling the Silva case and Tigran Vardanyan's slaying. Virginia Beach PD is investigating your wife's death…with my input."

Detective Mapu's comments seemed to provide Bri some degree of satisfaction. Normally, she's tough to please. For me? It was less about prosecutorial progress and more about a sense of relief than any satisfaction. With Detective Duke Mapu taking over Rafi's case and monitoring VBPD's homicide efforts, it meant Bri and I could hand back the investigation to the pros.

With that news, I expected to feel like a million-pound boulder had been lifted from my shoulders. But my relief was only partial. There was a second million-pound boulder. A rock of guilt I was carrying. And deservedly so. Marissa's death was on me. At some level. And though I wanted to believe I was not directly responsible, I knew I shared the blame. That load, that tonnage wasn't going away any time soon.

"For amateur investigators, you three know how to *geev 'um.*" Detective Mapu backslapped Bri and Jorma, almost knocking them down with his *aloha*.

Indisposed as I was in a hospital bed, there was no

back-slapping for me. Instead, Detective Mapu said, "Proud to call you, *braddah*, Thaddeus Hanlon. Even got something for you."

He returned to his chair by the window where he had parked his stuff—the video camera gear, his overnight bag, and a big plastic department store sack. He reached into the sack and pulled out the best Christmas present ever—my red combo backpack briefcase. "You looking fo' *da kine* bag?"

"*Mahalo*," I said. "Come here." I gave Doogie Mapu the best thank-you-hug I could manage. I only winced twice.

Jorma said, "I hate to be a buzzkill to mellow times but aren't we missing something? The fake gold bullion? Who's looking into that?"

Chapter 45

"The United States Secret Service," Detective Mapu answered. "They handle counterfeits. My office says that includes gold bars."

"What about the two bars in the briefcase?" I asked. "Especially the gold-dipped tungsten?"

"Seized as evidence, *brah*. MPD Crime Scene Investigations is processing for trace evidence before handing it off to the Secret Service."

Bri stood and rearranged her skirt. "Can we back up one minute? Something's puzzling me."

There was a chorus of uh-huh's. Three head nods—Jorma, Detective Mapu, and me.

"Out of curiosity," Bri said, "when you questioned Secretary Beck about VersaChem very early this morning, Thad, what did she whisper to you? I need to know if Rafi was fantasizing when he told you he thought he had stumbled on the scam of a lifetime? Or—"

"Is the scope of the gold fraud no bigger than two bars?" I said. "Is that what you were thinking?"

"Something like that."

Bri knew how to cut to the chase.

"What if," I said, "there was no VersaChem?" I swear I could hear the room deflate like an unknotted, overfilled balloon, latex lips flapping.

VersaChem had been my go-to test throughout our

amateur sleuthing. I used it as a code phrase. I thought I could tell from listeners' reactions if they were complicit in whatever Rafi had discovered. I quizzed everybody. The Dodge Whitney LA Office Managing Partner, Donnell Warnick. Secretary Beck. My senior manager, Tigran Vardanyan. And even Agent Jaxon Casama.

Not one person I asked ever flinched.

Because Rafi had never said "VersaChem" when he called.

The night he reached out to me I was in the middle of downtown LA traffic, wheeling through high rises. Cell reception was spotty. My connection with him garbled. Somehow the snatches I did hear got combined in my head as a single phrase. I assumed Rafi was referring to some corporate player, that VersaChem was the name of a company responsible for the mega-fraud.

"So then," Bri said, "what did Rafi actually say?"

Before I could answer, Jorma fired up her MacBook Pro. "I got to get this down."

I waited until I heard the clatter of her keyboard. "Reverse Alchemy," I said, "or, more precisely, *Operation Reverse Alchemy*." My bandaged shoulder started to itch. I scratched and wished I hadn't. Made the gunshot wound unhappy. "Beck explained Reverse Alchemy was a shell corporation within a shell, nesting so deep we'd never discover her covert op."

"But Rafi outed her," Bri said.

"He thought he did. But he only had one piece of the puzzle, micro in comparison."

"But not too small to get my fiancé killed."

I closed my eyes. The pain meds were messing with my ability to be situationally aware. When I said "micro" I hadn't meant to minimize Bri's pain, to mock her grief. "I'm sorry," I said.

Detective Mapu handed Bri the box of Kleenex. She grabbed and dabbed, clutching the tissue in her right hand.

"The covert op thing is good. I can use that." Jorma was talking to herself out loud. She licked her lips and looked up from her keyboard. "So...Thad," she said, "I just have to ask this. Reverse alchemy—the undoing of the magic. It doesn't make any sense. Why would Beck want to turn gold into base metal?"

Good question.

Detective Mapu and Bri raised their eyebrows.

"The op," I said, "was Kennedy Beck's ticket to permanent appointment as Secretary of the U.S. Treasury. She was tired of playing Acting Secretary and felt it made her less effective in her responsibilities as Chief Financial Officer of the U.S. government. The only problem with her plan was that the U.S. deep storage gold—the bullion that was going to back the country's return to a hard-money currency—honestly wasn't gold."

That really got everyone's attention.

"I knew it," Jorma said. "Knew it, knew it, knew it. I broke that story last year in my blog on "Fort Knox: Piggy Bank or Crime Scene?" Just give me a minute and I'll show you. It's right—"

Bri interrupted. "So, what you're saying Thad, is that it's all fake. The bullion in Fort Knox is gold-plated."

"Umm," I hedged.

"Where'd the gold go?" Detective Mapu said. "Who took it?"

"I honestly don't know," I said. "And neither does the Treasury Secretary. Her only concern was swapping out the fakes at Ft. Knox and elsewhere for the real deal. Her plan? Ensure the inventory at every U.S. Mint depository site matched the original record books, serial number for serial number. Otherwise—"

Jorma jumped in before I could finish. "The gold conspiracy theorists, like me, would have a field day."

"Not exactly. That's not where I was going." My throat had dried. I took a sip of my leftover diet soda. It was warmer than I cared for but wet. "It's bigger than that."

"A larger puzzle?" Bri said.

I explained that Beck wanted to hand the president a way to fire up his political base for his re-election bid. She knew he was interested in a return to the gold standard. "But," I said, "if the U.S. doesn't really have any gold—"

"Beck had to quote-unquote 'borrow' it, didn't she?" Jorma stretched her fingers, then reapplied them to the keyboard, ready to key my response.

"That was Beck's justification for Reverse Alchemy?" Bri asked.

Detective Mapu raised his arms in the air, shaking them back and forth. "You lost me. What did Beck borrow?"

"The gold from the half-million bullion bars in the New York Federal Reserve Bank," I answered. "Temporarily, of course."

I walked everyone through how Beck and her stealth corps swapped the good bars for perfect fakes, how by calling in favors on a supply chain she had built behind-the-scenes with Sunstake Extractive Industries, she took the pilfered gold, had it re-smelted, and smuggled into Fort Knox and the other U.S. Mint depositories to replace the bogus bullion in inventory, making her dream of "In Gold We Trust" possible. Pure genius. Almost.

"How temporary is *temporarily*?" Detective Mapu asked.

"Until she—"

"Can we back up for a second?" Bri said. "I need clarity. Rafi's files—the spreadsheets Jaxon never found? Are you saying that was the forensic proof of Beck's scheme?"

"I think so." I took another sip of my drink.

"I know so," Jorma said. All eyes shifted to her. "At least, I think I know now. That is if you overlay Beck's scheme with what Rafi had pieced together—all the ins, the outs, in every vault compartment."

"Documentation, maybe. But not proof positive," Bri said. "I'm not buying it. Why would they kill Rafi for a complete data set of every Official Joint Seal action at every U.S. Mint gold depository? The Treasury already had that info. There *had* to be something more."

"And I think there was," Jorma said. "You remember in our first meeting you asked me to look at the data files to see if my background provided a perspective?"

"Vaguely," Bri said.

Jorma looked to me for corroboration.

I closed my eyes and tried to summon heroic powers of recall—never my strength—and faintly remembered Jorma making a big deal about how it would take some serious data crunching to uncover

Rafi's secret. "Yes," I affirmed.

"I pushed the numbers, hard," Jorma said. "Re-did all his math. I think Rafi stumbled on the smoking gun."

"And…" Bri said, "what would that be?"

"Your fiancé was a genius," Jorma said. "He used algorithms to massage the raw data. He discovered patterns. He figured out exactly what Beck had done, transaction by transaction, in her epic financial sleight of hand. That's why they offed him."

I wished that were the case, that Rafi was simply an innocent who had stumbled on conclusive evidence of massive fraud, but I knew better. I looked over at Bri. "As Rafi's best friend, it kills me to say this, Bri, but Rafi was not guilt-free. He used his discovery of Operation Reverse Alchemy to blackmail Secretary Beck. That was the *plan* he referred to when he called. That was what he wanted to talk to me about that night."

"Beck confirmed this?" Bri said.

"Rafi was desperate for my input when he reached out. Maybe I could have talked him out of his scheme."

"So, the money in his wallet? The money Jenny counted?"

"I think it was a token down payment to see how much Rafi knew."

Bri's jaw tightened. Her eyes got fierce. I had seen that look before when she went on her kicking spree at the lab after realizing Agent Jaxon Casama's role in her fiancé's death.

"Jaxon didn't have to do what he did," Bri said. "My Rafi didn't deserve to be tortured."

"No one does." I wanted to give Bri a hug, wanted

to commiserate with her, but I could barely move. "Jaxon," I said, "was twisted in a way that you and I can't understand."

Bri shut her eyes. She stood silent for a beat before saying, "Jenny went home, Thad. Her parents took her back to China. I still have questions."

"Maybe it's for the best." When we had confronted Jenny about being with Rafi the night he died, Bri had sensed she was holding back, that there had been something more.

"She gave me this." Bri held up a wrinkled two-dollar bill.

I smiled weakly while my head bobbled. My brain was fuzzy from the painkillers in my system but not too fuzzy to remember the missing money. Rafi had $2,502 in his billfold that night. When Bri picked up his effects from Evidence Control, there was only $2500.

"Two-dollar bills are rare," I said. "People carry them for good fortune. Maybe, in her own way, she was wishing you luck."

Or helping us tie up loose ends.

"You know, *brah*," Detective Mapu said, "you're going to have to do this all over again, swear to everything so I have it on tape." He stood, fiddled with the video cam, and dropped in another digital media card. "You up for it now?"

"Can we pick this up tomorrow?" I asked. My strength was flagging but I still wanted to check on Junior, let my son know how pumped I was to be his dad, and that I would be ever-present. And after connecting with Lil' Dude, I was determined to see my wife, hold Marissa's now-cold hands, stroke her braided hair, and whisper "love yous" one last time even though I knew she could no longer hear me.

"I got no beef with tomorrow, *brah*, long as you stay put."

"For reals, Doogie?" I did a head tilt toward the ankle monitor.

Detective Mapu smiled. "*Mo' bettah*. Anyway, I go catch some waves while in VB. Surf's up." He took down his equipment, put the tripod and camera away, and collected his bags. "You know, *brah*. You still owe me one surfboard."

I had completely forgotten about that, about how I busted one of his primo boards when I went berserk at the pier. No way the board could be repaired. "You take credit cards?"

Detective Mapu waggled his head, the curls of his pompadour bouncing as he walked out. I overheard him give a situation report to his replacement. The second officer took up protective watch just outside my room.

Jorma seized the lull in the conversation. "Thad, I'll make you a deal," she said. "You give me that quote you promised and I'll bug out too."

I put my head down to think and flashed through the last forty-eight hours, frame by frame. I kept coming back to Beck, to her ambition, to the covert operation that she revealed once I took away her sight.

"Shakespeare was more than a playwright," I told Jorma. "He was a latter-day prophet."

"How so?"

"Because he foreshadowed the likes of Operation Reverse Alchemy in the *Merchant of Venice*. You know the part where Portia, the gorgeous heiress of Belmont, challenges her suitors to a riddle? Three caskets—lead, silver, gold—only one of which holds her portrait and the key to her hand in marriage?"

"Vaguely." Jorma tapped her keyboard. From the reflection in the lenses of her trendy fashion frames, I could tell she was searching online. "Is this the story where the Prince of Morocco goes for the gold?"

"It is. And to his surprise, when he opens the gilded tomb, instead of Portia's portrait, he finds a skull. And in the eye socket of that skull, a small scroll that reads: 'All that glisters is not gold.'"

"You mean *glistens*?"

"Not to be technical, but in the original—the 1596 edition of the play—the wording is glisters. However, as glistens is a tad more euphonious, it has superseded the original phrasing."

"Accountants," Jorma said. "Always in the weeds with details."

She had a point.

Jorma slapped down the cover of her ultralight notebook and left for the evening.

Bri could see I was starting to wither. She rolled a wheelchair next to my hospital bed and called a male nurse to help me sidle into it. I couldn't get comfortable but that didn't matter, I was going to spend precious time with my family. Final moments with Marissa. And a newbie dad's first real contact with his son.

Chapter 46

Life is a consequential act. You can bob forever on the surface of the ocean, scanning the horizon for swells, and take whatever waves come your way. Or you can choose to make your own waves.

I did.

Make a wave, that is.

Turned out to be a tsunami.

Riding a tidal wave is not for the faint of heart. There's the endorphin rush. The moment when you are fully alive, master of that freak wall of nature, sliding down the face, trailing your hand along the shoulder of the swell, tickling the surf gods.

But riding a rogue wave can never compensate for what you sacrifice. My fidelity to my best friend cost me my wife.

Marissa, I never meant for any of this to happen. Guilty me. I'm to blame. And I'm the reason our son will never see his mother's smile. Might you forgive? Can you? Will you?

Talk to me, please.

A still, small voice will do.

It's been nine months now and Marissa Petrovski Hanlon has never spoken once. Unless you count the times I called her cellphone to hear her voicemail greeting. I've prepaid her phone bill for the next two years so I can keep listening.

Marissa, if you could write on my heart, I'd feel comforted. Maybe an inscription like this:

"You are stronger than your grief. Don't let it cloud your thinking. You weren't responsible for my death. Jaxon was. You were just in over your head. Way over your head.

"Repeat with me: Wipe out seven times, paddle out eight. *Thad, will you do that for our son? Will you get back in the water?"*

"Thad, there you are," Bri said, disrupting me mid-revery. "I was looking for you." She was wheeling a tandem bicycle with a high-tech baby seat in the middle. "Hop on."

I scooped up my son who had been playing in the Santa Monica sand and secured him into the bike baby carrier. Lil' Zael tilted his head up as I snapped on his bike helmet. For a preemie, his little body was catching up quickly and was now in the ninetieth percentile. By the time he was two, we'd be tandem surfing for sure. Attached to the bicycle built for three was a surfboard carrier, solo board in tow. I jumped on. We rode.

The coastal bike path stretched for miles. As we pedaled, the twilight gave way to the promise of blue skies. The SoCal sun peeked over the horizon. A pelican or two floated low over the water.

We stopped at Bay Street, a little less than a half-mile shy of the pier. I parked the bike while Bri spread out a patchwork beach quilt. She broke out the sunscreen and dabbed it on my son. I lathered up.

"You know, Thad," Bri said, "you can't go back to auditing for Dodge Whitney. As soon as you open your first spreadsheet, you'll start yawning. Have you considered other options?"

Other than recuperating from the gunshot wounds and powering through grief moments, that's all I had been doing lately. Exploring career options. Trying to manage life without Marissa. Examining alternatives for my son and me. Sifting through work-life possibilities.

"We were pretty good together in DC, you and me," I said. "I was thinking—"

"Stop," Bri said, "before you say something really stupid." Zael started fussing. Bri reached across the blanket and put the binky back in his mouth. "If you're thinking, I'm your option…I don't do Sugar Momma."

I kind of figured that. I also knew I was no Rafi—strappingly tall, dark, and handsome. Except for my buff shoulders, I was kind of lanky and prone to freckling.

"This is going to sound totally wackadoodle," I said, "but I was considering getting a PI license. I thought, maybe, I'd hang out a shingle as a Private Investigator. Only thing is, Bri, I would need a good sidekick. Interested?"

"And what would we detect?"

"I'm still working on that."

About a hundred yards from the shoreline, I could see a swell building on the Pacific. I unzipped my surfboard bag and took out the seven feet seven inches funshape. By now, the baby was snoozing. It looked like an opportunity for me to catch a few.

According to the morning's Surfline report, the offshore buoys at Bay Street were picking up some solid energy. Forecast: a south-southwest pulse offering two to three-foot waves. Overall, plenty manageable with a few fun, racy barrels. A perfect day for an occasional ride…and making sandcastles with preemie Junior.

"Go," Bri said. She tossed me a bar of board wax from my surf-gear box and settled in to sunbathe.

I couldn't say no.